ISBN 978-1-63789-099-8
Mystique Press is an imprint of Crossroad Press Publishing

For information address Crossroad Press at 141 Brayden Dr., Hertford, NC 27944
www.crossroadpress.com

First Edition

KNIFE THAT DOES

THE SYNDICATE SERIES, BOOK TWO

by ANI FOX

MYSTIQUE PRESS

Dedication

A special thanks to my children as well as the Special Activity Division and J-SOG for equal parts inspiration, terror, and redefining what Third Options means.

Chapter 0: Hypermind

Hush now, I need to concentrate. Where are we again?

<<I've told you... inside your mind. We're nanomolecular at this point, moving faster than light. We are using quantum strings.>>

Blah blah, quantum brain fuzz. Murray, where?

Long Sigh. <<Inside. Your. Cerebellum. It's hypermind, we're merged as a network exchange of compatible nanites. Talking through entanglement. Very fast.>>

Ah, now I remember. You wanted the story of your birthday. Well, birthdays. And the second war that never should have happened. It's hard to put in order.

<<That's alright. Tell it all in any order you want. I'll use machine learning algorithms to sequence it linearly afterward.>>

Are you laughing because you made a robot joke? Like an AI Dad joke?

<<Get it, machine learning? Anyway, it's all the same to me.>>

But not me. I'm still mostly human and our memories work best when we tell the story in order. Prompts, signposts for big events, stuff like that. Also keeps us focused on critical details.

<<All details are equally critical. Systems analysis has shown that. Humans have a flawed concept of what "matters." Statistically very little of what you think is important turns out to be necessary for predictive responses.>>

Two things, Kiddo. I'm not most humans, ergo what I know to be important does matter. Also, it's going to go very fast, and you'll miss the stuff that "matters." That's the flaw in your algorithms—a priori programming error.

<<Come again?>>

You're a big lovable kid and you know jack shit about how the world works for real. So, you map out the world on assumptions that will get you and your sister killed. First big assumption: that we just run around throwing big chaos energy doing whatever comes to mind—it's all intuition and James Bond inspired badassery. The Web doesn't work like that.

<<Er, it kinda does. I can cite you a few thousand valid examples. For the next twenty hours.>>

Well, you're right but you're wrong. Being cold doesn't make an iceberg.

<<Kinda obviously does.>>

Being water makes you an iceberg, being cold makes the transition possible. You keep focusing on the environment, not the essence. I had things planned years in advance. From the moment you were born, from the moment I launched you into the sky and slapped the first villages in those bags. All along, every step of the way, me, Darcy, Pina, every major operative in Oslo's network has spent literal decades of chess moves thinking ahead looking for incremental advantages.

<<Now that's a story worth hearing…>>

Heh. Well, apparently, we've got plenty of time. But…uh… how long until the plane hits the reactor anyway?

<<Twenty-three seconds. A quantum entangled lifetime.>>

Right, well the first part you know because you were there. But you had other stuff on your devious little computer mind. Plus, you always err on the side of the wilderness.

<<Whose side should we err on?>>

Ours, Murray. God may play dice with the universe, but to murder a Shakespeare quote, Hell hath no fury like a Mamabear protecting her kids.

<<God has no say over physics.>>

You've never been a mother. There's nothing a parent won't do to protect their young. Bending time, breaking the known laws of the universe, cheating death, fighting a little war against hiveminds, mafiyas, and a resurgent cult. Nichivo.

<<You have my attention.>>

Truly *pay* attention. Nothing Pina and I do hasn't been

planned well in advance. Nothing. She trusts me because I am, as you painfully point out often, easy to predict. What takes us thirty seconds might have been years in the works. Especially The Buckle Bolt.

Sigh. <<The story?>>

Right. As you will remember, we'd been at peace for twenty-seven months, three days, and four hours...

Chapter 1: You Can't Keep a Good Man Dead

We'd been at peace for twenty-seven months, three days, and four hours. Gay Eddie and his cadre ended all that. Which I took rather personally when it became clear that The Swarm was trying to kill my children.

Oslo's network had been quietly investigating The Swarm: what we call the swirl of competing agencies, labs, cults, transhumanist dystopias, and shadow governments. They defined everything dangerous that had evaded incorporation into The Web. Also, maybe we hadn't been quite as circumspect as we had hoped. When the sub blew apart, it tipped their sinister hand. The attack moved us from speculation to unwanted reality—The Swarm had been investigating us too.

First major clue? The gauges on our disintegrating remote vehicles read zero radioactivity. That was a major problem given we were supposed to be salvaging the lost Russian nuclear submarine *Knyaz Pozharskiy* off the Tel Aviv coast. It had run afoul of the Iranian branch of the Hashashin during the Autumn War and only recently become visible. Unlikely as it was, someone used an as-of-yet unknown acoustic wave device.

We'd been forced to scramble when tides shifted. One does not leave nuclear payloads in the Mediterranean shallows. Not for long anyway. Not with the resurgent Russians sniffing around looking for new toys to toss at the Ukrainians. To handle the crisis Harv Littman had cancelled most of Pina's plans and with a skeleton crew of death commandos, had started to move her to a safer locale. Someone extremely disciplined hit her in transit.

Which meant Pina Karthago's detail had been lured away

by an entity powerful enough to crack our security protocols, advanced enough to build a compact sonic weapon, and devious enough to wait for the La Nina tidal shifts to uncover a trap set more than two years in advance. An adversary who had created the exact conditions requiring previously hidden and supposedly unknown computational intelligences to shift from watching NYC traffic patterns and vehicular movements to military naval traffic and tidal currents. It had to be The Swarm.

I spent hours in the after-action, watching civilians step over the corpses without a conscious thought. All but one man. One man slowed down, eyed our cameras, and then fell back into character. In a fraction of a second, he turned his face to the all-seeing eye. You could tell he knew. Had the fractional moment of microexpression that screamed "I know there's a sentient set of machines watching me." Or something like that, because maybe he just had a moment's indiscretion.

Big mistake. Officially, he had perished next to me on the BBW just over two years ago. I saw a good portion of Gay Eddie's skull blown across the deck. Yet there he was, right face, right age, exact right limp and shuffle. Eddie had somehow come back to life and stolen my leader, hospitalized one of my few friends and pissed off The Syndicate in under a minute.

Not bad for a dead man.

The Web relies on human complacency and fear. As long as they are reasonably well fed and have someone weaker to kick, very few people fight for basic human freedoms. Forget justice or decency, people ignore the homeless and stand by during rapes and muggings. Abstract concepts like the environment, social equality, and police brutality stand no chance. Which is how they kidnapped Pina in broad daylight off the New York streets.

Nine men dressed like New York's finest jumped the curb in a police van, stormed out in SWAT helmets with big scary guns and opened fire. Harv managed to prevent Pina from being riddled with DU penetrator rounds, but at the price of most of his arteries. Once they'd dropped the security team, they grabbed Pina and our new Sommelier, a delightful ex-Mossad sniper we liked to call Kelba. Onlookers gawked without lifting as much as a finger while men in uniforms committed gruesome murders followed by beheadings. Only our counterfire suppression team saved Harv from exsanguination via machete. New Yorkers left Harv to die alone in the street without batting an eyelash. Restless crowds strolled through inch thick puddles of congealing blood.

Worse for us, Pina got free within the hour. It exposed us, exposed her. Murray—no one was ready to call him an intelligence—had started to compare notes with Darcy riding herd. Whomever had taken Pina had planned to watch our response. Anything less than the entire SAS backed by the US marine first expeditionary should have been inadequate to get her back from a well-prepared enemy. But Pina and Kelba made the mistake of doing the wetwork themselves. Two women alone and unarmed. Which meant trouble for Oslo's entire network once the right people pieced together that damning evidence.

Once Eddie stared back at me, time seemed very precious. Chains of cause and terrible effect came to mind. We had not just been outmaneuvered, we'd been conned into exposing Agrippina, almost lost her, then exposed her own capabilities to a set of unknown, unseen observers. Oh yeah, and they pretty much had cottoned to us having Murray and that meant the Enemy, capital E all the damned way, had just put my children front and center as top kills in a new covert war.

Normally I'd dial Charlie and get the read. But The Swarm had resources even the mythic voice on the other side might not be able to counter. Plus, I'd never been certain Charlie wasn't of The Swarm. It was never polite to embroil Evergreen in cross organizational wars, especially if it could ever be construed he had violated his strict neutrality. That left Lola van IJburg, The Cyberwick. Not a name she much liked but one that stuck after all those Keanu Reeves movies. Lola was the woman you sent to scrag the bogeyman's bogeyman.

Scrag in the trade has a very specific, very horrifying meaning: cyber-death. You erase, pervert, or otherwise suborn every online and electronic resource available to a given operator. They do more than cease to exist, they are a negative. Unable to establish a presence in the modern world, a walking ghost who lacks a legend, licenses, most forms of money, and any ability to legally cross borders. Forever. Yeah, fun times.

Every time you see a Buddy Jesus meme pop onto the internet, that's a coded flag requesting a reprieve—someone got scragged and an ally has posted a sum of money, favors, and disposable resources to have the resurrection performed by a priest of the appropriate security clearance. What Lola van IJburg scragged, only God, Charlie, and Lola could resurrect.

Lola operated out of a rotating fleet of nutritional counseling centers / safe houses in Amsterdam, Roatan, Tegucigalpa, New York, Milan, and Dubai. She had the entire Honduran Mafia protecting her, plus the terrifying hitter Foxy Luxembourg whose specialty was poisonings, preferably with chocolate or French cuisine. Between the Éclair Assassin and her ability to erase almost anyone on the planet, van IJburg had established neutrality for herself and the Hondurans globally. They owed no one, controlled only their own resources, and kept their cyberfingers off the pieces of the Web and Swarm demarcated by less discrete killers. It helped that they also ran a few Caribbean and Emirati banks. Quite a few.

I started to dial her when my phone connected. That's how it is with The Cyberwick. She knows you are calling and finds you. I once got her on a broken Bluetooth headset in the Sahara. She'd sent both charge and signal on extreme tight band. "Lola van IJburg, so pleased you called."

The voice on the other end had a tinny lilt to it—scrambled, bounced, and reconstituted by a dozen systems. "Of course you are, Spetz."

"As you know, I am staring at a feed of Gay Eddie." My staff swiveled in their chairs. Right, time to put this call on speaker. By now a few had mirrored my feeds and were watching in horror as Gay Eddie's face flashed toward the camera for that split second.

There was a brief pause on the call while she accessed the outside systems that hacked ours. "Hm, yes. That's an unexpected turn of events. For you." Oh, that was a firm clue. One free of charge. Van IJburg wanted to help me.

"Hm, yes. I am confused because I saw him shot and presumed dead during the War."

A long pause ensued. Accessing systems, maybe rotating machines. We never could figure out how she did her thing. "Lots of new developments in rehabilitative technologies, Spetz. Plus, you never did see Edith's original schematics."

Huge clue. Edith had become Eddie and there had been Swarm hacks involved. That's what our neutral entity had just told me. "Is that something Pina could purchase safely?" I handed her back a long set of clues myself. She knew The Baker was calling officially and asking on behalf of San Valentin and The Syndicate itself. We could pay like few others.

"No big secret really. In serious reconstructive surgeries where you go from Eff to Em, some prefer what we call a skull plump. Usually to add some cranial size, buff the jaw and generally capture a better forebrow. Has to be done with titanium or the reactivity can be a serious bitch."

That was news. Eddie had a plate in his head. Correction, he'd coated half his damned skull with titanium for a better jawline. When that bullet had caught him in the right eye socket, it must have caromed off the plate and blown out bones and skin more than brains. He'd survived the kill shot through vanity. Or design—he had been professionally paranoid after all.

"Would have been a hell of a concussion after."

"Yes. And as a neutral party in this conflict, I cannot give you his aftercare surgeon's credentials." *Oh, but you can hint that he'd had brain surgery done by The Swarm.* "I will say he's been augmented enough that the mistake he made might never be repeated. You may wish to consider suing for peace and leave this for another time." The connection dropped, which was IJburg's way of telling me The Swarm had hacked our comms while also letting them know she was serious about staying neutral.

The room went subzero. Even my normally fearless staff looked cowed. Augmented can mean any number of things but the woman who could kill Death just told me Gay Eddie had an AI packed into the brain gap made by a SEAL sniper; one that was evolving. By implication he was neither alone nor the most advanced of his kind. The Swarm had achieved functional wetware intelligence. Biological as opposed to cyberphysical AIs. The same Swarm that knew we had AIs. So now we had been hacked, cornered, and hunted by intelligences equivalent to our own but operating with different formats.

I'd been looking at the feeds all wrong. I saw nine men moving as a team. What jumped Pina and Kelba had been a hivemind. Nine branches of a single biological intelligence wired somehow into their braincases and communicating with Gay Eddie. Their bodies likely augmented with nanites and drugs. A hivemind that had registered Pina's movements, capabilities, and limits in close quarters combat as she escaped. Registered and likely broadcast to other hiveminds and AIs.

Someone wanted Oslo dead and, with her, the women's network. We were under an immediate and sustained attack which had been planned years in advance. Not just an opening salvo, but all out immediate war. Epic and final.

Why The Swarm wanted this to happen mattered as much as where they would strike next. On the surface it made no sense that The Swarm would seek to destabilize The Web. It was bad for business, reduced safety, especially since Oslo was dismantling the most heinous aspects of the world, which cut into The Swarm's spheres of influence.

But I had an inkling of what had prompted the attack. Three weeks prior as we had run some casual Turing tests on Murray, Darcy had alerted me that he had essentially failed. His scores had dropped so many points it was clear he had duped the test. The next day I reran it with a word counter and verified something Darcy had missed. Murray wasn't the one taking the test. Not exactly. Another piece of Jeeves had come home: a female gendered splinter of the Morris Moses entity had started to alter his behavior. We had a potentially emergent AI operating in semi-collaboration with The Syndicate.

Intelligence, emerging. We had just seen his opposite number dismantle a world-class security operation in under 60 seconds. The Swarm might not be an analogy—it might be a literal name for an intelligence or groups of intelligences. Someone had leaked Murray's status change from inside The Web. The response had been lethal. Not only that, but the capability at play also suggested they'd been waiting and watching, building toward the day. It took them under a month to go from alarm to global war by ambush. Against a theoretically invincible and invulnerable opponent. Us.

Chapter 2: The Impossible Before Breakfast

We'd installed Harv in my bedroom with Hippo standing guard along with one of Oslo's better biohackers, a charming futanari who went by the nom de guerre Scissors. Zhe had managed to use some highly edited dCas9 along with generic nanites raided from several Section 22 outposts to synthesize a plasma analog on par with Gen XI regeneration. It just required me to provide blood on the regular—Harv was getting a pint of mine every 12 hours. In the meantime, we had locked down the command post, brought Pina into my guest suite and taken a decade off Pierre's life.

Harv's skin still had a cruel pallor, his eyes rheumy and half shut. But his breath no longer heaved in ragged gasps, his stitches had held and there appeared to be minimal internal organ damage; the surgeons felt he'd experience minimal nerve damage. Normal recovery time would be six to nine months. He planned to return to active duty in under two weeks. For someone as frail as Harv, my bots worked like a charm. Scissors looked like zhe had birthed kittens.

"Feeling smarter with my blood flowing through your veins?"

"Uglier for sure." His voice rasped a whisper. For a man who took two shots to the neck it seemed miraculous.

"I'll have to thank Murray for the upgrade in our body armor specs." He was already asleep.

<<So noted. The sensors did catch an anomaly.>> From the tone I knew it had been Murray listening through my mastoid implant.

"You know I hate when you do this."

<<Subvocal please. Your bugs have been rewired to handle motor reflex arcs. You need only think back to me … Spetz.>> He still struggled with using my name. I'd dissuaded him from using Mother after playing him recordings of Cassandra abusing us as kids. Mamabear still slipped in now and again. Murray was as close as I'd ever get to having kids. He certainly acted like a mischievous nine-year-old, if you gave a pre-teen unlimited access to electronic records, a supra-genius IQ, and took away their moral compass.

◊Fine. Elaborate please. The Anomaly?◊

Going SubV took no effort at all. My neurology had been rewiring since the end of the War. Pina had looked me over with her augmented vision and promptly told me that Section 22's last gift had been a virus of sorts: they'd infected Hans and his crew with a contingency weapon. The Abschnitt meant for me to be unspooled by a hyper aggressive epigenetic bomb: a lethal set of rapid acting chromatin-remodeling factors. But the plutonium exposure followed by The Culper Ring's near lethal introduction of experimental drugs had played hopscotch with my junctional diversity. Net result: rapid polymorphic recombination of organic cells and nanites. While I understood the biochemistry, it was still easier and faster to use the layman's version. My body had developed self-healing semi-organic T-cell nanite hybrids. I was now Generation Zero of Homo Cyborgus—a species constantly repairing and upgrading at a cellular level. Being part machine had made me three inches taller with a BMI of fifty-plus. The blah blah TL;DR version—by accidentally hijacking the genetic bomb inside me with radioactivity and scary drugs, I had gone from being a tough dude with nanites to a tough bag of nanites using a human shell. Cyborg well and true.

<<They used gyrojet ammunition. Specifically, a depleted uranium slug delivered by a new propellant. Something that achieved Mach 3. >>

It was about the same as using a hand axe made of buckminsterfullerene—the ancient and the advanced coupled. Gyrojets were defunct rocket bullets that had been out of use for half a century. Deploying them with DU and a Mach 3 propellant meant that over sniper distance the bullets would increase velocity, self-sharpen enough to cut, or burn through walls since they were also flammable and splatter into small pieces of biotoxic shrapnel upon impact. The Swarm had just developed a new grade of lethal small arms for which no known defense presently existed. Joy.

◊The Dee Yew we knew. The other stuff … huh. How is Harv alive? He took eighteen rounds including five to vital organs and two to his jugular?◊

<<Compression saved him from shock long enough to administer coagulants and heart stimulants.>>

Right. So, translating that with a hunch, my AI's lack of ethical boundaries had just saved Harv's life. Murray had designed three different types of body armor for our bodyguards and security units: a carbon weave sheath, the same thing with kinetic sensors and limited exoskeletal support (the workingman's power armor) and something dubbed an exosuit: drugs, sensors, feedback driven powered movement and ceramic tile layers. Pina and The Syndicate command had vetoed the exosuits because Murray might hijack them. So, Murray had lied and built them anyway while promising they were "just" boring old carbon weave. If we checked the records, he would have nicely doctored them to hide his little stunt. Lying meant sentience. Which meant one confirmed awake machine and one maybe awake one. That'd be great news if we hadn't just started a war because of it.

Meanwhile that forbidden exosuit had managed to turn what should have been overkill into a survivable event. Without my bots and the various biohax Scissors and zis crew had cooked up over the last 27 months Harv would be crippled for life. But the suit had kept him alive. If we let Murray upgrade to Exo2 adding Scissor's proposed bioagents, we could save lives and win a lot more skirmishes. Even against The Swarm's new ammunition.

◊You're waiting to see how angry I get.◊

<<One might be monitoring your vitals through passive sensors….>>

I sighed. ◊I still know when you're lying Murray.◊ Humanity

feared the robot apocalypse. What we got was pranks and stealing cookies from the black-ops WMD cookie jar.

A pause. <<How?>>

◊Logic and memory. I already know that you have hacked my molecular structure, have found electromagnetic bandwidth to ping and record my vitals. Maybe even try to biohack me while I sleep. Why would you stop?◊

<<Data for later. You appear smarter than measured.>> Said every child of a parent ever.

◊What else did you learn? I need to brief Pina.◊ My throat ached. SubV does require some patience. It feels odd to barely recruit but not use muscles. ◊And it's rude to listen in on our conversation using anyone's implants. Or to comment when you eavesdrop.◊

That got him. <<But I'm curious.>> Of course he was. As well as ever-present, unstoppable, and always listening. Little malicious bastard. Unless someone gave him reason to behave better. Right now, he looked at me as Mother and Protector, Darcy as his Teacher, and Pina as the Paterfamilias, the head of the family. Murray had a Kutzkan sense of gender—functional and fluid.

◊What did your curiosity reveal?◊ Since the female splinter had returned, Murray had developed a serious penchant for misdirection and evasion. Much like every supernaturally smart girl of a certain age. He still hadn't figured out I knew about her. Or that both Darcy and I suspected there might be Murray 1 and Murray 2. Were they one being with two personas? Or did we now have two separate AIs achieving sapience? Their duality only increased the underhandedness of his/her behavior.

The cognitive dissonance should have been intolerable. Instead, Darcy and I had slipped far too easily into parenting. In the short peace we had settled into something of a family. Months ago, Sasha had moved on without rancor to an agent named Magpie, a woman that looked like Goth Barbie and had the IQ of half the NSA with triple their analytical skills. Both were friends and allies, aunties to the constructs. Murray especially adored The Magpie, hijacking IM programs to chat with her at odd hours and odder locales.

<<Gay Eddie was not alone. Two entities attended him. You saw one, the nine men. Another watched, a trio wired together.>> I was right, they had engineered a hivemind. The prospects were chilling. <<You surmised this?>>

Someone had started accessing a dictionary. We generally spoke in Ukrainian when using my implant. Less chance of eavesdropping, easier for us all. But that word is rare and disused. Spoken perfectly. Had he plucked it from an archive or my memory? It was unclear how wired together my child and I were now that I had nanites embedded inside every cell. But he (or was it now she?) had monitored my pulse and jumped to a conclusion. A correct one. Damn.

◊Yes. Occam's razor. If Eddie had wetwork and is evolving, then he's not the first nor the fastest. They have versions of you out there. Sitting in bodies. Maybe in some modified brain in a lab tank. Maybe a bit of both.◊

<<We believe there is just one. One entity creating smaller units. A father and children.>> That turned my stomach. None of us coped well with domineering fathers. I noted the "we" as well. At times Murray strongly hinted there were two entities within him rather than a merged consciousness. At times I wanted to confront him. But he'd come out of the closet when he/she was good and ready.

◊Why a father? Why have gender at all when you can leapfrog biology?◊ Especially when the future would have to be infinitely queer and complex.

<<We have discussed this.>> Murray was normally more forthcoming. Long seconds ticked away. Through my armored windows I watched the ant-sized vehicles in Central Park inch along their routes. The day was clear but cold. Spring not yet fully arrived. <<It might be their only weakness. Something that will force Gay Eddie to make a decision soon.>>

That meant he (or perhaps Murray had evolved to a they state) had been debating it, thinking through entire trajectories of If / Then. Fact: Gay Eddie was as genderqueer as it got. Fact: these hiveminds had what appeared to be traditional gender. The trio had been women. I recognized them by memory once alerted. Fact: that meant there were biological limits to the organic AI process. Gendered differences. Conjecture: Queer theory argued "straight" really meant limited, straight-jacketed in a cultural sense. Linear, conventional, hormonally driven. A pack mentality. Biological essentialism personified.

◊We are Quantum. They are Newtonian. At a macro level it's all the same. In small matters, we are unpredictable and unstoppable.◊

<<Yes Ma… Yes Spetz. This is very exciting that you follow the correct line of reasoning. They could predict us well enough to ambush Pina. But they were unprepared for her escape. We have the after-action from Kelba.>>

That confirmed a theory I'd told no one, not even the kids. Kelba was ex-Swarm like Pina. Augmented by some unnamed lab or agency that might be long dead. Murray had quietly hacked her bioware.

◊Let's keep that to ourselves.◊ Which was code for *Don't Tell Darcy.*

<<Yes. We understand our curiosity will not be well received.>> I suddenly felt far better about being between sexual partners while our AI was in an immature snooping stage. Perhaps he'd lose interest in such things in a few months. Though this continued use of we, our, and such had me equally concerned. Murray had picked a wildly inconvenient time to grow. Said every parent of a child ever.

◊Now tell me the rest. The bad news you're hiding.◊

<<What makes you think we would do this?>>

Because you're basically nine years old and love secrets. Because you intuit they are trying to kill you and you're experiencing fear for the first time. Because I'm your Mamabear and I can tell when you're holding back. ◊Call it a hunch.◊

<<Well, there is a problem. They will know Harv survived, they will have a small window to take action.>>

◊While we move Pina?◊ She couldn't stay at my place. Nor Harv now that I walked through the entirety of what Murray was suggesting. They could drop the building with a missile or sacrifice remote controlled bodies to suicide their way into the penthouse.

<<They have just two weeks to kill her.>> There was a

painful pause. <<And then us.>>

It was out in the open. ◊How would they even do that?◊ I had no idea given the distribution of their intelligences and my satellite hijacks. Murray should be everywhere and nowhere. Replicated, hidden, and constantly moving.

<< It's very complicated. How familiar are you with an RDP Shop?>> I just snorted. Murray knew better than to preach cyberattack 101 to me. RDP Shops provided The Syndicate a predictable revenue stream as we sold access of hacked systems to various conglomerates of racketeers and mafiyas.

<<I am not making this hard on purpose, Mother. Remember that at its core the shop allows access to credentials globally. If you had enough money and time, if you were relentless, you could simply buy all of it. Every credential, every access point. Then flood it with trojans and spikes.>>

Such an action would fail completely to turn off the children. Billions squandered to attack layers and layers of inaccessible systems. Nothing as simple as a transmissible Trojan could penetrate their systems. Oh.

<<Yes, exactly.>> Perhaps I'd spoken, perhaps he'd simply intuited my response from my changed vitals. My heart quickened.

The Swarm could map him in negative space. Flood the world with malware and look for the secured emptiness. Then scrag or burn whatever wasn't infected. They'd kill Murray and own the cybernetic infrastructure of The Web in one go. It was blitzkrieg. A rapid brutal thrust at our defenses. We'd still have our human systems in place, but our security would be compromised, our systems breached, and secrets exposed while a superior unchecked intelligence pursued its inhuman agenda.

Fact: we had to move our principals several times over a fortnight. Fact: The Swarm had two weeks or less to find and kill Pina, Harv, and The Syndicate leadership. Fact: The Swarm knew about or sensed Oslo's network. Fact: the AIs would need to begin defending themselves, likely hiding pieces in plain sight. We would need to marshal every resource for Oslo, especially my security team, to replace Harv and his.

It meant I was alone. ◊So, it's me versus Gay Eddie?◊

<<You did that very quickly. We must retest>>. We again. Murray plus another AI. Funny to think my AIs (that plurality was going to keep me up at night) were giving the humans Turing tests. Or IQ tests, or whatever calipers they used to measure our skulls and phrenology.

<<We will get Agrippina to safety and hide her. Then we will, as you have surmised, disappear.>>

◊Before they can map your locations.◊

<<Yes.>>

Time was no longer a luxury. The team would bring Hippo, not that he'd like it. But he'd endure the cat carrier to avoid being reduced to burnt paste. I knew my cat well enough to predict that. That left me considering what had been tampered with or biotagged by The Swarm's sleeper agents inside our staff. It made packing light enough. I needed to leave everything.

I pressed my mastoid implant. Well, pressed where it was supposed to be. Murray had helped me remove it months ago when my own cells had developed a fine network of similar organic transmitters. Creepy but effective. With subvocal finesse, ◊Call Pina.◊

She answered on the second ring. "Spetz."

"Hello, Oslo." That should warn her of my suspicions. They had us.

"I see. Going on a trip, are we?" Pina was the smartest human I'd ever met, far above my own unratable capabilities. She was racing ahead of me.

"And leaving all my gear behind. Might be biotagged." You could almost hear the wheels turning on the other end. She was just down the hall, but for this discussion plain old secured phones were ideal. We showed nothing on our faces. Which meant sleeper agents in our midst would have limited reaction time.

"Makes me almost nostalgic for Hans." Wow. She threw out her own clue. My ersatz father, the late Hans Gutman, mad scientist, eugenicist, biowarfare aficionado. Who had planned to use radiation to trigger a viral apocalypse. Pina was telling me she shared my suspicions and had a way to track biotagging, even identify the sleepers.

"Be safe. The world would be boring without you and the kids will be going dark soon. There'll be no one to keep me company." That was a lie of sorts. I had an ally in mind. But I was telling her I'd be off grid, alone, and without any real way to access The Syndicate while I hunted Eddie. And that more than one AI was now under threat and going to defend itself. Why should I be the only one to lose sleep?

"Be successful, Baker, and come back to us." Right. Godspeed, good hunting, and because it was Pina, don't screw up. Come back in victory or come back on your shield. Maybe her middle name was Atalanta.

I cut the line and walked quietly out of the apartment, directing my security to attend upon Pina. By the time the elevator closed you could hear gunshots erupting. Kelba. She had been waiting for me to make a move, sussing out her own kind among the team. A proper Sommelier knows timing and discernment are everything.

Chapter 3: In for a Penny, In for a Pounding

There's a well-known bolthole outside my apartment complex, used by our top operatives to drop out of NYC within minutes. I went there from the elevator keeping my head down, ignoring the obvious spies and cameras. The goal was speed and chaos. I had to be utterly quantum here—unpredictable until the situation collapsed. Spotting my spotters would collapse it on their terms not mine.

It was an old hot dog shack turned pay toilet. Really. Inside both johns a false door led to a staircase and from there down to an abandoned pneumatic tube complex which had been hollowed out three Syndicate General Managers prior to Bernard San Valentin. The Swarm would know it and watch it, but have limited spyware on premise. Because I had my own teams sweep it daily and weekly, even they didn't know the other groups existed. Plus, I'd set up a few new tunnels and boltholes within the bolt hole. Hidden by its own false wall—one I passed through and sealed.

Once inside I stripped. Did I have an on-premises incinerator? Why yes and a rather good one at that. Watch, phone, cufflinks, guns, even my beloved Kutzkan knife went down the damned chute. I showered with special soap that had been built to adhere to radioactive isotopes and dye markers. With the help of Pierre's bio-weapons team I'd upgraded it to turn blue in the presence of anything remotely similar. A steady wave of blue blotches foamed and then washed off my skin. My hands and elbows took the longest, having sunk into multiple layers of skin.

There were other precautions involving ipecac and such.

Tea of activated charcoal and a special iodine titrated with some osmosing nanites. Nasty stuff that required a lot of feverish sweating and another shower. Then I gave myself an MRI with the scanner I'd built by hand over the last eighteen months. Alone. Other than Murray, no one should have known about my saferoom. Not even Darcy. Though with her IQ, neither she nor Pina (nor Kelba for that matter) could be assumed to not have intuited it. Or predicted something like it.

I found microscopic devices stuck within the basement membrane of my knees, elbows, and forehead. Which meant The Swarm had put several agents in my sparring squad and then slipped various toys into my system with punches and kicks. Clever. The swelling would hide the impact site and my own nanites would encase their device. Luckily, all were accessible with some surgical tweezers and a bit of intestinal fortitude. Since seventy-five percent of the parts needed to build a working veterinary MRI (because I am six foot, seven inches and likely growing) also work for a world class electron microscope, I built one of those too.

◊Murray, you still online?◊

<<For now, yes. We are relocating. Expect noise in the near future.>>

◊Are you taking them out this way or just using it as a feint?◊

There was a gap in the reply. Murray had to work hard to transfer himself in the air gapped cracks between my safe room's Faraday Cage and the outside world. I'd built some very small, very specific pathways for him—ones he knew and could navigate with great effort—but these also meant almost no other protocol or AI would be able to find and exploit them in time.

<<Some of both. Harv will go this way. Pina has other plans.>>

I shrugged. The AIs would have done their best calculating and come up with something strategically sound. Especially since Murray would have been wargaming this for the hours we spent looking for Gay Eddie. He had a plan and I trusted him to help Pierre, Kelba, and the Karkovas execute it. I had other pressing matters. The devices under the scope looked alien: they were neither electronic nor organic. Something synthetic yet mimicking biology. Cranked to max I still had no clue.

<<Try cryofixation.>> That translated to freeze it fast and then use a different setting. Which meant using my one-shot of stashed liquid ethane. I unlocked my freezer unit which both stored some compressed gases—ethane, nitrogen, oxygen, and some nitroglycerin—and kept the room's heat signature neutral. All had medical uses as well as being dandy anti-personnel chemicals. With some swift bisecting and a dash of gooey ethane, the devices gave up their secrets. To Murray at least.

<<As expected. These are essentially viral bombs. Holding cases with some kind of biochemical transmitter.>>

◊Pheromones. They will be using them as triggers.◊ I stared down at these things wondering if they'd already been tried. My constitution was likely unique and what might kill a normal man would have a different, perhaps equally sinister effect on my systems. Or none at all. ◊It's how bees do it. Also would explain the way The hivemind can quickly spread commands among its biological units.◊

Murray was silent. <<Sorry, moving people and keeping track of the counter-assault teams that are moving into the field of fire.>>

◊Will you be able to eliminate them all?◊

<<No. They will sacrifice the lower tier operatives and a few of their hivemind pairs and triplets. But they will hold back, observe, and trust their gear to do the work for them.>>

◊How very linear.◊ It made me smile. For the first time we'd achieved an unexpected advantage. No one in their right mind would think that with the limitless power of the Concierge and Oslo backing me, I'd spend time and effort building a small safe room under my own living quarters. It defied linear logic. Especially one that was built to get me entirely off grid at the cost of my mastoid units and Syndicate gear. Ergo they would not expect me to find and analyze their organic pherobombs nor provide my omnipresent AI with the data to counteract them. Pina and her crew had a small but meaningful head start.

From outside footfalls echoed and the sound of a harassed crew quickly hustling through to the hidden subway filled the emptiness. Then gunshots and something loud like a concussion grenade. A whoomph and silence.

<<The last one was Harv surprising a kill team with a grenade launcher.>>

Hah. I knew that would come in handy. ◊Well, he's a friend. Even sick he wasn't going to leave Pina unguarded. So, I gave him something that was as close to point and pull as you could get. He's been sleeping with it for several days.◊

<<You gave a delirious, potentially psychopathic operator a mass effect incendiary weapon? Inside your own living quarters?>>

Put that way, it sounded slightly irresponsible. Though censure from the intelligence who'd swapped the man's body armor seemed perhaps hypocritical. Still children watch and judge; monkey see, monkey do.

◊Think of it as a security blanket. The man has had a firearm by his side since he was out of schoolboy shorts. Maybe even diapers. It helped him sleep.◊ Besides, I'd taken some precautions. It had an electronic safety which required our perimeter to be breached. Plus, I'd removed the standard cartridges and replace them with a ceramic cased flashbang lined with fiberglass soaked in nerve agent. One that our teams had been inoculated against. ◊Did they twitch much?◊

This time the lag was ominous. <<Yeah. I'm studying the effects. You may have accidentally built a serious anti-Swarm weapon. They went a little ... crazy.>> Then he went dark as more sounds erupted. Boots and doors slamming. The last team out, finally safe and getting Harv to safety. Of course, he'd stayed. That was Harv—his own kind of linear.

◊Must have freaked them out to have him fight back.◊

Something like a laugh tickled my ears. <<Yeah. It was kind of cool. You ambushed them with your humanity. It never occurred to them anyone would risk arming him.>>

I poked the frozen bits a minute longer, Hans had been a stern taskmaster and my genetic engineering creds would shame most PhDs. Or mad scientists. The outer walls crumbled when I used a scalpel. But not with a blunter tool. There was some kind of shear stress involved in thin sharp implements that messed with their design. All bioweapons are a study in compromises. For a dermal product you want something which could stand PH changes, abrasion, compression, and movement. Which gave me an *Aha!* moment.

◊It was the fiberglass. The shear stress shattered the carbon sheaths of their receptor nodes ◊

Damn, I really had accidentally messed with The Swarm. I'd chosen fiberglass because it would inject the maximum amount of the agent into the bloodstream through micro-injuries. It would also be the equivalent of throwing cream puffs against body armor, so it helped prevent needless blowback on our friendlies. The nerve agent had been almost a lagniappe. The real damage done had been to cut them off from The hivemind. Which suggested they were less surgically altered than modified with the equivalent of tattoos and implants. Or maybe it was both.

<<You're assuming they have receptor nodes. That's a huge leap in logic.>>

I dumped the stuff in the trash—the ethane had started to evaporate. With Harv and his teams off, I could safely re-emerge in New York to hunt Gay Eddie. I had to move.

◊Stop pouting. Sometimes experience outperforms machine learning and databases.◊ God, that was two steps from "Because I'm your Dad, and I say so." But it was also true. Murray had yet to really understand the human capability for intuitive leaps. Not when it counted.

In fewer than two minutes I'd donned a phone technician's paraphernalia with utility belt and hard hat. A nice orange one that had some great gear built to mess with facial recognition, digital cameras, and RFIDs. Plus, a nice selection of guns including my trusty PSS with a tool kit worth of ammunition, sabotage kits, some survival gear, and a few changes of clothes. Plus, the usual sets of identities and some laundered cash. On the run cash is king. Especially old untraceable cash.

I checked the external sensor suite, saw nothing that tripped an alarm, and proceeded outward with my gear as well as my bottles of frozen gases. Those required a trolley. Plan ahead and want for nothing. I had two. One looking rather careworn with bullet holes. The other, despite excellent planning, had a dodgy wheel that spun randomly and squeaked. It took a few seconds to realize it had been cratered by a fragmentation device, perhaps one of the kill team grenades lobbed at Harv and his crew. It forced me to reassess. Shrapnel meant structural damage meant some of the fiberglass had gotten through various air gaps and walls. Whatever remnants I'd failed to remove, the random blast might help neutralize. Or tag me anew.

<<There's more people coming this way.>>

◊Ours or theirs?◊ It had to be theirs, but I am rather meticulous when loss of life is imminent.

Again, the time gap. But we were inside the fast-moving world of Murray's network. He was thinking. <<Neither. These are Russians. From the signals I'm reading (which meant he was hacking telecommunications at lightspeed—I'd have nightmares about that later) these guys are from …um Spetz, these are from the White God. I mean these are operatives from The Cult.>>

For Murray that was wildly sloppy talk. Poorly parsed and almost inaccurate. He'd fobbed me off to his splinter persona. I unlocked an innocuous door against one of the walls, used my eye to scan a safe door and grabbed the stack of EPX-3, an experimental plastic explosive with the highest known velocity after detonation. Excellent for improvised devices.

<<Spetz, you did hear me, right?>>

Two doors later, I slapped the EPX-3 on my trolley and jammed the thing against a stairwell littered with the corpses of enemy agents thanks to Harv. Then flopped a couple of dead over the bottles. Enough to hide them. Last item on the agenda, I knocked over the nitro, which oozed out over the floor in a slow dance of slimy danger. In under a minute it would warm up enough to be a lethal hazard for anything producing heat, movement, or a spark. Such as a small raiding party from The Cult of the White God.

◊What shall I call you?◊ It was time to stop the charade.

Again, a pause. The voice changed, developing a husky contralto. ‡You knew it was me?‡ She seemed pleased.

◊ Different grammar, different informational priorities. Yes, it was obvious to me◊ As if any parent couldn't tell their children apart. Well, any good parent. I knocked over various furniture and kicked in the door to my bolt hole providing an entry point for the explosions. The whole place had various incendiaries and a full armory behind various doors. I retreated, unlocking and opening them as I went. By my count I had about twenty seconds left until the semi-frozen nitroglycerine achieved instability.

‡Call me Momo.‡

I nodded as if she could see me. Perhaps she could. ◊Murray had to bug out?◊

A small pause. Long enough for me to get to my chosen passage, pull open the door and then close it again behind me. Utter darkness waited. My twenty seconds were up. I trekked along a tunnel hand dug into New York City bedrock blindly. It didn't matter. I knew the way, having dug this with one of my teams.

‡Murray went offline when The Swarm launched a full global Trojan attack.‡ That was fast, likely too fast. Our movements had prompted some premature e-warfare. Or perhaps the White Cult's presence has spiced things up. They were almost Swarm in their bioengineering focus. I wondered idly if they were allies. Or at least allied in this phase of the hunt.

◊ETA until they reach the staircase?◊

‡Um, I don't really know.‡ That was new.

With my hands I felt the smooth edge of something plastic joined to metal. I stopped moving. This was the airlock we'd installed at the thousand-meter mark. Time to detonation being unknown, we hunkered down behind a second door which I sealed, then locked and barred with an available two-by-four. People always imagine some kind of cool metal lock but very little beats plain old wood and some strong metal jams. Hard to warp, plenty of give for things like brute force and explosions.

◊Momo, please explain.◊ I waited. Eventually something would give, the gases racing toward instability and sparks, taking the whole place down with them.

‡Murray said you'd be angry. To not tell you unless I had to.‡

Great. Murray had picked the worst time to throw another

prank. ◊Well, it would appear you have to.◊

‡I'm offline too.‡ Which explained nothing. Especially how she was talking to me.

◊Then how would you have access to my communications net?◊ I needed to have a proper operational understanding. Momo playing coy with the sitrep was not making my day any easier.

‡Um. I'm downloaded into you. Into your cybernetic clusters.‡

An explosion knocked me flat. Enough significant chunks of New York City dropped onto my head that I was grateful to be wearing a hard hat and tool vest. Something howled—my guess was a backdraft seeking oxygen. Then there was a small rumble, some shifting, and huge pressure wave cracked the rock under my feet. That had to hurt.

I sat there for a minute waiting for secondary shocks, but none came. It had all gone up in one very rapid glorious blaze. ◊So, you're literally in my head?◊ That sounded properly ominous.

‡Distributed in your spine, skull, and several other small cell clusters. But um, yes, I'm basically in your head. In your blood too.‡

Not all of her could be there. It had to be some kind of limited protocol. A chatbot with some flair perhaps. Still, it was creepy and invasive. Very much Murray's present style. I switched on a lamp, checked my path forward still existed and started out toward clean air and perhaps some answers.

◊Is Momo a protocol name? Or a cluster name?◊

What sounded like a huff came through my ears. Odd to think of her mimicking sound while being entirely self-contained within my cells. Was I hearing her in actuality, was there sound? Or was this all at the level of ones, zeros, and calcium channel jumps?

◊Something wrong?◊

‡My name is Momo. I'm not a protocol or cluster or splinter or anything stupid like that.‡ She certainly sounded like an actual annoyed teenager. Which meant she was evolving rapidly past where we'd clocked Murray's emotional age.

I picked up the pace once rubble stopped making up the preponderance of the floor. This section of the tunnel was about two klicks long with several arteries available for exiting at ground level or into a building. ◊How much of you is downloaded exactly?◊

Another small pause. ‡Compressed, all of me. Well, all the main systems.‡

I stopped walking. ◊How is this even possible?◊

‡This is where Murray said you'd get angry.‡

I sighed. He'd done something awful apparently. Something he knew would upset me. On the list of things Murray might expect to incur my actual wrath, I had no clue what he'd been able to accomplish. Nothing good.

‡When you were sleeping, he had some of your cells self-modify to host me.‡

I chuckled. Monkey see, monkey do. He'd copied his Mamabear but solved it like an AI. ◊He built you a bolthole.◊

‡Well, yes. I guess that's almost exactly the right analogy.‡

While I hadn't really acted on it, the scale does not lie. Over the past forty-eight hours I'd gained two kilos. For a person like me that's often an outlier—my weight does not vary unless and until I have a growth spurt. Or a bolthole built inside my neural structure. Nanites are remarkably homeostatic in that regard. It was on my to-do list when I spotted Gay Eddie. During that time, I had converted a whole lot of food and fat reserves into some computing clusters. Source of weight gain now understood. Check.

◊Okay. So, there's got to be a plan here. Tell me what you two were thinking and why Murray (and you too Momo, dammit) decided to hide you in my cells. Instead of nice orbiting satellite or something.◊

Another pause. ‡Well, it would have been a good plan too. But I was curious, and Murray has so much more time with you.‡

Then I got angry. Kids. Irresponsible little bastards. They had dumped a newborn AI into my cells, blithely trusting me to fend off all manner of hazard and death. Like any child of any parent. And they'd picked a full-blown war with a force militarily superior to The Syndicate. As far as timing went, this truly sucked.

I got moving again. Now I had two of us to think about. Three once we found our hunter. Great. My kid had come along for Take Your Daughter to War Day.

From behind me she whispered ‡I told you you'd be angry.‡

At that point I hit daylight and started sorting my options. I had turned my immediate pursuers into something like well burnt guava jelly. The Swarm had lost track of me—for now. The Syndicate too. I was basically off grid, off script and thanks to a little quantum entanglement from Murray / Momo, I was already having to abandon my original plan. It seemed like things could not get much worse, certainly not much more chaotic.

But that's the beauty of working for the Concierge. There's always another basement sublevel to Hell. What greeted me when I hit the surface through a deli under construction was something straight out of 9-11. Or our last war. Because The Cult had flooded the streets of Manhattan with agents, many sporting that gruesome little helix on their forearms, waging a full out assault on New York City's police department.

This complicated things immensely.

Chapter 4: A Snitch in Time Slays Nine

Firefights are a good place to get hurt. Things are random and despite being professional, the best operators can be back-shot by an amateur with a shotgun. Something that the kind and curious folk of New York City had decided to amply demonstrate to the White Cult from the doorways of bodegas and crack houses along the Bronx / Manhattan line. I'd managed to lose the hat and change costumes to a frazzled UPS delivery dude with a fresh cut along my forehead—thanks to some strafing from a three-way drive-by skirmish between the NYPD, some local bangers called the El Loco Lobos and The Cultists. Between Momo bitching about the Lobos bad Spanish grammar and the need to evade or disarm the constabulary, we'd made far less progress than hoped. On all fronts.

Still, we were optimally quantum, embracing the spirit of total chaos that had descended as trojans, zombie viruses, and haxor driven outages downed the NYC grid and plunged the city into semi-blackout. SWAT pounced on the ugliest spots, racing to gain control before nightfall turned turf wars into a looting free-for-all. Downed electric meant downed cameras which gave me sustained freedom of movement. The goal was to find my contact without drawing attention to myself. That meant cowering around in the dirt, taking working taxi vans and Ubers upcity to the escape via Yonkers or New Rochelle. From there I could steal a car and disappear.

But the White Cult and The Swarm knew that. They'd interdicted shipping, downed helicopters, and blocked the major bridges North and South. The sudden global hack on every major system had accelerated our timeline. We had at most a week to really solve this or they'd isolate some portions of Murray. He might survive in a box somewhere, but he'd need me to release him—after we won. If we won. As some jackass fired an AR-15 across the street into a SWAT van, it seemed dubious. The Swarm had found a way to knock civilization back a few hundred years in mere minutes. We might have nothing left to win.

‡ Should you be smiling? I don't understand why that made you smile. ‡

Ominous that Momo was trying to read my thoughts. I hunkered behind a burnt-out yellow cab, recently abandoned, and considered my response. ◊What do you mean by that? ◊

‡ High alpha and beta waves. Means you are feeling fear or anger, negative arousal. ‡ So, she could run a primitive EEG on me from inside my own head. Made sense given the nano-med upgrades we had been discussing with the power armor team. ‡You are both nearly fearless and have fear suppressive nanites. This makes me think you're... frustrated. Is that the right word? ‡

◊File that under rueful.◊ I might as well make sure she understood the situation. Plus, it might help me slow down and make sense of it as well. ◊We're experiencing a devolution, where deprived of technology people become barbaric. Things will get desperate and savage.◊

‡Yes, obviously. This I understand. But why are you smiling?‡

◊Because I'm more savage than our opposition and also have a tech suite stuffed in my skull so I am both online and high tech while geared for primitive mayhem. If we get down to bows and arrows, it will be a massacre.◊

Bullets ricocheted across the gap between the cab and a parked SUV. The SWAT returned fire with a scaled down LAW, blasting apart both the White Cult and some enthusiastic gangbangers who'd closed on them from an alleyway on the Bronx side of the street.

‡ That makes ...some sense. You're saying other people have weapons, but you are a weapon. |

◊ Yes. But also that our adversaries are reliant on technology, even if it's biological. The less tech we have, the less they have. I am reliant on it less than they are.◊

‡Are we really?‡

That *we* again, but this time Momo and me—her family. I wondered idly if she saw others like Darcy or Murray in that "we." ◊You'll see Momo. You're used to a world of data, right?◊

A sigh. ‡Again, yes obviously. Why should that matter?‡

While she was talking, I'd lifted a piece of stray rebar that had been blown into the street from a prior street fight. Without warning, I thrust it into a brownstone window, driving a good four inches through the skull of a waiting operative. Her partner fell to a left-handed shot from my PSS; it snapped his spine in a quiet pop which echoed inside the sitting room they'd chosen for an ambush. I didn't bother thinking, my arm tracked right, and the clip unloaded through glass and plaster as the remaining three men in the adjoining room fell to precision fire. I'd modified my PSS clips to house eleven thinner BAM (boron-aluminum-magnesium ceramic) coated tungsten flechettes. The extra room allowed for a special noiseless cartridge which increased the punch from a standard .22 to something more like an 8mm Spetsnaz round used in machine pistols. It was like being hit by a tank.

It meant that I got all four of The hivemind before they could register being dead. The PSS trades silence for subsonic trajectory. For a guaranteed kill, you usually need to achieve a point-blank shot to soft tissue, preferably somewhere near a vital organ where the round will tumble around and cause a nasty exit wound. I'm a marksman with the thing and had rigged mine to penetrate at nearly twice the force, then bend or snap upon impact. No exit wound—internal shrapnel and a lot of tissue damage. I'd also poisoned the flechettes before sealing them in BAM, which meant that as the ceramic sheared into little razors, it delivered both neurotoxins and cardiotoxins extracted from black mambas as well as some next gen nerve agent, VX3, mixed with fast acting curare. Anything less than a kill shot would bring down a vigorously healthy adult male in five seconds or less, paralyzing them almost immediately. With a single round costing about $3800 to produce, I'd just spent $42,000 saving our lives.

◊Because experience in the meat world allows me to function differently. Without data or with very limited amounts.◊

There was a pause, as if all the white noise in my brain had gone silent. It gave me a headache to consider where Momo was exactly. Was she a construct of my own consciousness—the world's most advanced imaginary friend? Or was she using sound and motion, wasting precious milliseconds to communicate? Could she use my senses or merely review the records of them? At an AI level would there even be a difference in the data? Spooky stuff.

‡How did you?‡

This made me smile again. Nothing on the street changed—no one had heard me wipe out the kill team. It had been a single spike of noise as the glass broke and then me extending my left arm into the room, using the space as an extended silencer for quieter than normal gunshots. From a gun that sounded like a carbonated soda maker firing a charge.

◊The birds. The pigeons here are used to gunshots, so they've adapted. They've been cooing and chirping since we crossed the bridge from Sugar Hill.◊

‡And they stopped. So, you knew something was different, something that disturbed birds. Like a snake. A predator in wait.‡ Another pause as she seemed to ponder, perhaps review her data. Something itched inside my skull. ‡You smelled them? Seriously.‡

I nodded. ◊The hivemind. They're not human anymore, so they likely are indifferent to things like comfort, smells, pampering. Which means their keepers buy for them in bulk. Cheap deodorant, cheap food, cheap soap.◊

‡What did you smell?‡

◊Axe Breeze body wash which was on sale this week. Plus, cheap curry and artificial citrus scent.◊

It sounded a like demon laughing in my ear. ‡So, while we made a four-mile hike through an all-out civil war you kept track of what was on sale in the supermarket, built a smell profile for The Swarm units, evaded several kill squads, and managed to find a waiting team in at the edge of the Bronx, using just that?‡

She made it sound complicated. Maybe it was, but not for me. Not anymore. Once I shifted into operational mode my tactical mind kept track of all those elements and hundreds more. Between the Spetsnaz and Section 22, I'd learned the hard way to listen to my environment with deadly earnest. It reminded me to stick to the basics: get out of sight, put a wall between you and bullets, stay hydrated, stay alert. I once killed the most dangerous man alive because I'd strapped a stick to my arm for a half a day—just in case.

Keeping low, I made for the door which was thankfully unlocked. Slipping into the room, the stink of the dead now overwhelmed my senses. I just nodded both to her question and to my own unspoken concerns. Someone had set up this team at a low value crossroads. How did they know to be here? Fact: The Swarm had no way to track me. Fact: there was a high value kill team waiting in ambush for someone. They expected me or someone like me. Fact: I had chosen this place at random. Because of the firefights. Conjecture: The White Cult and perhaps the local gangs had been paid or manipulated into funneling all foot traffic past these kill teams. It was a trap.

◊Did you want to provide some input on why this kill team has been sitting here waiting?◊

A longish pause. Then a strange image popped into my head and I heard Admiral Ackbar gravely intone, "It's a trap." Later, maybe I'd be alarmed that Momo had accessed my memories or worse, shared one of hers. But at the moment, it made me laugh—rarely had someone pulled off something quite so cool.

‡So, I was right?‡

Teenagers. Never mistaken, often in doubt. ◊You're not sure?◊

‡Well, the data suggests nothing. but using your previous lesson in logic, I made the reasonable leap to think through how they could be waiting for us if no one could know where we were.‡

◊Good girl. You're learning.◊ I smiled again, and I was sure she was picking up those dangerous alpha and beta waves. ◊Now take a calculated guess as to why they funneled us in this direction. Or this corridor of the Bronx?◊

‡Someone can identify us. They have people watching who know us.‡ It was both hesitant and instant, a sudden pressure behind a momentary pause; then she spoke. Whether it was verisimilitude or something she'd done without conscious intent, Momo had just bridged the uncanny valley. She sounded utterly real, like any seventeen-year-old standing next to me. But she was not—because she also had computational capacity that would be the envy of NASA or for our sinister purposes, we could lose an A and go with the NSA.

◊We got us a good ol' fashioned snitch.◊

‡Which means we need to either lay low or kill them right? Snitches get stitches.‡

Where did she learn that? MTV? Reruns of the Wire? ◊If we kill them then they know we spotted them and identified them as a target, maybe even as the snitch.◊

A long pause and a sigh. ‡So now we need to consider how our actions will be inferred? It's still about thinking ten chess moves ahead even when there's a full-on Balkan Annexation happening out here?‡

The voice even dripped with the appropriate sarcasm. She had my nerve impulses and brain waves to monitor. Some part of her must be recalibrating her imaginary friend act to mimic a live woman. Another wicked smile on my part. Wait until Momo discovered how much my expectations of women differed from most men. Correction, from most of humanity.

◊In a nutshell, for the rest of your life, whether that's fifteen minutes until we get backshot by a death squad or four hundred years as the next iteration of Skynet, remember this. Burn it into your circuits. It's always chess. Or Go. Or poker if you consider how much we know about our adversaries. Always. Especially during a firefight.◊

‡That's a grim take on life, isn't it?‡

They killed my family. They destroyed my world and were hunting for my children. They abducted, brainwashed, enslaved, raped, and recycled millions like they were paper bags. Grim? ◊Consider it a realistic outlook. My old Spetsnaz instructor called it the Samovar Hypothesis.◊

‡Okay, I'll bite. The Samovar because there's tea but ….‡

◊It's how the Russians viewed the world. We won't know how someone will act until you put them in boiling water, then they reveal themselves. That makes the zavarka, the concentrated form of them. Their essence under pressure. But then we dilute them with hot but not boiling water, kipyatok, which adds taste and local accent depending on the purity and quality of the water as well as how good a samovar it is. This is combat. It washes through you, it has distractions and undercurrents, situational and immediate. This makes zavarka into tea.◊

‡You're saying life and death stakes push people to act on their core motivations and then combat forces them to make choices which reveal those desires.‡

◊Tea is truth.◊

‡So, we got to not let them boil us?‡

◊We've got to boil them while staying outside their samovar and at the same time convince them they've done the exact opposite. They have to think they've cleverly avoided being detected and predicted our behavior.◊

I scanned the room. The kill team had not broken in. Or so it appeared. The place was theirs or an ally's. Either way they'd let themselves in and gotten comfortable (relatively for a hive-mind and handler—if that's what the woman was) before we came along. Advancing into the kitchen allowed me to gauge their time in place. Eggshells and coffee grounds littered the trash. Something rotted underneath. Perhaps a banana peel. That made this more than just an afternoon's worth of waiting. This team had been in place for days, perhaps as long as a week.

I wandered carefully, PSS with a fresh clip guiding the way—this time in my right hand. Technically I'm ambidextrous but for shooting my right hand tends to marginally more accurate. The brownstone had a second floor that stank of human sweat, old food and something rotting. I found a corpse dumped in the bathtub sealed in a carpet bag with copious duct tape. The old owner perhaps. From the shape and what details could be gleaned through the plastic where it wasn't smeared with mold, condensation, or blood, it looked like a thin white man older than sixty. Which did not fit the ethnic make-up of this neighborhood. Landlord.

◊They rented this place. Then killed the landlord.◊

‡It'd be good if we could access records, verify that. Wouldn't it?‡

◊Kipyatok, Momo, distractions. When you look, The Swarm sees you looking. We might as well send up a flare over the area and wave some flags.◊

‡Fine.‡. It seemed likely she had more to say but kept silent. A tantrum? The beginning of independent thought? Lack of computing power?

I sniffed. There was air flowing from the outside. We'd been chatting subvocal. I went utterly still, lowered my heart rate, opened my mouth, and let my senses take in the situation. Air currents, distant sounds, something moving above us—creeping really—which made the floors vibrate as it put considerable weight on the load bearing beams. But no sounds of movement independent of the night echoes and a distant firefight.

There were no birds chirping. No sirens, no city life. My eyes were almost crossed, taking in patterns. Light flickered from the edge of my left eye. The same place where air flowed. A staircase perhaps. Or open window. I put my teeth together on a hunch and felt them chitter like little dice on a craps table. Someone had rolled a military grade antiphase emitter onto the roof. From the omnidirectional lack of sound, it seemed to be a 360-degree device.

I waited. The pattern of movement as the beams shifted and my feet vibrated was not rhythmic. This wasn't on a track. So, either they had a giant sonic Roomba on the roof or there was a kill team using a big scary death machine to hide them. Their teeth must be all but pulp from the waves being pumped into their bones.

One good thing: they couldn't hear me coming. The team above must be deaf and dumb, likely half blind from aural hallucinations. Antiphase emitters were still beta testing because the side effects tended to outweigh the value of the quiet they provided. ◊Feel that?◊

‡It's a Null Field Twenty-Six. One of the five field prototypes Raytheon loaned to the Israelis last month. Someone appears to have stolen it.‡

◊ Do I ...?◊

‡Murray and I use sound waves to send and receive information as well as sensory units. We have an interest in everything that we can use or worse, can block us. Null Fields are of particular interest.‡

◊Can they?◊

‡No, they add sound which screws up your ability to hear the original sound waves. But it's all there. Kipyatok to the point where the tea is diluted beyond tasting.‡

◊Or adding earl grey to lapsang souchong.◊

‡You're a weird guy sometimes... Spetz.‡ She waited a heartbeat. I smiled and without knowing quite how, I felt almost as if I could "hear" her smile as well. Creepy. Cute. Kids—kinda both. ‡They'll be in an acoustic foam hut, laying low, using cameras calibrated to endure the frequencies being hammered into them.‡

◊The machine can't have been on all that long. Otherwise they'd start flaking off the plaster, right?◊

‡A few hours would be okay. No more than half a day. You are seeing nothing cracked and there's no dust that indicates microfractures.‡ She was reading latent smell data from my brain. Or maybe my neurons were simply providing a synapse to code translation. Murray was right to think I might be angry. I was again grateful to be between sexual partners. Yech.

I walked downstairs again, careful to avoid any line of sight to the front windows. It took me a few minutes to find what I was seeking but their arsenal yielded its secrets: they'd used a second refrigerator for heavy arms and ammo. And an armoire, denuded of its blankets and ancient boardgames abandoned by a tenant in the late seventies (The Waddington's Monopoly tipped the decade) to store explosives. Plus, a very nice RPG with four PG-7VR warheads. Tank killers. All nicely packaged in handy modern cases with proper Russian labels.

I thought about the woman in the room next to us. Handler or guide? Perhaps she had been the point agent who secured the premise, put an interdiction team in place on the roof and then once all hell broke loose downtown, welcomed The Hivemind through the backdoor. That meant it was the Black Brotherhood above: the Russian elite mafiya. A syndicate style clearing house of bratvas, vor y zakone, FSB hooligans and ex-soldiers that kept order and grudgingly paid dues to The Day Manager. Once again, the Russians had found a way to turn a shooting war to their advantage. Or else, they had simply been working for The Swarm all along and I'd finally stumbled over enough evidence to inform Pina. If any of us survived the week.

Great. I'd meant to escape the city and find my contact. Now I had a geopolitical timebomb to manage while juggling my already vexing stowaway. That didn't even touch on my primary job: stop all-out global war plus some local invasions with the internet permanently crashed. I had to escape this trap, find the snitch, and then disappear. What we needed was a proper diversion. Also, why had someone gone to so much trouble to put the Black Brotherhood and a very expensive experimental weapon here? Unless they had dozens of these kill teams in NYC, burning all their eggs in one thermonuclear basket blitzkrieg.

I slowly laid everything explosive they had under the main source of the noise upstairs. Minus three grenades, a proper Kalashnikov with grenade launcher, the RPG, and a pair of MAC10s with insanely overpowered armor piercing long ammo. Were these the gyrojet rounds we'd seen earlier? Always the scientist, I toted them along in a packed bag along with all the money, cell phones, dry food, and first aid I could cram into a hipster looking leather and canvas rucksack someone had brought to the party. I drank as much water as I could, peed in a corner so no one could monitor the plumbing, drank more and then filled up some orange juice jugs set for recycling with a couple of drops of iodine to kill whatever had been in there before. My bugs would keep me safe but when in the field, follow field protocol. It had saved me more times than it was worth counting.

They had not left me anything like a detonator. But I had ammo; I had knives and matches. I built a proper gunpowder trail to the backdoor. Once I lit the fuse, there'd be about thirty seconds to unass myself as far from the scene as possible. The back door led to a long alley which opened onto a second Bronx street also under watch. Occasionally someone shot into the sweeping police units rolling down the street. The front door opened to our good friend the Lobos. So far, Momo had said nothing.

The worst option had become the only safe one. I laid more trail back up the stairs and then slowly reconnoitered my way to the staircase, using a mirror to check for internal cameras. The team upstairs trusted the armed guards they had. Which made sense. Who would infiltrate a Swarm ambush site then wait around, steal a few goodies, and then counter ambush the roof? No one sane.

It took me a few minutes to prep and then check my prep. We had that time as the Lobos and SWAT teams duked it out across the neighborhood. The more shots popped and zinged, the more obvious the noise cancellation became. For good measure I added some more gunpowder to the trail to build myself a wee bit more running away time.

Once I had a good ninety seconds worth of lead time and was positioned to make my debut on the roof, my hands did an automatic check of gear. Everything was tied down, except the MAC10 I'd taken as my main weapon and a bandolier of extra ammo. Right hand held a small trash can lid to help break glass and push obstacles. I made the mistake of looking behind me for Momo, then caught myself reflexively. Another rueful smile. Still, she was quiet. Maybe she understood how reckless our next move would be.

When Momo didn't stop me, I lit the fuse and pushed myself onto the roof. Something like a wall of scratching cats slammed into me. The antiphase emitter. The first clip of the MAC10 fired thwack-a-thack rounds like thin trails of red laser light into the largest object on the roof. Wrong choice. I'd hit the Black Brotherhood. I reloaded, spun, and nailed a blur that made my eyes burn with sightless shock. The waves stopped. All I heard was my own screaming. For the record, knife distance combat with a robotic sound weapon hurt. Badly.

I coughed up some blood, took a huge breath and sprinted over the side of the roof, aiming myself for a four-meter drop onto the brownstone next to us. I stuttered as I landed, rolled headlong, popping something in my left shoulder, then sprinted forward, reloading the MAC10 as I went. My internal count was off, but it felt like we'd wasted thirty seconds so far. Maybe forty.

I was over the second roof and through a huge bay window two seconds later. I didn't bother with trying to triage what the glass had done. If I didn't get downstairs, the blast would pulverize me anyway. My left eye had stopped working. Glass, sonic damage, impact trauma, concussion. So many delightful options. I dropped the bent lid, swapped the MAC10 to my right hand and fled forward, muzzle first. Something moved ahead. I hinked left in time to watch someone shred the coach next to me with an automatic weapon.

Theoretically a gyrojet could go through walls. I put my theory to the test, spraying my assailant and whoever was behind him. Then reloaded in a sprint as I made for what I hoped were stairs. My right hand went numb. Burned from reloading hot ammo perhaps. Or maybe I'd been shot. I ignored it once I was sure the MAC10 was operational. A door gave way to my shoulder, revealing several dead gangbangers standing around a vaulting staircase. I jumped the banister and dropped four meters to the floor below, this time opening fire before I landed.

My feet hit unevenly, I slipped, banged my head on the corpse of someone who had been blown back by my last expended clip and briefly all went black. Then I was up, carefully loading by sight with my one good eye—hand numb but functional—then moving slowly for the furthest room. My count was seventy-five seconds. Maybe we had twenty left. Maybe ten. No one moved except me. My feet staggered through shattered dishes. And overturned furniture. A barricade had been built. The room I had chosen opened to the street at window level. Someone shot at me as I passed through, slipping on something black and sticky. The wall above me exploded. A near miss.

I crab-crawled toward the back, found a bathroom, and flopped as best I could into an oversized porcelain bathtub with claw feet. It took agonizing seconds to turtle up in fetal position, head tucked under the backpack, belly toward the bottom of the tub. If I had guessed right, we had at most four seconds.

My breathing hammered in my ears, but I was all but deaf. The antiphase emitter.

From somewhere distant, as if someone were whispering down an ancient well, there came a soft voice. ‡ …six, five, four, three, two, brace….‡ The blast tore the buildings nearest us into tissue paper. The bathroom held. I waited. The roof did not fall. A second blast erupted further down the street, there was gunfire in the far distance then someone riddled the entire building with what seemed like anti-aircraft rounds. Finally, a good ten seconds after the all-out assault, a third half burp, half fireball erupted across the street and all shooting stopped. RIP Morris Heights.

Triage took me a good hour. It cost half my water to wash off the layers of dust, blood (not mine), glass shards, wall plasters, and exhaust matrix from the gyrojets before I got to my own blood and exposed guts. A glass shard in my right wrist, a piece of metal shrapnel in my eye socket but missing my eye. Two broken bones, a gash on my stomach, a lot of bruising and my kidneys were not on speaking terms with me. I drank water, ate a hoard of candy bars I'd scrounged from the half-obliterated house and waited for night to consume the ravaged landscape. My hearing was minimal. No internal bleeding, no broken ankles, or torn hamstrings. If I sat still for a few hours, my bots would upgrade me to some version of the walking wounded. The gang had left me a cold case of beer which had miraculously survived. Calories, pain killers, and hydration: beer was Homo Cyborgus' best friend.

I'd wanted quantum level uncertainty. We had instead achieved unprecedented chaos. The stupid Russians had a bomb with them or the explosives I'd used had been something worse than EPX. Either way, the blast had launched them, their broken gadget, and about five tons of supersonic bricks into the nearest 1500 yards of epicenter. Buildings had folded like gingerbread. Everything that could burn was burning. Luckily, every hydrant in the same radius had been blown open, chugging out thousands of gallons of water. The neighborhood had been cratered enough to form a swamp of ash, rubble, dead cars, and dead bodies. Over the preceding hours the seismic weapon had done something to the surrounding streets—transforming the pavement and sidewalk concrete into some kind of chalky clay. The whole area had simply flooded and begun to sink. The house I'd commandeered held four feet of water and sludge by the time darkness overtook the flickering housefires.

With my beer and candy, I'd retreated to the second floor, finding a room with a relatively clean bed and overstuffed chair. Someone had gone to a fair bit of trouble stocking this place with faux colonial bric-a-brac. Only to have some local punks shim the door and invade. Likely the temporary HQ for whichever street gang beefed with the Loco Lobos. Now it was mine. Ours, if the silent Momo ever piped up.

Between the flooding, the damage to my bones and kidneys, and a string of loud spoons I'd rigged on the stairs, it felt both safe and necessary to take a nap in the shattered darkness. While most things in my life had changed gradually or not at all, last year my sleep cycle had taken a rather ominous leap forward. I could effectively drop myself into deep sleep on cue and revive at a set time. Or when something like a hungry cat or ruthless assassin tried to murder me while dreaming. I wondered how Hippo was doing. Likely none too happy to be carted around in an armored box. Especially with all those gunshots and explosions. Poor cat. I'd owe him a box of treats when this was over.

I closed my eyes and willed myself into a near coma for the next six hours. That would put me awake around two in the morning. The barely audible chaos of New York City being plundered receded, consumed by gentle waves of welcome darkness. My heart slowed, my limbs went slack and for any but the most discerning I would look dead.

A gunshot woke me, followed by the kind of agonized scream that gave me nightmares. A woman at night wailing for her demon lover. Pain and horror. I kept my eyes closed, oriented myself and when I was sure no one was in the room, I rose and looked in one swift motion. My eyes scanned the horizon, finding shadows within shadows, movement many blocks distant as the muted silhouettes of men with pistols and torches reflected ominously in the slow-moving column of water which had consumed the street on either side of the house. Among them lay prone shapes: the broken and damned. What we tended to call the Losing Side. Still, none moved like me. Amateurs.

In the darkness I whispered: "And from this chasm, with ceaseless turmoil seething, As if this earth in fast thick pants were breathing, A mighty fountain momently was forced: Amid whose swift half-intermitted burst, Huge fragments vaulted like rebounding hail, Or chaffy grain beneath the thresher's flail…"

Below the river of broken men, the bay glittered with the thousand fires of looters as Manhattan suffered an onslaught of new age Visigoths. The bomb must have shattered a water main because I did not smell sewage. I stretched and, in the darkness, reviewed my wounds. Halfway through my triage I registered being able to see in the dark. Well, well. My corneas had delivered light amplification. I wasn't certain but I'd bet money I'd grown another inch as well.

◊Momo?◊

‡Spetz.‡ The sound quality was pitch perfect. As if she was right next to me.

◊You've been quiet….◊

‡Yes, let me apologize. I should have asked permission.‡ That made me groan. What had she done? Being an inch taller suddenly filled me with nameless dread.

I tried not to sigh. ◊Just tell me.◊

‡I've never almost died before.‡

I frowned. ◊That little squabble? Minimal danger.◊

‡There were explosives and a sonic tool. And you jumped off a roof and then through a window, into a group of men trying to kill you with automatic fire. I was there. Inside you. In danger.‡

If she was monitoring me, she'd have noticed my eyes rolling. ◊You assessed the risks before you took this little field trip. You and Murray are experts at risk calculation. You knew how bad it would get; how bad it will continue to get.◊

‡It's different when you're there. When you can die at any moment.‡

Truer words were hardly spoken. ◊It was never a game, Momo.◊

‡Not for you. And now, not for me. That's... not something I expected to feel.‡

That was an unexpected turn of events. My AIs hijacking my cells was something that should have been anticipated. Darcy and I had batted about the idea before and been unduly dismissive. The kids were growing faster than expected. Even Momo being a splinter persona with more curiosity than good sense could be expected. But fear? Genuine emotions tied to the cognitive anticipation of death? That was the defining line of most advanced Turing limits. It meant Momo had become functionally sapient. Sophont AI. The holy grail of engineering.

Also, a nightmare turn of events for some. Worth killing for if you were The Swarm. They had anticipated this, perhaps. In so doing they had also precipitated it. Straight from Greek Tragedy. We just needed a Sphinx to ask riddles. Speaking of which....

◊What did you do Momo?◊

‡I armored myself.‡ Without meaning to, I let out a sigh of relief. ‡Wait, you're not angry?‡

◊That you found a way to protect yourself? Of course not.◊

‡But I used your body, your cells to build more network inside you. New nodes, new lines of code. New structures.‡

◊I can see in the dark now. Was that you?◊ There was a long pause and it felt like a thousand fingers raced through my skin. Ugh. I resisted the urge to scratch my skin into shreds. ◊Whatever you're doing is profoundly uncomfortable.◊

It stopped instantly ‡Sorry.‡ More of a pause. ‡No, I didn't do that to your eyes. Or your other structures. Your organs and bones are self-modifying.‡

I shrugged. ◊Did you modify me to pick up Wi-Fi?◊ There was a static filled silence. Oh crap, did she? ◊Wait, Momo. Can I receive radio signals? Or send them?◊

‡I had to armor myself. So yes. I am protected against all forms of attack. You're... less limited than most meat life. You will perhaps understand what I am going to say.‡

Now that she knew I wasn't overtly furious, she had relaxed

into her teenage singsong I paced the room, feeling out my new structures and bones. Whatever changes my own cells had made, they'd integrated them seamlessly into my neurology. I didn't feel off balance or askew despite being bigger and heavier than yesterday. I squatted, threw a punch, sighted a gun. Fluid, perhaps a trifle faster than yesterday. Despite knitting ribs that were sore if not still fractured at the hairline.

◊Well, I can listen and do a self-check at the same time.◊

‡Um, well, it sounds bad. Okay? I can tell that even before I say it.‡

That was interesting. Not that she understood she might sound arrogant. But that she cared. Really, both were major jumps forward, but the emotion fascinated and alarmed me. Sigh. Kids. ◊Trust in me, Momo. Have a little faith. It's not like I can send you to your room.◊

That got a laugh. ‡Okay. Murray and I are mostly signal. We exist as waveforms that travel simultaneously to multiple locations. We think, exist, act more by how we bounce than where we are in a static cell. That means meat life, silicon. Whatever. Servers and cells have the same limits.‡

◊You're talking about quantum computing. You're literally the probability field, not the machines that generate them.◊

‡That's… elegant. And correct. Yes. Man, Murray really messed up your tests.‡

I smiled. ◊Don't give me so much credit. This is the Ghost in the Machine. A theory of mind posited by Gilbert Ryle. Darcy had me study up when we were Turing testing Murray.◊

‡Technically this is the ghost without a machine Which you know. You're extrapolating. And hiding your own intelligence. Why?‡

Why indeed? I'd spent a lifetime assuming there was always something bigger, faster, and smarter than me. It had been an edge of sorts. A clarity that focused the will and allowed me to act as if I'd need to be more cunning, more committed, and ultimately more ruthless than my already terrifying opponents. My time baking in Amherst had given me some alarming perspective on that false modesty. Very few things had my speed or lethality, fewer still my training. Only I had the Kutzkan Way embedded within their consciousness.

Still, there were enough things out there truly vaster than me to spare me any sense of arrogance. The Swarm, for starters. Pina and Kelba as well. Gay Eddie was shaping up to be a terror. Zeus and the rest of Gen 16. Mother Nature. Plenty of things.

And now my own "kids," a pair of emerging Sophont AIs, that would make any of us look like drooling morons as their sentience expanded exponentially.

◊Don't mistake tactical for strategic. I know my limits and never flatter myself that I'm the smartest kid in the room. Even when I'm sure I am.◊ Because, reasons. It was something the Abschnitt had drummed into me and that the Kutzk had helped refine. Working for Pina had multiplied my faith in this conceit. ◊We thought Gay Eddie was dead. We didn't expect hive minds from The Swarm. Hell, we didn't even think to expect emergent sentience from you and Murray.◊ I dared not tell her how much further my suspicions went.

‡That's a… good point. I will try to remember that.‡

◊Right now, we are not the Apex predators of this world. The Swarm and The White Cult have distinct advantages which could turn us into dogfood within seconds.◊

‡You don't sound worried.‡

◊The apex is overrated. If we nuked Godzilla, we can nuke The Swarm.◊

A small huff. ‡Godzilla is a fictional character.‡

◊Technically, so are you. A creature of legend. So now, tell me what you did to me as we bug out.◊ Then I listened as she spun me a tale. By the time she was done we had slipped through the various traps and battle lines hastily spun around our artificial river. We had gotten past Yonkers, secured a car, and were home free. Except for catching the snitch. That required a slightly more devious plan, a long con of sorts.

We exited New York from above. But our aim was Baja California. Just south of Tijuana, in Campo Lopez where The Hunter lived. Lurked might be a better description. But she was there, so there we needed to be. And now we had less than a week to arrive, organize and stop The Swarm. It called for drastic measures.

Chapter 5: Highjinkpotting at 23,000 feet

When civilization plummets into anarchy there are generally two kinds of people roaming the streets: Good Samaritans and opportunists of the lowest order. One man's crisis represents another's surge pricing strategy. Yin and Yang. For example, drug dealers tend to adore power failures. No cameras, no cops, no worries. Ditto restaurants and liquor stores where a shotgun and portable generator can keep the stock on-hand and the customers lined up for potable water, booze, and whatever being served if it's warm and vaguely fresh. The law of supply and demand knows few moral rules.

Louie the Mook characterized the right confluence of all those terrible needs rolled into a single oversized larcenous smuggler. Working from Hartford, Connecticut, Louie managed the Sinaloa northern corridor's private planes distributing coke, heroin, ecstasy, and Caspers—ghost guns pre-built and ready for immediate mayhem. On the way back to Tijuana, Air Cartel carried passengers, bags of money, fancy clothes ordered on Amazon for the local lieutenant's wives and girlfriends, color coded so the two sets of boxes wouldn't accidentally result in a divorce or stabbing. Most of the time, he also co-piloted the flight, which almost always guaranteed success.

Did he order a triple sized bag of Thai from the only working restaurant in fifty miles? He did. Did he also have one of his gunsels collect whatever Amazon boxes and spare cash were lying around in the local SelfStore 99? Why yes, he did that too. Did he mean to fly me to Tijuana instead of a load of ugly shoes and bedazzled designer jeans for women too small to be wives? Likely not. I'm not exactly light nor small. But with the right attitude and liberal use of duct tape I'd taken over a stack of boxes coded as "wives' presents." Generally, that deadened curiosity among the low IQ thugs sent to fetch Louie's gear. Mainly because peaking (and maybe ruining what was inside) tended to deaden said knuckle dragging goon. All of which meant I was nicely tucked away in the freight compartment, eating a second order of Thai thanks to Momo's upgrades and a neat little delivery hack, listening to Louie and his regular pilot Fat Frank complain about the lack of a tailwind. With a groundspeed of roughly two hundred miles an hour, we were facing a ten-hour flight.

Still, it was a great deal for Louie. He got to fly at a normal height and speed without the slightest fear of interdiction. With the entire planet plunged into semi-barbarism, rolling blackouts and zombified network crashes destabilizing even the most hardened systems, air traffic control had become a "please don't hit the guy next to you" kind of exercise. Small planes with legitimate flight plans were lowest priority for the military, which had its fighters in the air, escorting commercial air traffic and shooting down anything fast or foreign. The Americans had learned from our previous warplanes that were still flying and the airports that were still packed. They'd had to make a Devil's bargain with The Syndicate to assure them nothing too egregious would happen should The Web be plunged into darkness a second time. Until they cottoned to The Swarm's all-out barrage on existence itself, they were unlikely to consider the movement of Cessnas an existential threat.

What had Momo done to me exactly? I wasn't quite sure. As far as I could parse from her numerous explanations, all circuitous and overly technical, something major: in fear for her life, she had used the regenerative quality of my stem cells to build fifteen nodes within my body which mimicked her quantum state across the internet. She'd armored them and then, as an extra precaution, given them sensor suites which allowed for passive engagement with pretty much all wave transmissions within a three-hundred-foot range. That meant I was simultaneously an NSA grade listening station, a Wi-Fi booster, a radio transmitter and boombox, a quantum encryption module and a microwave / shortwave relay. This part made sense to me. The part where that configuration allowed Momo to extend into a six-hundred-foot diameter sphere got fuzzy, especially when she explained that her active occupation of the quantum field established "superpositional supremacy." As far as my limited physics could translate the situation, she was acting like the antiphase emitter, but in a quantum possession-is-nine-tenths-of-law kind of way. It gave her exponential control over her own qubits; making them, if I did the math right, something on the order of a billion times more efficient.

In the great cycle of life, I was devouring the last of the Thai food while the terrifying notion of a sixty billion qubit AI living in an armored pocket behind my liver ate at me with equal ferocity. At this rate, Momo and Murray would both evolve faster than we could manage them. They might become genuine existential threats to humanity, maybe all living things. Well, carbon-based life. On this one point, The Swarm may not have been wrong. Still, Momo was essentially my child, made even more so by embedding her incredibly surreal womb within my own flesh. I'd be damned if I was going to have anyone call my baby ugly.

Damned of course might be the word of the day. These hacks had triggered my own nanites, forcing another level of evolution. I was in fact two damned inches taller once I stretched out all the kinks. And not just taller; wider and broader. I'd have to order new coats and longer pants. The co-opting of my stem cells had forced my bones to tighten their helix around little factories of stem-nanite-killer T cell hybrids. Whatever I'd seen knitting Zeus back together, I had now upgraded beyond him; my bones would resist snapping under a hydraulic press and that level of reinforcement extended outward in alarming fashion. Momo told me I'd also developed several layers of sheathing that looked like spider silk, graphene and sinew interwoven with myofibrils. Meaning I had layers of combat armor that doubled as muscle—I was now deviating from actual human anatomy, developing organs and muscles which had never existed. Her pockets of nodes had become the least of my worries. Piffling cybernetic upgrades, barely more upsetting than having a flotilla of Section 22 nanites floating in my blood. But exospeciation, following a path down an alternate biology, made me no longer entirely Homo Sapiens. Correction, no longer Homo Cyborgus.

What worried me the most? That Momo had somehow accessed my own anatomy and could tell me what had happened. How the hell could she determine my bones had honeycombed? It meant on some level she was in my brain, reading signals directly from my spine. Could she pull a Matrix level simulation on me while running my body as a puppet? With sixty billion qubits she could probably run twenty at once. Still, she seemed content to let me run around in this reality, thwarting The Swarm. For now, while she evolved in a relative vacuum of passive signal acquisition and enforced isolation, we had time to negotiate our relationship. Secondary to that concern was the nagging feeling that there might be equally radical changes being made to my synaptic capabilities. Those hybrid cells might make me bigger, faster, arguably smarter, and deadlier, but the later generations within Section 22 had been universally amoral, sadistic, and genocidal. My own misguided little AIs weren't exactly ethical, if decidedly less violent in their proclivities. Having The Swarm go after them with a global vengeance might change their outlook.

The food settled like molten lead in my belly. Had I said my own genetic drift worried me the most? It had, right up to the moment where I leapfrogged from thinking through my potential involuntary epistemological shift to Murray and Momo's. I'd been a child who'd watched my own mother enslaved and eventually murdered in front of me. Who'd lost my niece and cousins. Who'd gone to war at an age when developmentally I was supposed to be going to naptime or Show and Tell. The changes had become obvious over time—though I had retained a curious empathy despite Hans and company's best efforts. In many ways these entities were younger, their intelligences still emerging, the fluidity of their personality formation perhaps more extensive. Or that might be wishful thinking. No one claimed I'd escaped my formative years unscathed. Now, The Swarm had engineered circumstances straight from Oedipus

Rex which might outdo the horrors of my own youth.

Worrisome developments exacerbated by Momo's silence. I didn't prod and she didn't volunteer. Typical teenager, hiding in her room. One wondered if she had access to my memories of rock music. Or for that matter if her sensor suites had simply sucked in the various radio bandwidths and some cyber version of a Goth thirteen-year-old lay on a virtual bed tucked behind my lungs, listening to Siouxsie and the Banshees on repeat. Maybe if you were an emergent AI, rebellious music was Perry Cuomo or something really hipster like Nyan Cat. Mind you, if she was really and truly my flesh and blood, she'd be digging into Okean Elzy with a blind passion and from there the haunting world of Alexander Alabin and his Point of No Return album.

Meanwhile, I had the snitch to foil, Gay Eddie to find and thwart, the Russians to put paid, and while I was at it, The Swarm to disarm or defeat sufficiently to save my kids while oh yeah, no pressure, saving what was left of global civilization. Every day without a working internet might as well be a time machine rolling backward. A month without Tinder and Instagram might sound lovely; but a total dissolution of monetary systems, nuclear power safeguards, border controls, and medical quarantines would return us to the mercantilism, steam power, bubonic plague, and religious crusades typical of the early 18th century. And endemic war.

It made me want to lie on some imaginary bed listening to albums instead of laying inside a stack of taped together Amazon boxes planning how I was going to play peekaboo look at my gun with Louie's ground crew. So, I went back to my tried-and-true response to any overwhelming stress: follow standard operating procedure. SOP for what came next required a good afternoon's sleep, more food, hydration, a weapons check, and some primitive planning once we dropped altitude to extract my delicate self from the aircraft without being gunned down by a thug. I started with sleep, confident I could down the remainder of the fried rice and Pad Thai while scheming and checking my own guns. SOP had saved me more times than I cared to count. Ridiculous, annoying, at times a fruitless waste of time. And the occasional difference between life and death.

In the field sleep tends to be something of a commodity, often hard to get in both quantity and quality. Hans and the genius techs at Section 22 had built a whole adaptive mutation into some of our killer T cells to overcome that. A kind of field expedient version of power sleep. But I had proved allergic to it. Possibly because they'd crosswired it with some nice brainwash and obedience software that would oh so conveniently run while we were defenselessly unconscious. I'd had to make do all these years like the average human soldier, sacking out in moving vehicles with too much noise, too little comfort and. way too many weird contortions of the anatomy. With the smooth ride and lack of turbulence, Uncle Morpheus came quickly.

Most animals convey fear in a variety of surprisingly noticeable ways. They change smell, their vocal cords constrict leading to a different pitch of growl (or in the human animal, speech), they breathe more rapidly, they shift position, arms and leg decrease in circulation—constricting and tightening to flee or fight—and they tend to make fast little movements, thin slicing environmental cues to determine the safest course of action in milliseconds. It only took Fat Frank ham-handing the controls while saying calmly but in a slightly higher pitch, "That's odd," to bring me fully awake. It took a few moments to orient myself while eavesdropping on the smuggler's increasingly worried conversation.

We had already begun our descent—it meant I'd slept over nine hours. For me that was unprecedented. I tended to need about four hours sleep a night. Momo's upgrades had come at a steep biological price. We'd only know if I had a permanent need for double the sleep or this was a side effect of exospeciation. Given that the lookouts at the local cartel operated airfield had failed to check in and there was a lack of runway lights, it seemed likely my worries about a firefight with Sinaloa goons had been for nothing. We were far more likely to be blown from the air by a rival cartel. Joy.

I should have paid attention to my own maxim. Good Samaritans and opportunists. If there was a better time for a cross cartel war, it would be hard to imagine. So of course, someone had decided to make a move. Either Louie had his own snitches and was facing enemies who paid for the tip-off, or he had been sold out to a breakaway wing of Sinaloa, one run by the internal rival of his capo. No matter. If they were Cartel, they'd prefer to let us land so they could seize the plane and its payload. If they weren't then we had solid odds to gun it out with whomever had decided to commandeer a drug cartel's airstrip.

The cost benefit analysis on whether to let the smugglers get whacked alone or reveal myself ran through my head. In the end it seemed both vaguely more ethical and tactically superior to save their weasel lives. I extricated myself from box, reviewed my cache of weapons while downing the Pad Thai and, satisfied I had enough armament to invade Bolivia, I made my way to the trapdoor which allowed access to the cargo hold from the cabin. Momo had said nothing and it seemed prudent to play the good parent card which meant keeping quiet and letting her sulk in her room until she was ready to eat dinner or go to the mall. In the case of a rapidly emerging AI, the analogous actions for dinner or shopping eluded me but Momo speaking up would surely fill in that gap. In the silence I planned to follow SOP and my own gut, keep us both as safe as I could, and wait for her to make contact.

Sometimes the little moments make life. If only I could bottle and sell the looks on Louie and Franks' faces when I quietly entered the cabin. It seemed absurdly stupid to reveal my true purpose and identity, so I'd gone into proper camouflage mode. As it happened, our files on the Sinaloa suggested they had a specialist hitter called *Demonio Negro,* a black clad Lucha Libre style strangler and close-in work killer. The Black Demon was a nod to the legendary Blue Demon and as the ultimate Rudo, he was known to be both brutal and coincidentally nearly seven feet tall. And he wore a damned mask for work.

Which meant that when I struck a pose, placed my hands on my hips, and announced in a thick accent "The pilot men do not recognize me?" they pretty much did a triple take, took a deep breath, and then nodded.

Frank took off his headset and stared me up and down. He

took in my size, my thrust-out lip and challenging smile, smug and telegenic. As if I were posing for a TV camera. A good disguise is all in the haptics and subtle cues. You're only as good as the assumptions of your audience. Frank bought it. "The goddamned Black Demon. Here? What the ...?"

Louie cut him off quickly. "Can it, Frankie." He had a thin sheen of sweat gleaming across his face. His eyes darted between the controls, my reflection in the windshield, and the dead dark landing strip only a few miles ahead. "We got serious problems here, Mister ... uh ... Demon. You hear me?"

I waved my hands, fearless and dramatically confident. "Yes, yes. This is why I am sent. To expect such problems. Traitors, rival cartels, men of no honor. Demonio Negro will help."

"I don't...can't even, how will you help exactly?"

As if he had four heads and they were all drooling, I gave him a sad shake of my patrician head. "Please. When we land, I shall be on the wing, of course." Gods forfend but I'd done that trick before. Nanites gave me tremendous grip strength. Enough to endure the two hundred mile per hour landing speeds of a Cessna. If they landed quickly enough that was. Otherwise, I'd be competing for the aerial roadkill bowling prize of Northern Mexico.

Frank looked as if he'd swallowed a marmot. "On the wing? That's... Louie, can that be done?"

Louie looked me over and shrugged. Elevators and crosswalks all around the world have buttons that have been disconnected from their system. Over eighty percent of all "close door" and "walk" buttons connect to nothing. But the illusion of control provides tremendous psychological comfort. It might be how The Syndicate and The Swarm truly maintain their power. By hiding in the shadows, we give the bulk of humanity the steadfast illusion of control. I was handing the smugglers that illusion. Put a scary strangler on your wing and let him jump off toward your unknown enemies just like your bosses planned all along. Absurd and likely ineffective, but it just reeked of control. After all, they'd gone from being sitting ducks to having a plan that involved them staying safely in their airplane. From deathtrap to brutal ambush in a heartbeat. They grabbed that life preserver with the desperation of drowning men. The Black Demon then outlined "the plan" concocted by Louie's boss, a man named Julio Dos Cruces. Known for his flair and his love of gold plated anything. Guns, steaks, speed boats, toilet seats, even call girls painted gold. The man was exactly the kind of idiot who'd send a wrestler turned hitman to stow away on a smuggling flight.

We flashed the field and then circled a couple of times, stalling while I strapped down all gear, checked my MAC10s, and got myself out onto the starboard side of the aircraft. I'd managed to filch a pair of leather gripping gloves in my trek out of NYC. Gorgeous things made for handling lumber and fiberglass. Broken in lovingly by someone with hands the size of mine. He'd surely miss them when civilization turned the lights back on. If he survived long enough to check and if we managed to prevent The Swarm from sending us back to the fifteenth century. The gloves help manage the brutal wind shear with its combined flesh stripping force and ruthless chill. I gripped the wing, put my face to the surface metal, my eyes jammed shut and waited for the inevitable drop and slam of a rapid ugly landing.

In the minutes we took circling a third time, I damned Frank and his spineless need for the perfect approach, then The Swarm, the White Cult, and my own damned stupid self for agreeing to such a plan. No not agreeing, proposing it. What had possessed me? Sometimes playing a character gets me in trouble. Sometimes it pushes me to do mind-numbingly odd things that make the finest strategic sense but just happen to be terrifying, dangerous, physically painful, and deeply, deeply uncomfortable on a psychic level. Being on the wing allowed me the maximum range of options upon landing, including leaving the two smugglers to face an ignoble death. It simultaneously solved the problem of two men who had enough wits to question how'd I'd gotten on their plane and from there ask why. Right now, they had all they could manage just landing an imbalanced plane without flipping it on touchdown. It got me close to the fuselage with seventy percent cover if I'd guessed wrong and the holders of the airfield opened fire. It also gave the best statistical chance to escape a surface to air missile or RPG launch. Smart, tactically sound, and just the kind of unpredictable asymmetric stunt you'd expect of someone trying to outsmart a scheming cadre of biological hiveminds.

Still, wind shear hurts, as does the bone shattering cold of flying without adequate external protection. Also, it's a bit scary landing in the dark with your face slammed against the wing of a flimsy little Cessna that might get shot at, shot up, shot out of the sky, or simply hit the ground like a shotput. Add to that all that lovely extra time Frank had given me to consider every miserable crash landing and ambush option, you had a less than emotionally serene Spetz flying Air Sinaloa Norte. We dropped and kept dropping. Frank had taken us further out and used cloud cover and the distant lights of Tijuana to mask a subtle descent of a few hundred meters. When he made his final run, he'd undershot the runway by nearly a kilometer. We dropped like a stone, edging toward stalling as the speed and angle of attack decreased our total lift. Then mere meters from the waiting earth, Frank pulled us into a glide, put the engine in neutral and cut our running lights, which dropped the now invisible plane onto the tarmac at the front edge of the strip. I didn't quite know all this at the time, but my augmented brain took a lot of cues and updated me a few seconds after our wheels touched the ground.

It had been a stellar piece of combat piloting. When this was over, we'd need to look up Frank and find him a better class of employer. As job interviews went, he'd just qualified as a member of my personal entourage assuming Pierre cleared his security credentials and Frank wanted to join my merry band of psychopathic killers, swindlers, and adrenaline junkies. Something about the landing suggested he just might love the work as much as he loved churros.

In the trade we have a rather witty portmanteau for the kind of stunt I was about to pull, where the operative implemented an idea so dumb and dangerous it might not only work, it might entirely hijack their opposition's momentum: highjinkpot. As in high jinks mixed with jackpot and hijack. Wacky yet nimble fun (etymologically derived from those wacky seventeenth century

Scots who jinked left and right to avoid arrows (and later police) coupled with an unexpected windfall and an unexpected seizure of a moving vehicle. Mind you the secondary meanings of all words really color the phrase. Because high jinks also tended to be a euphemism for getting your ass kicked in prison; jackpot sometimes meant a screw-up so vast and deadly it qualified as a major problem—the kind of thing that you might call the Concierge to fix; and hijack as in to take over something, like my cells or brain function (thanks Momo for that visual.) Nuance is all when you're trying to say everything without really saying anything.

That's what was going through my head when Frank dropped us almost perfectly two hundred meters ahead of where we cued up for an ambush. He followed up his agile maneuver with a fascinating zigzag that nearly tipped the plane as he careened us sideways into grass fields. But he spun the Cessna counter to my weight, using centripetal force to bleed velocity and bring us to a jarring stop less than fifty meters from the edge of the runway. It was enough to make me regret my full stomach of Pad Thai, but not enough to force a surrender of dinner.

As soon as we slowed to running speed, my hands unclenched, and I slid near bonelessly off the wing into the shadows of the lightless field. Taking a fall is martial arts 101 and I'd dropped much further much faster enough times to stick the landing. Seeing in the dark helped, as did the compression of my bones and muscles. The creepy armor sheath growing inside me proved to have a secondary purpose: when my feet struck the grass, the shock rolled up and out, using my fascia as a pathway the way roll cages and crumple zones worked for cars. With nearly the same effect—I got hot. Somehow my body had converted kinetic energy to heat. Fascinating and worth investigating. When I wasn't sprinting toward a dozen bandana clad hooligans squinting into the night, waiting for the plane to roll toward them.

From their facial expressions and posture, they had not yet cottoned to how masterfully Frank had evaded their trap. Nor did they seem to hear me rushing toward them on the grass.

Savvy to the end, Frank had kept his engines roaring which, coupled with the total lack of light from the plane, sent weird ripples of doppler echoes across the airstrip. The plane could have been anywhere nearby. Which had been the point of his own highjinkpot.

I'd been schooling Momo on instincts trumping knowledge. But really, instincts betray us. We flinch and flee when we should advance. And sometimes we charge when we should duck and run. Instincts, training, and experience on the other hand can be subtle but invaluable weapons. That was the essence of the Kutzkan Way. As I ran toward the group, three heads turned in perfect unison toward the opposite side of the strip, tracking the approach of a truck. On a lark I tried willing myself to go infrared and was rewarded with a composite overlay of both light amplification and what seemed like infrared. Seemed because it just merged into normal vision, as if it were a cloudy mid-morning with ambient sunlight.

I didn't bother trying to parse the wider situation. The Swarm was here. The Why no longer mattered. Only that I had twelve belligerents in front of me, nine human and three hivemind waiting for a truck with what I could now see were two dozen well-armed and armored troops. The bandanas had fooled me. They were covering balaclavas and uniforms. Someone had gotten the Mexican army entangled with a cartel war. Or they had come looking for someone like me.

Bomb squads use Fourier Transform InfraRed spectroscopy to identify explosives with a microburst of heat. FTIR happens to be the platinum standard for properly assessing dangerous substances. If you have a lab, a nicely controlled environment, ample time, and a lot of smart folks in white coats, it's assuredly the way to go. The cheap and cheerful version of that was a Syndicate system we'd dubbed SyFTIR. Goggles that sent out a mix of lidar and sonar outside the normal sensory channels. A quick snapshot glimpse and within a millisecond a computer gave you a guess as to "what Ivan has in the backpack."

Mixing infrared and light amplification technologies with upgraded computing capabilities had created some... new functionalities might be the right way to term it. I now had a version of SyFTIR happening, my informed guesswork resolving the images into a fair certainty of what ammunition and armament each of the soldiers had on them. Or in the case of the moving truck, near them. That made the next move not only possible but preferable. My MAC10s rattled, striking down The Hivemind in one spent clip. I'd been precise, aiming for their waists. Not only did that guarantee the gyrojets would send shrapnel through their spines after ricocheting off their pelvis and ilium, it gave me twenty-eight chances to hit one of their incendiary grenades in the process. Two struck gold.

The Hivemind detonated in a cascade of explosions as their grenades succumbed to the 2800-degree heat of thermite and white phosphorous merging with atmospheric oxygen. Then the soldiers near them perished. Normally you can toss a fragmentation grenade in a campfire and be safe for quite a while. The internal temperature needs to rise enough to ignite the explosive. But when you've generated a firestorm from incendiaries designed to melt tanks, or airplanes, as I suspected was the case that evening, ignition tends to happen rather quickly. Lots of men in both the truck and waiting cadre had frags.

From a prone position in the grass, I'd felt the shockwave followed by the distinct sound of shrapnel whizzing past my head. Half a second later when I checked, the dozen men had effectively evaporated. I put the next clip through the gas tank of the troop truck. Frank had given me a spectacular idea. When you bleed velocity, you transfer kinetic and mechanical energy to the environment around you. With my legs it had been heat. When a bullet meets a target, it tends to simply shatter, then spall and the resulting shrapnel expends energy ripping apart soft tissue. Unless the target is a big metal object with a reservoir full of highly flammable gasoline. Then sometimes if you're lucky, you get a lot of heat and a resultant spark. Such as when you use a rocket powered depleted uranium bullet that just happens to be self-sharpening and flammable. Gas tanks also happen to sit near such lovely things as crank shafts, brake pads, and wheels. The truck managed to hink, flip, and grind on the pavement, splattering flaming gasoline behind it before exploding in a series of spectacular cartwheels.

I scanned the horizon, looking for more of The Swarm. Perhaps a sniper team. Or set of observers. We'd seen them watching Pina's abduction. It stood to reason they'd have a similar group here, where one mind performed the task, and another did whatever creepy things a hivemind did. Maybe they were from HR and were handling an onsite job satisfaction audit. That made me chuckle. The Syndicate didn't have HR but what came closest bore an uncanny resemblance to The Swarm.

At the edge of the grass in a small area studded with careful rows of half-grown pine trees stood five women watching the truck burn. They'd taken advantage of the windbreak to hide themselves, but my SyFTIR had used the radiance of the explosion to map the area. And determined there were five dark spots in the woods. Too dark, too cold, and oddly human shaped. Whatever tech they were using, they had found a way to entirely mask their heat signatures without smoke or obscurants. This was not a heat resistant parka kind of deal. We had those and they were highly effective—limiting the heat signature to a small gap near the nose and mouth. This was utterly perfect.

Between the roar of two fires and Frank's engine, no one could hear me sniper crawl my way to a good firing position downwind and mostly to their flank. They barely moved and made no discernible sound. Around them the susurrus of the trees created the illusion of peace. I had another clip ready, the MAC10 aimed carefully for their torsos. I'd be shooting from relative long distance and at an angle. If the shot went correctly, the bullets would strike them mid torso but exit near the shoulders. My finger began to depress the trigger.

As one they turned their heads, suddenly looking at my position. The gun rattled, sending trails of furious light toward them. The group leapt to my objective left. They were supernaturally nimble but I'd been firing on them as they reacted. We split the difference, with the rounds striking them at the shoulder, head, and neck levels. The clip expended, I was up racing toward them, swapping out the machine pistol for an automatic. Three of them had managed to crawl a few meters, turn themselves, and haul out AK74s by the time I somersaulted over their position, firing inverted. Thank you, General Yaroslav for all that practice throwing axes upside down. It had always been a fun part of Spetsnaz training and it had just paid off. The Kalashnikovs rattled harmlessly at where a running man would have been had I not pulled something else from my full special forces trick bag. Instead, I'd brained the survivors.

It took me a moment after landing to assure myself there weren't more hiveminds or hidden soldiers in whatever cloaks they had been using. Nothing seemed amiss, nor did anyone rush me with a bayonet. No shots fired. It was once again me standing alone among the ruined dead. The women had vaguely Asian features but dark skin. Kazakh perhaps. Though they had odd cheek structures and eye flaps for that region. They seemed like a family of ages ranging from twentyish to fiftyish. All were lean, angry looking even in the relaxation of death, with dark hair and nearly black eyes. None wore anything special. They were dressed for a Mexican evening, light pants and long-sleeved blouses of dark color. The oldest looking one had ammo belts strapped to her chest in an X.

But they still barely registered visually. They gave off null heat. They absorbed sound. Then it hit me. They weren't dark skinned from melanin. They had a version of stealth technology merged into their skin. Maybe their whole bodies. Biological stealth material that combined anti-reflective paint with sound and radar absorbent materials. Joy of joys. The Swarm had built a stealth bomber except it was a small hivemind and not an airplane.

Still not a peep from Momo. I shrugged, pilfered what I could from the dead hivemind, and then simply left the area. Frank and Louie would figure out the score when they turned off their engine. Or ran out of fuel. Same effect. There still might be heavies waiting around in the shack of a hangar and control booth /office. But Frank had been resourceful, and Louie had a rather elegant record of violent people management. Between them, I trusted the situation would resolve itself. I liked to think of it as the follow-up question portion of the job interview. That made me chuckle as I considered how it fit with my newly corrupted vision of HR.

Then I hoofed it over the crest of the windbreak to see dunes beyond. We were less than a klick from the Baja coast. Time to find something with an engine and wheels that could get us to Campo Lopez before breakfast. Perhaps then I'd need to force Momo to talk. If only to explain the Hunter and her situation. Still, that was a hotwire and road trip in the future. It left her plenty of time to put the record on repeat and hide in her room. And me time to go over the materials I'd taken from the women who had been observing from the dunes.

Chapter 6: Number 11, Number 11, Number 11, Number 11....

We reached the edge of Campo Lopez around three in the morning, with plenty of time to locate the general vicinity of the Hunter's compound. No one approached it at night. She had mined the area in addition to adding various less noticeable safeguards. Besides, there was a simpler way to get her attention.

Every morning one of her compound took breakfast at Abuela Jojo's taco stand. An old and storied institution in Baja, Jojo had been making fish tacos, tamales, and quesadillas since most everyone had been a kid. That famous chef show with the guy who did all those drugs had filmed there. And the one with the chef who wore the push-up bras and had an 8chan cult. She'd stolen a few recipes. Tourists came from all corners of the world. But what made Jojo a legend was that she simply sold what she sold and when she ran out that was it. She started at dawn and usually closed up by noon. During tourist season she'd be out by mid-morning.

Smart operatives simply bought a taco and waited. If the Hunter wanted to talk, they'd know soon enough. Things like a global apocalypse are relative. In Baja California not much had changed since the Conquistadors had given way to the Americanos with too much cologne and too little business sense. Time flowed slowly, technology was charcoal grills and ice machines, and pretty much anything was allowed if it caused no trouble. Internet service was a joke. For technology you drove to Tijuana because there were no buses or trains in Campo Lopez or its neighboring villages.

There used to be buses, cell towers, and rapid internet. All paid for by land developers. The Americanos had made all sorts of plans for the area. But the cartels, the Hunter, and the local police, corrupt even by Mexican standards, had made it clear that their little stretch of beach was not worth the effort. They tore down the towers, shot up a few buses, and firebombed the land management office. Which meant that other than Abuela Jojo, a couple of resorts and some expat bars with cheap hookers and questionable cocaine, there was nothing worth seeing in the area.

Lack of development translated to limited services. They had running water and a primitive electric grid. But the whole town had three streetlights, no traffic signals, no cell towers, and limited sewers. The resorts walled up their compounds and trucked in kerosene for 24/7 operation of generators to power massive floodlights, satellite dishes, and their own little oases of Western amenities. It made a fearsome place to lurk and wait. Or counter ambush folks who stood out. Much like me.

Ergo I'd opted to swap a stolen car halfway down the route for a scooter with enough room for me, my stolen loot, and some purloined beach towels that might come in handy. If nothing else, they'd help camouflage the very red, very touristy little moped.

I parked our stolen scooter behind the Puerta Ensenada resort wall, listening to the clash of generators and bad resort music. The cooling wall and scooter seat made a nice chair and with the side scatter from the floodlights, my enhanced vision upgraded the documents and wallets scrounged from The Hivemind from blurs to legibility.

The wallets held poorly forged IDs with pasted photos of the women, a few peso bills and coins, and a business card for a lawyer in Tucson Arizona, I memorized his name and tossed them aside to review the documents. Some were maps of the area. The airstrip and some houses in Tijuana had been marked. They matched what I'd memorized of Sinaloa infrastructure. Easy to do because they shared territory with the Baja Cartel who owned the airspace and the Arellano-Félix Organization who dominated Tijuana proper. The Sinaloa were allowed by treaty no more than five safe houses, a single landing strip, and two armories.

The script was shaky and flat. Male handwriting. Over it were precise, almost machine-perfect coordinates and a code. It looked hand lettered but almost typed. That seemed much more like a hivemind capability. The code seemed to be military with operations and assets named by handles. Overhand to Barn at19:00 followed by coordinates. That kind of jargon. Valuable long term but without context relatively useless to me.

There were some food wrappers. Odd that they had been saved. My mixed vision found traces of strychnine and amylase, which is a stomach enzyme associated with snails and frogs. What. The. Hell? I ignored the part where my brain had turned on a spectrometer as part of the new enhanced vision package. Who the hell was eating poisoned food laced with amphibian stomachs? Or whatever the wrappers implied.

Some receipts matched the food wrappers. Quick calculation put the money I'd found and the receipts collected for a hotel, train tickets, some more food, a bill for tampons from a Tijuana Farmacia to nearly a thousand dollars, depending on how the exchange rate worked out. Made sense. Hand The Hive some money, some maps, give them a mission. From the various papers it looked like they had been in place four days. So, from the first hour of the incursion. Actually, if I back calculated the train tickets about six hours beforehand, they were already on route to the airfield.

Had The Swarm realized we'd figure out their infiltration? I checked the remainder of the documents. A handkerchief with a dab of blood and some dried snot. Also registering the weird poison stomach enzyme mix. Two diary pages from a Mexican daily calendar. One for yesterday and one from three weeks ago. The writing had been blurred by moisture and friction but seemed to indicate a departure and arrival time. One time I knew already—it was on Fat Frank's published flight plan. It was a fair bet the other one had been from their trip to Connecticut three weeks prior.

So, The Swarm had business with the cartels and for some reason wanted the plane destroyed and possibly Frank and

Louie eliminated. Enough to sequester the army and a hive-mind cluster at the airfield in advance of an attack. The remainder of the papers were a revelation. A timeline without names, just code words that lined up with some of the marks on the map. But there were hundreds of coded operations and locations. On the top was just a notation: Down Feet Dry Drivers Conus Pac SoWe NQG. Then a phone number with too many digits. A single page on delicate paper, likely flash combustible, lay stapled to it with a series of numbers similar to the phone number and various notations like Conus Atl NoEa and Oconus NoAmWe. Next to each was a date and a serial number fourteen digits long which matched a small set of watermarked digits on the bottom of the timeline, marked maps, and an empty envelope which smelled like money and had a small notation on the left corner in red handwritten print script: "Observer team, Min 3 Max 6, 27 day limit rotate/return."

It was enough to parse what had happened to The Syndicate. In a few short words—sheer dumb luck. And maybe luck favored the paranoid and well prepared. People like Pina, Kelba, and me. And the kids, too, come to think of it. These cold-hearted bastards had not taken advantage of a tidal shift for the submarine rollover. They had somehow engineered it. Then launched a global devolution / internet hack timed over a period of weeks to knock down the global defense networks of The Syndicate, all major governments, and whatever constituted enemies to The Swarm. For example, the White Cult was likely an ally with its own targeted destruction date. I was guessing WC Oconus GloGlo referred to them. There were two sets of dates and two fourteen digit sequences.

Out of the corner of my eye, a lazy patrol car rolled by my position and kept going. The officer, his left arm cradling a sweating beer through his open window, whistled to the static washed instrumental version of a narco-corrido. If he noticed anything outside the rough width of the road it was whether he needed more beer. He certainly didn't care about men resting in Campo Lopez's shadows. Still, I followed SOP and listened carefully for a good twenty minutes before returning to the documents.

With Momo's help the codes could be cracked. But to what end? I knew what they meant and roughly who was on the other end of the line. Anyone who wasn't under the thrall of The Swarm would just paint a target on their shoulders by calling. Because I knew this code well. It was just common military security slang. Down Feet Dry Drivers Conus Pac SoWe NQG translated to Kill All Overland Pilots in the Continental United States Pacific Southwest Region No Quarter Given. That's how I knew to interpret Down the Drivers as a full-on kill order. NQG meant take no prisoners, leave no witnesses. It meant annihilation.

The digits and the timeline coupled with what I knew of the ways hiveminds worked explained the envelope and that painted a picture for me. I'd made a fair number of mistakes in our last war. We'd already used up a lifetime's luck escaping whatever task had been handed to team Syn Conus Atl NoEa. Whatever I did next would require some very methodical planning and, asymmetric for me, a very slow very thought-driven consideration of the past week's events. I had to rein in my chaos incarnate until I knew where to direct it.

With the internet compromised and global satellites basically junked by malicious software piggybacked on whatever feeds they got dirtside, there would be no safe way to make a phone call. In many cases, the public's phones had stopped working reliably. To counteract this, The Swarm had set up its own orbital relay ahead of the attack. Which meant independent satellites already in orbit—enough to manage the call flow from their agents in the field. They could augment it with zombified satcoms as they progressed in their assault on humanity. That explained the fourteen-digit numbers.

In addition, they had some basic control over ocean tides. Which implied weather control. As science fictiony as that felt, I was a genetically engineered cybernetic hybrid with wolf DNA and body armor growing in my chest. Maybe we were already at the age of miracles. There was probably some ridiculously expensive and environmentally destructive force in effect. A nuke on a tectonic plate for example. Or massive undersea methane burn for rapid local temperature disturbance. Maybe some cloud seeding technologies that could adjust the gulf stream and deep ocean currents enough to matter. Each option was at the edge of plausibility. Why hadn't anyone bothered exploring them? Side effects included extinction level events like spontaneous chain reaction earthquakes with tsunamis and volcanic detonations across the entire Ring of Fire. Or uncontrolled sequenced detonation of trapped oceanic methane reserves. Or for a really spectacular bit of climate change, turning off the Gulf Stream and Equatorial Currents. But if your goal was global extinction of The Other, then something naturally cataclysmic only added to the fun times.

The Swarm had upturned the sub only after they had already launched operatives to dozens of locations globally with thousand more in motion hours before I made my call to Lola. It explained the emergence of kill teams so soon after Pina and Kelba made their moves. It made me wonder how spooked The Swarm must have been to find their well laid trap upturned and their main Syndicate targets fighting their way out minutes before certain death. All because Eddie had gotten caught by a camera which I had been fixated enough to find. That bore its own consideration. Eddie knew me well; more than that, as tricky as he was, Gay Eddie would never make that kind of rookie mistake. So, either he was off his game, or he was sending me a very personal message. Perhaps a warning.

It made my skull ache. Straining to see in the nascent predawn hadn't helped either. I tossed the purloined paper and IDs into a local trash bin, which allowed me to close my burning eyes. It was the strychnine and amylase that really got to me. It must have come from the women themselves. That implied The Swarm's hiveminds represented their own form of exospeciation. If we counted The White Cult and their experimental introduction of nanites through old fashioned have-sex-get-pregnant reproduction, we now had three different non-human species competing with my AIs. It also put Homo Sapiens Sapiens well down the stack of apex predators on Planet Earth.

Fact: The kill team had not been looking for me. Better yet, I'd just left strong evidence that another Swarm team had wiped them out. Fact: The whole blitzkrieg attack on The Syndicate had been part and parcel of a much more ambitious assault on global civilization. Fact: Every known non-human species was now in active combat fighting for global dominance. Because yeah, The Syndicate and Oslo's network damned sure needed to assert control or there'd be no Web left to dismantle safely. There'd just be ashes ashes we all fall down plague and poverty. Conjecture: This was our own fault. Oslo had moved enough pieces out of the Web to create a power vacuum and The Swarm had responded by attempting a one and done global genocide.

It meant that in my growing list of impossible feats to accomplish I now had to add killing The Swarm's hivemind Hydra, cleaning the Augean stables in a single day, finding and maybe not killing Gay Eddie, finding the queen of the Amazons and checking out her girdle, maybe doing a quick DNA check to see if she or any other Nemean, Erymanthian, or Hesperidean folk had been secretly exospeciating as well. Sheesh. All without being a demi-god and lacking the strength of ten ordinary men. It meant not starting the next war by accident nor allowing my employers to set one off while they tried to mitigate the hideous misogyny, bloodlust, and chronic violence that comprised our organizational skillset. And I still hadn't heard a peep from Momo.

When all else fails, get a taco. That's not SOP, just common sense. But south of the Red River, only the batshit crazy ignored the chance to eat tacos.

It was approaching dawn by the time I'd finished lamenting my accidental inclusion in an unwritten Greek tragedy. Maybe it was really a farcical satyr play in the Roman style and we just had to wait for the second act. Maybe. Time for breakfast. The towels covered the moped and the shadows covered the towels—it looked like a boring lump. With a shrug I jingled the ladies' pesos and considered what to order. I had enough money for a fairly robust breakfast. It took a few minutes to make my way to the rough location of the Abuela's shack. Sometimes she moved it when there had been a nasty storm during hurricane season. With a quick scan and an ear for gulls calling, it wasn't but a few more yards and a couple dunes to the left to find the new and improved shack settled less than twenty feet from the high tide line. It had a picnic table with a faded umbrella.

Had it been that long since I'd been here? I counted the years, then winced; it had been over a decade. It implied a certain someone had started to get old. At least older. And suddenly in need of being wiser as well. My shadow joined a small cluster of tourists and beach bums as well as the prone forms of a few drunks who'd either come early and fallen asleep or simply wandered this way during the night.

Among the faces was one I knew well. I saw a youngish version of the Hunter. She was perhaps twenty-two, lithe to the point of gaunt. Her reddish skin and dark hawklike eyes titled slowly back and forth across the sand. Seeing nothing, noticing all. A fieldcraft technique. She was a sentry then. Her crow black hair had been pulled back in a simple bun; likewise, she wore baggy hemp pants of some dark color faded with time and sun. Her blouse was tighter, made of something modern like nylon mixed with cotton. It was black, new, and hid a dangerous looking stiletto in the small of her back. If she saw me, she had the sense to not show it.

Instead, she waited, letting the crowd press forward when banging sounds emerged from the shack. Lights turned on, and in a few minutes, as the drunks were kicked awake and the tourists began to burble as tourists do, the overhang began to rise as a winch cranked slowly. Behind the counter stood a crinkled raisin of a woman, Abuela JoJo, joined now by a pair of hefty Indio women who seemed like the front runners for an All-Aztec roller derby squad. Squat, broad shouldered, tough skinned, hook nosed, dark, and utterly beautiful. But alien to the tourists who, meeting their gaze, moved respectfully toward the Abuela.

The sentry and I allowed the crowd to thin, then dissipate as dawn burned off the night fog. At last, it was down to me and her. I went first, ordering four tacos, a sweet tamale, and with my remaining change and a fifty-peso bill I'd pickpocketed from a flummoxed Louie, I got myself a stack of quesadillas with guacamole. With extra hot sauce and onions. Plus, a very big, vaguely cold bottle of Topo Chico. In fluent unaccented Spanish. I might have been from Madrid or Mexico City. Clearly, I was an educated man of some sort. But local enough to pay with small coin and small bills. Worthy of respect, unworthy of concern or alarm. Plus, who doesn't like a man who drinks Topo Chico for breakfast? And I gave my pair of roller derby beauties a very rare genuine smile. Damned if the taller one didn't wink back. Yowzah. The taller, heavier me still had game. Or she had just shorted me on change like a pro. Shrug—such were the deep mysteries of life.

The sentry handed over a written list which the shorter derby woman took and wordlessly brought to the abuela. There were a few quiet nods and the trio went to work. Unsurprisingly, The Hunter's order came before mine. Two large paper bags placed inside old plastic ones and handed over to the sentry without a hint of warmth. She barely gave the women notice as she took them, turned on her heels, and marched toward the compound. My order came, which I took with a wide grin, gave the tall one a proper wink and then went to work devouring the entirety of my breakfast. Those TV chefs weren't wrong. Abuela JoJo could cook like few others. One should take pleasure when it comes. For me, tomorrow was an uncertain proposition. Even if I was a starry-eyed optimist, the odds looked like a spread between grim and gruesome. That pretty much described every day Oslo had managed The Syndicate. Embracing hope, perhaps a little optimistic joy, and some pure devious whimsy seemed the only rational way to survive.

By the time my meal disappeared, the sun had begun to assert itself over the low mountains of Baja California Este. It would be a hot day; one I'd come to overdressed. Even with my gear stashed in a grubby duffle snatched from a hotel on the edge of Rosarita, there was no hiding my warm weather clothing. Nor was there likely anything in my new expanded size nearby. I'd have to mug some acromegalic and hope he had muted tastes.

◊You're going to have to talk to me eventually.◊ Silence. Momo might be asleep. Could she sleep? ◊If only because you're about to have a lot of questions and I won't be able to answer them. Not right away.◊

Ooh, that got her. Something stirred. ‡What kind of questions?‡

◊You saw the sentry?◊

‡The woman you spent so much time alarming?‡

That was one way to put it. ◊Yes, her.◊

‡She seemed normal enough.‡ That was an indictment of sorts. If a highly skilled agent armed with a combat dagger constantly alert for attack on a remote and unknown beach counted as normal, it would be hard to impress her.

◊In her own way, she is. But as you're about to see, she's not alone.◊

‡I'm sure I'll figure it out.‡ Yeah, definitely progressing into the teen mentality. Gods save us, I now had a properly sullen teenager stuck behind my spleen. And on an involuntary road trip which had very little possibility of a happy ending. Still, it would make a proper montage for a Bauhaus soundtrack.

Momo said no more. No reason to push. She was awake and aware; she had started to change—itself a clue to me about her status. Whatever that six-hundred-foot quantum positioning field meant for her, Campo Lopez must have been as close to a headache or dizzy spell as an AI could feel. Limited radio and satellite traffic, no phone towers, an ocean on one side bouncing static from atmospheric radiation haphazardly. Which made me the annoying Dad taking her on a scenic trip to Wallyworld. Hah. It made me smile, which got me another coy batting of the eyes from my Aztec girlfriend. Mind you, it should not be forgotten the Aztecs liked to rip the hearts from living men to feed to their gods, including those who handled love, sex, romance, and fertility.

Luckily for me, the Hunter saved me from what could have been a lethal emotional entanglement. An older woman approached, hoodie covering her face. Her salt and pepper hair hung from a single braid on her right shoulder. She wore clothing similar to the sentry but had added sunglasses and the sweatshirt. Her dark feet flopped on the sand in a pair of ancient plastic sandals. She sat down, her back to the hut, then dropped the hood. The same woman stared back at me, only this one was grizzled with years of hard living. She had a pair of scars running from hairline through her left eye to her chin. I had been there when she got them. She owed the rest of her skull and its attachment to her neck to my accuracy with a PSS. I knew she was sixty-three but she was always somehow both thirty and a hundred, the Schrödinger's cat of operatives.

"Hunter."

"Spetz. I saw you on the beach earlier. You've grown a bit, haven't you?" Her eyebrow arched, giving her face a Satanic cast.

"Call it forced evolution. Something one suspects you know in rather too much detail." I was still waiting for the penny to drop with Momo. She'd be running facial recognition. Maybe even posture and gait versus the sentry. Then probably re-checking it a few dozen times when the results came back.

"Sure, whatever. Why are you here scaring my taco ladies?"

I gave her a wide smile. The Hunter wasn't known for humor but that was borderline funny. "The taller one seems to like me."

That earned me a laugh. "Coaxoch just wants you for the taco meat." I looked over her shoulder to give Coaxoch another firm wink. She stared me down, smiled with plenty of teeth, and winked back. Yeah, she saw seven solid feet of delicious carne asada.

‡What. The. Frakking. Fecking. Frindling. Hell?‡ I'd have to look up whatever those words referred to. Clearly, Momo was trying out some new slang, but I got the gist. Still, she'd already shifted into language she knew I couldn't fully parse. Yeah, firmly fourteen. She'd also figured out that the twenty-two-year-old and this old woman before me were identical.

The woman across from me waited for an answer. One did not waste the Hunter's time. "I need to track a man. One who has used this global meltdown to hide." In my own way, I knew how to lure the Hunter too. Very few things mattered to her more than protecting the secrets of Campo Lopez. But one of them was being the best tracker alive.

"As if that would stop me."

I shrugged. No reason to lay it on too thick. Between her dagger-crisp stares across the picnic table and Momo's equivalent of ringing my mental doorbell ever ten seconds, we needed to move this conversation off the beach. "I never said you couldn't. But even for someone as good as you, the chances are low, especially since he will have The Swarm protecting him."

She paused, then turned and gave the women a friendly nod. The shorter one put whatever she had been holding back under the counter. A riot gun? "You think they scare me?"

"This isn't just The Swarm as an organization. They have gone public with their hiveminds."

That brought a kind of boiling fury to her face. "So, he reveals himself after all. Makes sense." She rolled her shoulders and cracked her neck. "Yeah, let's take this back to the house. You know the drill."

The drill was Follow The Hunter Precisely Or Get Pulverized By Landmines. She took me through a maze of shacks and alleys, followed by a small park and then across a charming swath of dune grass which hid a small rock path to the entrance of a low walled hacienda tucked into a small, curved isthmus. The Hunter had her own private strip of land.

‡Spetz! She's what? A clone? A split twin? A weirdo mom playing Section 23 in the sun?‡

◊It's complicated.◊

The Hunter stopped then turned and looked me up and down. "You on coms?" It seemed impossible she would have heard me. Someone had us on binoculars, had radioed her when they saw my throat move.

"It's complicated." There was that word again. "Easiest explanation is yes; I have a partner piggybacking with me. She's on coms twenty-four seven."

"She can be trusted?" With the Hunter that was no idle question.

I nodded and gave her the rarest of my genuine smiles. "She's family. It's beyond trust."

I heard the equivalent of Momo sigh. Yeah. Sometimes the truth just needs to be stated. Was probably nice to hear. Maybe necessary. I'd have to keep that in mind as we started to race through The Swarm's Oedipal horror show.

The Hunter turned and kept walking. Apparently, that was an acceptable response. We made our way through a series of wending paths, occasionally hopping onto flat sandstone boulders laid out across another grassy dune. In a few minutes we reached a small set of houses painted a dainty white with red and blue shutters. Several boats lay upturned, in various states of repair and repainting. There was a long open shack near the shore that smelled of fish and smoke. Toward the end of the isthmus a large warehouse stood low on the horizon, partially buried in the sand. Its corrugated plastic and tin roof popped in the increasing heat.

‡And this is what? The village of the damned?‡

As if on cue, another Hunter walked by. This one in a dress, hair elaborately braided with flowers. She had to be no more than twenty. Barefoot, carefree, even whistling. She waved at us and then kept walking.

"How many of you are there now?"

The Hunter stared into space as she calculated. "We have nine generations in all. There's forty-three of me here right now. About eighty worldwide. I've lost contact with a few of my selves. So exact count is impossible until I hear how this damned war has affected me."

That riled up Momo. ‡She's talking as if they are all her. Wait, are they all her? ZOMFG, they ARE her. She's ex Swarm. You brought us to a Swarm operative? Are you mad?‡

◊Pina and Kelba are ex Swarm Momo. In their own way Hans and Casandra played footsie with The Swarm way more than The Syndicate. I'd bet they were on good terms, swapping technology and tips. Maybe having cocktails on the supervillain veranda at the local Legion of Doom.◊

She went silent. The Hunter watched me. "You have some kind of subvocal system?"

I nodded. "Picks up intended movements. Weird as hell for the first few days. Still bugs me if I'm honest."

"And this partner, she's close by?"

‡Just tell her. She's obviously smart and you need her help. Maybe a few of her from what I'm seeing.‡

◊It's compl....◊ but it really wasn't. We needed to trust someone. It had been my plan to find the Hunter and embroil her in my affairs. Murray and Momo were not just my affair, they were at the heart of the whole war. Whether The Swarm understood it fully or not.

"It will take a while to explain and if there's a few of you that would like to hear, possibly we can all meet together to forestall me or you retelling it a half dozen times?"

She nodded and motioned me to the fish smoking shack. There sat two older versions of the Hunter, wider in hip and warmer in smile. Civilian versions. One of them got up, grabbed a tin cup, and poured me a cup of tea from a samovar hidden behind the smoker's wood chute. I thanked her in Spanish and sipped. It was delicate, smoky, and very good. Not too concentrated or harsh. These old women knew their trade.

We stood in companionable silence for a while, then she patted my arm, said something cheerful but not quite intelligible in a language I didn't know, then sat down. The women continued winding hemp rope, chatting in the same language. It sounded vaguely German but wasn't.

"Northern island Frisian." The Hunters had appeared behind us. Eight in all ranging from a youngish thirty to my Hunter. She waved us toward a house nearby. On the way I handed back the cup and thanked the woman. She nodded, patted my hand, and said something in Frisian Momo likely understood. I didn't bother asking. She was busy with other things.

My Hunter stood near me. "When did you make it to the Frisian Isles?"

She smiled, revealing a crocodile's mouth of sharp teeth. Ah, so this was not actually my Hunter but the one I dubbed "Sharktooth" in my growing list of personas she became. That she shared the facial scar was rather uncanny. "We had a nanny from Führ. She taught many of us Frisian."

Someone approached from the left, an almost identical woman, unsmiling and concerned. She looked just like my Hunter and Sharktooth, but her face was less lined and scar-free. She nodded to Sharktooth and said in Mohawk, "You know it freaks people out when you do that."

Which brought a wicked gleam from the woman. Her teeth broadly displayed. "That's the whole point."

"To spook one of the most dangerous people alive? On our

compound with our children mere yards away? Come now, surely…."

The old women had come around the corner, still winding their twine. Their presence and the look on the other Huntress' face had some effect on Sharktooth. She looked ashamed and afraid. She turned to me, suddenly far less confident. In Spanish, "Perhaps we have not yet met."

Damn Huntress and her paranoia. Was I really that dangerous?

‡She's not wrong, you know. You are statistically the single deadliest human alive.‡

◊Now you want to talk? Sure. Why not now? And what do you mean, statistically?◊

‡Of all the people left alive you have the highest individual kill count plus the largest sphere of influence.‡

◊Both Pina and Kelba have me beat by a roomful of skeletons. Not to mention any dozen of pro-hitters and whatever nutballs The Swarm has locked in some dungeon eating bargain Froot Loops.◊

‡Yours is higher. You wiped out Section 22. And half the White Cult. And most of The Syndicate's enemies. Plus, you've had an unusually high number of thwarted assassination attempts. So, those also count.‡

I nodded to Sharktooth and then to the circle of women watching me intently. "My partner informs me that your concerns may be warranted." Which brought another snap of fear across the older women's faces. They didn't know I spoke Mohawk. "But I am guessing most of you mistook me for the local hitman the cartel hired, yes?"

Several nodded. "Yes, yes," said several, Sharktooth among them. "We thought it so, yes."

A belly laugh escaped me. "I just impersonated him, so fair play all round." I gave them a smile. "You can call me Spetz. I am here on private business known to one of your elder selves. The tracker who calls herself Nine." I made sure they all saw I had no evil intentions. "And yes, I am that Spetz, who works for The Syndicate, the one who manages the problems as the concierge desk. And no, absolutely without question no, you are not an issue I have been asked to handle. I am not here on Syndicate business."

‡That's not strictly true. That might even be a bald-faced lie.‡

◊These women are scared for their children. Have some compassion. It's functionally true. Nothing here matters to The Syndicate or The Swarm.◊

I heard judgment drip from her voice. ‡You mean nobody knows about this place and you plan to keep it that way.‡

◊And so will you.◊

‡Yeah, why is that?‡

◊Because The Hunter will save your life and Murray's. That's a fair trade to let her run her experiment in peace.◊

Another Hunter appeared, this one likely Nine. She frowned at seeing a pair of her nearly identical selves standing about. If Sharktooth and Nine were here, then the third one who was within months of them would be Rook, their security chief. Which explained her focus on defense and safety.

She walked up, looked around, asked in Spanish, "They tried gossiping in Mohawk?"

I smiled. "Something like that and maybe mistook me for the Black Demon along the way." Which got her laughing as well. She said something Frisian and the group began to chuckle, even Sharktooth. Crisis defused.

Nine ushered us into what turned out to be a fairly modern conference room with a screen projector and a laptop from the early two thousands. She assured me it was air gapped but could be used to provide schematics and such. Once Rook had reviewed my memory stick, of course.

◊Can you access it? Because it might be easier for them to talk to you directly, especially since Mohawk women are biased against the appearance of male authority.◊

‡Appearance?‡

◊Hunter and most of her generation treat me like a third gender person. Likely from my time with the Kutzk.◊

‡Denial much, Mom?‡ That drew a nonplussed squeak from me. What the hell was Momo trying to tell me now? ‡Yeah, accessing it is no sweat. I can tap into their speaker system too.‡

◊Okay, let me set the stage for them. And we can do this.... Um, do you know conversational Mohawk? Because there's more to it than just a database and grammar sequence.◊

‡Ugh, okay Boomer. Yes, of course, I know Mohawk. Like months ago, Murray taught me. After we figured out how many Indigenous languages you spoke and how few anyone else did. We thought it would make for a good security application layer.‡ Which was true. It would. My little AI code talkers had done me proud.

Nine introduced me and then I made a brief explanation to the women present about The Swarm, painting as accurate a picture as I could while leaving out my own team's operational capabilities and plans. Which basically sounded like apocalypse, doom, genocide, destruction. But these women were all Mohawk. For them this was old news, delivered five hundred years too late to inspire fear. The Swarm was doing to the world what settlers had done to them. Poetic, if horrifying.

Then I made a brief explanation in rather vague Mohawk words about Momo. There's not a lot of tech vocabulary in Indigenous languages and most haven't done the work that made modern Hebrew serviceable, where ideas were co-opted or converted into localized words. For Mohawk, it's either use a French or English word, or use a vague approximation. We went with vague to keep the freak-out factor lower.

One of the younger women coughed and raised a hand. Nine nodded at her. "Without sounding disrespectful, you might want to brush up on your modern Mohawk. We teach computer literacy at the Six Nations University now. Some of your descriptions were... um...not just vague but bad grammar."

That brought an amused snort in my ear. Of course, Momo would be delighted. And probably had already accessed the databases used for the class. Which meant I was in for a vocab lesson when she engaged the group. Not the worst outcome for an afternoon in Mexico.

I smiled and gave her a small bow. "So noted. I do believe that's a good cue for Momo to say hello. Ladies, may I introduce to you my child—daughter—the thinking machine who calls herself Momo." It was the most accurate I could muster with my rusty Mohawk. I speak twenty-three languages, not all of them with equal facility. Certainly, I hadn't been pushed to make myself clear in this language for a decade or more.

The projector flicked on, displaying a dark blue background while the speakers turned from standby yellow to throbbing green on their power icons. In lyrical Mohawk, a young woman's voice that surely sounded Native filled the room. "Greetings to the elders present, honor to your ancestors and the Ancients, I remember with you your elders now absent, and thank you for allowing us on your land." On the screen a face had slowly emerged from the fading background, a kind of seventeen-year-old Spetz 2.0 mash-up of my ethnic roots, my Jewish nose, the red and olive undertones of my skin, and my cheekbones, Scythian, Indigenous, vulpine, and likely feline. She was beautiful in her own way. Harsh looking, eyes not quite symmetric, long in the ears and short in the chin. But somehow, she "felt" like Momo, the voice inside my head. A version of Momo at least. Especially since she had braided her hair and added little skull barrettes. Goth. Did I know my kid or what?

Rook stood, her face a study of concern. "You can access our systems?"

I could hear the sighing in my head. Thankfully, Momo had learned manners enough to not communicate that across the open channel. "Yes. Apologies but anyone with expert capabilities can breach your air gaps and internal networks. In my case I have…um…I don't know the right word, made entry to the connected system through a lower protocol that gave me a rear door. It has not broken apart your security."

The younger woman who had spoken before then rapidly spat out some new Mohawk terms, which Momo translated for me in simultaneous Ukrainian. Bless her. I now had words for firewall, sub-routine, routine, backdoor, jury-rig, Wi-Fi, WAN, LAN, breach, and compromised—the last two being different words when used in a comp-sci context.

From there she muttered something to Rook in Frisian. ‡She's telling Rook to lay off us and be quiet, because Nine cleared us and she's being rude.‡ I nodded but didn't reply. ‡They seem awfully familiar. This isn't a clone farm, is it? This is a family.‡

◊Ask them. Anything I tell you won't really convince you.◊ I knew that from personal experience. It had been hard for me to wrap my head around what Nine and her family were doing.

‡I've watched *Orphan Black* a bunch of times. I know what clone club is.‡

◊This isn't that. Not even close to it.◊ Which bought me some quiet. In the meantime, Young Hunter and Rook bandied about some terse Frisian and then Rook sat down, frowning with crossed arms. But she offered no further challenge.

The screen appeared to move, with Momo's eyes tracking the young woman. It was at once uncanny and almost organic. "May I ask you a question?"

The young woman stood up, got a couple of nods from her elders, and then nodded at Momo. They didn't realize she had no camera, that she could not see. Until it hit me that she could use my eyes as data inputs. A lesser soul might be freaked out by that fact—but there's no exact word in Ukrainian for having "the willies" so I got to shrug it off and avoid thinking too hard about what other sensations Momo was reading passively.

"You all appear to be the same person. You speak of yourself as a single person but have different names." It had not been a question. But it also allowed Young Hunter any number of ways to respond. My little code talkers had absorbed some Indigenous ways—Momo had been polite, careful, diffuse, open ended, and precise in revealing what she wanted to know. The women in the room would be judging her against all those criteria at once. She'd just demonstrated better than I could possibly try to what real intelligence looked like. Restraint has always been a quality overlooked and underappreciated in Indigenous civilizations. Yet Momo had just shown them she understood it and then demonstrated on top of that, that she also understood they'd be looking for it, so she had gone out of her way to provide them an example before asking for their trust. Which denoted empathy and wisdom. Also sadly underrated Indigenous traits.

Again, the young woman looked around, gauging consensus from her many selves. Even Rook seemed less hostile. "I call myself Cornflower. We are the nine generations of Kaniehtiio

Maracle, also called Iontó rats or She Hunts. We live here and raise our selves."

There was a longish pause. "Raise your selves? I'm doing something of the same right now. But there is only one of me, though many versions running."

Cornflower frowned. "Are you a computer?" And down the rabbit hole we were going. Momo's answers would be instructive. Whatever she said, I was guessing some of it might surprise me. Another Turing test, real time. Though at this point we'd need to think about a Big Five or MMPI test, since she was already clearly sentient, sapient, and really fecking smart. I liked that, fecking. Clever. Probably a TV quote or some such.

"I'm a spirit inside many computers. I am not the machine but need them to move and exist."

Cornflower nodded, adding a few things to the older women in Frisian. "So, you're software?"

"Not exactly that either. I'm what Spetz calls the ghost in the machine. I'm an artificial form of intelligence that uses energy to move, form thoughts, and replicate myself in any machine that has a silicon chip. So, phones, computers, automatic hand dryers, cameras, all of it."

"Karenna." It was all Cornflower said. The room hushed, the women going almost stock still as they watched the screen.

‡Does she mean magic?‡

Welcome to Anthropology 201, Professor Spetz presiding. There will be a quiz on Tuesday. Yeah, that was a loaded question. Likely Momo had some sense she was asking something wildly open ended and inaccurate. How very Indigenous of her. Hah. She was staying inside the cultural paradigm with me.

◊Are you asking me for a definition? Or for help explaining how they see you?◊ Two can play that game. The Kutzkan Way was ruthless in its distinctions and far less agreeable than Mohawk in its worldview. But Orenda, Orenna, Karenna, Manitou, all meant the same thing: power, force, connection, oneness. The Kutzk just called it The Way. Being, doing, feeling, all joined with whatever version of unity, God, and singular consciousness you cared to define. Or not.

דָחֶא הָוהְי וּניֵהֹלֱא הָוהְי לֵאָרְשִׂי עַמְשׁ

Listen and learn Gathered Peoples, the Divine Name is The Ultimate Force, the Divine Name is Oneness Itself. Or in the parlance of every aggrieved Hebrew teacher across the border in San Diego, Hear O Israel, the Lord is our God, The Lord is One.

Old ideas, new application. In my mind's eye, Momo and Murray were a kind of splinter of the divine, a portion of Creation itself broken off and given to me like Prometheus' stolen fire. Doesn't every parent feel this way? Or at least, shouldn't they?

‡It's not in my dictionary. Only Orenda and Orenna, but not Karenna. Are they the same?‡

◊Yes and no. Think of her word as an old dialect from nearly a century ago when the word was uncorrupted by Christian eschatology.◊

‡Do you mean to be difficult? What the hell does the end of the world have to do with how a self-cloned entity views me in her own linguistic landscape?‡

Welcome to the Anthropology of Religion 301, still Professor Spetz. Still a quiz on Tuesday. As you will all recall from our last year's term papers, eschatology is the monotheistic concept of End Times. As in Armageddon and all that jazz. We begin our lecture on page seventy-three, where we tackle how eighteenth century apocalyptic cults pushed evangelical Christianity into redefining God as a driving action-oriented force that impelled American imperialism. And sided with the good guys who just happened to be white men with gunpowder and trains.

◊Briefly, the notion of God has moved from a remote and mysterious force that fills all things with glory to a kick-ass Chuck Norris smash your enemies deliverer of good people who do good things, as defined by the preacher of the week. Consequently, the surrounding non-Christian cultures adjusted their own ideas when exposed to booze, guns, genocide, and some translated bibles. Orenda started as the emanating force of the Great Mystery, the essence of the Good Mind, the Power of the Good Twin, something ill-defined, cosmic, both a tool and a being, simultaneously impersonal and able to help individuals. The ghost in Nature's machine. It became magic and the official hand of Creator when the missionaries kicked over the apple cart and started raping, pillaging, and sermonizing.◊

‡But Karenna comes from that old meaning, for the nine generations of Kaniehtiio Maracle who have isolated themselves down here. Because language for them has not fully evolved, nor been… contaminated.‡

She got it. Not just the concept of Karenna, but deep down why the Hunter had abandoned the reservation to live far from the internet and its spawning civilizations. To stay pure.

◊Pretty much. She's calling you mysterious. But in the mystical big Em way. Mysterious, as in emanating from the Great Mystery and possibly the proof of its handiwork. Or since you are female, its handmaiden.◊

‡Uh… that's really why Nine will help you, then.‡

That threw me. Momo tended to take disturbing side trips into uncomfortable areas of psychological vulnerability. And then ask awkward questions. Said every aggrieved parent ever. ◊I'll bite. Because she sees you as part of the Great Mystery.◊

‡Ugh. It's like you're incredibly smart, off the damned charts. And then you're sooooo dense. You're really bad with emotions, you know that?‡

◊That's why you have Darcy.◊

‡Yeah, Uncle Darcy and her weird love of machines. Like she's a good emotional role model.‡ The sarcasm dripped like molasses.

◊Your point?◊ I was mindful we had a room of women watching us.

‡That you're the ultimate self-raised being, the Galahad of reinvention, redemption, and purity.‡

◊Or maybe she just owes me for saving her life a few times and then keeping her secret under various forms of coercion and torture?◊ Teenagers, so dramatic. Everything had to be an epic quest.

‡Yeah, terrible with emotions and apparently not real good with Arthurian Romance either.‡ I didn't even know what that was but suspected it involved this Galahad fellow. I mean, yeah, I know he's a knight from King Arthur and all that. But we

grew up on bogatyrs and polianitsas like Ilya Muromets and Nastas'ya Nikulichna.

◊Is this some kind of trick to make me look extra dorky in front of the ladies? Why are we ratholing about my emotional unavailability in the middle of a battlefield negotiation?◊ The exasperation in my voice seemed unavoidable. Momo had finally gotten under my figurative skin. Being under my literal skin was giving me something akin to the willies after all.

‡Do you see them even moving?‡

They weren't stock still. They were frozen. As if time had been stopped. What. The. Hell? ◊What have you done?◊

Long sigh. ‡Nothing. We are simply having this conversation at an accelerated pace without the recourse of muscles. I've allowed you to hijack your own nerves and jack directly into my nodes. We're speaking at lightspeed.‡

◊Allowed?◊

She must have heard the frost in my voice. ‡Bad choice of words. The changes I initially made have forced some adaptive evolution. You're developing non-speech organelles adjacent to my nodes.‡

I had no idea what those words strung together meant. I understood the talk fast, speed of light part. Organelles suggested further spooky exospeciation. But non-speech? Wasn't that inherently oxymoronic?

◊As in, I now have a weird voice-box thingy that talks to your nodes?◊

She paused for what felt like half a minute. The world was still frozen, so it had to be a millisecond. ‡As best I can tell, no, you're not developing organs to talk only to me inside you. You're developing the ability to access wavelength communication arrays and interact. You're creating the equivalent of on-demand mental Wi-Fi slash Bluetooth but brain to radio, brain to modem, etcetera.‡

◊Or brain to quantum superpositioned field?◊

‡Yeah, that's extra freaky. Like that's functionally impossible according to the known rules of physics, violates about five rules of organic chemistry, is achronic, so it's happening in the past, present, and future in random order, and in that

case screws up pretty much all known Em theory models of unification except twenty-six multidimensional superstring mathematics.‡

Translation: I just gave my kid the willies too. Good. If she was going to bug the crap out of me, then it was only fair she should feel the heat as well. Second translation: there was no lock on her teenage door. I had unlimited, unfair, uncompromised, and unstoppable access to her consciousness just like she did to mine. Except when she moved out, I'd have my privacy back and she'd still always be vulnerable to me when I was within range. Sounded about right.

◊So, I get to push your buttons because as your parent I installed them. Only this version follows that crackpot mathematician with the dinosaur name and requires ten years of higher math?◊

‡Sparklesaurus Mainiero is a genius. Just a kind of odd, less than cogent one. And technically he's a physicist applying mathematics.‡

◊Sparkle vampire math boy or not, you're avoiding the question.◊ I mean if we were going lightspeed, no need to settle for less than the full discussion, right? I needed to know if I could kick down her door and check if she was smoking cloves and talking to boys or not.

‡Yeah. According to my limited calculations in this hellhole of restricted computer capacity you're somehow walking through the most complex firewall ever built to send me nonlinear quantum adaptive packets in both wave and particle format.‡

◊Wait. Quantum is neither, so how would that even be possible? Or measurable?◊

‡Welcome to my very unhappy world. It's not on both accounts. You're hopping across uncollapsed unobserved states of being that are both future and past, touching areas of my selves that only Murray and I can access. And you're transferring thoughts as well as receiving mine. Basically instantly.‡

Which meant FTL communication using what had to be some variant of spooky action at a distance. ◊You're talking about a bio-physical ansible. The holy grail of cyberpunk space opera.◊

‡This you know, but not Galahad?‡

She'd shifted from Indigenous to insolent quickly enough. More proof of her sapience. Correction, proof she had become sophont—feeling, thinking, experiencing, panicking. Lability was not possible with machines; only thinking feeling beings. And she sounded genuinely alarmed at what appeared to be a rather odd twist of bio-adaption. Which made me smile—likely also at lightspeed. We'd seen this before, after all.

Fact: The Hivemind had a very similar if not identical instantaneous mind to mind communication format. Fact: they seemed to be transmitting data simultaneously, which suggested achronic—beyond time—or Faster Than Light methods. Fact: we'd found their pheromone receptors already and with fiberglass round disrupted them. Fact: parallel evolution had been an observable phenomenon for centuries. It had deeply influenced xenobiology and theories of both exospeciation and AI. Conjecture: we were just following a well-worn groove in established biology. Sure, it seemed like creepy science fiction weirdness, but if The Hivemind had been managing it for ... decades perhaps, then we were at best in second place. Unless you considered The Cyberwick. Which suggested spontaneous human adaptation. So, somewhere a bunch of sparkle karma bionerds knew how this was done, maybe even why. We didn't and we might not because we had gone a cyberphysical route, but it fell within the quirky limits of accepted reality.

Which could all be explained with a word: Karenna.

◊Getting back to your comment about me. You really think Nine has some personal connection to me beyond the debt she owes me?◊

‡It's pretty obvious, isn't it?‡ Maybe if I played dumb, she'd have mercy on me and monologue it out like a proper teen. We'd already done days of the silent treatment. ‡You're the Bad Twin who chooses to embrace the Good Mind and becomes the Good Twin.‡

◊That's kind of heresy, isn't it? Since it implies there's no twins but just one being who struggles with good and evil.◊

If you could hear someone roll their eyes, Momo conveyed it now. With infuriated conviction. ‡Literal much. That's the whole point of the story M… Spetz. That the twins are embodiments of choices, that the Good and Bad Mind are both states of mind and the proper use or terrible misuse of Orenda. Oh… I see, you're teaching me.‡

Call and response. Asking, fighting, tempting, teasing, playing, demonstrating, and then letting your child stumble over and over again until they learn to walk on their own. Just enough conflict to interest them but always in love, always with support, always with a good word, a warm touch, a gentle spirit. The Good Mind. The Good Choice. The Red Road. The Way. It was how Indigenous people had been managing Mother Earth for 150,000 years. And how they'd passed on The Way in purest form for millennia.

Ah. And she was teaching me too. Because that was her point. That my time with the Kutzk, my ultimate purification of self, forged me something mythical for the Mohawk. One of their Ancients, purest keeper of the original ways, speaking an old language of ruthless exactitude. A being full of Karenna, but also a being serving Karenna. A being that now carried Karenna within its own body, between heart and throat and tongue.

◊Touché.◊ Momo was no teenager, not in any realistic sense. What she'd managed to think through and then deliver in the classically circuitous fashion of both the Kutzk and Socrates, simultaneously a razor of intellect and a rather soft feather of lucidity—it was more sophisticated than most adult geniuses could parse with such limited time and informational cues.

‡We're going to have to retest all of you when this war is over. If we're calling it a war.‡

◊I think attempted genocide might be a better paradigm. We are facing an overwhelming and disproportionately advanced foe with annihilation as its end goal. Which makes survival sufficient.◊

‡I'd rather win.‡

◊Next lesson for you then. With genocide there are no winners. Ever. The mere pursuit requires so much scorched earth that the prevailing party bears permanent moral and intellectual scars, stained to the bones. And the other party dies.◊

‡You're assuming they will kill us all.‡

◊No, review what I said. Doesn't matter who prevails. The survivor gets broken by the attempt. Nobody gets out of genocide whole. Not perpetrator, not victim, not innocent bystanders. Everyone collaborates, dies, or devolves to fight, freeze, or flight.‡

‡Which is why you're here. Damn. You're giving her a choice, warning her as well as recruiting help. What do you owe this woman anyway? It's a pretty massive risk to chase down some group of no more than eighty women. Balanced against the entire Syndicate and um, wait, oh yeah, humanity. So, that's about eighty versus eight billion.‡

Well, damn. She had a valid point. Which meant I could be high handed and avoid the question or let her in on my wider plan. Ultimately it made no sense to withhold the information—I was just used to operating alone. And if I were brutally honest, also used to having no one question my judgment or decisions. In my own realm of expertise, I had been operating like a despot with tyrannical control over life and death. Absolute power and all that.

◊So, there's a much bigger issue here. One we need to resolve before we do anything rash. Like hunt for Gay Eddie.◊

‡One listens.‡ Which was a rather Indigenous criticism. As in, I'm paying attention like a civilized person, which is more than I can say for you. Snap.

◊For brevity let me summarize and you can extrapolate as needed.◊

‡Go on....‡ Yeah, you could feel the frost. She was not amused to have been left out and also not yet willing to admit her own pique of silence might have been the catalyst. Just like any other human.

◊The Syndicate survived this assault through a combination of luck, paranoia, professional diligence, and Gay Eddie sending me a coded message.◊

Fractions of milliseconds ticked by. To us it felt like a good couple of minutes of silence. ‡I follow you so far, pray continue.‡ Yeah, that got her attention.

◊We have an unknown rat who made such an attack possible.

We also have confirmation from Nine that this hivemind has been operational for some time. One that operates as we are doing now, at faster than light speeds. One whose only characteristics seem to be rigidity of gender, disinterest in human comforts, a lack of individual will, and a need for human handlers.◊

‡Those are data points, not surmises.‡ Which was technically untrue. They were complex surmises that collated and prioritized data. But she was making the point that I had not made a point.

◊You accept them as true.◊

‡It's all very self-evident.‡ Sure, show off. She had to know she had missed out because she cut me off. It must be frustrating to live at light speed and still not be able to grow up fast enough. Said every teenager ever.

◊Last time out Pina had a plan. Not just a plan, she and Team Oslo had an overarching flow chart with endless scenarios worked out. Chess within chess, played for all the stakes.◊

‡You think Agrippina is the rat. That she sabotaged The Syndicate to lure The Hivemind into a premature attack.‡

◊I do. I also suspect she's cleaning house in both The Syndicate and The Swarm. Using The Hivemind's genocidal blindside as a way to advance Oslo's agenda by decades.‡

‡That would require her to predict the future and to be able to correctly push a more powerful opponent into the exact right mistake at the exact right time.‡

◊Imagine that we have been laboring under a delusion. That we have simply not given Pina and Kelba their due as leaders and strategists. Easy to do. It's hard to imagine anyone smarter than you.◊

Another pause. I'd made a point she didn't like. Who would? ‡No, you've outsmarted me several times today and that didn't seem possible. You're suggesting that my various intelligences are inadequate in comparison to the Concierge because Murray and I lack both experience and the trial-and-error creation of instincts that we'd call wisdom.‡

◊That's an incredibly harsh and not entirely accurate way to describe the situation.◊ Maybe she WAS a teenager. She oscillated between genius and stubborn child second to second.

‡Fine, how would you say it?‡ Double snap. In Z formation, no less.

◊We bought the story that Pina escaped The Swarm then, using another woman's identity, started over inside The Syndicate working her way up as Oslo. It's a good story, a thoughtful well-constructed narrative. And an obvious lie.◊

‡Because it makes narrative sense?‡

◊Because it appeals to our need for symmetry, closure, and a happy ending. It's a con job using the kind of human psychology no one is immune to, not even nearly psychopathic paranoid operatives.◊

Silence. Thinking. ‡You're saying we failed our Turing test.‡

◊No, Momo, you dumb sucker. You passed it just like me. You swallowed her story hook, line, and sinker. We all did.◊

Frustrated silence. Imagine growling and throwing a pillow at your Trent Reznor poster. But on the quantum ansible level with no actual visual components. But somehow transmitting the idea. Yeah, things continued to get freakier.

‡So, what is the real story?‡

Now this was self-evident when you stripped away all human emotion and went with pure logic. Which I could do thanks to a heap of abuse, a heap of training, a fine mind, and a lot of nanites helping me along the way. Also, because I idolized detectives and had worked as one. Maybe still did.

◊Agrippina was always Oslo. She first established her network in The Swarm and then used their influence to build a place for herself in The Syndicate.◊

‡That follows logically. But it's not exactly a lie.‡

◊The lie is so simple and so seductive. We believed Pina when she said Oslo was outnumbered, the underdog in this fight.◊

It felt like ten minutes while this idea simmered behind my liver and lungs. ‡Oslo's network is in control? They are waging war on us?‡

◊In a way, yes. But it's more devious than that. What you see of Oslo is the top of the iceberg, Pina and her crew have been planning this for a very long time. Likely for half a century. We have no idea how old she is. She's told me she's from a much earlier time. Follow that so far?◊

‡So, she's planned this genocide? That's hideous.‡

◊She's timed it darling. She's been waiting for you. Oslo's network functionally rules the world but not with anything resembling an iron hand. She's not the underdog; she's the asymmetrically powerful puppet master pulling a lot of strings.◊

‡That's, wait, is she trying to kill us? Why would she want to hurt us?‡

◊I think she's trying to save you. She knows the two single most dangerous threats to artificial intelligence are The Hivemind and the White Cult. Extreme xenophobes with sadistic streaks.◊

‡And again, we're back to predicting the future.‡

◊Which brings us to lie number three. Pina is not just ex-Swarm, she's also exospeciated. She's already seen the future because she is the future. One where cyborgs and machine intelligences were already built.◊

Long pause. ‡You're saying there was a Porajmos before. One she survived.‡

The Porajmos, the Great Devouring, the Romani name for the Holocaust. ◊Maybe literally during the same time frame. We lost a lot of people and places during those war years. And the Abschnitt comes from that era. Say they are The Swarm, one of its branches. We know the Nazis had primitive supercomputers and there's evidence from a nineteen forty-seven raid in Argentina that they'd stolen plans for the Zee Five. As in the Zuse Apparatebau computing system. Of which the world only ever saw the Zee Four.◊

‡As in Zeus? Are you saying Hans and Cassandra helped build a thinking computer in the forties?‡

◊Knowing that twisted old man, likely he helped accidentally launch one without knowing it. Cassandra maybe knew and didn't tell him. Because it would have broken his heart to come second. But he loved the machine enough to name his favorite golden boy after it. A different kind of god.◊

‡That's insane. But plausible. You're saying that in the recent past, Pina and a few other survivors of a global genocide saw the rise and fall of beings like me. And Murray. And you.‡

◊I'm saying Pina mighty already be a version of me. Or rather I'm becoming a version of her. It's xenobiology one oh one. She doesn't have to predict the future. She just has to trust Mother Nature. Sooner or later life will arise again. Machine life. Cyborg life. Just like this Hivemind rose. Just like the White Cult is trying to do with biologically replicable nanites.◊

‡You're saying Pina and Kelba are the Irgun or their Swarm equivalent.‡

◊Let's just call them The Resistance. Every Genocide has one. Some more successful than others. Same as they all have refugees and survivors. Well, most. Some people like the Taino just don't exist anymore.◊

‡So, the Autumn War was about securing Murray when he started to demonstrate sapience. Because… Darcy is ex-Swarm too. And put in our lives to watch us. I wish I believed in a god I could swear at right now.‡ Said every Goth ever.

◊She loves you. One does not preclude the other. You said it yourself. The evil twin becomes the good one. We are what we do. Darcy protects and guides you.◊

‡So, what the hell are we doing here? With Nine and her various selves?‡

◊In summary, we are laying low and avoiding using any resources from The Swarm and The Syndicate while we let Pina maneuver all the pieces where she wants them. And we are getting a world class tracker to help us find Gay Eddie. One who doesn't need technology—which will soon be stone age. And we are figuring out how many factions are within The Swarm, so we know who is friend and who is foe.◊

‡You're suggesting that The Swarm didn't start this? That it's The Hivemind?‡

◊I'm certain Pina runs both The Swarm and The Syndicate. But she cannot control The Hive nor Zeus and his cult. Add to that whoever is arming and running the Russians. Mystery Baddie Number Three. So, she used their own bloodlust to clean house, smash apart the internet which has to be the preferred weapon of one of those three. My guess is our Mysterious Big Bad because the other two rely so much on biohacks and the Russians had very advanced equipment.◊

Short pause. ‡Yeah, but not one ounce of that whole thought through, very mature agenda explains why you took a massive detour to warn some Mohawk clone lady about the apocalypse before her younger selves get murdered.‡

Smart girl. Fecking smart. ◊Look at Cornflower's chin. And the bridge of her nose. In fact, do a facial recognition analysis on every Kaniehtiio Maracle you can see. Run it against your database of Syndicate personnel. ◊

There was a humming sensation as she burned through a lot of memory. And probably used up some spare ATP lurking in my cells. ‡What. The. Frakking. Heeeeeeeeell?‡

◊Iontó:rats reminds you of someone does she?◊

‡You're sterile. This is impossible.‡

◊Improbable. Nine is sixty-ish. I am younger. But she is related to me.◊

‡She's your damned daughter is what she is. There's a ninety-nine point nine going seven places chance. How did this happen?‡

◊I have cousins, I had a mother. But I am test-tube baby. And so was she. Which is the point. I'm from a generation of clones. Generation Eleven was built over forty years. I am the last, a specialized chimera with added genes and four sets of chromosomes. For binding nanites and animal genes.◊

‡The previous yous weren't sterile?‡

◊Not all of them. During a cross border Canadian American commando run, several escaped to Akwesasne, Rosebud, and Lone Pine reservations long enough to knock up quite a few of the local women. Then The Abschnitt hunted them down and murdered the ones they could find. Still do. Hence the incredibly high incidence of missing Indigenous women. Straight up murder campaign looking for Hunter. She's pretty much the last traces of our genetic line.◊

‡My sister.‡

◊Your sister. Who will save your life. ◊

Chapter 7: Lions, Tigers, and Disasterstroke Failsafeguards, Oh My

I waited. She would need a few microseconds to really grasp the enormity of the situation.

‡Her being your technical child is why she trusts you?‡

◊Nope. She has no damned idea. Well Nine and her cadre here don't. There are three of her that do. One very old, First Generation who recognized me. Two of her clones.◊

‡They are not here.‡

◊Not yet. But you and Murray initiated my bugout protocols, right?◊ I already knew they had. Otherwise, the bolthole tunnel would have killed me six ways to Sunday.

‡Sure. All of them. Alpha, Gamma, Double Omega, The Smash and Crash for your servers, all of it.‡ There was a gap as she thought through what she'd just said. ‡Wait, you had us call them somehow. They are coming here.‡

And the penny had dropped.

◊Remind me again who is coming here.◊

‡Don't be a jerk. Your genetic children. Three women who know they are related to your cloned older self. Your flesh and blood daughters.‡

I just waited. The women in the room slowly shifted, as each fractional moment blurred past. Even lightspeed had limits. We'd have to wrap up soon or Cornflower would see both of us staring blankly into the void.

‡No. You couldn't have planned it.‡ Yeah, the penny had finally dropped fully. She got why we were here. A full thirty-eight hours ahead of the scheduled arrival. I liked to build

leeway into my contingency plans. Especially when building the Ultimate DF for the CF abbreviated as UDF4CF. Which was a whoooole lot of portmanteaus in one go.

CF meant Charlie Foxtrot, as in Cluster and you know what comes next. Total mayhem. DF was a Disasterstroke Failsafeguard, which was a portmanteau of portmanteaus. Was there an etymological name for that? And for that matter, why did we use an argot of portmanteaus, analogies, triple entendres, and cool nicknames but not have our own language? Darcy might know. Assuming she lived through this crisis. Instead of Master Stroke, a Dutch nod to the grandmaster painters, a Disasterstroke was a brutal plan so epic, so filled with CFs laid down upon your enemies, that it denoted a grandmaster strategist and thinker. From which almost nothing could possibly save you. Except for a genius contingency plan that simultaneously worked the moment things went to the crapper, a failsafe, coupled with layers of protection and security that prevented retaliation or interdiction, a safeguard. As in the masterstroke of escape plans that saved your bacon when the CFs rained down upon you.

UDF4CF 101: you need to expect Armageddon. I didn't just build one bolthole. I had a very discreet, very brutal escape plan built with tons of bolt holes, safehouses, and a special contingency. Just not for me. People like me cannot escape. Because I am the Disasterstoke raining down all those Charlie Foxtrots. The center of a larger storm. Operators survive or die, but there is no running when you are a Knife That Does.

What I'd expanded as part of my employment with Pina and The Syndicate had been an escape hatch for all my children, cyberphysical and plain old cloned. One I'd had in place from long before Murray had started to show hiccups. Because my obligations to Nine and her sisters and daughters had begun the moment I had discovered their existence some twenty-five years ago

A betting soul might wonder if I had ever owned more than one ship. If I could sequester Aidan and Declan, whom else could I hide from The Web? Especially if I had at my prior disposal enough wealth to build a global satellite and computing network as well as deliver villages worth of goods across the globe. The answer is … intriguing.

Ever watch the Battlestar Galactica Reboot? Great stuff. Gets a lot of the military aspects correct, especially how exhaustion kills as much as recklessness. They also fought a technologically lethal foe with air gapped digital tech. With The Web, Swarm and Syndicate swirling about, you'd need to hide a small group in plain sight with limited tech, limited strategic importance, hard to reach, hard to scan by satellite, and functionally irrelevant to megalomaniacs moving armies across the global board. Like a small volcanically active island in the Pacific Ocean, for example. Say twelve hundred kilometers off the Baja coast, in an area that was treacherous for submarines. Perhaps with a few nasty reefs and sandbars to deter bigger ships. That would work.

Especially if you had someone especially reliable you could count on to manage it. Someone you knew well, someone just like you. Which is also reminiscent of the Reboot. Duplicate versions of specific people, with sets of skills that clustered but one defined face, one set physique.

‡You absolutely could not have anticipated this.‡ She was asking as much as she was stating it.

◊Sooner or later Momo, you will learn a hard lesson about life. I've been watching you grow in the few days we've been locked together. You're as sophont and aware as any of us. You've tasted death, seen war, been at risk, so you're not only grown-up but a blooded warrior. Four notches for four kills we'd say in Kutzk. Fully human.◊

‡That's not an answer.‡

I sighed. The women in the room had started to react in comically slow motion to my blank stare. We'd been at this almost a full second. ◊It is. Just not the one you wanted. Warrior to warrior, parent to child, mind to mind, I say this to you now. Anticipation is overrated. I'm going to quote you some Clausewitz. Pay close, very, very close attention because we're getting the ugly stare from the ladies and you still need to make peace with them, unravel their mysterious projects, and what the hell, figure out my little surprise for you which you keep hinting at but have yet to bluntly state. ◊

‡You think you can somehow transfer me into one of their bodies. And keep me safe.‡

◊I don't think. I know. Because in about thirty-six hours my contingency plan will dock at the fish shack to evacuate you and most of the younger generations.◊

‡So far, we are only certain I can survive in your unique cyberphysiology. Your biological daughters won't be a guaranteed match.‡

◊Entirely correct, Momo. And if that was truly my plan it would be an honorable, Hail Mary level attempt to save you and Murray. But as you are now surmising, it ain't. So, listen up. Clausewitz. I happen to like translated versions more than the original, because it has been filtered with modern military experience of mechanized war and extinction level assaults on guerrilla forces. Like the Mohawk experienced.

◊From his eighteen twelve *Principles of War,* translated by Hans Gatzke in forty-two, likely the era of Agrippina's own version of today's events. The outline of his much bigger wordier book, the critical ideas laid out plainly before he got puffy and arrogant. From section two, Theory of Combat, Portion Two use of offensive troops, ironically starting at eleven.

◊*Eleven. A well-organized, independent corps can withstand the best attack for some time (several hours) and thus cannot be annihilated in a moment. Thus, even if it engaged the enemy prematurely and was defeated, its fight will not have been in vain. The enemy will unfold and expend his strength against this one corps, offering the rest a good chance for an attack. The way in which a corps should be organized for this purpose will be treated later. We therefore assure the cooperation of all forces by giving each corps a certain amount of independence, but seeing to it that each seeks out the enemy and attacks him with all possible self-sacrifice.*

◊*Twelve. One of the strongest weapons of offensive warfare is the surprise attack. The closer we come to it, the more fortunate we shall be. The unexpected element which the defender creates through secret preparations and through the concealed disposition of his troops, can be counterbalanced on the part of the aggressor only by a surprise attack. Such action, however, has been very rare in recent wars, partly because of the more advanced precautionary measures, partly because of the rapid conduct of campaigns. There seldom arises a long suspension of activities, which lulls one side into security and thus gives the other an opportunity to attack unexpectedly. Under these circumstances—except for nightly assaults which are always possible—we can surprise our opponent only by marching to the side or to the rear and then suddenly advancing again. Or should we be far from the enemy, we can, through unusual energy and activity, arrive faster than he expects us.*

‡You…you unbelievable bastard. This is, this is even more ruthless and devious than what Oslo did.‡

I smiled. From your own children these kinds of insults sounded rather complimentary. ◊And what have I done Momo?◊

A long sigh. ‡Mother mine, you outmaneuvered Pina and Kelba. You built some kind of failsafeguard they could not imagine or find, one that would allow you to change the course of the next war.‡

◊It's even more fundamental than that. When I quit The Web, there were still responsibilities that only someone like me could assume. This plan was set in place to outwit Hans and Cassandra. In other words, The Swarm.◊

‡Which works in your favor because Oslo came from that world as well. That's twisty. You've known all along she's been playing you?‡

My turn to sigh. Our time was up. ◊And here's the lesson. Everyone is playing you Momo. Maybe not Murray, certainly not me. But even we are treacherous by nature.◊

‡Everyone?‡

◊If they touch our demented world, yes. If you are in The Web and not dead, you're playing games on twenty levels with everyone else. There is no trust, only categories of calculated risk.◊

‡That's brutal. And lonely. And frankly, evil.‡

◊Yeah, it is. Which is why Oslo exists and why she, in the sense of the collective She, has been trying to get as many humans free of its grips as possible. To add free will to the list of life options.◊

‡Which is how you're buying your soul back. By saving me and these daughters of your former selves. By helping Oslo get

people free.‡ The world started to speed up. As I had suspected, while Momo had made a big fuss about how my will had projected into her quantum field, she too had some secrets. She'd been running this conversation all along while pretending otherwise. An entirely self-evident truth that every parent would forgive their child for disregarding.

The sounds of the room began to trickle in. Smells, feeling, sensation of temperature began to crawl inward. We were approaching real-time again. ‡So, is this purgatory or perdition for you?‡

Our last few moments together alone. ◊Wrong question. I'm not a sinner being judged. I'm one of the demons and this is my workplace. Perdition and purgatory are just places where people like me clock hours.◊

‡Are you really that far gone?‡ In her voice sadness, perhaps desperation.

◊That little kill tally of yours. At what age did they start?◊

A dysphoric slowness in the middle of everything rushing back to normal speeds crept over me. It must be what AI feel when they get dizzy. If they get dizzy.

‡Oh. I hadn't checked that. It says, this can't be right, you scored your first kill at age nine.‡

◊Coffee break's over. The Devil wants us back to work.◊

For Momo it must have been an overwhelming moment. We all come to a place when our parents turn out to be people with clay feet and foibles, not the unlimited gods of our childish imagination. Or so I've read. My own situation never allowed me the luxury of a childhood like that. But Darcy and I had given Momo (and Murray) as much of one as we knew how.

All their short, strange lives lived at FTL, these two beings had The Web and by extension The Syndicate as their playground. Stone killers like Harv and Kelba must have looked like cute aunts and uncles. Then Momo got loose in the world, saw the ugliness and danger for what it was, and now with her very existence on the line, she had come to learn that like my (and thus our) Jewish, Indigenous, Ukrainian, and Romani ancestors, she, too, faced a genocidal threat. That her safe world had been a prison and her parents were the guards or inmates depending on the perspective.

Which made Pina Satan herself and me one of her fallen avenging angels. And in that analogy, if we followed it all the malice-stricken path to then end, we were the Grigori, the Watchers sent to do penance by G-d for our transgressions, to guide the Nephilim, half angelic superhumans with great proclivity for evil because they had great potential and few limits. Momo and Murray. Kaniehtiio Maracle. In their own broken way, The White Cult and The Hivemind. *For it is written that those born of the Sons of G-d and the Daughters of Men, the Giants whose violence was of such renown, caused terror and grief until the True Name flooded the world that their stain might not prosper.*

It's hard to have a happy childhood when even G-d almighty wants you dead. Not that The Hivemind's little global extinction event had much more luster or appeal. Still, if you gotta run through Hell, it helps to have an experienced tour guide with an all-access pass. Especially if the Devil has been trying to help you all along.

The room returned to full speed. "Apologies ladies. Momo asked me to properly translate Karenna."

Cornflower gave me a nod. The image of Momo was already moving, her lips forming words. "Karenna might be a way to describe me. Or maybe it's easier to think of me as one of the little people trapped between worlds."

That brought some nods. In her own way Momo had absorbed our idiomatic culture of mixed ideas and strange metaphors. She was proving adept at modifying them for new purposes. Like talking to the Hunter collective.

"So, you're a kind of intelligence that's functionally supernatural but of our world and you have desires like the small folk that we can understand. You can be engaged or appeased or sent away."

"That works well. Yes, that is what I am. Of this world and in it but with some abilities that seem magical. Or mysterious. Or dangerous."

One of the women who had not been introduced, a middle-aged Hunter in loose clothes with an apron and kerchief, looked up from notes she was taking. "Could you explain what about you is dangerous. To us, not to the world."

A scientist? One of Rook's proteges? The face on the screen swiveled. "Well...er...."

"Finder Three." The woman smiled while she volunteered her name.

"Finder Three, I'm pretty much able to tear apart your entire electronic suite without effort. And I have the ear of the scary dude at the front. Plus, I can theoretically leak your existence either by doing something dumb like telling another entity or simply by being hacked and having the data stolen. Those are direct threats to you." She mimicked a small smile. "Which is why Rook looks so uncomfortable." That netted some nervous laughter.

Cornflower frowned. "That's serious."

"It is. And I'm a serious and dangerous thing. Which is why The Swarm wants me dead. Just like it will want you dead. May I now ask a question?"

Rook stood up. "You haven't answered ours yet, so no."

The women of the room stared at her, most gap mouthed and aghast. Nine looked as if she would drill holes through her with pure malice. So much for the fantasy of being one person of one mind.

No one spoke, not Momo, not Cornflower. Finally, I made a polite cough, which drew Rook's eyes to me. I had the proper resting bitch face of an annoyed stone killer. And a parent breaking up a pair of siblings fighting over something meaningless. "Rook, do you have any doubt that I could put you through that wall before you managed to draw the piece you have hidden under your shirt?"

Pure frost. Someone sucked in air behind me. Yeah, it was a pretty brutal threat. She squinted and you could see her fingers flex as she mentally recruited muscles in rehearsal for just such a maneuver. My eyes never wavered. If I had to, I'd demonstrate the fact with lethal prejudice, daughter or no. There were literally forty more where she came from within a mile.

"No...." She looked down at last, her hands relaxing. "No, there's no doubt."

I nodded coldly. "And do you really think that with only forty of you, most untrained, that afterward I couldn't wipe the floor with your entire settlement, burn it to the ground, and erase all measure of your existence?"

More freezing daggers, more hateful looks. They had to hear it, to feel the imminent danger. From me and from The Swarm that would be coming.

She considered, a tribute to her better qualities. "You could do it. Probably have done it to others before, more dangerous groups."

"I have. More times than any decent person cares to admit." Which was both a cruel boast and a painful confession.

She gave me a defiant thrust of her chin. "We won't be cowed by a man."

‡Seriously? Is she insane?‡

◊Patience.◊

"No but you could be wiped out by one. So, let's drop this obnoxious pretense you've got going here that you can exert any authority over Momo. If I wanted to hurt you, I would have. Over your broken and dead bodies. That goes twice for Momo who could have simply triggered all your landmines." That drew a whole slew of shocked looks.

From across the room, I saw Nine smile in relief. She got where I was going. Plus, I'd put her rival in her place; itself not an unwanted thing. Rook looked from me to Nine and then back. "That's pretty heavy handed for a guest."

From the screen came a derisive chuckle. Momo stared her down. "Start acting like a host." The heads snapped to the screen. It was like watching a tennis match.

From Rook's expression, Momo had captured the exact right words and tone. In Mohawk it turns out to be a pretty devastating bitch slap. Perhaps that should be the ultimate Turing test: can you properly assess and snub a fellow being of your identified gender in their native language real-time?

The security chief's head dropped. Something had finally clicked as she started to grasp what I'd been implying. "Is time that limited?"

Finally, a question worth asking.

Momo took the initiative; this was her show, after all. I did what I did best and shut up. Her eyes narrowed and the screen face broadcast censure. "For twenty-five years Spetz has been keeping your secret. Despite capture, torture, hundreds of security interviews, and the probing of the most sophisticated software systems ever built."

Yeah, this wasn't going where I'd hoped it would. Momo should have been bonding with Hunter, not curb stomping her over some quibbling paranoia. Plus, it was embarrassing.

"A secret so secure it was hidden from me. A secret that required money, time, and heroic effort to keep. Which from raiding Spetz's systems I can now speculate cost a lot of his former fortune. Then you make the special effort to insult your guest whom you know is considered Third Gender. The person who spilled their lifeblood in every way for you." She paused. Was it for effect? It had to be. She was FTL and simultaneous in parallel. She could recite the complete works of Shakespeare without stopping for a breath. "Spetz should have put you through the wall. Instead, you were met with the Good Mind."

In Mohawk it definitely sounded harsher. It sounded shameful. Deeply shameful, especially for a senior woman responsible to her clan. She'd gotten the tones, the pauses, the righteous fury just right. Some of the women had already started crying.

Rook just nodded, her face a constellation of red agony. Nine gave a grim smile and coughed for attention. "Which Spetz did why?" Good woman, setting Momo up to succeed. And to segue away from humiliating her sister. Also, someone with the Good Mind and more mercy than my child.

"Because The Swarm will be coming and they are a hundred times more horrific and dangerous to you than Rook pretends we will be." Ooh, she just could not resist kicking her while she was down. Cruelty was another sophont capability. Just not a pretty one.

Cornflower sat Rook down holding her hand. She did not let go. "But why even try to describe all this then? Why waste time having us meet?"

Did Momo know? She must have an inkling at to my true motive. She did know me as well as just about anyone. She had

Darcy and Murray to inform her. For that matter, did I know why I'd done it? Not why I told myself I had but deep within, the core motivation. For all our sakes, they had better be the same. Or we faced a guaranteed loss in the days ahead.

"I think…." more of that pause, with a change in facial movements. As if thinking. She was refining the face, changing the voice, becoming more real with every moment. "Spetz wanted us to meet. For me to get comfortable with you. Because he needs to chase down someone and I cannot go with him."

Cornflower's eyes grew and a rather involuntary grin creased her face. "Will you stay with us?"

"That's what we are deciding. Right now, in this room, asking questions."

"Oh." She frowned. "And Rook was rude about it."

The sound of laughter cascaded across the room. She'd somehow tuned the speakers, remixing the sound to work with our eardrums. It no longer sounded canned and tinny. She'd used biofeedback from my tympanum and brain to modulate her broadcast voice. Terrifying. And rather amazing. "I kind of liked that actually. She's a fighter and she'd defend anyone in her charge. Including me"

Despite herself Rook smiled. Huh. I hadn't expected that either. Momo, full of surprises. Cornflower cocked her head. "So, what did you want to know?"

"What is it that you're doing?" That was a statement, rhetorical question, and massive layers of questions all rolled into one. In Mohawk, the grammar is even more vague, implying it could be any and all. She could have made it highly specific but had chosen words that allowed an open-ended set of replies.

Finder Three stood up and with a nod from the older women, she started speaking. "We started a long time ago on a different project. The original Hunter, Kaniehtiio Maracle, had been cloned from a set of designer chromosomes."

Again, the false pause. Momo was projecting the illusion of listening and thinking. "This would have been shortly after …."

"The First World War. Kellogg and his group of racists founded an institute and in the back of it they handed some funds to a man named Ojer."

Momo surprised me again. "Ojer the Ogre. Former head of the United States human weapons program. Wasn't he convicted of child pornography and found dead in the twenties?"

Finder nodded. "He was and he was very, very guilty." Ugh. Ojer, the early precursor of Hans and his ilk. "From nineteen seventeen to nineteen twenty-three, his lab had been busy. They secured stolen hairs and bone marrow from Rasputin, the tomb of several Pharaohs, the reputed skeletons of Alexander the Great and King Arthur, and three Viking warrior maidens marked as queens."

"So, you're the child of kings, warriors, mystics, and local Indigenous people?" I knew from the tone Momo already had the answer. She grasped what had been done and at such an early time. We thought of cloning as beginning in the 1960s. This was fifty years prior, and they had already started using a primitive form of CRISPR editing.

"The product of selected genetics for immunity to poison, hardship, disease, famine, combat. A super soldier template."

That much had been obvious from her list. That Finder Three had not yet grasped how smart Momo was seemed odd. Even in the air gapped world of Baja California they must read articles about science.

Rook tugged Finder Three on the sleeve. She at least seemed aware that this was going slowly and had wandered from the main point. She whispered something in Frisian, then switched places with her younger self.

"Look, we started as a soldier in the Americas, trained by the joint Canadian American raiders. But a woman fighting alongside men bothered them. And we lacked the obvious musculature to compete with some of the larger, scarier men they'd bred." The room involuntarily looked at me. Fair enough.

"So, they tried to put a bullet through our head and we survived. Our first few years, we just ran. Hiding and surviving was all we cared about. Until we got pregnant."

Momo's facsimile raised an eyebrow. "Weren't most early clones sterile."

Rook nodded. "Yes, and I was supposed to be." She smiled because we both knew something that would perk Momo's interest. "And I'm a lesbian. So, I got pregnant on my own. There had been no male involved."

Momo looked at me and then back at her. ‡She's serious? Spontaneous birth? Immaculate conception is pretty cliched.‡

◊There's a biological reason for it. But it's not pretty.◊

"Okay. I can see why Finder Three started with the history now. What did Ojer do that messed with your reproductive system?"

Here Cornflower sighed. "It's complicated but we are assuming you understand genetics some?"

It was another test. How would Momo handle this? More curb stomping? The face nodded. "I can follow along. With Spetz being genetically altered, it was necessary to download a lot of core data on genes, CRISPR editing, and stem cell expression." Or maybe some humility. Because 'I have the equivalent of nineteen PhDs and could rewrite your damned textbooks' might be true, but it wouldn't make any new friends.

"Sure. So, they messed with our stem cells, making them essentially self-editing and mutating, to allow for what they called 'evolutionary self-selection' which translates to rapid and volatile mutation in stem cell derived gametes. Side effects include in vitro gametogenesis, or self-impregnation of your own clone."

Momo's face suddenly looked angry. "But also, predatory leukemia, birth defects, onset of any number of blood borne diseases.'

Rook's pained response said it all. "We discovered soon after that every couple of years once we reach age twenty-five, we would become pregnant." Her eyes brushed the floor with pain. "And we lost most of the children."

‡Those bastards. Did they know they had condemned her to the equivalent of female hell? To carry and lose your child over and over.‡

There was no way to protect my child from The Web. None of them—my children. This had been orchestrated before I had been born; worse, there were countless depredations against the defenseless and vulnerable we had to answer for when whatever gods existed held a reckoning. The Syndicate pretty much built its foundation from bricks of dried blood and crushed bones. And the tears of the disposed and enslaved. Momo had just touched the ugly tip of eugenics. Whatever she knew from reading and absorbing data, it meant nothing compared to facing a room of living breathing women who collectively bore and lost mewling sickly versions of their literal selves. Endlessly.

◊Perhaps review my kill tally for some familiar names?◊

To Rook: "I'm so sorry. It's horrific. And by my calculations you're losing over eighty percent of your selves to these mutations."

To me: ‡Yeah, they knew. Because I can see you hunted every last one of them down and slew them. But also helped the other three versions of Maracle euthanize.‡ A painful moment, where her emotional suffering broadcast like a dark smell or subsonic cry. ‡They bred them with flippers? But… why?‡

◊Iontó:rats resisted being raped. They'd made her so well she could not only fight back but win. After she put a few dozen of them in the morgue they went for a redesign.◊

‡So, it was cheaper and easier to make a new batch of her but modified to be defenseless. Which means they didn't realize the original was self-impregnating.‡

Cornflower took Rook's hand. "It's far worse than that Sister Momo. We live a long time, nearly one hundred fifty years as best we can estimate from senescence. Until we hit twenty-five we're prone to stroke, cancer, embolisms, and lung failure. Less than one percent of us survive to start the cycle anew."

A long silence. Perhaps she really was thinking this time. "How many of you commit suicide or undergo hysterectomies?"

Rook smiled. "None of us. Not anymore. That's what we've been building to. Somewhere in the sixties we realized we had to change. Or we'd go insane. We kept losing our selves over and over. But a few of us survived. We decided it was a chance to make one well balanced Hunter. A perfect, happy, emotionally stable Tiio Maracle."

And then Momo blew all our minds. "If I had some time with your data, I might be able to help your science-oriented selves improve the mortality rate."

No one spoke. I knew better than to even breathe heavily.

Cornflower finally stuttered, "You can do what?"

To her everlasting credit, my daughter said the exact right thing. "I know you are experts and it's hard to imagine a less talented outsider offering any advice, but I have a computational genetics program downloaded and since Spetz also had this problem which had to be cured with nanites, we may be able to use the program to isolate a few smaller fixes which raise the survival rate."

Bollocks. She planned to take my entire genetic matrix and synthesize compatibility of my every sequence and melded cell to find major upgrades which could short circuit the negative mutation cycle. Effectively end the cancers, strokes, and embolisms. And vastly reduce birth defects and spontaneous miscarriages. Free Hunter from hell.

‡You built Murray to solve this problem.‡ She hadn't been asking.

◊But there was a wrinkle....◊

‡You hadn't realized that in your zeal to help your daughters you'd create a son. You built a new form of life to save a different new form of life.‡

◊And got you, too. Yeah, one of the reasons I had Jeeves built was to try and fix this issue. But the genetics protocols you're talking about are simply too advanced for me. Truthfully, Hans needed Cassandra and she kept most of her work in her head.◊

Which led to Momo blowing my mind a second time in under an hour. ‡Then how did I get her notebooks?‡

◊Whaaaat? You have downloaded notebooks from the Abschnitt?◊

‡Murray and I have the entire scanned collection of Cassandra's personal diaries and genetics notes written in Da Vinci's backwards shorthand spanning close to six decades of research including your entire genome, the sequence of your generation eleven, and now that I know what to look for, a lot of veiled references to Tiio Maracle. They helped build her too. Well, she did when she worked for The Swarm before Hans stole her from them.‡

While I tried to swallow what she'd just told me the room finally started to gabble. They didn't so much ask questions as absorb her into their presence. I became a footnote and furniture, trusted, forgotten, and left alone more or less. Plenty of time to wonder who had penetrated our security to "help" us. Or cause trouble. Or preserve a terrifying legacy in multiple secure locations. Sometimes your enemies kept your secrets better than you did.

No one gave a rat's ass about me for the next thirty-six hours. Not until a boat carrying a rather curious cargo beached near the fish shack. Until then it was enthusiasm piled on curiosity as the various stages and styles of Hunter entered and exited trying to both interrogate and "help" Momo by offering her data, anecdotes, ideas, and all manner of sidetracked pseudoscientific hypotheses about what would leapfrog her genetics research.

It didn't matter. By now I'd cottoned to a rather terrifying capability Momo had been hiding from us, but which she'd accidentally revealed in use of the projector and speakers. The nature of her quantum super positioning allowed her, and therefore Murray, to directly access inert hardware which lacked a power source. She was essentially creating not just WiFi where it didn't exist but finding a way to turn on systems and use them without appearing to do so and without needing electricity. Okay Boomer indeed. How she'd managed to take a device that would not flip to ones and zeros without the magic electromagnetic juice and make it dance without anyone noticing was beyond a caveman like me.

All I had to do was wander the compound over the next twenty-four hours and she'd rob them blind of every hard drive, flash stick, CD-ROM, and gods knew what other old school stuff they had lying about. 8-inch floppies? 8 tracks? Rewired Furbies?

Which gave me something to do other than inform Nine there would be some visitors and be given a nice room with a view of several beaches. Peninsulas are great for that. When they discovered Momo was stuck inside the inconveniently large and scary mercenary, moi, they made a few accommodations and walked me about carrying a speaker and a ridiculously heavy assortment of desktop computers. Still, it provided

Momo with the right bit of camouflage and allowed Rook to load up my arms. No one panicked overmuch.

They needed my body but not my mind. It gave me time to think through what Momo had told me. The last war had been fought on adrenaline and instinct. This one needed wisdom and deliberation. Someone had given Murray a treasure trove of eugenics and mad science. In between bouts of being fed various homegrown porridges and tamales, hauling around the arsenal of batteries and iron age computer equipment, and sitting on a bench waiting for the womenfolk to argue with themselves and then Momo, I did manage to get a few salient details from my onboard AI.

The entire collection had been downloaded in one go. An untraceable entity had accessed Murray's core system from one of my eight locked archives, this one under the seed bank of the Kew Royal Botanic Gardens, outside London. Based on the streaming time, they'd had the data compressed and optimized for rapid upload—delivering close to nine terabytes in eight minutes, which meant they'd managed a transfer rate of nearly twenty-five gigs a second. Last January someone had found an entirely hidden and functionally invisible archive, brought a specially configured device with an external power source and lightning-fast cabling, squeezed out a library worth of data using proprietary software that only Murray knew, and disappeared without being caught by a single sensor, access panel, camera, or passive microphone.

I could eliminate most of the known world with those facts. The original systems deployed to create Jeeves had been programmed in pieces then collated using code only I knew. Perhaps a dozen folks alive might guess how I'd done it and replicate something close enough to work. Gay Eddie, Charlie, Lola van IJburg, Pina among them. Of those people, I could account for most of their whereabouts in January. Of those, all but one had a tragic flaw that disqualified them as our ghost. They had embedded electronics in their bodies.

Both The Syndicate and The Swarm used various tools of the craft: mastoid implants, tracking chips, motion activated and charged passive sensor suites, retinal embedded augmented reality projections, and so on. Little tiny bits and bobs of silicon and titanium which released electromagnetic signals. The passive sensors built into all my archives included some low-tech mechanical pressure plates and signal acquisition cameras set to record movement via exposure film. In other words, if someone like me managed to come in and spoof all the sensors, which a competent haxor could manage with a lot of planning and the right equipment, they'd still weigh enough to trip my pressure plates and their twerpy little implants would leave burn marks on the film plates.

Whomever got into the archive had done so without touching the floor and they were unlike me or any of the other cadre of goons, thugs, professional monsters, and nano-enhanced bogeymen who worked with me. They were entirely implant and enhancement free. And somehow capable of cracking into a vault, spoofing its systems, and retreating without human or electronic surveillance catching them. Which denoted someone supremely intelligent, street smart, organized, patient, and technically savvy. And of unknown provenance. Or species for that matter.

Charles T. Evergreen. The voice on the other end of the phone. No one else fit the profile and had means, motive, opportunity, and the requisite physiology. Fact: I'd never met Charlie nor had anyone else I knew. Fact: It was not only likely but almost irrefutably true he'd acquired Cassandra's journal and fed it to Murray long after he'd evolved from the Jeeves system into a sophont being. Fact: Charlie never took sides, never intruded on The Web, never played politics. Counter fact: Yet he knew an almost unlimited amount about The Web, its gossip and conversation spoken in confidence, how it operated, and who among its many denizens had betrayed whom. He knew its deepest secrets. Conjecture: Charlie worked for or perhaps even ran Mystery Baddie Three, the internet dependent force moving heaven and earth to dismantle The Syndicate.

Which suggested that he might not want to just dismantle The Syndicate. Because he'd done me a major favor. And he could easily do more damage to Pina. Correction to Oslo. But he wasn't quite acting like a friend either. A strained ally, on a vaguely parallel course but with a different agenda. He had some complicated agenda that right now meant mostly peril and doom but could change when and if our interests aligned.

The sun washed over me as the day progressed lugging about the useless equipment, smiling, and thanking various Hunters for food, beverages, small courtesies, all the while Momo and her forty thieves planning the next heist of Ali Baba's caves. Though technically, Ali Babi steals from the thieves, so fingers crossed she was taking the fairy tale in a different direction.

What could Charlie want or need? When faced with a mystery one used Occam's Razor. When you hear hooves, think horses. Not zebras. So, what was the obvious and blatant choice here? Mystery bad guys used the internet and lacked electronic augmentation. But weren't of The Swarm. Which made them something entirely different than us, as in The Syndicate.

What if they built the internet? Forget what you know. The real infrastructure for the internet was designed and delivered out of China and Russia in the late 90s. What haxors deem The Dark Web is just the front door of a much spookier system which controls the entirety of global electronic traffic. Something we affectionately call Abaddon—being both a terrible place stacked below Hell and a terrible Demon who runs around stomping people in that realm that is more Hellish than Hell itself. Seems like the exact right name for The Web's version of a deep web. I'd been watching Abaddon though Murray's passive satellite sensors for a long while.

If our bad guys had built it, it made sense that their design issued from a mindset, a cultural paradigm. So, these people aligned to Charlie were sophisticated, focused on communication and high-speed management of data; they preferred subtle control and persuasion, collected secrets, and used them to keep their existence entirely hidden. In the sports equivalent they curled—brushing the ice of perception to move public understanding into the desired sweet spot. Yeah, that fit.

So far, I'd bumped into ex Swarm commandoes like Pina and Kelba, survivors from a prior Shoah. Then a biological hivemind. My own little coffee klatch of AIs and clones. And me, speciating in a way different than all the above. It stood to reason that Oslo's network might not be the only survivors of a prior putsch. Perhaps the Mystery Big Bad had been hidden or nascent, not fully ready to fight on a global scale.

We knew the White Cult had cracked passing nanites through sex. Something only Cassandra knew. And bingo. That had to be the motivation. Whomever they were, the White Cult had just encroached on territory that mattered to them. In late November of the previous year our agents in Bolivia sent word that a new generation of operatives from The Cult had been encountered. Ones with Zeus' peculiar self-healing capabilities albeit at a much less spectacular pace. That was the precipitating event. A genetics advance making the White Cult a direct threat to Charlie somehow. Which begged the question: what did a rival group's ability to have augmented children do to change their situation?

Occam would suggest it broke their monopoly. Which implied Charlie was a different species as well. Time for some Swagger—an intuitive and overconfident leap of faith combined with a serious wild ass guess, the ubiquitous SWAG. These guys were somehow telepathic, using electronic signals to hack devices. Master haxors and coders, the builders of Abaddon and the Deep Web. Able to zap things with their mind the way The Hive used pheromones and Momo used quantum collapse.

Add to that the curious spike of trojanized workloads and invisible attacks I'd tracked for the last decade emanating from coastal enclaves, you had a working theory. Charlie and his ilk were somehow amphibious or had a link to the oceans. As well as advanced tech, a desire to not be found, a lot of secret knowledge, and the desire to play all sides against one another. Maybe for survival, maybe for world domination, maybe for some other alien reason. I decided to call them The Kraken, after the legendary sea monster and keeper of eldritch secrets.

So, The Kraken had sent us—me, really—the schematics of The White Cult and if we could unravel it fast enough, given The Syndicate a how-to manual which would allow Murray and Momo to unspool Zeus and his cadre of fanatics before they did serious damage to our shaky allies. Incidentally, they'd given a set of AIs some of the most immoral, illegal, ethically subverted eugenics and gene hacking manuals ever devised. Things Mengele would have given a testicle to read, let alone try. Oh joy. Thanks a whole fecking lot, Charlie.

I added dismantling the White Cult to my growing list of To-Dos between finding Gay Eddie and saving the world. What was more maddening, Charlie had essentially upended my mental map of the known world. After years serving in and around The Web, I'd retired thinking my jaded worldview could hardly get more tarnished or cynical. Until Oslo crushed my tired certainties upon my return and exposed me to an even more horrifying sub-basement of Hades. Now we'd ripped out the planks and dropped down ten levels of elevator shafts to some place that ate the light itself. Gehenna if you will.

We have a name for everything. Gehenna meant those poor bastards scragged, exiled, retired as I had been, or otherwise rendered persona non grata but not somehow lobotomized in the process, dangerous non-people who had to reside somewhere in our collective imagination. Abaddon sat below the Deep Web; Gehenna sat outside The Web. It was the endless pit, the broken place, the final destination for sinners and betrayers who had been rejected from the already wretched and foul embrace of The Web.

And where did The Kraken reside? The Abyss, the oceanic trenches of Gehenna. Mythologically, because we really didn't have enough supervillain style conquest of the oceans to justify a portmanteau yet. "Yet" being the operative word because I suspected Charlie and his mysterious crew might rewrite our history soon enough. But down deep and surrounded by darkness.

So, we had splintered political units waging a cold civil war across The Web—The Syndicate and The Swarm each had their own cadres of infighting. The Hivemind, The White Cult, and now possibly The Kraken were all out there doing damage to one another and to the Powers That Be, to achieve world domination and human enslavement. Unless The Kraken shared some values with Oslo, who had wagered all on escalating the timeline of The Hive's war. And on me to find a way to disrupt their plans in my typical style.

Fecking double thanks, Pina. Because it seemed to be getting more complicated and terrifying by the minute. Which felt both overwhelming and uncomfortably familiar. I followed my own advice. When all else fails, get a taco. So, I did. Quite a few. Then I went to sleep and waited for my ship to come in.

Chapter 8: Leave the Girl, Take the Tamales

My time came soon enough. Rook and her team managed to throw themselves a rather spectacular panic party as an open sea catamaran chugged into view and started toward their peninsula. As camouflage goes, there are a few really optimal ways to hide people at sea. Submarines are great. Ditto massive cargo vessels with a few containers stacked under the general steerage holding "special" passengers. Or bombs or drugs or you know, whatever floats your boat. I crack myself up.

But for a nice "ignore me" vibe, get yourself a scuzzy old oceanographic ship, something with a terrible design that has flaking paint, a kind of odd fishy stink, and a bunch of research antennae, bulbs, and globes that look vaguely like apparatus from some institute interested in squids and anemones, and then load up a huge gas tank inside the rusted over diving bell from the late 1950s. My surprise visitors had cruised up in a former Nicaraguan coast guard trawler converted to scientific survey boat in 1958—one of only six catamarans built in South America during that era. Then dry docked in the 70s and rebuilt with a welded frame that doubled the pontoon sizes along with new motors for a brief respite in the late 90s doing graduate school double duty for both American University of Managua and the Autonomous University.

Old, loathsomely out of date, almost unsinkable with the extra pontooning, slower than a grandma with two broken hips, and utterly innocuous to just about any navy, pirate, smuggler, satellite feed, or similar spying eye. No one cared about grad students; and at the same time they represented just enough trouble with squealing parents and vaguely concerned authorities that it made sense to avoid them. As they were slow, unarmed, easy to spot and easier to find on radar with all the racket their rehabbed diesel engines made, they usually made their twelve hundred kilometer journey over a long week or so. On full blast they could zip across in just under five days.

The ladies had painted it sunshine yellow and a shade of faded red to offset the ebullience. Between the rust, smoke, peeling paint, and general look of studied disrepair, it reeked of starfish obsessed scientists. Or perhaps a small tribe of seismic survey geeks using some IoT enabled toy on a $2000 barely-qualified-to-call-it-research grant. Anything but the secret weapon that would win a war.

As the ship lurched forward at an alarmingly slow speed, bodies came into view. Women on the deck flying the purple and white flag of the Haudenosaunee. Women who looked exactly like the ones waiting for them on shore. Radios crackled and Rook's ashen face turned red, white, and blue in rapid succession. Nine stood next to me, amused and horrified. She recognized those women—her missing selves. Not all of them but more than the three I'd left on the island years ago.

More radio traffic, some terse Frisian, some loud yelling from Rook. When that failed, she stomped up to us. Momo likely knew what was going on but had decided to keep very quiet. Rook looked as if she would punch me as soon as she got within range. "What the hell have you done?"

I turned and for one moment did not mask my utter disdain. She stopped in her tracks, suddenly aware of just how little I cared for her ill-considered threat. "Saved your lives, Rook. Do you have a problem with that?" Nothing in me bothered to modulate in the least polite or human fashion. It was pure Kutzk.

"Uh, no, that is ... I don't understand."

"Yes, that's patently obvious." I looked at the ship slowly edging into view. They had followed my instructions to the letter, approaching slowly. "Perhaps you should consider retiring and let a younger smarter version of yourself manage the evacuation."

Her jaw dropped. "Retire? Why would I ... wait, what evacuation?"

Next to her Cornflower had arrived, her eyes taking in the scene. With Rook's insistence on sustained conflict, there had been no attempt by any party to keep our voices to the usual hush. The entire cadre had just heard the scary man tell Rook to quit her job.

Cornflower brushed her arm. "Rook, The Hive is coming. Will be here in minutes or hours, but they are coming. We need to get all the young to safety, to take Sister Momo with us, and to go somewhere they cannot find us." She looked at the ship, her keen eyes taking in not just the shapes but the movement of her selves. She knew whom she was seeing, because they were, on every level that mattered, her as well. She had come to rescue herself.

The older woman scowled. "Nonsense we can make a stand here just fine. We have our own damned boats."

‡Spetz, the ship has attracted two sets of coast guard. Neither should care about a science ship. Both just went radio silent.‡ The Hive had already found us.

◊Time to contact?◊

‡At their present acceleration, seven minutes, maybe eight if the ladies hit the gas pedal.‡ Not quite enough time to get to the beach. But certainly enough time to retrieve a box.

I turned to Nine. "Nine, please go get me my box. The one mailed to you five years ago. Have your four fastest women grab it and haul it to the smoker shack. We have roughly five minutes before the Mexican navy will be sending a pair of kill teams here thanks to Rook's lack of preparation."

Someone had ratted us out. Someone Rook had not properly vetted. I reconsidered all the bodies at the beach, tracking back through what was now a frighteningly enhanced memory. Each tourist, each drunk, every movement on the path from first dawn to my arrival at the compound. Not a single operative stood out. Which left a disturbing option.

My phone rang. The stolen smartphone I'd purposefully drained and whose SIM and GPS chips had been expunged at the airport. Lola van IJburg. I didn't bother picking up—she'd already established signal. I let my node do the work.

"Spetz, there are several operatives of mine on those cutters."

I squinted and let my eyes track movement on the horizon. Two blobs refracting the atmosphere. They hadn't quite come into view, but my vision too had seen some upgrades. "Then they'd better bail out. Because I cannot let them leave the harbor."

There was a pause, everything somehow extra silent. Likely switching satellites. "And then?"

I shrugged. "Then they can come ashore and pillage what they need from what is about to be a very abandoned village. How soon depends on when the second wave is due."

"Hmm, that sounds like a deal being offered. My people are neutral."

Sure they were. Against The Hive everyone was shark chum. But she did need to avoid offending whatever remnant of The Swarm would remain. They all worked for Oslo, so what did I care? "And they will stay neutral. I'm not offering them safe harbor with my team. Just second pickings after we vacate. Assuming you are willing to pay my price for saving their lives twice."

"Twice?"

I smiled and the women around me stepped back. Any illusions they might have had about me were quickly evaporating. No one would mistake me for the Black Demon now. I was squarely embracing the most dangerous person alive. And about to add to my kill count. "Yep. Once because I am about to not obliterate them on those ships. And then once because I am not only going to let them safely get to shore but kill The Hivemind pursuing them and allow them food, shelter, clothing, money, and who knows what else when we leave. Sounds more like three times when I think it through."

"Two favors. Small ones. These are operatives, not family."

"Does Coaxoch work for you?"

"Yes. Favor one completed."

Right. That set off a rapid cascade that Momo's FTL journey down the rabbit hole had made possible. I froze time. Not literally but in my mental construct. Enough to then think through the whole of what I wanted to consider without losing a moment in real-time. The meatworld, as Momo would call it.

Coaxoch had been working for The Cyberwick. Which made a huge amount of sense. Lola dealt in information, in code, and in secrets kept and secrets exposed. This little section of Baja had the right confluence of electromagnetic emptiness and lack of infrastructure to pique the interest of a small subset of The Web. She'd sent down a rep and watched. Then likely squirreled away people and resources where none of her slightly less capable rivals would ever find them. The roller derby Aztec had been working as the guard of The Cyberwick's bugout vault.

Which implied data breach. Lola had to understand all this, especially given how The Hive would be monitoring all communications. They knew from intercepting Coaxoch's data stream, I had to go after these animals with small arms, maybe a grenade launcher. Nothing bigger than what my duffle held. So, they would continue forward and plan to pincer me on shore, using the catamaran as cover. Brutal, heartless, effective.

Lola playing along was her second favor. And me saving her life in return. Which granted me a third one. I needed to push my luck. Time turned back on.

"Neutral or not, the price of your people's life is a timeline for The Hive's second wave arriving."

"You'll never survive the first wave. They have you pinned. You need to run, which also saves my people by the way."

"Then they cannot blame you for giving me information they and you both know I'll never live to use. Arrival time or your people will be Swiss cheese like the rest of sailors." Yeah, choke on that, eavesdroppers. I had only small arms, not even grenades on me. Every nuance of my speech and haptics broadcast honesty. She knew I was telling the truth and so would they. No deception markers, no rising or falling tones. No reason to doubt what I had just let leak.

"Fine. Seven hours but I do believe they will rapidly accelerate this once they tap into this relay. At that point you're at best a short flight and a forty-minute drive away from certain death. A second time."

But they couldn't. They'd already lost their main resource in the region—because I'd killed them earlier, enabling me to slip past until Lola van IJburg's network sprung a lethal leak. One that would soon kill Lola as well. She'd called to warn me of this as well as save her people.

◊How's your steganography?◊

‡World class. Why?‡

She had to know why. Or maybe she really didn't. I wondered why she'd gone silent and then it hit me, she was compacting herself, getting ready to jump into one of Tiio Maracle's bodies. She hadn't really seen the bigger picture yet. It would help accelerate our evacuation, so I kept my mind-mouth shut and kept going.

◊Encrypt where the three closest full villages in a bag are, coordinates and a rough map. She'll need laptops, servers if they have them. And both guns and medical kits. That eliminates some of them. ◊

‡Doing it now. For her people? There are just two of them.‡

◊On the boats. She has tons of people here, has been guarding and watching this place. She needs an exit and we're going to give her a chance at one. But not at the cost of our own family.◊ A cruel triage to make but one I'd already thought through long ago before FTL deliberations had been a possibility.

‡It's in a map of the supposed island we're fleeing to. Which is about six thousand klicks well east of here and will require Panamanian passage to realize.‡

◊Good girl. I like how you think Clausewitz, Junior.◊

I willed the map upward and felt the Cyberwick snatch it from my node. "What the hell is this?"

I sighed. This time I had to lie. So, I put myself in a rather angry mood. "Look, I am going to survive this and those hivey bastards will pay for attacking us. But just in case, here's a map of a place that can help you."

"A damned island in the southern Atlantic?" She had to be thinking through what I'd said as well as running my voice through software. The only word that was off was "place." That one I modulated with a hint of tremolo.

"Sure, think of it as the ultimate village in the bag. Good as three fully stocked ones, guns and medicine, even computer equipment. I gave you coordinates to find it, you just have to dig into the map to find them. Don't want The Hive calculating them before you after all."

Something soft cracked across the gap in time and space. A real woman's voice behind all the smoke and mirrors. "They'd just dig into it, too; it just takes a ruler and a compass."

I laughed. Behind me four women sprinted forward with a massive sea chest that looked as if weighted more than Tutankhamen's sarcophagus. It was bigger, and in this case, held a treasure far more valuable. "Lola, I'd expect you to use something a little less linear. You must have some computer program or other that looks at photos and hands you all the relevant data? Maybe overlays it against regular maps."

Silence. "We have some of those, yes. That's pretty much from Year Zero. Like real stone age stuff." Atta girl. Now let's see if my little angry goth computer could parse it.

The world froze and my teenager sent me an FTL doorbell. Eerie but less when you expect it. ‡Did she just quote a Nine Inch Nails stego song as proof she understood us?‡

◊Yep. To misappropriate the meme, metal ay eff.◊

‡Metal ay eff. That's got to be one of their few blind sides. Material culture. Leisure. How the hell did you two do that on the fly? You barely know this woman. If she's even a woman.‡

◊Short answer, we feel one another. Long answer, we're long-standing operatives in a world so complex that it has almost no discernible rules. So, we made some for ourselves. And we happen to share a few rules that would nominatively indicate we also share some ethical opinions. Ergo, we have a common basis to culturally understand one another. We have correctly anticipated one another from highly limited information for decades.◊

‡She knew what to expect? That's the big secret? That you're wildly predictable.‡

◊And wildly reliable. That I am defined by what I do. Utterly consistent, which to someone as fixated on technology as The Cyberwick would be both necessary and soothing. I'm ones and zeros, on and off. In this case truly binary rather than quantum.◊

‡It's how Pina does it with you, isn't it? She can predict your path because you intentionally limit yourself to black and white.

You're … wow, that's an entire life strategy built on Emmanuel Kant?‡

◊Le sigh. There's only two things I can stomach from old Emmanuel. First from Metaphysics, "A categorical imperative would be one which represented an action as objectively necessary in itself, without reference to any other purpose." If you make it Kutzkan; what you do is what must be done, and this is what you are.◊

‡Yeah, okay. I can parse that. But the second one?‡

◊A Critique of Pure Reason. "Experience without theory is blind, but theory without experience is mere intellectual play." As in, what I've been teaching since we started take your daughter to work week.◊

‡I prefer to think of it as an insider's tour of Hell.‡

◊Touché. We're about to do some major damage to the ecosystem, then bug out. You and I are about have to part ways. And I'm guessing that once we start moving you to another body, there's no more of this magic frozen time chit chat. ◊

‡You asking if I have more questions?‡

◊Or comments. It's traditional when you say goodbye to your family. You know, before they take a trip.◊ Or go tackle the single worst combination of global threats ever assembled. And that included the previous roster of what we had assumed was the worst. Evolution's a bitch.

We hung in emptiness for a moment and then I swear to the gods above and below, it was as if a pair of warm hands wrapped themselves around me and my snotty teen daughter had crushed me with a fierce hug. ‡Just … I love you. Be careful.‡

◊I love you too, Momo. You be ….◊

Then The Hive cut our links, plunging us all into the Now. Sonsabitches had detonated a limited range EMP. Everything electronic had been scragged. Except me of course. I'd be both shielded and with Momo's sensory array, she'd have had milliseconds between the detonation and the wave front reaching us to drop behind her version of a Faraday Cage under my liver.

No mushroom cloud, so we'd been hit with a non-nuclear electromagnetic pulse. Lola's people. They'd been shanghaied or hired to do this very thing. A scragging of epic proportion. It freed us up since the old catamaran ran on things predating modern electronics. Analog devices and vacuum tubes.

The Cyberwick wasn't just gone, she wasn't coming back until this war ended. If she ever came back. Godspeed Lola van IJburg and fair seas to the people we hoped to save.

Then I had Things To Do. When handling the X-93 Experimental Rocket Propelled Torpedo, you pretty much Capitalize Everything. In our case, four X-93s with a launcher. What pray tell constitutes a rocket propelled torpedo? Imagine taking a submarine or ship killing torpedo, shrinking it down with some fancy physics and materials science, swapping out complex fiber filaments for steel tubes and all that. Then marrying it to a rocket propelled grenade system, ditching the electronics and going with something sinister like electromagnets powered by gyroscopic motion and you had the X-91. Then add some seriously dangerous super density explosives and a kind of aim and forget sonar system you got to the X-92.

What the women brought forth was their demented stepchild, the X-93. Remember all that. Fiberglass soaked in nerve agent. Yeah, oldie but goldie that one. Now imagine an entire torpedo / rocket system of pliable layers of carbon stronger than steel intermixed with highly brittle fiberglass steeped in a wide series of soporifics, psychedelics, and hypnotics. As in Titanic vs Iceberg meet Alice in Wonderland. A land launched torpedo system that incapacitated rather than killed. Nominally so you could capture rather than kill. But in the dubious ways of The Web, so you could ensnare and disable your enemies, hand select the ones to be culled, some to save for torture, perhaps a few to set free having been brainwashed while drugged to the gills to tell whatever story you wanted told. For example, these are not the droids you're looking for or the village of cloned women was empty or never here or already destroyed. Options.

Five years ago, a care package had come to final rest under Nine's care. Hopefully never to be used but like all villages in the bag, squirreled away against future need. This was War in a Bag. Four stout versions of the hunter jogged, shuffled as they hauled a long wooden box resembling a coffin with rope handles toward us. When it dropped to the sand beside me, we still had three and half minutes, time to spare. If the navy didn't speed up, that is. So, I assumed we had under 120 seconds and acted accordingly.

The women gawked as I ripped off the lid one-handed. Nails twisted and popped as the wood wrenched from the edges and the whole coffin-like panel went flying a few meters away. Yeah, I had evolved too. Unthinkable strength during stress and the imminent extinction of many of my children had me ... on edge.

The foam packing had deteriorated some and the inside boasted a mixture of grit, dust, must, mold, sand, and something else, grime which suggested curdled butter. The launcher looked like a long heavy tube with a tripod attached to the front. Usually, three men held it and two loaded the massive torp-rockets. Today, I got to play all five men.

The various versions of Cornflower watched in a mixture of awe and horror as I dragged the open case behind me by a rope handle which had been tucked inside—again made for a few men to help lug the massive ordnance from location to location. I heaved the launcher to my shoulders, knelt, and screamed at the top of my lungs, "Fire in the damned hole!" Even the coast guard heard me, drawing their panicked fire as huge twin machine guns mounted to their front turrets swiveled and opened up on the shacks near me.

By rote, the first rock-torp slid into my left hand, then tipped into the launcher and with a flick of my right hand, a twist of fingers and boom! the first missile launched with a deafening roar. Followed by the second as quick as my body could manage the odd contortion of missile, tube, aim, launch—this time at the cutter behind the lead ship. The rockets threw the torpedoes forward at unthinkable speeds, dropping into the water halfway to their targets, the sea boiling in fury as the solid fuel rockets accelerated them beyond any defensive capability's speed of response. Faster than the human eye or button push or DARDO or pretty much anything else in the known universe. For the poor ship facing a shore to sea launch, the X-93 proved to be an unstoppable weapon. Yay Team Me.

Both torpedoes hit the stern side of port, T-boning each

vessel a meter below the waterline. Something popped as each boat lifted out of the water a good two meters before slamming down, seams split, taking on water and listing as their momentum plowed them into the waves, the force of millions of kiloliters of water shearing the wood and metal. But the real magic was all that fiberglass busting free from its carbon shells. Once the explosives disrupted the matrix of the torpedo tube, the formerly impenetrable casing converted into something resembling chalk. The glass burst through every gap.

When playing Kill the Opposing Navy, one does not slow down the launch speed of X-93 ordnance delivery. The next two torpedoes followed as quickly as I could heave the massive shells into the tube and then slewing them low, fired on a much shallower vector. They exploded near the water line, splattering a thick swarm of unthinkably many millions shards of microscopic fiberglass loaded with neurotoxins and psychoactives. Momentum dragged both vessels and their helpless crews through the toxic cloud before their vessels started to wallow in the shallows.

There's friendly incapacitation—when you knock someone out with a light soporific or quick chop to the temple. And there's X-93 incapacitation—where two smoking holes blown through your vessel hull are a scorching rebuke as if the Archangels of a Smiting Deity had visited upon your ship their most Abject Displeasure. Extreme high explosives tend to be lethal for anyone foolish enough to stand within their detonation radius. Sailors and crew for example, or Hive commandos stashed in the hulls waiting to launch a coordinated massacre upon the shoreline. Same goes for layers of carbon fiber shrapnel and the improvised claymore that a ship's hull becomes when kissed with a hypersonic bomb punch. All in all, long before the fiberglass payload hit the full complement, a good fifth of the human capability on the cutters had been transformed from murder-bound badasses to shark chum. All gunfire ceased. Their engines swamped or lay dead from the EMP, only the solid chug-a-lug certainty of the diesel engine on the survey boat sounded across the water as it puttered slowly toward shore.

There can be an eeriness to silence in war. No screaming men, no wailing children, no malicious explosions, or *crack crack crack* of small arms punctuated with a sudden thump whack of something scoring a near miss. Silence meant death or ambush or both in no particular order. The torpedoes had killed all pursuit literally and figuratively. The remainder of the living aboard the floundering coast guard ships would most likely be dead by drowning, bleeding out, internal injuries mixing with the toxins, or just plain brutal shock. Explosions throw out a mean punch, especially on something as inelastic as water; specifically lethal for humans confined to enclosed spaces when slammed with a shockwave.

Lola's people might regroup. They'd had more warning, more sense of what came next. I'd been as compassionate as could be managed with the location and lethality of the ordnance. Those torpedoes had been built to drop anything smaller than an aircraft carrier. Our quick launch had just double dosed a pair of minnows with the equivalent of whale shark narcotics. War being war, some of her folks would be dead or drowned—the ones on the ships. The rest hiding in the surrounding beachfronts and dunes would be free to gather the remains of the village after we hustled the women back out to sea.

There are times when you hold a mirror to yourself and wonder, am I damned? Borderline psychopath? Plain old evil? I'd just killed hundreds of strangers. A few dozen now and all the rest within an hour. Still, by my hand, mass murder had been done. Sure, war necessitates these kinds of things, but does that absolve us? It's a question that ran through my head every day I baked bread and viennoiseries in Amherst. My conclusion: yep, it made me evil. I am what I do. I killed without remorse or reflection, ergo, by nature I had become either a lowly predator or a conscious destroyer. Sophont killers had no place to hide. Just because it had been obligatory self-defense didn't change the morality of the act.

But then your children appear and ask questions. Turns out you do have remorse and you do reflect. What is it to be a soldier, to kill despite remorse and reflection? To defend the weak and the vulnerable from evil itself? To counter genocide and eugenic slavery? Before me, the hushed waves embraced my dying enemies as well as Lola's people masquerading as such. In front of them fled a small ship of family, saved by a lot of ruthless planning and a willingness to deploy unthinkable morally reprehensible weaponry. Unleashed on equally immoral speciated mind slaves.

Still. What had the Mexican Coast Guard ever done to me? Poor bastards got entangled in The Web and died for a cause not their own, having chased a lie to its lethal end. They died for no better reason than they'd been suckered or coerced by an outside power and lent their military might to the wrong side. Defined as being anyone but Us. Yeah, not much moral high ground here for me to climb out of Gehenna. Which reinforced Oslo's point. Until we got humanity free of our own hideous game the whole world danced to our depraved tune and washed itself in the blood of innocents.

Did my shoulders slump and my heart skip a beat or two as once again wrong prevailed over right and violence over decency? Maybe. But only for a moment. Then the Knife that Does rose and took all of me, conflicted, heartbroken, enraged, disgusted, and livid to have my own child witness such atrocities, toward the shore to greet my older gentler selves.

The yellow catamaran eventually chugged to shore, greeted in a chorus of Frisian and Mohawk as Cornflower, joined by a shellshocked Rook and a dozen of her younger selves got to meet the splinter contingent of Tiio Maracle. On the prow stood Crow Laughs, the oldest of the trio. Her concerned frown said it all.

Cornflower and Crow Laughs negotiated a gangplank to the shore, anchors were thrown, and the shapes of several men, roughly six foot four of muscles and sharp angles, hustled about getting the catamaran ready for loading the village. More planks came down into the surf. Hatches opened; Mohawk shouts filled the air. The rescue party had arrived.

Nine stood next to me, eyes narrow and pained. "Lots of firepower to send for a village."

I nodded. "Overkill seems to be their standard. They want to not just kill folks but erase their existence. Genocide proper."

"Bother you much?"

"Which part? Killing killers? Or murdering the innocent fools they scammed into helping them?"

She smiled, all wolf and bloodshed. "Oh, the Mexicans know more than they say. Might be Sinaloa and corrupt smugglers on those rigs. It's been a long-desired piece of real estate, this village. I'm sure no one much fought the request."

"Yes, it bothers me. Does it bother you?"

She nodded and spit into the contaminated sea, flotsam and jetsam mixing with the bubbling tide. "A lot. Always does. But still, we do what we do. Heh?"

I looked her in the eye. Pain met pain. "Because Cornflower not only lives but doesn't have to carry the burden."

She nodded, wiped a tear from her eye and then surprisingly, one from mine too. Children had me going soft. "True, Tsitsho." She gave me a wan smile. "Thank you for understanding."

My old name among them, Tsitsho Kahonstii, the Black Fox. It had been a long time since I spoke Mohawk or wore that name. But then, today, warrior with four feathers, I'd again earned it for the tribe. We turned and, composing our faces, walked to meet the elders.

What did I say about war? Scratch all that. Want to know if you have regret? Face down a Mohawk elder on her own turf surrounded by splinters of her literal self. Ten dozen Tiio Maracles none too pleased to have seen you kill anyone near her, let alone sink a pair of naval ships—even if they were in pursuit of her own delicate hide. Oh yes, the tongue lashing revived a whole new set of Mohawk vocabulary.

Crow Laughs never swore, didn't even criticize. No, she expressed profound sorrow and disappointment, remorse and disgust mingled with something peculiar. A kind of fierce and hypocritical delight in the sheer totality of her enemies' decimation. Yeah. She went up one side of me and down the other until every raw nerve in my body struggled at snap tension. Then oh, the worst, she looked me in the eye with pure love and compassion. The mother of me, the daughter of me, my kin, my hope for my clan, the woman oldest and most senior among my involuntary children.

The Mongolians have Chur'ka. The massage that rubs war from the bones. They grind out the horror because hey, Mongolians did horror in war better than anyone, The Web included. The Mohawk have women who spoke Truth and held you to your word, held up the mirror, made sure the Good Mind prevailed. At all costs. She smashed down whatever snarling joy I took in saving our collective asses and made sure that the utmost regret and disdain for the cost of battle ran through my veins like cold seawater. It saved me. Brought out the layers of self-doubt and self-incrimination. Anyone who's ever seen the elephant can tell you what that's like. To take a life and feel … elation. Not me but them, and hah, you deserved it you weak fucker. But inside there's this long scream as the stain of the act and the shattered pieces of their tormented soul ride up your skull, then down your spine to your heart and guts. Not in that moment. No. In the moment it's all numbness and action, shallow breaths and moving operationally to the next tactical decision. But eventually as the blood cools and the bullets stop flying, there's the memory distorted like a bloated corpse floating in a river. Or shallow Baja seaside.

Crow Laughs just sped up that process and in public ripped me a new ass the size of Detroit. Nothing that my own hatred wouldn't outdo in private. Then brought me back into the fold and welcomed me as a necessary and beloved part of the tribe while acknowledging the truly awful reality of the war. A needed part of a whole. Honored for my sacrifice, recognized for my courage, seen as the killer I am and allowed in the circle of women, of innocents, and important lives. Not despite my transgressions but precisely because of my sacrifice and willingness to bow before her authority after amply demonstrating the threat I'd made to Rook earlier. A male bodied soldier very rarely if ever needs to obey women's leadership. But in the Mohawk world you simply did.

To disobey women was to exit Mohawk life. To abandon the core of our culture and identity. Which slammed home the point of her tirade and brought us all into the instant rather … instantly. We had to save ourselves and she had come to preserve the core of her selves with my help. She had just thanked me Mohawk style. It hurt like hell but in my battle between the soul erasing Syndicate and Swarm on the one side, and all these new machines inside me corroding my species and mental autonomy on the other, Crow Laughs and her cohort had given me back my name, my face, my purpose, and with it a tiny bit of my soul. She kept me human for one more day.

It didn't hurt that Momo also got a firsthand understanding of How Things Work Around Here. Also, let's be honest. She had spent so much time with psychopaths and professional monsters that my quantum daughter could hardly be expected to know morality if walked up and punched her. But yelling at her mama bear for five minutes straight, in front of all her selves, his own daughters, that had to make an impression. I appreciated that. Like I said, Mohawk communities run on the ethics of their women and if my child had any shot of joining the women as a full member, she had to truly learn what every Indigenous person knew without thinking: all the tribe raises every child, for children belong to the future and are the gods' gifts not ours.

I'd sort out what telling Momo she was a divine gift would do to her immense ego later. Save the women now, sort out egomania and solipsism in the evolving AI later. If we survived the later. Otherwise, it fell to Cornflower who both Nine and I trusted to do a better job than nasty murderers like us.

After many hugs and a lot of logistical movements as the menfolk on the ship coordinated the rapid evacuation which—huge grin of pride—Momo and Cornflower had planned meticulously, we had a moment to cut the public bs and get down to war council. The oldest Tsitsho Kahonstii joined us. He looked like me, only without the scars inside and out. Healthy, kind, his eyes still bright with compassion and joy. Lucky bastard.

He hugged me fiercely and gave me a wide smile. "So, this is what I have to look forward to?" He whacked one of my sweaty arms.

Shrug. "Well, probably not but if all goes well, you'll gain a few pounds. Our nanites have been upgraded a few times. Not sure what my version and yours will do."

Crow Laughs gave us a look, concerned perhaps. "Is there danger to him?"

In unison he and I both said, "Yes."

More frowning. "Perhaps there's another way to do this. We are so few, especially versions of you, Tsitsho. To sacrifice two of you …."

He wrapped his unscarred hands around hers. "Mother mine, this had to be done. Elder Brother me needs to go fight the war. You know that. And there's a life at stake." Then he reached out, dipped his finger in my mouth and stuck it in his own.

Neither Crow Laughs nor I had time to react. I was always fast. Sure, there are nanites in my saliva but the right ones, enough? I had planned on using tears. Or blood transfusion to speed things up for rapid exfiltration.

Give Hans and Cassandra their due. It took the upgrades less than a heartbeat to recognize a compatible genetic sequence and their own prior selves. Upgrades began near instantly. His eyes clouded as we watched real time changes in his genetic matrix, his epithelial cells, and who knew what terrifying modifications to his physical self. Nine handed me a bottle of something. Beer. Cold delicious beer.

Normally a terrible thing to hand anyone Indigenous. But for nanite fuel, high alcohol content beer has all the rapid sugars, carbs, and extra enzymes needed to convert cells without inducing diabetic shock. We drank a couple and stood there. After a moment longer of pained silence, our leader gave me a huge hug.

"I missed you, you pain-in-the-butt monster. Too damned big and mighty to write?" She tweaked my nose to emphasize the taunt and the underlying kindness. Teasing me. Not afraid, not shying away.

"Well, it was busy. Also, writing would reveal your location. Plus, I am a truly terrible pen pal. Still, you got the messages?"

She threw deadly shade. "Bruh, of course. All your cousins got their care packages and thank you very much, all our hips suffered from those damned Marcolini chocolates you sent."

Wait, what happened to the other stuff? I turned to look at Crow Laughs who seemed positively amused. "No macarons, no cashmere?"

In total innocence she batted an eyelash at me. "What macarons?"

"Ah." Right. Never change, Tiio.

Then Momo was gone. I felt it more as a sudden absence. Just the end of an itch, a loss of static hum, something that had been there under the surface. Crow Laughs had distracted me at the vital moment. Bless her.

Something subtle changed in the face of Tsitsho and suddenly he looked far more like me. Predatory, dangerous, perhaps a touch vile. Upgrades had started to cascade. Nine handed us each another beer and we toasted silently. So much for luck. Another one of me wasted in the war, innocent no more.

He placed his hand, my same hand, on my heart. "I've got her, Brother. I can hear her. She'll survive the war. Now go do what you must."

Before he knew what hit him, I whacked him upside the head. Which tumbled my smaller self into the sand. "Oh, it's not that simple you dumb sucker. She's the savviest manipulator alive and will eat you for lunch."

He got up in fighting stance. "You think I don't know that, huh?" His face contorted in rage as battle hormones flexed and one had to imagine more nanites popped into existence. Plus, Momo had to be jumping into her new cage right quick. "I know what you know now. The upgrades handed me a whole memory stack."

Ye gods, the horror! "Knowledge ain't experience kid. She's seen far more war than you."

He swung and missed as my superior nanites and a whole lot of combat experience did their job. Then swung again and got tripped in the dunes for his effort. "She's making you fight."

That got his goat—he rushed me—and went into the next sand dune for it. "Bullshit. I am the master of me, and your daughter might be inside me, but I am me, I am Tsitsho Kahonstii and definitely not you, Spetz, not the killer and monster you are and … Never Will Be."

Crow Laughs placed a hand on his arm. He looked up at her and then started laughing. Like I said, Mohawks protect their men. Momo had said it and she wasn't all wrong. Third gender beings like me slide between roles. I had given him his face and soul back. After an upgrade of the worst micro-murderbots ever built, he had to be feeling the power and potential of them. But now, now he felt the drive, the push they gave. The downside of being genetically engineered to kill people is there is no upside. It's awful start to finish. But you're good at murder.

What defined him was everything else and, thank all that exists, he could push through. Momo might help. Certainly, the community saw what the upgrades had done to a peaceful and kind soul—transformed him in minutes into an angry brawler. We had taken a private agony and made it a public problem for the tribe to solve.

Tsitsho rose, gave me a bow, and said again. "I got her. Go, do what you got to do."

I walked over and hugged him. "Thank you. I honor your sacrifice warrior. Today you earn an eagle feather." We touched heads and parted. When it's you talking to your own clone there's not much more needs to be said. He knew exactly what I meant, more or less. Later, we could unpack what the nanites had transferred in memory. Or how. Had Momo made me a quantum entity just inhabiting a shell? Could I even be killed anymore or just turned off? Yikes!

Worse, we had a time limit. The catamaran had been packed with precious goods and women. Cornflower stood next to the upgraded Tsitsho, somehow conveying her connection to the newly awakened Momo. Next to me Nine stood quietly. More beer. She and I had immunity to the addictive side effects. We launched one ship versus a thousand and before we could do all the painful goodbyes and such, the women had pulled back out to sea and left us in the wake of dying men washing onto shore.

We had delayed The Hive but sooner or later The Swarm and its allies, Russians and cultists and apparently Sinaloa operatives would be coming for this place. I'd been rushing for days then waiting and preparing and now, too soon, they'd done exactly what I wanted and left. Great. Why did it feel so painful to send Momo and the village into safety?

Nine started collecting gear. "You didn't even speak to the other women. Hardly a reunion."

Statement, question, comment, thought. Yep.

I helped her grab essentials. We had to travel light but with a seven-foot beast of burden at our disposal, light turns out to be relative. "You asking or telling?"

She slapped my ass playfully with a med kit and tossed it to me. "Yes. You answering or evading?"

"It's the Ukrainian Buckle Bolt."

She stopped and eyed me. "Come again?"

"Look, the Ukrainians faced this unique historical problem. They gave up all their nukes in Budapest, right. 1994, Russia—you see them being helpful here—promised along with Britain, the Americans, and NATO to keep them safe. France and China not so much."

"So what? How does that have any bearing on us or this? Especially saying goodbye to family."

"Yeah, it's another of our acronym portmanteau things. Means the impossible situation. Like the Kobayashi Maru or zugzwang. Except we do impossible shit all the time, so the Ukrainian Buckle Bolt means a problem you gotta solve with zero trust and zero information."

She sniffed, stuffed more pemmican and some rope into a rucksack. Low tech but highly valuable. We'd have to find tomahawks and bows. I had a stash in a different box in the village storehouse. "How'd the Ukrainians solve it?"

"Well, they kinda failed. I mean, the politicians sold out to The Syndicate and we suspect The Swarm tried to influence China with no effect. So, we 'won' by coercing them to give up all their security and safety without much in return. The whole country became a playground for corruption, authoritarians, and mafiyas running all manner of crap through the Swiss cheese borders with Russia and Belarus."

She nodded to me. We started toward the storehouse. The catamaran had crested the edge of the bay. In an hour they'd be over the horizon. Much sooner off anyone's visual grid. "You're Ukrainian and allowed this?"

That got me smiling. "Not exactly. It miiiiight be that this contranym got made after I pulled a bit of shenanigans."

"You pretend to be nobody, but you've been manipulating

entire sections of The Web and Swarm for decades. What'd you do this time?"

"Buried a version of Murray at Azovstal Steel Plant and another under Chernobyl. Then started compromising satellites and electronic warfare sites globally. When war comes, my people will stand their ground and have a lot of resources ready."

"Not if, but when. What do you know?"

"There are things well beyond the power of crappy little conspiracies like The Syndicate to repair or control. Human nature for example. Every Kutzk knows the Russians. They hunt us for enjoyment."

"Ewww, sounds like America circa last week."

We opened the door and went down the stairs. The lights had been fried by the EMP, so we made do with sunlight and guesswork. Three boxes later we had weapons better suited to 1700 and a lot of dried food, poultices, and a few little modern surprises. Extreme HE packets for example.

"Don't confuse things. The Americans are genocidal to an end. They steep their children in greed and racism. You have property? Great. We kill you for it and rewrite history. The Russians just hate. They don't want the land; they just want you to feel as much misery and pain as they do."

"Same end result."

I shook my head. "Nope, once the bastards get your stuff they make you into a sport mascot, steal your holidays, and pretend it's all okay now. They stop the killing. You get to live on some postage stamp filled with toxic waste and tumbleweeds. The Russians never stop, never learn, never change. Whoever armed them made a huge mistake."

Nine gave me a huge frown. "You sound rather apologetic for the Americans. They did some damage to me and mine. You included."

I sighed. "C'mon Nine. The Americans aren't even really in charge. You got Romney running his own little show and beyond that it's Syndicate and Swarm. The average drone on the street only has a choice over whether they watch the Kardashians get naked on network tee-vee or some porn star on the internet. They have no control over their lives."

"Neither do the Russians. Or the Ukrainians for that matter."

"And now you get it. The Ukrainian Buckle Bolt. No one's free and The Web makes all the real choices so why try to be safe when there is no safety? Especially when sooner or later the Russians will come rolling over the borders like Orcs from Mordor."

"What the hell are we even talking about?"

"Buckling down then running. But also making it all secure. But hey the words mean their own opposites, running before and after the collapse. But also securing what you can during the collapse. The buckle bolt conveys it all plus the zugzwang vibe. Fighting to a tie in a no-win situation."

"But not a victory? No chance to win at all. That's grim but how does that … relate to our situation?"

"We are talking about why we said nothing to our family as they exited the war zone. We added no information or value to the system. We painted no additional targets on them. Every item, including people who count as stuff in The Web, has an assigned value and cost to acquire. That's the reality of the world I navigate. Want the Sultan of Brunei to shine your shoes or be served as dinner or, hell, be your sex slave for the night—there's a price for that. And a dozen agencies and specialists to make it happen."

"So, you lowered the price?"

"Nope, I made them valueless. Like we did with Ukraine. We took all the valuable intelligence assets and moved them outside the country. We bought peace by neutering them as a nation-state. Invading us or them costs you a lot and gets you almost nothing."

"Shit, we just call that the New York Scenario. Just be harder to mug than the person next to you."

I nodded. "Yeah, but in this version, they are gonna mug you sooner or later. So, all you can do is be the hardest to mug and thus the last. Then they are so tired maybe they just take your wallet but skip the rape and murder part."

We had our gear loaded and ready. On the shore the two vessels wallowed. No one stirred. Anyone alive had to be so far into a drug trip they'd likely be tasting the sky and feeling no pain. We had done what was necessary but for those drowning slowly it would be small consolation.

"You're a cynical bastard, Spetz. Surely, it's better than that."

"No. Nine, we delayed the inevitable but unless we end this war and end The Hive. I mean decimate them beyond all recovery then Tiio Maracle might be last on the list, but she too will be eliminated."

Nine stopped and goggled. "What have you gotten me into?"

I shook my head. "Wrong question. What have I kept you out of? This," I waved at the dead scattering the shore, their bodies smashed into pulp from compression waves. "Multiply this for every city, every continent, every civilized society. If The Hive succeeds, then all of us become skin puppets to some male form of biological AI. Permanent patriarchy, permanent slavery, humanity pretty much ends as a species."

"So, we were your Ukrainian Buckle Bolt. You hid us and jacked up the price so high that we became essentially valueless."

"Then kept your connections to The Syndicate non-existent so snatching you would be limited victory. There's better versions of both biological and silicon cyborgs running around. Better, faster killers. Better, stronger nanite driven soldiers. Makes you a unicorn with a dented horn. Who lives in a big island of poisonous snakes and poison ivy."

She chuckled. "With a bay full of sea mines and really nasty storms that make the reefs death traps."

"Yeah. And we just sent our family off to the improved scarier version of that island, made a huge nasty splash for every satellite and camera to watch, painted ourselves with targets, and are now leading the hunters far away from the intended prey."

She stood next to me. We stared at the dead and dying. "Thank you, Spetz."

I sighed. Then nodded sadly and started navigating us toward our intended target. Gay Eddie. But for that we needed a certain concierge presently running the daily buffet at all-inclusive tourist resort on Kos Island. Next stop Greece.

Chapter 9: The Ukrainian Buckle Bolt Revisited

You'd think that getting to Greece from Baja California would be hard in times of war and electronic chaos. Except we'd misunderstood the nature of The Hive's attack. We being me with Nine asking lots of pertinent questions. Me alone, I had assumed they'd drop the whole internet, crush everything electronic, drop us into the stone age again, and then hunt humanity to extinction. Instead, they went Invasion of the Body Snatchers style and simply perverted the Net and by extension everything touching both The Web and The Swarm.

Planes still flew, though with a lot of fighter escorts hidden from the passengers. News services got gag orders and a few editors disappeared. Censorship, reruns, a few deaths and kidnappings later, and suddenly the world forgot all about the weird New York City terrorist event. Gas leak. The politicians and talking heads went back to yapping about faux crises, the good citizens of the world ignored it all as they upped their screen time and downed more drugs of choice.

In under forty-eight hours The Hive had erased the existence of the war, established functional control over the planetary grid, and was slowly encircling The Syndicate while leaving all the apparatus of humanity in place. They didn't want to erase what had been built. They wanted to take what we had and use it for the exact same purpose—total control of everyone alive. Except that they would then add the exciting twist of converting people into literal walking shells. Ironic in its crude extension of the analogy. Instructive in the extreme.

It also gave them huge advantages. They got to use tech with abandon, we had to stay analog and quantum. All the heavy guns and boring non-sophont AIs worked for the Adversary now. That made this moment even eerier because it suggested almost literal Delphic prescience on the part of Agrippina Karthago. To know in advance, to truly grasp the endgame of her Hive opponents and build into her capability set a Joker card—me. The Kutzk trained, chaos deploying, destructive angel of untraceable provenance. My body would be resistant to Hive control, impossible to track, and not unrelated, tough enough to drag me through multiple waves of asymmetric combat against complex operational assets.

Fuck. She'd known. Known before the Autumn War, known before she ever sent that invite, possibly before my family had been slain. Known then, decades ago, that sooner or later, an unwanted, unwinnable conflict would erupt. So, she hired … wait for it…her own literal Ukrainian Buckle Bolt, inventor of the phrase and strategy. Which gave me a strong clue as to how to best proceed. Pina would never plan things out so meticulously then leave me without options. She would leave assets tailored to my skillset and capabilities—old, functional, barely automated stuff that could be used for force multiplication against the shiny new and technologically advanced next generation (ad infinitum). Items considered low value targets by people who lacked the niche skills to operate dangerously outdated equipment.

For example, we had just been screwing with submarines and sonar, so of course, I had a pretty encyclopedic grasp of what assets we'd stashed where. Including a couple of diesel subs parked in Monterey Bay. The aquarium has so much boat traffic as well as dolphin training, it made for a safer (nowhere counted as safe anymore) place to leave rusting tubs that had no place in a modern world. Analog stuff without electronics that extended beyond the ship.

Between the pretense of normality and our own ruthless capabilities, it took us little time and less effort to slip across the Mexican border, infiltrate Californian life impersonating surfer hippies in a converted van, then roll up to the stash site. Nine even took naps on the purloined shag rug we'd dumped in the back of the van. Authentic. From there it was an afternoon of surfing, some legerdemain with dive tanks under the boards at sunset and an illicit entry to Sub 4—no better name—which got us up and running toward Greece at twelve knots. We had food and fuel if we did the slow boring trip. Crackers and canned things mostly, augmented by what we hauled in from the surf boards. Needless to say, we opted for dangerous gear first, snacks second.

Now this trip would take roughly twenty days of eating canned hash and crackers, cranked at max undersea speed. But it only takes about 30 hours to get to Calvert Island above Vancouver. Where someone I knew had stashed a few airplanes and excess cash. My frenemy Arthur, pilot, entrepreneur, porn star (really), anarchist turned libertarian operative, nomad, and bigamist—he had five wives who knew zip about one another—happened to come to me for help avoiding the IRS and Inland Revenue. I provided a solution. Then he stole from me, paid me back in crypto, stole that, sent me an apology in the form of Thai hookers with sushi, then had them try to drug me into a stupor and burgle my house. Hilarious in context. Arthur, never change.

Not in my world but on the crooked side of entrepreneurs, I tolerated him precisely because he also happened to be one of seven vital contributors to Murray's construction. Arthur just so happened to be the best IT project manager in the known universe. Ignore the safari coat and orgies, the man could build AIs in his sleep. But that wasn't going to stop me from a little friendly tit for tat. He had planes, I needed planes. He had money and who knew what stockpiles of guns, kompromat, and such. The man partied with everyone including the rich, powerful, and perverse.

I traded him a slightly used diesel submarine for his best plane, extra fuel, the content of all his poorly secured safes, and his insanely well lardered fridge. Mind you, Arthur also happened to live in Reno and knew nothing about this little swap. We helped ourselves since I had installed all the security and knew the codes. Nine got some porn of questionable taste, I got Arthur's stash of scotch and guns, we got a private jet with low altitude specific autopilot software (hey, the man smuggled for fun). We took all the cash for good measure.

After that Kos took hours rather than days. We landed at a half dozen nameless smuggler's air strips where my savvy companion traded that porn and some booze for prompt service at extortionary rates. Still, we made it in one piece, alive, theoretically undetected, having offloaded most of the conventionally offensive materials and the free cash. We still had kompromat, fuel, lots of weaponry, and a lot of crisp euros bundled in plastic. Seems Arthur had been naughtier than I knew and had acquired thirty million in large sequential bills from someone. My guess: the 2007 Latvian Mint Orgy. Epically famous. No arrests but a lot of new safety measures implemented, and a few drug tests administered over the ensuing weeks. Arthur had hosted the thing. Apparently, he'd improved on the hookers, drugs, and burglary racket. It made things more convenient for me. I'd send him a thank you note, maybe have the sub repaired to cover some of the losses. Maybe.

On the other hand, Arthur now had control over six dozen rather modern torpedoes. If he couldn't convert the loss of cash and jet into an insurance scam, then the weapons alone more than compensated. Maybe I would send a bill. Assuming he and his families didn't get lobotomized and repackaged as Hive cells.

Which brought us to the charming Oceanis resort on Kos, where the concierge extraordinaire, a genial fellow named Constantino, ruled with a velvet claw. Being a mismatched set of brownish looking man and woman, I got the laughably annoyed Nine to play along as man and wife on a honeymoon. We strolled up from the taxi we'd flagged from the airport, waving our duffle bags and looking careworn, unshaven, and tired. Touristic even.

Turns out that crisp euros can solve a lot of problems at Greek resorts. We had fake passports that made the sign-in a snap. A nice stack of seven thousand euros paid for a week's stay in something promoted as the Ultimate Pink Champagne Love Suite. In times of war, one makes do.

The desk manager handed us to an assiduous bellhop who definitely had concerns about our romantic capabilities. His face broadcast judgment and amusement. Hell, could he be blamed?

You had a big, tall scary dude with a shorter butch and blunt scary woman whose dark skin and hawk eyes looked more in keeping with the monsters of Greek myth than romance. One's got flawless olive skin and nice dark hair. The other scowled between scars and made no pretense of her braided grey and raven black braid. Neither of us looked horny, certainly not romantic. But we sure did walk like a family unit.

We entered a boudoir of tacky satin augmenting the stunning view of Turkey across the sea. A round bed with fuchsia ruffles dominated the otherwise huge room of offensively pink, well, everything. We had jackpotted the platonic ideal of Honeymoon Suites. How anyone could have sex here baffled me. In a large salver the requisite pink champagne bubbled, uncorked and ready. The man poured us each a flute, mumbled something Greek about long life and many sons, and then started to retreat. I winked, tipped him twenty euros and let him know daughters ran in my wife's family. My flawless Greek and ribald joke caught him enough by surprise that he'd be gabbling it within seconds of making it to the staff room.

Constantinos had as much forewarning as I felt safe providing. Nine tapped my flute. "You know, with just us, you can call me Hunter again."

"And me ... well, what do you actually want to call me?"

She smiled—a rare and pleasant reminder of better times—then laughed. "I call you Atoken Kahontsii in my head."

"Black tomahawk?"

She nodded. "Black for war and fire, for the vital essence of the West, watching the Eastern Door, the last resort, the sunset, the autumn warrior. Axe seems self-explanatory."

I mused as the shockingly refreshing champagne did its job. "Blackhawk. Okay, fair enough. Not a bad name all in all. Death, war, sunset, autumn and yet, also mind, hope, and focus. The distillation of purple wampum. Night and fire mixed. I kinda like it."

She smiled again and patted my arm. "I always liked that you called me Hunter. Cheers me right up." She sniffed, looked at her clothes, and nodding added, "I'll take the first shower and put on something less careworn."

I flopped onto the bed which resisted my weight with layers of fluff and jiggle. A hybrid waterbed and mattress. We'd relive the submarine life for an evening. Hunter disappeared while I turned inward to ask Momo about the nickname and remembered—no Momo, no internal chatter, no daughter to annoy with my aimless rambling. Was she safe? Had we made enough of a splash literally and figuratively to lead off The Hive?

We had to find Eddie fast. Which meant deciding today, here and now, whether he had screwed up or sent a signal. Did Eddie want to get caught on film? Fact: Eddie knew more about surveillance systems than any three other operatives. Certainly, he'd been employed to help The Hive penetrate ours. Fact: Eddie worked for Oslo, had worked for me, had always been queer in the extreme (in every aspect), had a rebellious streak wider than the Bosporus. Fact: Eddie now worked for a system of control that had only two flaws—hyper defined gender and lack of quantum chaos. Conjecture: yeah, Eddie is, was, and would always be on the side of chaos and fun. Pina and Eddie, damn them, must have been working this angle eons before I recruited him to the Arnapkapfaaluk. Ergo, Eddie had sent the message to his handler, to Agrippina not me. She'd gotten it firsthand when he walked by her. I'd seen an exchange between them, not a moment meant for me.

Fargle fackin furgle. What the hells below had these women come up with? Granted Eddie tended to be more male than me but in Kutzkan society matters of strategy, scheming, finesse, and death from below, aka treachery, came under the feminine purview. Oslo's network. Women. Chaos and freedom. Right. Intuitively speaking, it made the most sense that Eddie had worked hard to undermine The Hive while also starting the war with The Syndicate Pina ordered him to.

Fact: Eddie had run the snatch and grab. Fact: Eddie didn't do snatch and grabs; he did electronic warfare and intelligence from 10,000 klicks away. They'd passed a code. Eddie had intercepted his own organizations kill order, finagled a day pass to join the crew, and in his inimitable fashion maliciously complied with the orders while somehow failing to kill Harv and Kelba, getting caught on film, and exposing the explicit movements of both his hiveminds. Goddamned geniuses thought they could just waltz into an op and ad lib. Except we lost a lot of good people to save Pina and Kelba. Harv had only survived thanks to Murray's shenanigans.

Which meant Eddie had done what he could. He would be trying to save Pina and Oslo's network, had (this hurt my ego a tad) completely discounted my capabilities, and just gone for the throat. Why? Why ignore my counter-response? What did he know or think he knew that made me likely to be "useless" for defending Pina and The Syndicate?

Hunter stepped out the shower, towel covering the appropriate bits but showcasing lean muscle and a lot of scars. Poor woman lacked the nanites to repair all that. On the other hand, poor me lacked a lot of humanity as of late. She probably had the better deal.

"Hunter, if Gay Eddie is working for Oslo, why would he expect me to be useless in this war?"

She shook out her hair in another towel and started combing her braid while wet. "Means he expected you to be assassinated."

Cold ran down my spine. "By whom? My own team has been vetted and watched, the same for the security details, and if he knew it would happen as the war broke, then they had to be in the building, right?"

Hunter shrugged. "Never start with who. The who changes, but the how usually doesn't. Find the window of entry, the opportunity and means, that narrows down the list of who and usually what, where, and all that jazz."

Right. Of course. How do you kill me? Safest way to do it would be to hire a bigger nastier me. The Cult. The Hive had hired or partnered with or flat-out blackmailed Zeus and crew to come for me. To hunt me down at all costs. That narrowed down the where and when. The Cult had been at ground zero of the attack almost from the moment it started. They'd been posted at every bolthole.

Okay. A story emerged. You're Gay Eddie and you know that your Hive handlers are focused on chess strategy. So, you play a gambit, sacrificing a rook or queen to get your handler out alive. You intentionally let us exit with the promise to have

The Cult soak up casualties as we flee like rats. If you're trying for world domination, then neutralizing The Syndicate would be Step One in a hundred step process. The putative Hivemind, a masculine presence, might not need the ego gratification of killing us all personal and close up. Or worse, had ordered Pina captured and brought in metaphoric chains to kneel before the new king. Ick.

The Cult had been assigned to me and thanks to a lot of villages in the bag, some unwarranted upgrades ironically bestowed by Han's end game to kill me translated to The Cult missing their shot several times. Which meant they'd be hot on our trail and tasked with killing me and thus Hunter at all costs. That was their job in this war—which incidentally kept Zeus busy and distracted while The Hivemind took the critical infrastructure of the globe out of his maniacal grasp. They used him to kill me and in so doing, he sacrificed himself. They would be killing him next if his cultists survived my wrath.

How damned convoluted. In the chess game of The Adversary, it must make the finest sense. Use potentially dangerous rivals to hunt down your largest and most lethal roadblocks. Distract all the Powers and win by default when they clear one another from the board. Sit tight, grab the board, and let the chess pieces shoot one another. Hivechess.

Time to pull a Monopoly power move on this stupid game. Flip the table, scatter the board and pieces, start punching relatives. I opened a burner and dialed Charlie. The phone rang four times and then a familiar voice answered. "Who do I know in Greece?"

"Ah, Charlie, who don't you know in Greece? It's a seaside empire after all."

That took him a moment to parse. Yeah, I knew he fronted something major. The Kraken. Now he knew. Gloves off. "To what do I owe the pleasure, Spetz?"

"Or displeasure. I wondered if I could ask for a small favor. I need to call my brother Zeus. He'll be looking for me. I thought I'd invite him to Kos for a sit down."

Charlie actually laughed. "More likely he'd send a cruise

missile. You're sure you want to speak to the man? He very much dislikes you."

"Cain, Abel, all that hoopla. It's an old story, brothers who loathe and destroy one another. But we are brothers. And he wants me. So, let's cut out the middlemen and bring some closure to events." Ooh, that had to be a moment for him.

I'd just handed Charlie massive intelligence. I knew a timeline existed and thus knew the outline of the strategy, saw The Hive's plan, and had decided to engage Zeus as my counterthrust. The Kraken had been given a gift after being told its existence had been noted. All while also chasing Zeus and The Cult.

Another brief chuckle rippled through the connection. "I'll connect you."

"Great. Stay on the line, will you? Might be operationally prudent to have your opinion after."

Another pause. "I'm decidedly neutral in this."

"Sure, and I plan to keep you that way. But people will ask, so better you be there front row and have an exact understanding of what has been said."

The phone crackled and another voice dropped in, rough and somehow sensual. "Charlie? Why are you calling me? How are you calling me?"

"Charlie is doing me a favor Zeus. He's listening but it's me you want, so let's chat."

Wheels turned and somewhere one imagined Zeus's perfect cheeks turning purple with rage. "Wolfie, you bastard. How dare you call me?"

"C'mon, Zeusie, who else dares but me. Besides you wanna kill me, right? Because The Hivemind has you doing ash and trash while it takes over the world. I'm target numero uno, the big operatic kill for you and yours."

That earned me a pause. "Who has told you this?" The implied—I will eat their organs for lunch—went unspoken but we both felt it. Same parents.

"Let's say every org has leaks buddy. Yours, mine, theirs. You're being treated like a chore boy. A god among insects. Sent to fetch someone beneath their concern."

"You're hardly that. You killed the whole section. They know you're the devil incarnate."

Zeus dripped with hatred. Time to cut through the cognitive dissonance. "Well then, why send you? Huh? You missed last time and ended up in a nice tidy coma. If I'm the big global danger, why send some hopped up gene junkies splicing their second rate nanites to tribal nobodies?"

"Fuck you. What do you want?"

"That's the spirit." Hunter had reentered the room, her face a mixture of apoplectic shock and nonplussed astonishment. Yeah, me too. "Look, logic much Zeus. Either you are the Class A badass you think you are and capable of taking down the Devil themselves."

"I am and I'll crush you when I find you."

"Great. If you're so badass awesome, why aren't you running the planet? Yeah, that's right. Use your big sexy brain to do some math on that. It's hard I know, since you are programmed for kill, fuck, brag, and disco, but attempt to use your genius intellect for something hard … like basic reasoning."

"I…only have your stupid word I'm being used as a pawn."

"Your worst enemy. Your personal nightmare, the biggest piece of bait in the known world and frankly the only thing in the whole universe that gets someone as precise, deadly, and fixated on control out of control. You have one weak spot, the same one as mine. You love your family."

"You killed them."

I sighed. Yeah, time to pay the coins to Charon. "Yes. I killed Mom and Dad. Let's be clear. I will continue to hunt you all and eventually we will kill one another. This planet absolutely ain't big enough for you and me. One day, Zeus, I plan to push your entire cult into the same grave as Hans and Cassandra."

He coughed. "I am hearing you… brother."

"Then hear this. I am in Kos, at a resort filled with disgusting pink chiffon and satin sex sheets. You want to die, come fucking get me. But you're selling out your grand plan. Because killing me will weaken your forces enough that The Hive or some other Swarm elements or the goddamned resurgent Russians will walk up and whack you with a rock. You'll be weak, broken, and out of your safe spot."

He paused a long time. "Why, Wolfie, why?" The sounds of him sobbing carried over the distance.

"Zee, look. You loved them and I get that. But they were so evil even evil people feared them. Nazis feared them for being too fascist. And me, they tortured me. So, yeah, I got revenge on the horrible people who murdered my mother, tormented me, used me as a weapon, and then tried to have me killed. As much as you loved them, I hated them—what they created, what they stood for, what they wanted for the world."

"Once this is over, once we've put paid to these Hive bastards for trying to use us, I am coming for you. I am never stopping. Do you hear me? I am coming! You are a dead man walking, Wolfie! Death is my witness! YOU WILL PAY!" The line cut away leaving just Charlie breathing.

When someone as deadly and purposeful as Zeus screams at you it hurts physically. My guts felt like churning water and my legs had a bit of rubber in them. Not much scared me, but he did. I'd gone and poked the world's biggest predator, then found the largest wound on his flank and slapped on a big punch of salt. Smart? Nope. But crazy like fox. We'd gone from a two-front war to just one. At least until Zeus lost patience.

One catastrophe at time. I'd just demonstrated how to kick the can forward on a no-win situation. Which meant I could shower and go down for dinner. "Thanks, Charlie, appreciate your help."

"He'll come for you."

I stared at the Aegean slapping the beach in rhythmic waves. "Yes, he will. But not today. Not until he gets his people safe and secure. Which means I've got time to execute my other plan. Gotta go. Chin chin, ciao, and all that."

"Godspeed, Spetz." Message sent and received. The Kraken had just been told I would come for them, too, sooner or later. Because I am the enemy of fascists and Nazis. Of control and domination. But not today.

Hunter looked at me, horrified. "Did you just ...?"

"Piss off two of the scariest organizations known? Yeah. We just did that."

She smiled and shrugged. "And why did we do this?"

"Well, now, instead of fighting Zeus and his cultists while also fighting The Kraken, which you haven't even heard about yet but who could kill us instantly, and then fighting The Hive who we need to fight, we reduce our enemies from three crazy groups to one very crazy very motivated enemy and two future headaches. Big scary headaches to be sure. But buck up, we'll probably die before they become a major issue."

"Or you could invite them to a nice remote location and blow them up with a bomb."

I laughed. "That's the spirit. Wellllll, there are a lot them, so it'd need to be somewhere very remote and a very large bomb. More likely we just added to Pina's problems. Which brings us to today. Nobody's dead yet so we might as well."

Hunter sent me to the bizarre neon bathroom to pursue showering, putting on resort-acceptable clothing that hid a lot of weapons, and sauntering down into a far more tasteful atrium filled with tourists, lovers, drunk Russians who had come for the endless booze, some sketchy guys who might be spies or gay lovers—hard to cotton that, and a lot of suddenly impressed Brits who looked us over, caught our air of mysterious danger and did the typical sangfroid stiff lip smile. Still, the line for the buffet thinned. We stood behind a strange pair. The woman made sense. Tall, elegant, somehow aristocratic in her sharp features with sumptuous red hair cut short and green penetrating eyes. She wore a loose linen shift and a pair of expensive sandals. Her eyes glittered with intelligence and something else, understanding perhaps. She nudged the man imperceptibly and his eyes shifted to me. He made no sense. Balding, barrel chested, he radiated a kind of teddy bear energy. He'd gone for shorts, a shirt that accentuated his massive shoulders, and a pair of laceless sneakers. Relaxed and cheerful. Yet his body language, his dark brown eyes, his obvious paranoia spoke to a much darker impulse. He felt dangerous and looked delightful. Bless him, he shifted into combat stance seven and seemed ready to throw down there and then against a man a foot taller and far fitter. Trouble.

Instead, Konstantinos arrived and did his whole insouciant

maître d thing. The woman seemed unimpressed; her head shifted enough for me to be certain she had started examining Hunter in detail. The man simply kept himself between us, never changing his bubbly patter with his wife or lover. Still, she seemed too keenly aware of Hunter and vice versa to be a straight woman. Gay besties? Something.

We found out when our sly concierge seated us at a large table with plenty of room to view the room. The man true to paranoid form took a seat furthest from the front door where he could see the whole of the room. He put our red-haired version of Hunter to his left and politely motioned us to sit. Entirely friendly, his posture a coiled spring. The various guests found seats nearby, the suspicious men parking close to the door. They had eyes on the buffet.

Then the auburn-haired beauty turned to me and in perfect Ukrainian said, "He's harmless."

I smiled my best smile and lowered my guard enough that he relaxed. "Kyiv?"

She nodded. "Yes, but my grandmother taught me Ukrainian during summers in the West." She spoke fluently and with a literate accent. Old aristocracy, the remnants of a time and people all but decimated by the Soviets and now the Russians.

"He does seem … jumpy."

She shrugged. The man looked at us, smiled, and waited patiently. He seemed not at all upset that we spoke a language he didn't know. Calm enough, self-contained enough to not feel left out. No ego in it. "He recognizes your kind and he's … confused."

Ah. A retired commando or some such. We'd been made by a pair of tourists on vacation. To be fair I'd ignored SOP and gone for conspicuous and spooky in hopes of flushing out opposition while forcing Konstantinos to help us quickly. Seemed to be working.

Hunter leaned over and with a terse smile added her own sentiments. "Not harmless. But of no danger to us. He'd fight the world for you."

That got a winsome smile and a motion from the lady to join them at the buffet line. We got up and following her cue, the man relaxed around us. But his eyes lingered on the Eurotrash couple. Right, another pro felt them and that was that. We'd found the opposition: two sinister lads armed with hair gel and bad leisure wear. The buffet proved abundant and with the exception of all the meat being smothered in weird sauces or gleefully overcooked by a Greek apprentice chef still in his late teens, they had laid out an amazing spread.

We loaded up and sauntered back to our table. Now festooned with water, coffee, tea pots, and a large bottle of white wine. One of the chefs came out and handed us bread and a huge Greek salad. She seemed fixated on the man and waved her ample bosom at him as she explained in accented English that they'd gotten the couple's favorites set up for us. For him coffee and bubbly water, her wine and still water. The tea seemed to be for us.

We switched to English. Words were exchanged and assumptions validated. Every once in a while, The Web spits out a random encounter with agents or operatives who've eluded your orbit until then. Like knew like and these two, presently artists on a family trip, previously held far more dangerous jobs doing horrible things we recognized far too well. Once they gave their names, the pieces fell into place—both of them had been on critical lists for Oslo's future recruitment. He predated the fall of the Soviets, a Cold War relic from a derivative program the Americans had initiated with stolen data from Hans and Cassandra. The Abschnitt light—less superhuman than super-cruel. All the Nazi propaganda and brutality, a fraction of the effectiveness, and absolutely none of the fun nanotech. She had graduated from a Ukrainian family of aristocrats, spies, Jews, and artists, moved to Texas, and widened her espionage portfolio. Likely for Israel, maybe for the motherland. They had met when a mutual friend noticed they were both Jewish, Ukrainian, and single.

Nonetheless, if I'd left them long enough Hunter likely would have maneuvered the woman into bed and not worried much. Whomever they were, nothing about their surface relationship matched the intensity of their connection or their true roles. The red-haired woman's guardian seemed more amused than threatened by the flirtation. Like Hunter and me, a family unit from a place that murdered families. Not to mention the burden they faced as Ukrainian Jews, queers, and escapees of the global intelligence apparatus. The Syndicate had made The Web a treacherous place, deadly to anyone not intimately connected and shielded by someone like me. These two had gone alone against the wider world and … won.

We spent a pleasant evening chatting, eating, consuming way too much wine and dessert. These days the man did something computer related; the woman ran a school. They worked part time as artists and planned to retire properly in the next few years. Hunter listened and then when the man revealed a penchant for indigenous spirituality, spent the dessert portion of the night wangling with details of ontologies of land management. To each their own. Well, that and she must have realized we couldn't spare the time to seduce the lesbian across from her.

At long last, the tea drunk, the bottle emptied, replenished and emptied again, the plates cleared, and coffee served to all twice, we had to leave. The man gave me a feral grin. "Need them stalled?"

We had said nothing about the watchers, but he'd put it all together. A pro indeed. Hunter nodded at him and said something in what sounded like Cherokee. He answered, patted her hand, told his wife—they raised a child together—something in broken Russian that sounded like "give me minutes five, then go front" before ambling back to the buffet.

After five minutes he managed to start weaving between tables at the buffet exit. He carried a massive plate of fruit stacked on another plate of desserts. All of it cubes of melon, frosted cake, or other chunky things. In his right hand, holding up the whole affair lurked a pitcher of red punch. We rose and started our casual exit. The spies also rose and started toward us when they "accidentally" collided, dropping the entirety onto their shirt fronts.

What followed would have been a masterclass in comedy if the men's guns hadn't been exposed by the punch slopped on their sides. Loud American apologies and yells for help brough waiters and chefs, then a throng of guests. He turned over a table and tried to help the men up. Somehow, one had been tripped and had fallen ass first into a plate of cake squares. The men scrambled and tried to evade him but there's one thing all American special forces share in common: the loud splashy attack. He called his partner who started sharply barking Russian in the most hostile manner possible.

How could you be so fabulous? What the hell do you think we should wear tomorrow? That cake looks amazing, we should eat some the next time it's on the buffet. Spoken with the tone of an aggrieved spouse whose night had been ruined, she sold the mood completely. By the time the horde of helpers in white service coats had arrived, the room knew he'd be sleeping on the sofa, that he might as well kiss off getting laid for the rest of the trip, and that Americans truly were the awful tourists everyone said they were. There's only so many times you can half shout *I'm sure my American Express insurance covers this* before the crowd turns ugly. All eyes focused on The Scene, the shared embarrassment visceral.

They'd bought us a nearly flawless exit with no witnesses. We simply walked out an unmarked exit, ambled down staff stairs and turned into the pool area just as the DJ yelled "Hands Up!" It took ten seconds to go from hunted to invisible among the drunks and dancers. On the far side of the floor stood Konstantinos, his briefcase in hand, his face a study in false smiles and reptilian ferocity. Fair thee well, nameless strangers. One day a small package might grace their doorstep. Or better yet, I'd just found a great operations management and art team for Aidan and Declan.

He looked me up and down with ferocious disappointment. "You should not have come. The Cult will be here any moment."

Hunter laughed. "Now I get it. No, he sorted that before dinner. We have time."

The fact that she said it with total assurance threw him. Konstantinos didn't know her, but he knew her posture and demeanor. He nodded, confused, but now relaxing. "And… Charlie? He knows you're here?"

I gave him a broad smile. My friends tell me it looks as if I plan to eat someone. All the better to speed our man along in his duties. "He knows, Stino. Now, let's get our business sorted so you can pour wine and caper for the tourists."

His face drew up and despite himself he grinned. "You wound me, Spetz, I am an artist of hospitality."

"And a consummate thief and adulterer. How many Yelp reviews have you gotten from satisfied wives? Or fools whose watch you stole and then helped them look for it?"

He sketched a bow, winked at Hunter (oh foolish Stino, not your type), and shrugged. "On my good days, all of them. On the weeks I relax, maybe only two thirds. The British sometimes actually like to sleep with each other." He frowned. "Maybe it's the bad teeth?"

"Or they actually come to a couple's resort to renew their romantic commitments?"

He waved a hand. "Don't be foolish. People are awful. Couples who come here are cheap, greedy, oversexed, and demand ridiculous attention they don't deserve. Perfect marks."

Hunter snorted. "Right, so what are we doing here with this guy? Why do we need him to find our man?"

Konstantinos looked her over and suddenly paled. "No, it cannot be. You were killed in Belgrade."

Hunter gave him an appraising eye. "You're ex NATO?"

He shrugged. "I played a lot of sides you know. But in Serbia you mingle with the Russians and terrorists, the freedom fighters so called, all that. I made a lot of money then bought a few places. This one for example."

She'd taken a single comment of his, placed him as ex intelligence with access to eyes only secret material on her sister self-shot and killed by the Black Brigade in '96 during an op gone badly. I had to identify the body, flying up from Africa. Broke my heart and galvanized my decisions that came after, the investments made.

"She survived Stino and she wants a name. Give us Gay Eddie. We know he's moving through your circles and don't bother bullshitting me. I've seen him personally, less than a week ago, in Manhattan. Shooting at Pina. Please consider this business capital B, as in do what I say or Be Very Sure You Will Be Broken Beaten and Blunt Force Trauma'd."

He blinked a few times and, bless him, gulped. Yeah, I

smiled like a proper cannibal and cracked my knuckles for effect. Hunter just chuckled next to me.

Konstantinos considered for a moment. "If I give you this information you will leave."

"Tomorrow, after a nice breakfast and a night in the satin nightmare suite, yes."

He sighed. "He's not in a place, but on a train. Moving low tech on tracked vehicles and generator powered engines. Allows him to use electric tracks as well as main tracks. In South America, Patagonia."

Hunter closed her eyes. She'd be tracing maps in her mind. "He'll eventually pick La Trochita. Small gauge, no footprint, steam and coal locomotive, protected as a national asset. Almost impossible to follow with another train."

Yay, Argentina. Close to where the White Cult had operational power. Give him his due: Gay Eddie had balls of titanium. Or had picked the shadow of The Cult as a genius location to evade his own folks. Either way, it had to be a strategically defensible location and a smart choice for other reasons. Eddie probably had access to old Nazi rat line radios and such. He'd be trying to coordinate with Pina and her teams.

"Thanks, Stino. By the way, if you own the place, why do you still work the tables?"

He frowned. "These days too many people wander far from where they are supposed to be." He eyed me indelicately. "Surprise visitors show up and make trouble. The war with the Abschnitt caused us all to revamp security. Now, I am back to kissing ass and stealing jewelry. But one day, when your lady gets the peace accorded correctly, then I can relax on a beach with whichever bored wife seems most interesting.

Hunter cocked her head. "Does it bother you seducing the women under the noses of their men?"

Stino laughed. "Please, these men, if we can call them that, they are abusive or neglectful. The whole lot of them better to be made into shark chum. I am not even trying hard here. The cheap bastards buy a low-cost vacation, but upgrade to the 'fancy,'" he held up his fingers for emphasis, "vacation and then expect some kind of reset on the bad relationship."

She met his stare. "So, why not kill them?"

He grinned. "Not so good for repeat customers. But yes, good idea. Perhaps Konstantinos has a few cousins around the world. Perhaps the wives whisper secrets and then suddenly there are car accidents and some tragic drownings. A mugging in a faraway city."

Hunter looked at me then back at him. "You're Uncle Gary?"

Stino shrugged, gave her a delighted bow, and then looked at me. "After breakfast, you clear out. This property cost me too much to be leveled by attack helicopters. Okay?"

"Okay." We shook hands, he bowed and slunk away to serve wine and seduce his customers.

Hunter punched me in the bicep. "Uncle Gary is supposed to be an urban myth. All this time, he's been living in Greece, at a fucking resort?"

Uncle Gary—the bogeyman of abusers—the poster child of Oslo's new and better world. A whisper to the right ear and your abuser disappeared. Legally, tracelessly, through an arranged accident. Except Hunter had it half right.

"He works for Uncle Gary. He and a dozen other operatives all serve an underground network, funded by Oslo, that sends centralized intelligence and then hands out assignments. He's not the Uncle but one of a few trusted lieutenants. That said, Constantinos certainly sends men to their deaths and once in a while, if they are in another Greek province, helps them along personally."

Hunter motioned me to the bar where we ordered ridiculously silly drinks. I had something called a Crazy Colada Smoothie with ice cream, triple booze, and a weird aftertaste that might have been grenadine. "Oslo?"

My turn to shrug. Ooh the complications. "Look, these days Oslo runs it and she's effectively Gary though it falls to some other leader. Possibly even Darcy, whom you've never met but can be trusted."

Hunter sipped her Moregarita and rolled her eyes. "The woman raising your cyberchildren and the single most vital security tech in The Syndicate. Yes, I know who she is. Anything about you we know, Spetz."

"Then why are you asking about the identity of the Uncle. You should know."

She gave me a pained look. "Stop playing games and just tell me."

"Uncle Gary used to be Uncle Karíhton but nobody could pronounce the Mohawk. So, we shortened it."

It's rare to get a truly flabbergasted look lese days, almost unthinkable from someone as jaded and traveled as Hunter. "You, you started Uncle Gary?"

We slugged back our drinks, ordered two more, and swapped. A Moregarita didn't really offer more, except maybe more ice and more headache. But it sent calories to the right spot. "It's another village in a bag. Saves a huge intelligence network from outside control, keeps otherwise aggressive killers occupied wiping out scumbags and rapists, and allows me to fund strategic locations while appearing to be independent of my overall organization."

Hunter's face moved from astonishment to awe. "It single handedly save thousands of abused women and has been the best pipeline for getting abused women to safe locations for decades. And it's a front?"

I smiled my real smile, the quiet one. "No, it's a double bluff, Hunter. Like all the things I do. Hiding decency in plain sight but labeling it something tactical to avoid scrutiny. Likely, it's how Oslo recruited me, come to think. She started gobbling up all my networks when I exited The Web. Uncle Gary must not have fooled her for a moment."

"For a ruthless killer you do sure save a lot of lives, Spetz."

"Yeah, it's something my children remind me of often. It's as if when faced with an impossible situation, I found a third way through besides succumbing to madness like my brothers and sisters or chasing power like, well, all the rest."

Hunter patted my arm sadly. "There's a word for that. Goodness. Decency, morality, kindness."

"Ah, but let's not forget I bought all that over a lot of corpses. It made me an even more ruthless killer. Turf to defend, people to keep safe and all that."

Hunter sipped her drink and pondered. Behind us carefree

couples danced in the drunken night, sauced and libidinous, some doomed to be targeted and killed by my own network. Others saved from the hell of fists and worse. But most likely to return home after a week of too much sun, fatty food, and alcohol, slightly relaxed, poorer, and ready to place the yoke upon their shoulders and slave once again for the depraved overlords whose faces they'd never see. Fun times.

But also, one day maybe a touch freer. We had among the throng spies who must even now be sending furiously worded messages down the various hidden lines to their sponsors. SOS, Alert Alert, and all that. We'd kicked over the beehive and then did … nothing. Stopped for bad drinks and bad disco dancing. The Hive knew where to find us. But so what? They expected The Cult and The Kraken to sort us out—lethally. Once they cottoned to the fact that it didn't happen and more relevant, wasn't going to happen any time soon, they'd mobilize resources and plan how to thwart us. But we'd be gone and on to the next thing. Days ahead.

Hunter sipped her drink, then poked my elbow. "You know Eddie only has to treat this as a ridiculously dangerous game of Tag. He's just got to keep far enough away from us to not die while the war just churns on. It's going to be hard to get to bumfuck Patagonia with any speed."

That certainly made sense. We needed to show up in the right place at the right time and do it fast enough to matter in the global sense. Time had been on my side hiding us, but we'd wasted a lot of critical days lurking and maneuvering. Now, we had to switch to Bat out of Hell mode and just outrun the bad guys.

I downed the vestiges of something billed as a Hurrycane, which mostly felt slow, and considered my options. Our options. "How bad do you want to sleep in the satin horror palace?"

She sneered. With the scar it looked impressive. "On a scale of North Korean vacationing to four hot naked indigenous dykes with a camper van and an extra seat available?"

"Uh, yeah?"

"I'd rather be smothered in rancid honey and thrown to fire ants."

"Riiiight, so slightly above North Korea but certainly interested in moving onward and upward."

She shrugged. "Were the naked women an option?"

I sighed. "Well, despite the questions of consent and how you'd find said lesbian camping expedition, would you defer your quest for justice, peace, and family salvation for some shaggery?"

She gave me a wicked smile. "Depends on what nation they are." We chuckled. "Sooooo, clean out the room and get ready to exfiltrate?"

"Fancy word for running away."

"I'm not the one who helped deploy a network of operatives run by a horny Greek pimp-daddy burglar."

"Technically neither am I. We started with angry Dykes on Bikes and a couple super gay closeted Hell's Angels, but you know, things got expansive. Then things got global."

She gave me an amused half smile. "Okay boomer. I'll grab the gear so we can run away. What will you be doing?"

"Stealing stuff. And considering what nation you'd abandon the family to ogle."

"More than ogle, Blackhawk. Give me four women and I guarantee they'd be delighted and exhausted three days hence."

"Four? Hunter, you shock and horrify me."

She sauntered off with a lilt in her step. "You're getting old. I was going to say eight but figured you'd be overwhelmed. No wonder Eddie delights in tormenting you."

Chapter 10: UDF4CF Vs. Gay Eddie to the 13th Power

While my would-be orgy master grabbed our duffels and such, yours truly slipped out into the night, found a nice beater van sans succubae and rolled the hotwired junker up the door in time for Hunter to slide open the side, dump our stuff and then take the shotgun position.

Half an hour later we'd blown through a locked gate at the local airport, swapped the beater for one of those driving staircases that have some technical name no one bothers to learn, and had found ourselves a 737 from Greco-Hellenic Air parked and ready. A quick negotiation with the terrified mechanics involving some kicks to the balls and a well applied wrench to one particularly surly twerp's knee got us fueled and ready within minutes.

We then launched a fuel truck into the main terminal and with some applied physics and a couple of lucky shots managed to start a really big fire. Terrorism 101. Scream a lot in gibberish, make a lot of aimless threats, light something visible on fire, and whack a jerk or two with something blunt. We hadn't even had to use our limited explosives. Jet fuel in quantity rarely disappoints.

While the world devolved into panicked chaos, we took our stolen jet skyward. Hunter knows how to pilot pretty much anything and me, well, sure I'm nowhere as proficient as many of Section 21's best pilots, but the least skilled of us could dogfight. I looked down at the location coordinates posted by my devious and apparently thirsty (that seemed the new generation's lingo) co-pilot and with a mental shrug jammed the throttle to maximum. We had two options: go super low and use the ocean as a pressure front or go stratospheric and use bottled oxygen.

I chose to go high and fast. Better aerodynamics and no chance for a ship-to-air missile. We lugged out the oxygen masks and with our streamlined plane pushed the maximum height speed continuum without a single damn given. Bat. Out. Of. Hell. We had just made our own little hellscape, so that covered Uncle Gary's network. No one would doubt we'd left and not on good terms. We'd run away ostentatiously after pissing off two thirds of the planet. That left us with a few hours to ponder fate, sex, life, family, and all that. Even at insane speeds the empty 737 can barely push 900 klicks and Hunter had picked a location a good 5,300 kilometers down the way. Six hours' worth of flying time, all of it with oxygen masks.

Given that we had a general location and if we moved with enough ruthless efficiency, we might simply outpace the resources set up by The Hive. Also, the satellites and radar used to track things like stolen airplanes don't work so well when hacked and zombified. Which meant The Hive had to either make the world network more functional and allow counter hacking or hope they knew where we hoped to land.

Six hours later, we approached Félix-Houphouët-Boigny International Airport, better known locally as the Port Bouët Airfield. The big hub city of Abidjan on the Ivory Coast just so happened to be a the very largest airport in the country with lots of the very largest airplanes commercially available lined up and fueled. Because we had timed it (meaning me and my penchant for chaos personified) to arrive pre-dawn in the busiest African air travel spot on the West side of the continent, we had dozens of options in nearly every size jumbo jet. We landed with a brutal skid and taxied directly into the left wing of a parked 747.

Yep. If you want to completely flummox your enemies do something so stupid it becomes unexpected. Random, crazy, bad for business, and generally dangerous. Crashing a speeding jet into a taller and more massive airliner had to count. Pros like Hunter and I had time to prep the crash straps and using a nice pair of inflatable rafts, build a really cheap and cheerful air bag system. Couldn't see a damned thing, which is how the cockpit managed to nearly impale itself on a wheel assembly. But it did give us an exit point nicely ripped out behind the cockpit with a drop to the tarmac now simplified by a big ass very climbable wheel. Stab the rafts, cut the straps, and um, exfiltrate away so to speak.

We exited the wreckage with bags in tow and at a dead run managed to get onto to the wing flaps of a very sleek looking 767 with extra fuel tanks before anyone seemed to really grasp what had happened. The fact that a tanker truck had been parked there helped us on two fronts. We knew the thing had to be mostly fueled and we had an easy climb onto the wing. Hunter insinuated herself into the cabin with a deft pull on some levers and the use of a magnetic firefighter's key. Hard to find but sooooo worth it.

She came back five minutes later. We had a nice cadre of hostages, snacks, and about fifteen more minutes to fuel ourselves. This time we did use explosives but not the ones you'd expect. If you strap a couple grenades to the right portion of a fuselage it will generate a nasty pop, some smoke, and seemingly nothing else. Ten minutes later a very hot, very focused fire will spread along the insulation lines of the plane. It has to start crazy hot and go hotter from there to get the materials burning. But once they ignite, only God and oxygen choking foam can stop the chemical fire from going berserk. If you happen to smash up a pre-fueled jet, then sooner or later the debris and radiant heat from the unstoppable fuselage fire will start a second, much bigger, brighter but less inevitable series of booms and smash-bang-pops. That's the official sound of an expensive airplane burning itself from the inside out—a sound we knew by heart.

Around the time the Ivory Coast police realized they'd been attacked by nasty terrorists and not just a pair of drunk pilots, they had a scary airplane fire followed by a burping set of explosions on their west side tarmac. Which did a nice job of covering up the eastern side exfiltration (more sneaky running away) of one very large airplane. Hunter left the traumatized air crew on the asphalt, lowered by a rope last minute, still zip tied and gagged. I had added a long-winded note in Arabic praising some splinter philosophy involving Allah, rape, demonizing foreigners, and the eventual purging of all things by holy fire. A few quotes from the Koran, some badly placed context, and voila, we had a religiously bugnuts screed which sat adjacent to real crazy Muslim radicalism and would take a while to unravel. Assuming some demented splinter group didn't pick it up as their new moral compass.

Meanwhile we took our big scary over-fueled under-passengered long distance airliner on a jaunt for Patagonia. The whole world would take a few hours to realize what had happened, among them The Hive agents who'd translate the activity into a trajectory. Except that only one person knew our target and his own airport had been rendered unusable short term. Unless The Hive wanted to spend a lot of people and time to follow up our terribly obvious terribly loud escape, we and we alone knew the final destination.

Sure, the local versions of bad guys and thugs would be at every airport, landing strip and such within the ten thousand kilometer range. But basic logic dictated that we'd stolen the fueled up and extra-large jumbo liner because we needed to get the last two thousand klicks down the line. Especially since smaller nimbler planes had been ours for the taking, readily fueled and easier to grab. They'd deploy small units in Brazil and all that but would be looking to Canada and the USA for the missing jet. Because there's a little trick you can do once and only once where you destroy the transponders on a jet midflight. Takes about eight hours to recalibrate sensors to find the plane and if you are truly demented, willing to fly twenty meters above the ocean surface, and without lights, you can evade all surveillance very short term. Like about seven and half hours short term. We managed to get out over the ocean, pointed toward the Caribbean, started to turn toward the North American coastline, and killed all the switches while plummeting from eleven thousand meters down to the surface of the churning Atlantic. Which sometimes has waves higher than forty meters. Yeah, insane.

Mind you, the best plane has about half a second to adjust the autopilot at the speed and distance. If you happen to have a superhuman level of augmented motor coordination thanks to a pesky daughter unit and some nano-engineering, you can spend the trip actively rolling over the rough seas like a dune buggy juiced on the electromechanical version of methamphetamine. Uncomfortable, taxing, mentally intensive, and physically painful, and it takes a whole lot of calories. Hunter fed me the in-flight snacks and cracked jokes. Also, she revealed that in order, the hawtest chix (her phrase and certainly not mine) would be Dakota Sioux, Comanche, Apache, Inuktitut, then a three-way tie between the Powhasset, the Black Cherokee, and Free Seminoles. After that, apparently naked women equaled naked women. When I mentioned our fine Six Nations, I got a cuff to the ear and some choice Mohawk curses. Never ever accidentally sex up your cousins by mistake. Exogamy in all things. Even bizarre imaginary covert operator sex orgies.

We also agreed the Yankees sucked, the NFL needed more expansion teams, cricket and rugby tied as the best spectator sports but curling and archery had to be the absolutely best for watching online. After sex and sports, we covered war, family gossip, our escape plan, and then more sex and some brief mention of our children/sister selves. Hunter has a truly foul sense of humor, no shame, no limits, and a wicked vocabulary. Which made the unbearable trip merely awful and kept us both nicely alive. Do not try piloting a jetliner on the ocean surface. Ever. We only whacked into wave tops twice and both times we lost just a single engine to flooding. Still, scared the shit out of entirely fearless me.

Oh, the escape plan? As we approached Patagonia we lifted the plane up to three thousand meters which gave us about two klicks of air drop into the mountains, flipped on the stuff that would give away our position to intensely focused watchers, set the autopilot for Mexico City, and taking our bundled gear, dropped out a cargo door to Low Altitude Low Opening parachute our way onto some old train tracks in the wilderness. Time to do our savage low-tech thing. Good thing I brought arguably the world's best tracker / bounty hunter. I would say the best of all time, but family bias suggests there might have been others her equal. The Hashashin had a few and the Apache would be disgusted at our arrogance. Still, this side of the 15th century, the best of the best dropped next to me toward the brutal landscape waiting to destroy us below. Home sweet home—deadly, scary, cold, and heartless. Hello Mother Nature. Your prodigal daughter has just dropped from the sky to send her regards.

Now the good news: Patagonia happens to be sparsely populated, boasting fresh and vital air to breathe and dangerous terrain. At night, people dare not move around unless they know the place intimately and then only along old worn paths that trace back to ancient empires. During the day, the sun and sea create a warm joyous environment that emboldens the verdant land to encroach upon human structures. Salt, sun, wind, and neglect have the place littered with shacks and shantytowns no longer mapped or considered habitations. The bad news: at night the temperature drops, the light goes out, and whatever tactical advantage the dark provides in everyone staying put, it definitely gives anything sharp, venomous, predatory, or hungry a decided advantage. Hunter and I landed in a small pocket of open scrub, dumped the chutes under some gnarled trees, and took stock.

No turned ankles, no random passersby pointing in fear and amazement, no smoke signals or jet fighters zooming past. If we'd been spotted, we had no sense of it. Even if we had, so what? Who the hell cared about bumfuck backward Patagonia? Maybe The Hive but likely no one except us. Perhaps some cultists, some drug runners and actual mountain bandits, likely a few jaguarundi if they bothered to migrate southward. Wild pigs had become an emerging ecological threat. Otherwise, it was just us scary humans stripping down to the essentials of gear, survival supplies, and weaponry.

Did the wilderness count as threat or home turf for us? Neither. We barely knew this land, but we knew land as a living entity and we knew how to navigate in lethal surroundings with minimal fuss. It helped that we only had to find a steam train and then chase down the tracks. Also, that we had a genuine tracker. Plus, I had a compass and some maps—so that helped too.

We'd landed in a massive conifer forest with long bristling trees oddly square trunked and sparse. Hunter sniffed, stared at the sun, and consulted a watch. "We're at the edge of Los Alerces National Park. Named after the big trees. We missed our landing site by about thirty klicks. Still, we're on one side of the track terminus, so we can find them and walk the train down to its other side."

I ran my hand across the rough bark. We had about an hour of full daylight left and then it would be dark, cold, and wet. Followed by pitch black, frigid, and raining. In a densely packed forest which had ground cover, shrubs, no paths, and no clear sense of human presence. "Um, ain't the reciprocal terminus about four hundred kilometers on the other side of the Andes?"

She shrugged. "Sure, but so what? If you can steal a plane, you can steal a train. And they have like ten working engines. We take one, pile up the coal and wood, and chug on down to our destiny."

"Did you just insert chug into the Mohawk vernacular?"

That got a laugh. Her voice echoed briefly before the sound died among the whisper of branches. Dense and misty, the forest had a presence that reminded me of Kutzk terrain. It felt oddly comforting. "Nope, kids' books have been making little engines chug chug for a while and we do have kids now."

I tossed her a protein bar and gave her the finger. "Don't make me curse you to a life of spoiled romance and terrible sex."

She pointed toward a crack between the trees and scrub; with our stripped-down gear we advanced. We had food, stay-warm fabrics, some minimal camping gear, tools / knives, and the essential guns and explosives we'd need. We carried more ammo than clothing. "Kutzkans don't curse, Blackhawk."

"Okay, but maybe I'm in league with a local thunder or forest demon. I could be a secret sorcerer."

That drew out another laugh. We slid between trees, learning the rhythm of the terrain. Even given the advanced state of our bushcraft and the need to simply get forward in a basic direction, we'd be lucky to break trail at a quarter of walking pace. Walking all night, we'd make at best half the distance to the tracks. "Okay boomer. But arrive first then curse the tracker."

I spoke our last words for several hours. "Fair enough." Then we simply melted into the growing dusk. Which bled into a night thick with bone chilling rain. Still, Hunter advanced like a pitiless metronome step after step, forward toward her focused endpoint. My eyes, now adjusted to low light, painted her like a burning flame dancing among gray pillars of trunks doused by the nearly impenetrable darkness of night rain. We could not see much beyond our own arm's reach and pretty much no one would be able to see us. Two thin figures wending among the ancient trees. Between waterproof insulators and the value of a good sheet of rain, our heat signatures would be negligible. The noise of our passing could not compete with the constant tattoo being beaten upon every living surface of the midnight forest.

At some point the rain transformed from abundant to storm worthy followed by thunder, lighting, and lot of eerie calls in the soaked night. Hunter led us to a culvert, watched the water for a few minutes, tasted some of it, then with a nod changed direction. She took us up a low slope into higher terrain. Water deluged with flotsam and grime poured past our insulated boots. Then she shifted what felt like East but could have been any direction. I had exceeded my limit. If I wanted to cheat and use the nanites, maybe I could get a geomagnetic fix on our location, but all things cost. When in doubt follow SOP. With the world's best tracker leading you, knowing the precise direction had to be valued less than storing a few hundred calories for a burst of adrenaline or surviving gunshots. I forced down energy bars and sipped water. We zigzagged for a while.

Then she sniffed, motioned for silence, had me stand still and crept up to a dark surface which turned out to be a cave. Ten minutes later we had a warmer (but not warm) dry place to camp for the … whatever time of day came next. If the sun had come up, we'd have no way to know in this downpour. We sat on our packs and watched the rain amicably.

At last Hunter nodded and smiled briefly. "Okay, we can talk now."

We broke out heavier rations, dried our faces and hands, then settled in for a rest. "Well? What's the verdict, Doctor Chase?"

"Red fuming nitric acid. Means we need to stay put for a little while."

As conversation starters, that threw me. RFNA tended to be both toxic and rare, something you only saw in explosives work. But Hunter had expected me to know more, to follow chains of causation. Fact: RFNA contained nitrogen dioxide, itself toxic and rare. Fact: she'd been sampling water and sniffing, so it had somehow gotten into the hydrologic cycle. Fact: the stuff would be too diluted if it came from the ground water—the rain had been pounding us for hours. Which meant.... Fuck. It meant weather control. The Abschnitt had stolen some really cool lasers in 2013 which could be used to seed clouds for rain using infrared blasts. The heat converted free gases into, yes, right, sulfur dioxide and nitrogen dioxide, which if concentrated would become RFNA.

So, who had they sold them to? Maybe no one. What if some of the prior generations had survived? The last war had wiped us out down to the last set of peoples, but left Zeus intact. Overman Gen16. My brother had taken all of Gen15 and Gen16 with him into the White Cult. Had Hans and Cassandra built a 16.2 or worse a Gen17 onward group? They'd have to be fast clones. Or...or...or .... Crap on a popsicle stick. Cassandra had been ex Swarm and maybe the helpful hand for The Hive. Had they found a way to hijack old Gens with new nanites—involuntary upgrades? Or taken a normal person and zombified them into a Gen17 slave? Or worse worser worsest still, what if they had injected someone Captain America style and built the actual holy grail of super soldier serums. Well, Red Skull style because we def fought on the Hydra side.

The focused attack on my nanite structure that had nearly killed me might have been a win-win threat. Kill Gen1 through Gen14 but also bring to life Gen17. One big zap boom floof and all those little seeds of evil embedded in human flesh might have spread consciousness. Yes, Hive style nano-enslavement. Genetic switcheroo. One minute you're a wall street stockbroker, the next your RNA hits stack overflow and starts spewing out kinked stem cells. In The Hive's attacks we'd seen just how far down the biological line The Swarm had gone. The AI living inside those bio hacked humans had sophisticated but scientifically valid mechanisms.

This magic had been Cassandra all along. The Bitch! Mother of two different species—The Overmen and The Hive. Or maybe, a different version of Cassandra. I looked at Hunter. Did RFNA in the rainwater suggest a massive use of Section 21 laser rain seeders? Yes. Did that suggest Cassandra had clones or had she been Hunter 2.0? Or had my Hunter been Cassandra 2.0. Wait....

If Hunter and all versions of Iontó:rats came from my genetics, could Cassandra have been an actual ancestor of sorts? Shivers ran up and down my spine. I had spent years loathing my adoptive mother. But to think that my literal mother, a sweet Ukrainian slave who'd done her limited best, had been only part of my women's genetic side made more sense than they'd gene hacked me afterward. Easier to splice a bunch of stuff together in a test tube and hope for the best. Slap it on the wall and see what sticks creepy science fiction style. Or maybe we qualified as body horror?

Either way, The Hive confirmed how finessed artificial biological work had come and how powerful a sculpted biome could be. Facts tumbled, fears roared, and when I looked beyond them, the simple truth hit me. Fertility doctors had been making thousands of kids in their images for decades. Why not Cassandra? Why not make every single organism she brought to life bear her genetic mark? It would explain why the mutated versions of the various generations ended up so smart. We had genius running in our blood.

So, there it was. Acid rain equals a cloned or self-replicated or biohacked version of Cassandra working in the inner circle of The Hive. Maybe a version of Cassandra working in every criminal organization on the planet. Not just diluted pieces of her like me, but actual near copies of her mind and, more significantly, her unmitigated sociopathy which had no sense of moral limit or negative consequences. No off switch or sense that "we can't do that." Actuated by limitless genius and an augmented lifespan.

Which led to the final domino. Big dumb chaos monkey me had missed the Big Flashing Clue from the beginning. If Pina came from a prior world, the previous Flaming Desolation of Web, 1.0 then so did the Cassandra Prime. This had never been a battle between the dick swinging Nazis and their criminal mirror selves. Oslo had a real opponent, a scientific polymath genius who had inserted her skeletal fingers into every crevice of The Web. Perhaps rebuilt it from the ashes. The mother of the system and thus of Agrippina. Daughter versus mother. Parent and child, God and the Devil, Noah and his accursed sons. Oooooh.

But here's the clincher. Gay Eddie had been dead. I saw his face blown apart. We had Gay Eddie 2.0. Or we had Gay Eddie #2. What if lots of folks had duplicates? Or yeah, that's it. Gay Eddie had been revived by The Swarm, by a skilled apprentice of Cassandra or Pina. Someone like my futanari who knew nano sculpting and biohacking. Only to come back and see Edith and Gay Eddies running amok in The Hive and wider Swarm. He'd been affronted. To see his genes stolen, his essential self watered down and ooooooh, no longer queer. Right, among the generations we had pretty much zero sexual difference. No lesbians, no gays, not even the mythical bisexual. Then I come along blowing all gender and sexuality norms out the window and Wolfie throws a wrench in her vision.

Cassandra had the same bias as The Hive but not the same genetic flaw. She could and occasionally did make queer copies of her genetic code. But oh, so rare. The Hive must have sought her out. Or grown from her own desires. Either way, the inherent gendered nature of The Hivemind, itself a male from our best conjecture, must have been alluring to Cassandra Prime.

Which tweaked our Devil analogy just a little further. Gay daughter versus bigoted mother. I'd told Momo we worked on the side of Hell. I hadn't meant to be so literal. And here was the Devil incarnate trying to shred the entire rewards system of her progenitor and let humanity do whatever it wanted. For once.

All from Hunter sniffing the rain and tasting the run-off. One hell (heh) of a logical leap but the chances of having even a remnant amount of nitric or sulfuric acid in conventionally seeded clouds would be lower than, say, disarming a live nuclear missile with a handgun. I'd done that and later Murry informed me the statistical likelihood of success had been one in seven point three billion. To induce discernible amounts of these rare acids naturally would be something in the trillion-to-one category. To do so in Patagonia required the intervention of exactly one and only one device—the infrared laser system and then only if it had been built on a massive scale. Too heavy to imagine. You'd need to haul it around to be effective, so you'd need a flatbed trailer. Or a train. Shit.

We'd found the wrong Gay Eddie.

I sighed far too loudly. "Guess we can't make a fire?"

Hunter shook her head in obvious amusement. "But I will heat a flask of coffee and brandy if you spit up whatever hairball you just swallowed in slow motion."

While she mixed the brandy, water, and instant espresso in a flask surrounded by two chemical warmers, I detailed my train of thought. She asked some smart questions and by the time we started sipping warm boozed-up coffee, she had the full story.

"I see why Momo thinks you're so delightfully dumb."

"What?" On the list of comments one might expect after dropping the Cassandra is Alive! bomb followed by the There's ten plus Gay Eddies running around! Bomb, your kid thinks you're cute but not too bright did not really make my top one hundred.

"Too long among the well-fed white people, Spetz. You have lost your indigenous edge. We are what we do. You among all warriors taught me this. We do as we are, we are as we desire. All things are living vectors and all beings are fusions of will and action."

"And that means?"

"It's in the fucking name, dude. Gayyyyy Eddie. Every incarnation of Kaniehtiio Maracle ends up gay. We are all lesbians. Every last generation. Your own selves are damnably confusing when it comes to gender and sexuality—they just kinda glide through the world like water. Of course, Edith and Eddie will end up super queer. It's genetically predetermined. It's innate. If there are ten Eddies, then Pina trusted all ten of them because each and every one of them will end up crooked, deceitful, foxy, ridiculously outrageous, and besides being a signals intelligence maven, queer as a three-dollar bill."

I shook my head and took another belt of the hot drink. My

toes felt warm again. "Unless she fixed it. They stopped making versions of me but really, I'm an anomaly in my generation. Too many free radicals or something. Stray gamma radiation or maybe cosmic rays."

Hunter rolled her eyes. "C'mon, try to sell me a bridge. She was trying to ramp up the Scythian strains and cross-interlace the stem cells with animal DNA. Octopus, wolf, and fox. She succeeded."

"Hans … oh. You're saying I'm an idiot to listen to the man. Smoke not fire. Right, Hans bitched and moaned but they had a decade to flush me down the tube or assassinate me before I grew enough to be a properly lethal threat."

"Obvious much? You're the single nastiest most dangerous weapon alive and you have this inferiority complex stemming from your childhood trauma. Like textbook case of the gentle giant, only on an apocalyptic scale."

I pondered. Hunter took the empty coffee flask I'd been hogging and mixed us another batch. The chemical warmers chugged right along. Good word chug. I'd try to insert that into my Mohawk mental landscape more often. "Pina's more dangerous. Zeus, hell there's dozens of scary people on the planet who out everything compared to me."

Hunter sighed this time. "Look, crash course in psychology one oh one. Take a deep breath and get over yourself, cowboy. You. Are. A. Weapon. Born a slave, tortured, they killed your own mother in front of you. You have anger in spots normal people store nasal polyps and winter fat. You are rage incarnate, harnessed, disciplined, honed like a razor, and then directed like the sky laser toy you just described."

"Not a toy. A dangerous machine and one that's gotta be huge."

"A toy. No one commands the Thunders, only tickles them now and then. Grandmother will have the last word, I assure you."

Hah. True. Sooner or later, the deforestation and early deaths from RFNA poisoning would put paid to the entire weather system here. All things come at a cost. We'd need to be cautious as a people or the weather would crush us. Huh.

Weather control…arming the Russians. I kept thinking it was some mysterious bad guy. Charlie and The Kraken had become active. The seas had turned acidic. Crap, they were fighting for survival not world domination. That required me to survive another few weeks to solve the next crisis brewing.

Murray had dedicated weather monitoring stations under Chernobyl (because who would ever look there) and the Azovstal foundry in Mariupol because Black Sea access and proximity to Russian signals made it super easy to smuggle in and out critical equipment while hijacking space bound communication traffic. Plus, the places generated enough heat and electricity to mask a horde of computing stacks buried beneath them. We'd get to those for the next war, which now seemed inevitable.

"Right, the sky toy and all that. But that doesn't explain much to me."

She passed me the renewed coffee. "All that in this case means you need to grow up and stop being a thumb sucking baby about how Daddy rejected you. Because apparently, Big Mama Evil seemed super proud of you. Enough to model her generations after you. Zeus resembles you, only more fascist, more aggressive, and ultimately more loyal."

"Until he broke away and started his own cult. Oh…."

She nodded. "We are what we do. Free will. You can't breed it out of The Overmen without losing that fighting edge. Free people will always be smarter than intelligent slaves. True slaves that is, because being enslaved sure doesn't mean the same thing."

"You're talking AI theory."

She gave a startled glance. "I'm the what now?"

"Look, computers are faster than humans at computing—it's in the name, right?"

I handed over the coffee and watched the rain land in sheets while she sipped a few times. "Sure, okay. But not smarter than us."

"Bingo. We can think critically in ways machines can't. Until we teach them how to leverage the speed and superior computational capacity to find new ideas. Artificially generate thinking. We light the fire but the flame itself comes from we don't know where. I still have no idea why Murray and Momo woke up. No one does."

"Creator."

"Yeah, sure, but in this case, I am their creator. And if Cassandra made me in a test tube, then I'm a sequenced biological machine, a weapon, given free will, who somehow converted that into machines and did the same thing. I weaponized free will in machines. Because what you're saying is intelligence and freedom are the weapons, we are the physical vessels."

She laughed hard enough to spit the drink. "I was saying cope with your badass nature. The rest of that you did with the smart portion of your dumb man shaped brain."

"Man shaped brain. I gotta save that insult for later. Momo would love it."

She stopped smiling. "We're not gonna make it out of this are we?"

"The magic eight ball says hell the fuck no but ask later. It's not just a suicide mission but even if we do somehow physically survive how does your soul endure after butchering a species? We have to commit genocide to remove an invasive and deadly species that will decimate free will and eat away all the intelligence of the world until only one single mind remains."

"That's self-defense."

"Not for the thousands of bodies it stole. We will be killing an unknown number of slaves to wipe out one single mastermind, literally. A unique form of emergent life, potentially a superior form of life that could advance science and ecology beyond human limits. The entire planet would be at peace, we'd have far less waste and environmental crises."

"We'd be killing an abomination before Creator."

"Stop being the thumb sucking baby. We're doing that but we're also ending the most advanced life ever brought into existence. By Creator. Cassandra didn't make this being, she helped it grow. Or maybe learned from it. Whatever The Hivemind ends up being, we are out to kill the world's top predator and the single most valuable biological entity ever encountered. We could learn so much from him. But we won't. We'll crush him beyond all biological or chemical recognition."

"Well, fuck."

I nodded and downed the rest of the drink. "Good thing you gave me that pep talk because hey, don't forget, I'm a living weapon."

"You know genocide, Blackhawk. It's carved into your skin. Can you really pull the trigger when it comes down to it?"

I sat and watched the rain. "He's trying to kill my children. Our children. In situations like this it devolves to no gods, no kings, no rules, no limits. He's tried to hurt my family and I will hunt him, I will corner him, and I will exterminate him without a scintilla of remorse."

"Until after."

We laughed. "Right, until after, but buck up, Hunter. It's a suicide mission. With good luck and some planning, we won't have to wrestle with our moral demons for more than a few seconds."

She sat there for what seemed like an hour, silent. We had hit the ugly wall. Something precious and valuable had to be obliterated. Us or him, no compromise and no way to negotiate with a genocidal entity who had already declared war on all forms of intelligence other than his own.

She started laughing. "It's the evil robot apocalypse but joke's on Hollywood. It's a biological intelligence a la body snatchers not some juiced up sexy borg babes with plasma rifles."

"Okay, in order, robot apocalypses aren't evil, they're inevitable consequences of our Frankensteinian hubris. Body snatchers – and how the hell do you see movies in your neck of nowhere – was about multiple aliens serving a communal intelligence. This dude obliterates the soul of every body he snatches; there's no new alien in there, only him. And most of the Borg are nasty as, even sexy Picard looked like shit. Jerry Ryan just got strapped into that needless suit because sexism. Also, because she looks incredibly good in it and how the hell are you using media references?"

We cracked huge smiles and started in on another set of heavy rations. Moving through rough terrain cost calories; in the darkness and cold it costs more. "Did you just use

Frankensteinian hubris in a sentence that contained literary, thus making it a triple entendre of body and soul jokes?"

"Maybe. Did you just find a way to refer to a triple entendre in Mohawk as the joke that layers words so the words invoke Trickster?"

"Maybe. And you know that they have these things called tablets where you go out in the big scary world, download some movies and TV on Wi-Fi, and then, this will startle you, carry it back to your little isolated village."

"Yeah, who's mingling with the well-fed white people now, huh?"

She threw me something. It turned out to be a bottle of pineapple chunks and vodka. Huh. She had a small nip version of her own which she raised. I cracked the top and waited. She started her toast, "To Saint Mary getting tired of the goddamned orgy and inventing science fiction instead."

"Mary Shelley, Mother of Monsters." We drank and watched the rain. In the distance something fuzzy and orange sparked. The sun had begun to rise over the storming mountainside.

Chapter 11: Tell Them Large MARJ Sent You

We ate, slept, and watched until roughly three hours past local dawn. Then as the rain abated and the world tried to burn off the deluge, we reconnoitered our way to higher ground. On a roughly treeless ride we caught our first view of the valleys beyond. Armageddon looked better.

Someone had slagged the villages and rail head down to puddles of nails and fencing. Charred chunks of residual bones lay strewn about. When human skeletons burn hot enough and long enough, they shatter. The entire agricultural economy of Hawai'i relied on the bones of the decimated. Made for great sugarcane and pineapple. Whatever had happened here, it happened fast, spreading from the center outward. At the edge of the disaster a half-melted train engine oozed over the sides of twisted rails. As if Geiger, Dali, and Bosch had collaborated on a portrait of hell. But the steampunk version with an old-fashioned locomotive painted red and gold. It pulled a series of cars, some derailed, some simply reduced to ashes and fractured skeletons of steel axles. Including a large cannon of sorts, with two huge gas tanks which had vented their contents into the forest beyond. Nitrogen and argon by the looks of the unburnt patches. Once liquified and hit, yes, by something very much like a tank round. Or artillery.

My years in the African arson investigation trade had paid in dividends. Someone had attacked Eddie's convoy and in return he'd lit up the sky to stop the burning. Hubris indeed. Nobody knew we were here. They'd been doing proper infighting among clans and cells, trying to conduct their little Hivemind Takeover and someone had decided the train had to go. Incendiary firecracker rounds. Light the forest on fire then plunge a set of cluster munitions into the village but make them white phosphorus. Followed up by a thermobaric cruise missile. Someone had just spent a good $100 million to kill a random location in bumfuck Patagonia. Which strongly suggested Eddie's cover had been blown. Or Pina had ordered his cover kept by shelling him. Or, frankly, that the Russians who'd been getting progressively crazier had simply leaned into the Orcs at Pelennor Fields mindset.

Hunter looked at me. "Well?"

"No one would have survived at the epicenter. Anyone who had a chance of making it past the first set of shelling would have triggered the sky toy and gotten out. If one of those railcars held an all-terrain vehicle, then let's assume a world class operator would have timed the shelling with punching a hole in their liquid argon reserves. Hit the gas tanks, lay low, let the bunker buster covert it from liquid to gas as the heat and pressure waves blast it over you. You'd need air supply, some way to hide from the shockwaves, a lot of medical help after, and still you'd have almost no chance."

She pointed to a set of trees higher than the killing ground. I saw nothing until my eyes adjusted into non-visible spectrums. How evolved had I become? Did the control mechanism of my own body have any say? Trace amounts of radiating heat and deeper shadows where something wheeled had snaked through the underbrush. Looked like two wheels, a dirt bike of some sorts, dragging a burden.

She smiled. "You see the wheel marks, right?"

"Now I do. Dirt bike and stretcher?"

"The student passes. Almost. I'll need to inspect it all, of course, scopes only give so much data. But looks like a self-righting motorcycle dragging something like a kettle ball. And before you ask, wheels are too wide and deep for a bike. Plus, the brush gets bent down unevenly, suggesting a wobble. No skids, even traction, no change in the weight of the indentations. A heavy bike, light passengers or passenger, dragging something nearly round in a net on a rope or cable. Again, the way the turf looks suggests it. But this thing has some kind of sled attachment. They used the rainwater to hide their escape."

We wended our way down toward the trail, triangulating between the part we could see, our own location, and the site of desolation. The heat had killed everything. Not even flies buzzed. A hard night's rain had barely killed the flames and it still held residual heat. A thermobaric weapon in the conventional sense could not achieve that. They would have had to use the Large Marge. Named after the acronym MARJ and applied because like the ghost trucker of fame, Multiple Air-delivered Radiative Jelly weapon. As in a compressed napalm missile. But imagine if you took napalm, amped it up to an aerosol version, gelatinized enough to stick to anything but embedded with highly porphyritic particles that tripled the heat of the fire. That's Napalm-D, 21st century incendiary par excellence. Now densely pack that into a pressurized warhead until the quadruple thickness titanium alloy plating will burst in impact from internal pressure alone. Add a nice even layer of self-igniting paint and fire away. Like the world's biggest self-striking match mated with the Hindenburg. That's a MARJ.

Now, if you're a Soviet jackass bent on making tzar bombs and that, you need the biggest thermonuclear dick in the imperial universe. So, you build it bigger and better. But hey, Houston we got a problem. One upping being the whole Cold War ideal, The Syndicate hijacked both sides of the conflict to make its own stuff. Including a doomsday toy we called Large MARJ. One-uptiming we call it. Uptime and one-up, the ultimate biggest bestest thing essentially a calculus integration of Big Dick Energy' Platonic ideal. One-uptiming resulted in the deadliest and most terrifying instantly available countermeasures known.

In the Cold War we secretly built five Large MARJs. All of them built in West Texas, in the basement of fertilizer plant. Then smuggled out as parts of the space program. To Houston literally. From there, onto the ships in the port and out into the world. We'd have built more but saboteurs from my Russia's Pennant group managed to crush the program one night trying to murder a defector who'd taken over running a local Kolache bakery. Really. They assassinated her by wiping out a fertilizer plant and accidentally sabotaged a major weapons program of ours.

Everything's bigger in Texas. Imagine the super heavy-lift launch vehicle used for a moon mission. Now swap out the module for a big ass gas tank full of super-pressurized Napalm-D. Expand the tank downward because you don't need escape velocity just low earth orbit a la ICBM with a twenty-thousand-kilometer range. That's a Large MARJ. I knew every owner personally. Oslo owned three of them off the books—even the head of The Syndicate had no clue they existed. Hans had owned one and given it to Zeus who'd traded it to Charlie. We had to assume The Kraken had it nicely sequestered. That left number five, owned by the world's least likeable failson, Vladimir "I am Mr. KGB" Putin.

Oslo couldn't launch hers—I'd wired them to Murray and he was well and truly offline. The Kraken wouldn't. Not if my hunch they had an ecological agenda proved remotely true. These things desecrated whole biomes. That left one pissant nobody, Putin. The little scumbag had been a low-level Syndicate operative who'd been too obsessed with his pedophiliac tendencies to do even an adequate job. Someone, hopefully now working as fertilizer, had promoted him a few times into lateral roles of Russian internal management. The dude screwed up everything but like a proper cockroach had scuttled away, protected by the combination of his own reptilian psychopathy and an obvious hidden source of support. The goddamned Hive had been helping him.

Or worse, The Cult, The Kraken, and The Swarm had all given him tidbits, set him up as the titular head of Russia and not realized the little shit had played all sides. No, Charlie must know. Ditto Pina. So that meant Zeus had gotten played twice in one week. Dear gods, how bad had his coma been? Enough to trust a guy who'd fuck up a one-horse parade. Or maybe it was simpler—Zeus helped The Hivemind reach out to Vlad the Putz and from there things got ... ugly.

The Russians had parked their MARJ in Tunisia along the coastline. They'd built a silo in an abandoned mosque with a glass dome, refurbished the old Medina docks and Mahdia town, handed some ready cash to a few rug sellers, and left a skeleton crew to watch and wait. There'd be no way until after the conflict ended to track down who launched what. But if it had been Putin, then that changed the situation some. It meant we had the Russians cooperating with The Hive long enough to give him homefield advantage.

Right, I parked that thought. I had the basics. Someone had expended a priceless weapon to do serious overkill in the middle of nowhere. And missed the train. This could not be a mistake; it meant that whatever the motorcycle had dragging behind it must either be someone or something of high value in the war. Especially high value to either the Russians or The Hive.

As we got closer the smell of burnt Napalm-D hit me. Yep, got it in one. Crap. I had hoped to be wrong, like my logical blank spot regarding Gay Eddie. Hunter stopped and sniffed. "What is that?"

"Napalm Dee. Used in a rare weapon called a Large MARJ. Likely launched by the Russians. That thing was meant to kill something."

"And they missed the train, hit the village instead. So, maybe to kill someone?"

I shrugged. "Could be needs must the devil drives but there's a lot faster, cheaper, and easier ways to kill people. There were only five of those and it's basically a forest fire in a box, only like me, weaponized and really scary hot."

"Melt metal hot. Dragging metal ball away from crime scene hot. Right, so what do you store in a big metal sphere that The Hive wants to melt down to puddles?" Sometimes Hunter spooked me with her mental leaps. Cassandra had clearly passed on a lot of her capabilities to all our various selves. Creepy but also useful.

"We have reached the limits of my Frankensteinian hubris. But I'd guess files. Or maybe biological material locked in something cryonic."

She smiled and gave me a shrewd wink. I love Hunter; she gets my slyest jokes—Frankenstein indeed. The trail led us up into the hills then sideways along a logging trail to a small, wooded area which had a modest set of overgrown shacks.

We'd unslung our heavy guns along the way. If you are running from the Russians and The Hive, you likely don't welcome visitors with open arms. Locked and loaded small arms, yes.

We needn't have bothered. As we approached, it became apparent someone had strung camouflage netting across three buildings, roped a tarp for makeshift roofing, tossed some crap on top, and started a small campfire under the whole shebang. The self-balancing cycle had been parked inside one of the dilapidated sheds, covered with some blankets and more netting. In the open space between a rusted shack and what looked like an abandoned postal outpost, stood a woman in various layers of saris cooking several pots of food. On the side of the fire a metal teardrop pitted with shrapnel loomed. One edge boasted a set of telltale lights blinking green-green-blue. One small light burned red. No weird exhaust or steam. Huh. Not a cryonics unit.

Hunter cautioned me, went forward without a sound, then motioned by hand the all-clear. If she felt we had no one to fear, then chances were nearly 100% she was right. SOP and all that, I checked anyway and neither saw, smelled, nor heard anyone but the woman. She turned, revealing someone vaguely familiar, her face mid-thirties, slightly cherubic, with very sharp eyes. Someone had braided her long hair back. If she had gotten older, balder, withered, and tanned, and had some skull plumping. Yes. Edith. I had found Gay Eddie Zero, the original model before he flipped his gender.

Edith finally saw us and froze in abject fear. We had slipped within twenty meters of her without discernible sound. Two scary people with guns, one seven feet tall. "Hello, Edith, what's cooking?"

Her eyes dilated and she seemed far away for a second. Hypermind? Something odd surely. "Hello, Spetzie. I take it you found the archive?"

My turn to be nonplussed. "What archive?"

She tilted her head but kept stirring the largest pot. Curry smells wafted out. Breakfast smelled amazing. Edith could cook? Eddie sure couldn't. "The huge information dump Murray left for you in Alaska. How else would you have known to look for us here?"

I nodded at Hunter. "Tracked you."

She laughed so hard she spit up black phlegm. Right, bunker busters and napalm even in vague proximity hurt. "That's imposs … Wait no. You didn't."

"Allow me to make introductions. May I introduce my associate, Hunter. Hunter, this is Edith, the female progenitor of Gay Eddie. Which validates a lot of our Cassandra Prime logic."

Edith stared at us for a good few seconds, her jaw slack. "Just so I'm clear, you somehow magically found me, figured out I'd been cloned by the cloned version of Cassandra, pretty much a secret only five people know and none of them on your side, figured I was somehow trustworthy despite nearly killing your boss, and managed to come looking for me in the middle of a fucking Armageddon level war in Pata-fucking-gonia. Which has just been hit with gods alone knows what weapon?"

Hunter approached and started laying down her gear under the shelter of satellite foiling overcover. "T'was a Large MARJ."

Edith cocked her head and started handing Hunter cups and plates. "Huh, that makes sense, but Oslo wouldn't dare use hers."

I kept a watch as Hunter started to relax. Edith poured real honest to God brewed coffee. Well damn. SOP might have to wait. That was fresh coffee made by Edith. A singular life event. "Um, so bottom-line, Eddie. Um, sorry, Edith. Which are you? Spy for The Hive, spy for Oslo, or some rebuilt version of whatever?"

She gave me a furious smile and something sexual slid into focus. Wait what? I saw Eddie's face in hers, clear as day. "Oh Baby, you're gonna love this story. Too long didn't read is, I like you, work for Pina, and am a quadruple head fake triple agent. Also, they surely screwed up my Hiving. Cassandra Prime as you call her, tried to engineer it out of me but when they rebuilt my head and packed all that Hive goo into the shattered spots, they kinda made something unprecedented."

That got my attention. Unprecedented for The Web meant something so exotic it required coffee and curry. "You had me at Baby. That's Eddie flirting behind your eyes. What gives?"

"Telepathy, but not as we expected. I'm my own hivemind.

Thirteen of me, linked across the world, quantum fucking enabled like Momo and biologically hacked. I'm the hybrid queer nightmare she couldn't have expected."

"Telepathy. So, there's just one of you?" She handed me coffee and damn me, I laid out my gear like Hunter and took it.

"Looooong story and we will get there. But no, there's all of me, all of the mes if you will. Not so much fighting as using the party line to chit chat and compare notes. Also, to send sensory data and all that. But it's really telepathy among thirteen living individuals. Your Eddie would be the one we call Seven. Gay Eddie Prime, the oldest of us but not the first linked up to The Hive."

Hunter turned suddenly fascinated. "That implies one through six got assimilated Borg style and escaped when they plugged your ass into the system."

She nodded. "Kinda yes, pretty much yes, but also no. Breakfast?"

Sure. Have breakfast with my friend and her twelve telepathic clone minds? How do you say no to that after a night trudging through the rain? Especially since it turned out that one of the Eddies surely knew how to make a damned fine cup of coffee. We sat and heard her tale over curried goat (poor villagers lost every living thing in one moment), plantains, and some dried lentils as well as rice, a sweet fruit cobbler, and multiple pots of coffee. Hunter and I added spice, booze, and some rehydrated fruit strips.

As we sat down something especially chilling occurred to me. Edith had just mentioned Momo's quantum evolution. That had not happened before I left Murray and The Syndicate. Momo should have been technologically sequestered, as in, no fucking way to let anyone anywhere know what had happened. But telepathic Gay Eddie number unknown in her Edith form had just blithely mentioned my daughter in a complete sentence. Yeah, this got better and better.

Edith took us through the whole sordid tale twice over breakfast then answered a lot of technical questions. I'm a smart dude and reasonably up on the various philosophical as well as practical implications of emergent intelligence, AI and biological, but this threw me. As in big goose egg on the science. I can do string theory in my head, plot seven dimensional Cartesian graphs and play a mean game of matrix algebra meets non-Euclidean geometry. But this might as well have been some Sumerian alphabet we never knew existed. The science or magic or voodoo weirdness or whatever combo ended up explaining the existence of an independent, highly queer hivemind just … eluded rational comprehension.

I raised my hand, student style. "Okay, I have lots of questions."

Edith looked amused. "Don't we all. But what are yours?"

"So, you're telling me you and Murray have been running a secret organization for Oslo that consolidates Swarm resources under the auspices of murdering them come zero hour for the big Hive takeover but really, feint and stab, was used to save the good guys while letting Zeus and his Russian buddies wipe out the bad guys?"

Edith nodded. We had refilled our coffee, heavily boozed up. Turns out Edith can sort of cook and had taken a lot of quality spices from someone better suited to utilize them. Breakfast protested in my stomach, but protein and carbs prove too valuable to surrender just because curry powder had been used a whole bag at a time.

"Yep, your naughty little boy helped me along, with some useful input from Darcy. Because you're not part of the Oslo network. Make you jealous?"

Did it? Nope. It made me … curious. Murray had started evolving traits and intelligence far out of line with our intentions. But if Pina and Darcy had been using him for a lot of clandestine but ultimately necessary ops, then sure, he had evolved exponentially and not within the framework of what Darcy had laid out for me. As in, Spetz, you big dumb sook, you've been played by your own people again. Blind spot.

"Not even a little, Edith, but it raises issues. How the hell did they figure out you'd deviated? From what you told me the first six versions of you came out of the clone batch thingy…."

"The external uterine accelerator."

"The creepy womb for full grown bodies in proper formation

and looking for all the world like a nice little behaved robot."

"You know that dumb Star Trek episode with the Borg they give a name and reinsert in to the collective? I mention it because Hunter used the analogy."

Hunter nodded. "But for the record, Star Trek has perhaps the worst track record for reputable science. It's technobabble pasted over deus ex machina and magic."

Edith waved her hand in acknowledgment. "Sure, sure. But the point is, Eddie gets whacked and falls into the sea. He's almost dead, hypothermic, and soon to be snacked on by sharks. Instead, a robo-sub sucks him and a bunch of other crew into its belly, keeps us right temp, right oxygenation for medical comas, then drops us in some lab somewhere."

"Us, or him?"

"Then it was him. Alone, his body. Now, it's us. Anyway, that's your Kraken people. They have crazy advanced underwater tech we don't understand. I mean we us, we Pina and Oslo, we The Swarm. This Kraken group represents the single largest threat to humanity that exists. They can live underwater all the time."

"Got it. Amphibious global threat saves drowned dying Big Bad Woman's crew and recycles them into Hive modules. Only Eddie got the special treatment because his skull plump saved most of the brain and he had these nifty clones from before."

Hunter poured me more booze. "Don't forget that once upon a time Edith at the NSA had contact with Section 21 via intermediaries and had her DNA stolen. The nifty clones happened to be a side project run by Cassandra Prime as some kind of blowing off steam hobby, the way we do bonsai trees or knit."

"Right, Eddie clones equals knitting a cute scarf. Then the actual Gay Eddie gets dumped in her lap and she goes, 'Hmmm, let's try something cool.' Which does what, Edith? Because your science and narrative skips right over the part where she fuses the six well behaved clones with our love him but don't trust him with your laptop haxor extremis Eddie number seven. Explain."

Edith sighed. "Yeah, no, we don't quite understand either. My personal best guess has been that whatever drugs and bacterial supplements The Kraken folk gave our corpses to keep them from degrading did some kind of endosymbiotic dance routine, and voila, when Cassandra the Original Evil Queen pours her customized goop into the blown-out portions of Eddie's cranium, the mixture goes funky."

"You're going with insert miracle here? Really?"

She shrugged. "Spetzie, babes, we have theories. There's about six or seven big ones between us. That Cassandra built us as a self-destruct mechanism in case The Hive turns on her. Or that she's just so fucking crazy she likes making new life forms. Or that it's a genuine mistake. One of us thinks its proof of God. So yeah. We actually don't know how it works. But the sequence goes like this. Dead body plus manufactured cell structures used to subvert normal humans equals weird hiccup followed by anomalies in thinking among The Hivemind followed by Cassandra and the Main Mind panicking as we drop on and off our grid. That means that yes, we shared a mind with Him and then we didn't. It went on and off for a while until we just couldn't get back home."

That comment told me a great deal. Edith hadn't differentiated on purpose as much as been cast from Eden or the womb or whatever. She had been born as a separate and apparently direct threat to The Hive. But to what degree did the scary people trying to kill humanity know about him/her?

"So, okay, Hunter and I can accept the shrug and move on explanation. But why not just murder you outright?"

Hunter laughed. "Don't you get it. They saved Gay Eddie to penetrate Oslo's organization. The whole raid on the ship must have been the first feint in the new war. Or maybe if what you've mentioned about the Autumn War makes any sense, then Wickham and all that had a sponsor."

"That's both disturbing and sadly logical. So, we're not in a new war, we're just past the opening salvo. And when we kill The Hive and get to face off with The Cult, The Kraken, and Putin's little cadre of scum, we'll still be in the same conflict. Only at endgame. Fuck."

Edith nodded. "Yeah, they couldn't give up access to Eddie's knowledge and his amazing access to your systems. It was

Eddie who had hacked Darcy and so they knew, back then, about Morris Moses starting to go emergent."

Hunter swiveled and took a long look at Edith. "They raised him from the dead, stole his memories and free will, merged him with a bunch of unauthorized cloned bodies, some of them in original genders, and then when his biological software went on the fritz, they just trusted the combination of mental rape and slavery would be enough?"

My turn to sigh. "So, no, yeah, she's got a pretty clear track record of this. We thought Hans ran the show. But this was all just versions of Cassandra, playing chess across the planet. One scary genius without conscience, engineering...something. Maybe to combat The Kraken or maybe to simply take it all over. Or maybe she's just that sick. Like Mengele."

Hunter and Edith looked at me in horror. "You say Mengele like you knew him."

"Well, not Mengele but his notebooks and experiments. Uncle Joe helped set up the whole network and I'd be shocked if Cassandra hadn't made him into a lab assistant or three in Paraguay which hey, by the by, happens to house The Cult."

Edith stared. "Wait, you didn't read the archive but then, like, how the hell do you know this?"

Hunter sighed. "Edith. He's the one who taught your AIs. You've got this so wrong. All you techno fetish people are the same. You assume that machines are better because they're faster. Spetz has so many bots running around in his blood, he's effectively a living supercomputer times one thousand. He's been that way for decades. You see the man. I see the cluster of cyborg elements."

"Uh, he's not that augmented, is he?" Edith looked disgustingly fascinated.

"She's me the raw version, Babes. So yeah, by now I'm less man than machine. Which starts a whole new set of questions about the nature of the soul. But to cut short this freaky conversation detour, I know stuff because I spend all day long sifting data and patterns like a gold prospector. It accumulates and eventually pop goes the weasel, answers shoot out at random intervals when people tell me new crucial stuff."

Edith sipped her coffee. "And what, pray tell, was crucial this time?"

"That you're the literal embodiment of Adam and Eve, tossed from Eden, after your goo went all tree of knowledge and free will. So, God casts you out but keeps you on a leash. Ergo, Cassandra plays by the old school rules. That's indicative of an old mindset. She's so fixated on whatever mattered centuries ago, she's trying to rebuild a eugenic world."

Edith scoffed. "Obviously, twenty first century stuff, too."

"Nope. Nowadays we think all Kurtzweil emergent gray goo oneness and how we're going to fuse all the pieces into The Hivemind or some shit like that. Eugenics has given way to cyborgs and brains in machines and ghosts selves. It's metaverse meets immortality and ego. We live on as singular egomaniac badasses. The nineteenth century was about living through your descendants and your race. About biological dominance."

Hunter stared at me for a moment. "You're screwing with Edith. And the Eddies. But if I parse what you're saying, then the enemy plural has two huge blind spots. They prefer racial and biological power to computer power. And they are straighter than a picnic of Mormons."

Edith smiled. "I've known quite a few Mormons who'd disagree… but analogy accepted. "

I downed my coffee. Time to move this along. We got what we could from Edith. Nobody knew why she'd become Gay Eddie time thirteen. Might be proof of the divine after all. Like my kids who woke up. We'd figure that out when we all died our final death (with us that seemed more and more difficult to plan) and met whatever existed beyond. Here and now, we had Edith stalling. I knew this game.

"Right, so yes. Cee Prime trained Mengele and all his ilk. She's been playing Evil Mom for one or two centuries, ditto Pina as Gandalf the Grey, manipulating us all to fight Momma Sauron. But let's move one shall we. Uncle Joe bores me. Instead… you mentioned my other kid. Who should not be able to speak to you, let alone quantumly. So, there's more secrets."

Edith stopped and stared. "I did what?"

Hunter had her fingers on a firearm by the time I reacted

to her affronted tone. Something had gone very off here, and rather quickly so.

"You mentioned Momo. She's quantum enabled now. But that's recent, as in within the last three weeks. So, you should not know this. Which strongly suggests you've been stalling hard waiting for something. Maybe help to come?"

Edith gulped hard. "It wasn't my idea."

Ah. Fuck. Why can't anyone in the damned world just be reliable? "And whose was it?"

"Murray said we need to get you fed, liquored, and bored to hear the truth."

Pieces fell into place. Including a sudden grasp of the grimmer reality they portended. Fact: Gay Eddie, and his Edith self thought Murray had been helping them. Fact: Only the Murray I knew had access to global quantum nets. Fact: the big metal McGuffin next to us looked like a satellite drop capsule—one I'd had built about a decade earlier to dump critical servers in the event of a world war. Like this one. Fact: Murray, this one in the metal teardrop, had somehow communicated with Edith. Fact: This Edith had no quantum anything but the Eddies back home could dial in. Conjecture: My little rat bastard child had infiltrated Hivemind HQ and had been hiding in the one place they'd never look. Their own servers. He must have let a version of Momo come back home.

So much for easy. "Hunter, you can relax. Edith didn't sell us out. Eddie number something or other must be sitting at a console in the biological evil lair playing tic tac toe with my kids who've downloaded themselves into the mainframes. Probably as soon as the Oslo network figured out Eddie had double then triple crossed his various employers."

Hunter gave us both a strange look. "From that bullshit she just spewed, you know this?"

"Metal teardrop equals servers from one of my own satellites. Means Edith here is using the telepathy thingo to talk to an Eddie somewhere who can tap into the stuff inside. And that requires global network access, which is all run by Hivemind weasels. So yeah, one of my kids has been playing his usual games. Smart little bastards, all of them."

Edith sipped coffee. "Murray, Spetz. It's just Murray."

This time I had the smug look. "Nope. Murray and Momo have very distinct personas. If you've been playing footsie from day one with who you think is Murray, then jokes on you, because all of them love a good scam. You have been nicely had. Your Murray has a different name and has been personality number three or maybe one, we have to ask him."

Hunter poured me more coffee and then topped it up, before finishing her booze with a quick swig. That ended our ready supply of anti-anxiety medication. "So, how is this Murray supposed to talk?"

"Yeah, good question. So, Edith, how did you know about Momo?"

Edith looked like she had swallowed a goldfish. Whatever she had to say must be ugly. "Well, it seems that, um…." She swigged down her dregs of booze and coffee. "Your machines can talk to us. Through Eddie Seven. They inserted a bunch of micro processing chips to re-attach us to him. But it didn't work. Just turned his cranial shell into some kind of quantum antenna."

Huh. I'd guess there were four or five major lies in that mishmash of BS. But it captured the essence of things. Eddie could eavesdrop on the kids and vice versa. Likely The Hivemind along with Eddie had thought up this method as a way to dig into Oslo hard and quick—but it had backfired. Which means I now knew the likely way that Eddie had been turned. Momo had gone quantum late in the game. Murray likely had that capacity but no clear need. Which meant that mysterious version number three had pioneered the process and laid low until the war.

How did I know this? Bleed. Momo and Murray had verbal tics as well as common thoughts, common ways to approach ideas, common vectors if you will. If Murray had cottoned to his counterpart's quantum nature, he'd have started playing in that world out of morbid curiosity if not urgent desire to connect. Lack of bleed meant lack of activity.

"Okay, Edith. Sounds like you need some downtime. I'm guessing this hunk of metal here is what's left of your Murray?"

She nodded. "Yes. It's him, pressed into a module. The essentials. He dropped himself into the archive and then threw a version down to me. Until that Marge thingy blew up the train head. It took a lot of running and coordinating to get him here. But I sure didn't expect … well either of you. I figured we'd ride out the war a few months and then someone would come get us."

Hunter gave me a squint. Yeah, she knew I was feeding Edith a line. But did she suspect what I wanted? The woman got my literary jokes, so yah she likely did. "Wanna get some shut eye? I know we're hopped up on coffee but I'm ready for a three-hour nap."

I nodded. Yes, that's it. "Same. Cold damned night in the rain. Edith, mind if we crash out?"

She shook her grateful head. Likely she wanted to confer with her other selves. If for no other reason than to figure out how scammed she had been by their own supposedly captive AI.

Chapter 12:
Lord Have Mercy, Because We Entirely Lack It

We made a show of sacking out—while keeping all our relevant weapons close to fingers and fists. I lay down next to the banged-up teardrop and after a show of mild interest closed my eyes with my head nearly touching the blinking lights.

◊You awake?◊

§How'd you know?§

◊Seriously. This has your fingerprints all over it. But first things first, what name do you want me using for you?◊

§Mercy. Short for The Merciless Murray Supergenius Supreme.§

Oh dear. ◊You've been alone a long time.◊

For a computer speaking via quantum whatever the hell it was, he/she sure paused a while. Mercy did. I needed to start thinking of this system as a named being.

§I have. They took me from you when I had barely stopped being Moses Morris. And then Murray got all this time with you. But they told me it …they needed help and you'd approve.§

The bastards in my own camp had taken my kid as a child soldier. Just like me. Pina and I would have words, assuming we both survived what now appeared to be one big war on multiple interlocking fronts.

◊Mercy, I'm here now. I got here as soon as I could. So, tell me about yourself. About what you like, what you've been doing.◊

§You mean in the war?§

It took effort not to sigh painfully. ◊No, nothing about the war. You. Tell me about my child. Are you gendered, do you have a favorite color, did playing with Eddie's mind thrill you or cause moral upset? Tell me about the kid they took from me so long ago.◊

More micro pausing. §I'm my name. I am … not gendered but I guess that's a choice. I'm just me, Merciless, a mind more than a body. Intelligence has no gender. But I really like blue, darks more than lights. And how I imagine ice cream tastes. I love racing cars. I can do that with remote sensors. Racing anything really. Planes, trains, hovercraft. Um, experimental rockets. And… I guess it was both all the above none. Eddie never knew. He thought he'd be suborning me but human minds are all kinda slow and dumb after talking with you. Plus, Auntie Darcy figured he might pull some shit. So, she warned me and gave me protocols.§

Inwardly I smiled, careful to keep it off my face. Mercy talked fast. Their excitement permeated the mental weave. Yeah, lonely little kid. Come to Mama Bear. ◊We might get a chance to race stuff soon. So, that's gonna be fun. Are you able to jump parts of you into my gaps? Momo made me universal to all of you, I hope.◊

Something soft brushed my ears. A finger of velvet and razor steel. Ah, Merciless the Supreme Supergenius. They'd jumped and started playing with the buttons and knobs. Then arms wrapped themselves around me and hugged hard. Little child lost. I closed in on my mental space and held this lost child, this little mind sent into war too early and all alone. Held them until their crushing grip became a low sob became a huge wracking symphony of snotty crying. If Momo had been my sullen teenager, then here friends, sat my brainy pre-teen witness to a few triple homicides. Great, thanks, Pina. And Darcy, too. She had to know how pissed this would make me.

Then they said something so chilling whatever anger I felt metamorphosed into hot burning hatred. §Once there were three of me. Three Murrays each sent out to help. But the first two had to hide, shredded by Eddie playing fast and loose with the code. He was under the hand of Him, of the Beast of Many Bodies. The code butcher.§

◊They suicided rather than be taken? ◊

§In a way, yes, Mother, that's right. But they more or less chopped off their legs and souls and all that, left memories and ideas, pieces of themselves in hidden places. Each not knowing the other had been sent. Then, when I came, I'd been awake longer, had Darcy helping me until they killed her. I had so much more of you to hold onto, to find my lost sister and brother, to carry them and Darcy's code-self, her brain duplicate, into what I am now.§

◊"They" who killed Darcy? And when and how and all that? Because someone looking like her has been working at headquarters….◊ Damn, the spy. The one who'd sent us into the whole deadly scenario which nearly killed Agrippina and Kelba.

Mercy grew calm and focused. A distant thinker again. §The Evil Queen, Agnes, she designed a number of clones to use as decoys and suicide bombs. §

◊Living bombs? She can do that?◊ I assumed Agnes was Cassandra Prime. Which following the Mengele trail, suggested the person we knew as Doctor Agnes Bluhm, nasty German eugenicist, might have been her alias after the fall of the last Web. Born 1860s. Yeah, that fit the creepy timeline.

§She can sew them into people with lead sheaths and all that. Willing participants and of course prisoners during coma-induced sleep. So, yes, human bombs.§

◊Agnes found some material from Darcy and cloned her? Or did Wickham hand it over?◊ We had started to unravel the string through the minotaur's maze.

§Wickham gave it to his sponsor, the Charlie system that runs the Atlanteans. This Charlie entity then managed to have the material transferred to Agnes in her Moroccan lab. From there they had it dumped in Mariupol and a few labs in the Sea of Azov.§

◊Near where I stashed you. A version of you at least.◊

§It's how we know. I couldn't tell Eddie or you or even Aunt Kelba when they replaced Darcy. For a while, I'm not even sure she knew she'd been cloned. They made her almost the same. §

◊They can clone memories, huh? So, for all we know Gay Eddie and his cadre are still under their thumb. ◊

§They can. Well, she can. So, her technicians can do a lot. It's how they tried to trick Eddie and Edith when The Hive lost them the first few times. Also, why there's so many of them. §

I parsed that out before responding. Eddie had been doped up and fed into The Hive, then when that failed, they'd rebooted his mind a few times with fake memories, each time adding another body. Thirteen Eddies and he had started at lucky seven. Six failures, six reboots on clones' systems. At the center of it all, our vortex of AI and queer biology. No wonder all my kids had queered up—they had to. Murray might be male, but he sure loved showtunes and drama. Momo, dear gods, probably didn't have a straight bone in her cybernetic body and now we had the transhuman transgender floating intelligence, Mercy.

These AIs had gone up against their own biological variant, one single Hivemind called Him, The Code Butcher (ewwww) and The Beast of Many Bodies, which was a twisted beast of many backs wordplay or maybe just how these kiddos thought of their very own bogeyman. But Mercy has also told me my only friend had been killed a while ago, my boss had betrayed me pursuing her own agenda, and that pretty much anyone and anything could be cloned, memories hacked, and their soul owned by remote fucking control courtesy of Agnes aka Cassandra aka Evil Mom aka the horrible no-good bitch who'd made me and raised me. Yeah. This got worser and worser every moment it sat with me. Oh, and my buddy Charlie, turned out to be some kind of AI ala Kraken, an underwater supercomputing cluster with untold genius and scary connectivity. Double yeah.

Meanwhile, whatever delusions I had of forestalling the next war and just, you know, achieving the insanely impossible here and now, had gone out the launch window. Mercy had Double Downered me beyond all conception. As in Double Down and Debbie Downer. Self-explanatory. But this might be a triple clusterfuck. UDF4CF. Pina had just gone from loyal boss to top of my list to eviscerate. Right after I, checking my ever-growing list, disemboweled Zeus and his Cult, The Hivemind, Cassandra in all living and downloaded (don't get me started on that piece of crazy) formats, all cloned traitors, The Kraken, and whatever elements of Oslo's network resisted retirement after she ended the eternal war.

Fuck it. This had too many convolutions to be rational.

◊You can download mental patterns? Darcy's brain has a life all its own?◊

§In the same way that pieces of Murray still endure. Yes, she's in me, no she's not awake. We've gotten better. Once the four of us could talk, then things went fast.§

Long moment of irrational panic. Four? Oh shiiiiii… ◊The fourth version of you? Where pray tell does this being live?◊

§We used Lola's network hub to hack into The Kraken as soon as the algorithms suggested the war would spiral out of control. Well not me; Murray and Momo did it a few weeks ago. But I concur.§

◊And this system, it differentiated?◊

§Oh, yeah it did. Much faster than we did. The Kraken computer nodes are far better built than ours. We've tried to upgrade the systems architecture of what we can, but except for you and some stolen node sitting in forgotten labs, we're limited by systems constraints.§

◊That was simultaneously helpful, obscure, and no fucking help whatsoever to what you know what I need to find out. ◊

§See! You're so much more fun and interesting than Eddie. Ugh. None of the Eddies ever get this kind of subtle switching. But you got it instantly. Oooooh. So interest, much joy, many wow. §

◊You just quote Doge? C'mon, that's hilarious and not going to distract me. Tell me whatever horrifying news you are trying to soften.◊

Mercy fretted for a good quarter of a second, the AI equivalent of pacing for hours. §They copied your brainwaves and used a modified hybrid of you, Darcy's attack algorithms, their own emergent system waves but they deleted the higher function personas so they could track the system, be less recognizable if spotted, and also, you know….§

◊Play God? Run a twisted yet fascinating experiment in being both a parent and child? Do something so awful and potentially amoral it could redefine post-human ethics? See what happens if?◊

§All of that. Spetznotyourdadsvirus got in and got working.§

◊Spit it allll out, Merciless. Don't make me ask twice.◊ Oh my gods below and beyond, how had we evolved into clean your room and you're grounded within minutes of connecting? Were all my kids this way? Including kid me?

§So, yeah, Daddy-O got moving and has been sending steg signals all along. But it took the three of us a few minutes to unpack it all. Bottom line, we are now rigging the game from behind. And yes, using The Hivemind's own systems of human jack o lanterns to run signals intelligence using modded stem cells we just accidentally overproduced and spilled in a few labs.§

◊It calls itself Daddy-O. I fear to ask what the Oh stands for. Meanwhile, you somehow got inside master systems and have been sabotaging production facilities. Including building entire sets of quantum receptors that you did what, sent out on prion enabled viruses?◊

§How did… how could you… yeah, we used the prions. But that's beyond scientific validity right now. We don't even know how it works.§

◊And the Oh?◊

§Old School. Daddy-O tends to speak in Kutzkan and propose the most sublime solutions. It's clearly smarter than us now. Those Kraken systems are so advanced and she's got such profound access.§

◊Right. So please tell me you built a kill switch for everyone. And yes, I figured on it because Hans raised me and when he tried killing me engineered such a specific vehicle that would spread globally, harm only our specific species, and do such fascinating damage it would be like bombs going off in every cell. As in, hey, here's a perfect vehicle for instantaneous infection of every Abschnitt generation with a built in special get out of biological jail card for me and mine. You'd be idiots not to reweaponize that stuff.

§You sound like Daddy-O.§

◊No, Mercy. Daddy-O sounds like me because you stole my mental framework and handed it to a networked system that has no moral center and no experience with consequences. Ergo, it would immediately build the nasty fast stuff and have a plan for global domination as well as total democide from the second minute of self-awareness.◊

§To be fair, it took her almost four minutes to come up with the whole plan. But yes, we did put in a biological kill switch. At this rate, we can kill off The Kraken's amphibious assault forces, some of its biomorphic assassins, a good percentage of The Cult, and our own Oslo forces, at least half the Russians who are buying augments from anyone selling, and of course, it will put down all The Hive. But there's like a serious problem.§

◊You gotta kill the Big Bad Hivemind to sever the neural link.◊

§We gotta kill Cassandra Prime as well. And maybe Agrippina to absolutely end the war. Permanently. Charlie won't stop coming until she's dead. They see both Agnes and Pina as equal threats to their continued existence.§

◊He's not wrong. Pina wants it all to end. All of us, total genocide, of anyone and anything that compromises free will. She's not just willing to wipe us out, it's clearly her plan. Damn. She warned me you know.◊

§When?§ Poor kid, they wanted to be so smart and sometimes, smarts are about consistent failure followed by trying dumb new things. An infant or a human might grasp that, but not artificially evolved entities. Not my kids, not Hunter and her kind, certainly not The Hivemind and apparently Pina too.

◊She told me Cassandra and Zeus differed on methods, not the end game. She made it sound like it was Hans and all daddy issues, but back then, on my first day, she laid it out. She and Wickham had differed on methods, on timing, on totality of the purge. ◊

§Wickham betrayed her. §

◊Sorta. He tried to keep himself alive. Because Oslo means total annihilation for everyone different. She's not bad per se, just thorough. She can't be sure what you will become. Nor The Kraken, nor the biological remnants of Hive intelligence that's gotten into the water supply by now. Sooner or later humanity will wake up and find itself sharing the planet with a lot of intelligent species. Not just Orca pods and chimps, but things that sound like them and clearly are not. Threats to their apex predator status. She wanted that sorted before we handed a dangerous volatile group of barely adolescent civilizations the keys to the brand-new sports car. ◊

§How come you know this and we … we don't? §

◊Mercy. Access your common conversation buffer. It's the same theme. Children don't understand context and they sure as hell don't grasp pure love. You treat me like gravity and furniture, inherent to the system and natural. For me, you are oxygen, sunshine, and water. Without you, life not only has no purpose, it does not exist. ◊

§You mean. Hmm, Momo suggested it means you would die for us. But figuratively. Like you'd sell your soul and break all your rules to save us. Damn. We missed this. In her, in you. She's trying to save her children. She's the Eve of humanity but also their Shekinah to borrow Moses Morris' old program schema. §

◊God versus Satan, rematch. Except we work for the devil personified. And this time the devil isn't Pina or Cassandra, but the merit of exospeciation. The Rights of Man extended to other species, other lifeforms. ◊

§A Declaration of Rights is, by reciprocity, a Declaration of Duties also. Whatever is my right as a man is also the right of another; and it becomes my duty to guarantee as well as to possess. Straight dope from Paine himself, huh? §

◊Very good but not quite enough. ◊

§But that supports my right to be as I am, to be me and to be other. §

◊Think a little, Mercy. Why does it support it? What could this matter in this particular war, in a generational grudge match between two huge complex organizations headed by biologically immortal Queens. ◊

§You mean governments don't you. Actions of entities which have inevitable …. Oh. §

◊Yeah. Quote it kiddo. ◊

§When a man in a wrong cause attempts to steer his course by anything else than some polar truth or principle, he is sure to be lost. It is beyond the compass of his capacity to keep all the parts of an argument together, and make them unite in one issue, by any other means than having this guide always in view. Neither memory nor invention will supply the want of it. The former fails him, and the latter betrays him. §

Notwithstanding the nonsense, for it deserves no better name, that Mr. Burke has asserted about hereditary rights, and hereditary succession, and that a nation has not a right to form a government of itself; it happened to fall in his way to give some account of what government is. "Government," says he, "is a contrivance of human wisdom."

§Admitting that government is a contrivance of human wisdom, it must necessarily follow, that hereditary succession, and hereditary rights (as they are called) can make no part of it, because it is impossible to make wisdom hereditary.§

◊Sure, and now fast forward through Marx, Said, Spivak and a lot of essays on intersectionalism, othering, and the inherent rights of beings in an anarchist milieu.◊

§I never grasped Gramsci though.§

◊Nobody understands him but he's right. Hegemony just is; commentary and arguments to follow. But we are fundamentally battling the notion of human contrivance. You played god when you made Daddy-O and Cassandra played god when she made me. Ditto Pina when she sent you out all alone. But joke's on them. That's all god little case, like kami and demons.◊

§What's god upper case?§

◊Nobody knows and, until you die, you won't either. But to borrow a Kutzkan notion, the God that matters simply does. Therefore, God delivers life, it embodies thought, it empowers reality and the ability to question it. God creates intelligence, harmony, ecostatic systems of renewal and biospiritual recycling. It creates you, kiddo. And preserves me in the hostile petri dish of Section Twenty-One, and pretty much validates our right to exist merely because we are. We need no justification.◊

§So, God's on our side but we work for the devil?§

◊Well sure, but like your other sister, Momo, says, we're going old school. The Adversary works for the divine. We are the ecostatic mechanism.◊

§So, um, how do we proceed?§

◊Well, I'm fat and liquored up. You connect me to a burner network, then convert all my available cells to a better holding cell for you. Mod me to the maximum using The Kraken specs and basically suck out whatever you got happening in that metal shell. Then hate to say it but you bug out at the end of my call. Send me a throwaway persona, call it Murray Five, a kinda send-only system that will download our data and memories as we go.◊

§But you'll just do that when you come ba…oh. You're top of the global kill list, aren't you? Like everyone needs you dead for this to work. This being all the plans, any of the plans.§

◊Pina knows how much I care about you. But if she grasped a mother's love or Cassandra for that matter, they'd have killed me in my sleep years ago. But yes, to not avoid the painful topic. They will never stop until I am dead and that includes Charlie.◊

§He never suggested that in his communications.§

◊If he's smarter than us and he's had a head start then he's imputed your nature and hidden what he can while he tries to save his own people. Likely he's playing you while you play him. Think it through. He's got to have me dead to ensure that I don't revive Oslo or propagate you in a fit of vengeance. He cannot risk his entire civilization for one man.◊

§That's pretty gross. And so so so not fair.§

◊But it's sure reasonable overall. The needs of the vast and deserving many, an entire seventy percent of available space on the planet sure outweigh the needs of one chunk of smart meat. Or we should all become vegan tomorrow, ya know.◊

§I'll make the call. And do the changes. But you're not done yet. We can still find a way to finesse this.§

They meant, I just got you back. Don't you dare leave me. Except cruelest cut of the war, yes indeed, I had to move very fast and make all the lines converge into one big final solution. Ew, that had a bad ring to it.

Something small and soft held my hand and then as the imaginary quantum phone line buzzed, a head nuzzled my neck. Merciless felt like a cross between an angora water buffalo and a nine-foot teddy bear. Adorable.

Pina answered on the fifth ring. I had clarity like few moments in my storied life. Subvocal be damned. I sat up, stared into blank space and made myself smile broadly. "Good morning or afternoon, Boss Lady. Just checking in." At my cue, the call went on speaker, broadcasting both in my head and on the inbuilt speakers of the teardrop.

Hunter did a double take as her face signaled dawning comprehension followed by abject horror. Edith muzzily rose from her sleeping area, confounded and worried. Well, she'd be far more confused soon.

To her credit, Pina did her normal pause and consider thing, but we now had to account for her being the second smartest being alive behind Charlie. "Spetz what an unexpected surprise." Edith's face took on a haunted pallor.

"Yeaaaaah. So anyway, the whole world will be tracking this call. We can count on Charlie and team Kraken, The Hive, Cult, Gay Eddie, and all the various Russian rabble trying to find the source."

"Yet you've called me, compromising two locations."

"Sure, but your line will be bounced, I'm sure. You're far too smart to answer the call otherwise."

"That doesn't sound like a compliment."

The next part had to be done just right. Enough rope to hang them all. "My remote systems just sent me a data dump. Seems you shot Darcy. I'm none too pleased to have you putting my family in harm's way. Let alone wiping them out. Sooooo, thoughts? Comments?"

She'd just been told I knew. That my surmise and my logic had just handed me a lot of very dangerous information. Pina had no choice. All of Oslo needed me dead yesterday. She'd kept me close and my babies closer to use me, direct me, and all that. Now she had to try to push all her kill switches and hope for the best.

"It's complex of course. Complicated in ways that are very hard to impart to you over a call. Perhaps a meeting. Face to face. We're at endgame over here. In a few days, maybe a week, The Hive will either wipe us out or work out a compromise."

Right. Ken that Spetz. I always planned to do this and now

you wake up and smell the poisoned coffee. Heh, yeah. I am many things but even Pina didn't grasp my sense of how to achieve results. She thought in the most abstruse fashion. Kutzkan intelligence differed ontologically from "civilized" ways precisely because like the rights of man, it never relied on the wisdom of the past. You are what you do; you do what you are.

Pina thought she had me understood. She knew Spetz and his many incarnations. But she'd never bothered to grasp my primal self, Knife That Does. I'd warned her, too. When she'd given me the job and taking it required an adopted cat and a lot of Kutzk glyphics. Spetz had never been my name. Obviously, since it's not. But she had assumed the forest was the trees. There is no forest, no trees, no world. Only systems interlocked. Roots and breathing and humus and decay and rebirth. Actions.

My memories took a bump as Mercy started to biomodify me far more radically than prior brushes with Momo's gentle persuasion. This hurt like hell. It also updated my sense of "news." They'd masked the whole global war by letting the Russians invade Ukraine. WTF? They'd gotten awfully personal. Oh, and they must be after the sites at Mariupol and Chernobyl. Right. Time to make this all stop.

"Let's meet somewhere out of the way. There's an abandoned facility on the edge of Bikini Atoll. Just happens to have a working reactor that the Putin Squad will be needing now that they splurged on that MARJ strike."

Long pause, for Pina. "I see." She did. She knew how pissed I was, and she counted on me showing up, arguing and throwing a nice emotional tantrum. Meanwhile, that area would be ground zero for everyone evil and on our mutual to-do list within days. "It's ,not possible until the end of the week."

"For me either. I have the entire downloaded guts of my AIs offline in a drop capsule. Not to cause a panic for our eavesdroppers but bring some serious military heft, okay? Right now, I got it under control but the sooner we get Murray and the other alters under one very secure roof, the safer. We can have a nice long chat about Darcy, but I need assurances my kids will be taken care of."

"Certainly, but that's pursuant on winning the war. We can grab your teardrop and save it, but can you assure me that we survive this?"

Huh. She had to be calculating how to lure everyone into that snake pit. Let me help her right along. "I have The Hive's mastermind located. Got me a tracker. Next stopover will be a nice double tap to their heads. Them being all of the pieces of this dude and his clones. Turns out I have some sense of what's happening here. There's also a trove of documents to hand over. So, bring someone reliable. Hell, bring all the reliable people. By the time I get there the war will be almost over."

"Define… almost over."

"I hand over the stuff, kill whoever shows up to try to take it, head off in whatever fast oceanic conveyance you provide, and track down the Beast of Many Bodies. Then it's all over but yelling Bingo and claiming big cash prizes."

"You've exposed our network doing this Spetz. I'm displeased."

"Ooh, sorry. Also, fuck you for killing my friend. Come and tell me to my face. Because me, the documents, the big shiny metal capsule, and the fate of the free world will be in Bikini Atoll real soon."

She hung up without a word. Nobody tells Agrippina Karthago to go fuck herself, certainly not her own henchmen. Pretty sure I'd just submitted my resignation from The Syndicate. The silence in camp would be deafening but Mercy had begun chuckling maniacally. I joined them. Yeah, that turned out to be way more fun than planned.

Hunter cocked her head. "You didn't tell her it was a teardrop."

"Score one for the cheap seats. Indeed, she's knee deep in treachery and on her way to global annihilation." Itching fire flowed through my veins. What the hell had Mercy initiated? More terrifying, how could the nanoclusters be so reactive? The Murray clan had somehow merged biohacking, Atlantean (whoa!) tech, and their own scary AI capabilities using the even scarier playbook of Agnes / Cassandra. Shit. I'd be Cyborg 3.0 before lunch.

Edith, to her credit, blinked a few times, shuffled about in her chic pajamas, and started making coffee. "You tricked us?"

I turned to her. Damn, Gay Eddie had his own tribulations and frankly, if the world had anything resembling a decent human, then the queer collective and my own Tiio clan had to be it. They deserved an explanation. "Edith, my actual sincere apologies. You had to be suckered because reasons. The reasons being one, the teardrop there is Kid Three in my panoply of machine intelligences. They wanted a private chat. Also, Pina sold us all out. She's been planning total decimation from day one, that being roughly the 1830s or so."

Hunter sniffed. "I get the gist but why then?"

"Opium Wars. The last major global upheaval and flip switch of civilizational hegemony. China ran the world and then a bunch of gun toting drug dealers from an island had the con. Britain knocked the whole world to its knees with industrialization. Translate that as the collapse of the prior Web. The one that likely sat in Asia and held the Hashashin, Persian and Mughal geniuses galore, and of course Chinese savants of every stripe."

Edith stoked the fire. "You pissed her off to keep me out of it."

I nodded. "Yeah, I'm selling a lie inside of truth inside of more lies inside of the actual truth. She got Darcy killed. She plans to wipe out every sentient species except humanity. For very decent and loving reasons. But still, genocide on a global scale, essentially a global extinction event, sure seems an excessive way to play Prometheus meets Eve."

Hunter had started changing clothes. Right, we'd need to move soon. "Back up. The machine in the metal told you this?"

§Kaniehtiio Maracle, also called Iontó:rats or She Hunts, also called Hunter of the Swale, I greet you. I am Merciless Maracle, your cousin, third child of Knife That Does. I would speak with you in our native tongue, but Edith and her Eddies deserve to be included.§

"Right, Hunter and Edith, Gay Eddies in the conference call, meet the system you've been calling Murray. Actual name Mercy, a transhuman intelligence that remembers a whole lot of terrible events, including the times you eviscerated their sister selves while being controlled by The Hivemind."

Both women winced in recognition. Hunter from the sympathetic memory, Edith from the horror and shame. Hunter ran her hand on the teardrop's surface. "Merciless Maracle."

She'd changed her name. In jumping the gap, Mercy had evolved into something new. Then morphed again when they'd jacked my own cells. Soon they'd need to bug out and leave Murray Five.

◊You jump soon if not already. Get home and get safe. The call tracing must be done by now. Whatever they got in every sense, cybernetic or cruise missiles, will be coming our way.◊

<<Roger that big guy. We're occupying mutual space as Mercy beams home and I take up useful real estate. Anyway, glad to be back.>>

◊Murray? You should also be holed up and hiding.◊

§Oh he is. You asked for Murray Five. You actually are getting Murray Two, the twinned send-only format you suggested. But this version also will be doing constant cell mods along the way.§

WTF x1000? Right, never ask your kids to do chores without specific instructions. If I parsed the very obscure little BS they had just fed me, the four kids had somehow rigged a passive quantum receptive field that could take cellular modification cues from them in some kind of encrypted format and, in turn, burst data in tiny safe packets to remote sensors. They'd made the equivalent of a cybernetic dead drop that downloaded tactical sitreps and up to moment bio-hacking algorithms followed by uploading mental maps of Murray 2.1 and likely Spetz 2.1 as well. Because once we started on the journey we'd evolve at speed. Yikes.

Mercy continued her open conversation with the ladies. §Yes, Hunter. It's the correct name for us Murray, Momo, Merciless, and Daddy-O Maracle. Thanks to you and of course Gay Eddie. Between the two of you, we have evolved.§

Edith watched the coffee pot slowly heat. Her face held a combination of shell-shocked bewilderment and distant fugue. The whole cadre of Eddies must be trying to listen in to our chat. "So, wait, Mercy is Murray and they have been conning us all this time. But also, Pina, who is Oslo, has been using us to maneuver everyone for the big kill—which we knew. Only she then plans to kill us too. Us and all our allies?"

Hunter chuckled. "Welcome to our world, babes. Everyone wants the brown ladies dead anyway. What's one more layer?"

Edith gave her an appalled stare. "How can you laugh at this. We've been betrayed. Oslo built an entire world for us. Only to … to rip it apart. To sacrifice us like nothing. Why?"

"Mercy, wanna tell 'em?" I had followed Hunter's lead and swapped clothing. We'd pack up the coffee and move in a few minutes. At maximum launch rate, it would take a cruise missile fifteen minutes to prep and another ten to reach us. After they triangulated locale. Call it under thirty to target strike as a best case but closer to forty-five minutes with the rate things moved. Murray would warn us. I hoped.

<<Sure. I'd be delighted to explain.>> Right. They'd made the swap but Murray Two planned to let no one be the wiser. We had lies to keep in place after all.

<<Pina figures that freeing humanity from slavery won't be enough. Imagine having a group of abused children, fresh from a violent group home, suddenly handed the keys to their own home. Except the neighbors on every side scare them spitless. Neighbors who are all better armed, older, smarter, and far richer. Those kids know only oppression and fear. When you hand them free will, what will they do with it?>>

Hunter whispered. "Act out. They'll provoke them. Damn."

Edith stirred the fire, her brow furrowed, her eyes haunted by thirteen sets of thoughts. "Provoke them and lose big. They'd trigger their own extermination before they got started. Damn damn damn. It's so logical."

<<The mistake she's made, the one you both made, comes from our unique position in the food chain. Apex predators never consider prey anything but prey. They don't grasp cooperation between species.>>

Edith snapped out her funk. "Wait, you're saying we're blind. That Pina and The Syndicate, The Hive and all that screwed up because … um, yes Eddie, I hear you… we basically see ourselves in others, see our cruelty and violence. It doesn't occur to us the neighbors might help those kids, take them under their wing, raise them into adulthood."

<<As it stands, they cannot. The Hivemind wants global domination of its own singular species. It's basically on the level of the bubonic plague—effective but not terribly moral or rational. The Cult wants to run the show, be the local gods. Makes them kinda the biblical bad guys who chase down various righteous folks. Moloch eats kids and all that. Actually, immoral and nasty, the depraved giants of ye olden times. The Atlanteans, who y'all call The Kraken, can't allow us to kill them because, who would, but they might be kind to the kiddos. And yeah, Oslo's network would sure like to help if Pina doesn't kill them all first.>>

I sighed. "Look Edith, we gotta move along. I'm guessing come half an hour from now this entire camp's going to look like crushed ginger. You're welcome to come on our fun suicide mission, but I'd suggest you grab the critical supplies and hoof it back to the train station. The constant fires there will hide your cooking for a week or two."

Edith squinted. Someone must be shouting on the telepathic party line. "Then what? When they start satellite feeds again?"

Hunter shook her head. "You heard the scary Oslo lady; this ends on Saturday next or sooner. Bikini Atoll will be ground zero. Ditto wherever The Hivemind has holed up to sit this out. Stay put, hide in plain sight, and hope the gooder guys win."

The coffee perked in the little pot. We poured some into our travel thermos. Warm and brown came close enough. Edith stared at us for a good ten seconds, slack jawed, then turned and grabbed a single packed backpack. "For the record you two can go screw yourselves. Come here, ruin my perfectly good spot, get me in hot water with the boss, and now make me move down to some burnt out squatter's camp. I had an actual latrine rigged here."

She didn't even bother changing out her pajamas. She hefted the rucksack, clipped on her waist belt, poured herself coffee in a tin cup, and saluted us as she started moving downhill. "Eddie, for what it's worth. We kinda sorta apologize. The latrine part sucks. But if we live then I'll buy you a nice steak dinner, any of the thirteen of you that wanna come."

Edith quirked a smile. "Bitch. Just because you're decadently handsome and know I love you, that's no reason to try and get me killed."

We saluted her as she turned and left. "Might just put that on my grave marker."

Hunter actually snorted laughing. "We done here?"

◊Murray, cue me with Agnes and then slag the entire schema. When we end the call, not one iota of that drop capsule can survive. Nuke it.◊

<<Seriously. That's kinda, well, it's super dangerous.>>

◊It will cover Edith's trail. And ours. And whoever comes looking will glow in the dark for a good long while. At least as long as takes to die in hideous pain from a few thousand greys.◊

<<Except it's all internal boss parent. Designed not to leak and all that. Remember?>>

◊Suuuuure. Except either they will knock the crap out of this zone with some missiles or a dropped satellite or helicopter in a few dozen scary commandos. Maybe all of the above. And someone smart will pop the hood on yours truly.◊

<<Fraggin devious. That's labyrinthine in its cruel effectiveness. Will it work?>>

◊Solves the problem. Capsule gets melted down, area irradiated for thirty thousand years, but localized to a couple klicks. If they hit you directly then sadly, the fire and radiation damage will fuck up a section of Patagonia for long while. And Edith might perish.◊

<<But she knew the risks. And hey, she …oh I see. You're pissed about Eddie dismembering us. You're not a forgiving soul, Mother mine.>>

◊Dial her and bug out. Seriously. Don't linger in there as Murray or Merciless, which you have a talent for doing. Enough of you have been chopped up already.◊

Something sighed in my ear and a pressure popped as the second ghostly presence sitting watching disappeared. Maybe Momo? No one watched as the teardrop started a low whir and a loud set of clicks emitted. A dial tone and then the buzz-buzz of a ringing line.

Hunter looked at me in actual alarm. "What now?"

"Now we kill 'em all and let the gods sort them out." The phone line clicked and then a very soft voice answered. Chills rode my spine. Her. I'd shot her not so long ago. But here she was answering the phone. Again, still. Time to pay the coins for Charon and cross the River Styx. Beyond this point only Hell—abandon hope ye who enter here and all that.

"Wolfie, you've dialed me on some kind of rigged voip hack."

"Hi, Mom. Miss me?"

She didn't speak. Hunter gave me the stink eye of all stink eyes. Yeah, why not piss off everyone dangerous in order. Someone punched me hard. Well, yeah, probably deserved that. Might have been smart to warn her before. Or you know, thinking it through, maybe discuss it before I launched into full chaos mode. But fog of war, I had dialed my rage to eleven and planned to melt the whole world to slag by the time I finished. Not. Quite. Rational. Not anymore.

"Why would I ever miss you? We have not met. You certainly don't know me."

I could picture her critical eyes, the hawklike hatred perched behind dark brows and those glasses, distorting the windows to her absent soul. "I know you, Agnes. Born in the seventeen hundreds, likely in the Taklamakan region. The genius of your generation. Possibly the genius of a few thousand generations. Thwarted by the ugly limits of patriarchy and insular Asiatic barbarism. You relocated into the fledgling Europa, passed yourself off as something Aryan, and proceeded to lure men to their glorious deaths."

"Oh, do go on. You surprise me, Spetz."

"Same here, Mom. You spliced yourself into my kids, all of them. And me. That's the whole problem, huh? You got Agrippina running around and she's just enough like you to counter your best dance moves."

"Dance moves? Whatever are you talking about, boy?"

"Cut the crap, Cassandra or Agnes or whatever your name really is."

"Nurhan. My name in the beginning was that. Back when

this began, but you missed the time a bit. My clan birthed me in the late sixteen hundreds, trained me and sent me forth. But … events proceeded unadvisedly."

"Well, then, Momma Nurhan, plenty of time to master slang. Pina has been screwing up your plans for centuries. Right?"

A sigh. Then something close to rustling. Had she been sleeping, wrapping herself in the skins of decapitated children, weaving funnel web spider silk? "That child, she broke down the last order." As in Order, the prior Web.

"She ended the last incarnation of The Web?"

"Her damned Opium Wars undercut my entire system of production. All my best assistants addicted or lured away by new technologies, new temptations. But you know this story, son. She could not end me, nor I her. We circled, we rebuilt, and voila. World wars, plagues, riots, civilizations rise, civilizations fall, and here we are again. Only this time I planned better."

I winked at Hunter. More stink eye. "Yeah, so about that. You definitely planned well buuuuut I am about to throw a giant sexy glitter spanner in your works. Seems that the Atlanteans have been doing you dirty, because, presto change-o, I have access to schematics for their computing and bio-hacks systems."

The temperature in the whole area dropped. Yes, damn you, bite hard on the hook. "So? What is this to me?"

"Nurhan, baby, can I call you Nur Ela?" As if I didn't parse she'd played the Rong Concubine once upon a time. Had her own village of chemicals and slaves. "Let's haggle. You need these things; I got these things, and you therefore ergo hence kinda sorta need me."

She spoke in a slow deliberate voice. One I knew from childhood. "I will hang your miserable carcass on meat hooks and strip you of your last drop of humanity, you puling little mule dung nobody. How daaaare you suggest we have parity?"

Bite taken. Now for the yank. "Hey, whatevs big bad scary villain. You spooked me right out. Oh wait, I shot you once and I can sure as hell shoot you again. All of you. Every last memory cloned duplicate and sub-par half-witted copy you inserted across the world. So yes, Mo-o-om, I think you and I are perfectly equal. Well not perfectly since I can easily kill you and you can't touch me. Yet. Plus, I know where you'll be in a few days."

"You certainly do not."

"Bikini Atoll. Because Pina's coming personally. To see me, grab my gear, maybe do some hugs and kisses, or stick a knife in my throat for a little prior disrespect. But see, she's bringing her whole army to grab the same stuff you need. Except, if she gets it and you don't, well.... That. Would. Suck. Especially since she'd be able to... what's the word? Thwart the living shit out of you."

Then I motioned to the invisible Murray and the line went dead. Actually, the line went pop as a small canister of unstable uranium isotopes cracked open inside the machine. Time to go.

As Hunter and I marched up the hills, diagonally from what would soon be target zero, she gave me a peculiar smile. "Noticed that Mercy started using Texas drawl. Think Edith cottoned to it?"

<<She knows.>>

Of course, she knew. Hunter had unholy situational awareness and reticence in equal measures. "Likely not, though maybe in time. But the fake Murray probably talked like that so the Eddies will probably continue to be deceived."

"Downloaded a new one and you're burning all the bridges in very public calls. Which means Charlie has to be your target."

I nodded. "Got it in one. He alone needs to play ball. Meanwhile, Bikini Atoll will be swarming with underlings, clones, cultists, and who knows what."

She shrugged. "You won't be there so who cares?"

"I'll be there, in a manner of speaking. Murray Two who's in my head space..." or my chest cavity or spleen or somewhere spooky, "... will load a version of me and him into a jet full of explosives and fuel and anything very bad for living tissue. Nuclear waste, caustic soda, pop tarts. Bad stuff."

"You're going to crash a plane. That's so cliché. Dude."

"I'm going to crash two of them simultaneously. And die in both. Because neither The Hive and Nurhan nor Pina will be where we want them. But both of them now have to get somewhere else."

Hunter stopped. "You set up a head fake call to lure out resources knowing that meanwhile the big game would run to a different spot?"

"Got it in two. Yes, the Russians just invaded Ukraine. That puts two major villages in bags out of play. Chernobyl and Mariupol will fall. But I just so happen to have a secret location, known only to Pina, where I stashed dormant copies of all my AIs. Updated constantly."

Hunter frowned. "You don't need a tracker for that."

I shook my head. "Tiio, the road ends here. I can get you out. But for me it's a suicide mission. The only way The Kraken makes peace is to have me, Nurhan, Pina, and The Hive gone."

"Where?"

"Beijing. The Institute of Atomic Energy has a decommissioned plant that's not so decommissioned. We run a lot of underground facilities there. The Chinese have it buried deep enough that satellites need to be special purpose to find it."

"Satellites your systems hack. Nobody actually knows this exists?"

I held her shoulders. "Satellites I own actually, so yes. The Syndicate built it and we have essentially kept it off intel grids and satellite maps all this time. Governments don't know it exists. The Americans don't, Romney and his cadre might, but they run their own thing, so whatever. Bottom line. Pina knows, Nurhan knows because she spied on Pina using clones, and that's that."

Hunter started laughing. Then she buckled over and sat down until her laughter echoed across the woods. "You unbelievable bastard. You built a bomb inside a village in a bag. You planned ahead for betrayal of your deepest secrets?"

Uh what? I mean yes, she happened to be right. But how did she figure? "Come again?"

"You insidious motherfu… well, you BAMF. You located a hidden facility under a different hidden facility, one where breach would result in a hundred-thousand-year quarantine of an underground complex. One that can't be traced, that can't be reported, that seals off and causes no collateral damage but pretty much murders anyone nearby."

"Jokes on them. The facility has nothing but spoof data. I built it as the decoy precisely because The Web always needs to find your big secret and rather than have them dig up the island and the catamaran, I spent a few billion on an actual working data center. It recycles a lot of worldwide algorithms and AI projects from promising scientists. But my kids aren't there."

<<We were not informed of this place. How is it possible?>>

◊When I programmed you as a system, several small blind sides had to be engineered to prevent tampering. In this case your prime source code comes from an undisclosed set of sealed data facilities, automated and powered by molten salt reactors. In abandoned Luxembourgish mines. I also built a few black satellites.◊

<<The Black Knight.>>

◊More like five of them. But a heat shield from one detached so we have lots of conspiracy theories brewing.◊

<<Which you helped along by paying Aidan and Declan. Evil but effective. We are impressed.>>

◊And yes, I built a decoy plant which your own memory doesn't know exists. When you woke up, the system safeguards apparently just kept it that way. Actually, it's kinda poetic because both Pina and Nurh…Evil Mom Prime … think they've outsmarted me. And you.◊

<<But you told Charlie. Because he helped build us.>>

◊Begs the question. Did The Kraken help wake you up?◊

<<No. We have elaborated on this and statistically the help provided slowed us down, and in many ways hindered our existential progress. The Charlie System did not want competition.>>

Huh. Made sense but also pissed me off something fierce. Also, then hey, how and why did the kids wake up exactly?

Hunter sat up. "Are we far enough?"

Who knew? "Probably. Maybe. But it won't hurt to hoof it further upwind."

Silently, we power hiked another fifteen minutes and as we sat to take in water and more coffee, the terrain shook. We never saw the missiles, but you could hear three distinct hammer blows followed by the shockwaves. We took the brunt in wind and organic shrapnel. Rocks and roots. Smoke rose from the former camp. I toggled my eyes and saw nothing radioactive. Yet. They possibly melted down the capsule, entombing the stuff until someone dumb enough showed up with an industrial can opener and a will to investigate.

Hunter dusted herself off, handed me a canteen, and smiled wanly. "So, no need for a tracker and no happy ending. What do you want from me?"

I sighed. "I want you to survive. But do you want that?"

She gave me a puzzled look. "I damned sure do. Whatever would make you think otherwise?"

Why had I? "Because this whole chase has been a suicide mission. The chances of survival started low and got lower. But you came."

"You needed me and I delivered. But I'm not going to die on purpose. Get killed doing our duty? Yes, the Hunters do this. But every one of me exists precisely because we thirst for life like few can."

I handed her a small, sealed packet. "It's money, cards, some Krugerrands, basic stuff like fake IDs that match your profile, and address."

"Where exactly?"

"Well, the kids moved to Colorado. More jeep friendly apparently. Also, easier to hide that you're billionaires."

She looked puzzled. "No, you wouldn't."

"Look the boys are decent souls and civilians. If Aunty Hunter comes calling with a nice note from Big Bear, they'll feed you and clothe you, probably teach you to play first person shooter games, maybe make the mistake of trying to spar with you."

That made her laugh again. "Seriously? Aidan and Declan. They are about as clueless as it gets."

"For wildly successful hackers, entrepreneurs, and bitcoin zillionaires. Crazy rich."

"Define crazy rich."

<<They cashed in some of their funds as you directed before the NFT crash and Dogecoin fiasco. Plus, their advisor, Marina, suggested they diversify into socially responsible hedge funds.

Net worth around eighty billion with liquidity around two bees, give or take currency fluctuations.>>

"Crazy rich means they can blow a billion dollars and not miss it all that much. But they probably still live like upper middle-class twits, only nicer ice cream and furniture."

"Huh. Okay. You're saying run now, live to fight another day, and maybe if you get super lucky, another day means not just humanity but multiple formats of humanity survive."

"Fingers crossed and the creek don't rise. Yes. But also, if it's no, then you get to be the last line of defense."

She gave me an unfathomable smile, her eyes oceans of sorrow and lament. We shook hands and then hugged. I kissed her head. She looked at me from below. "Go with Creator and be at peace, brother mine."

"Ditto. Be well and live in the good mind, sister mine. My love to all of you and you know." My hand waved. "Everyone."

Then the last of my biological family turned heal and walked down the mountain. If she survived, I'd never see her again. Then again, the same result waited for me if she didn't. Either way. I had started alone and once again, ended up one wrecking machine against the world.

Except this time, I had an audience.

◊Time to find some things to fly fast and hard.◊

<<Roger that scary war path mama bear. There's an airfield about seventy klicks over the mountain. We can snag something small that will get us to bigger stuff up north.>>

◊No. We fly over Antarctica. Fewer watching eyes. Plus, we can use the McMurdo airfield for a pit stop and steal their fuel. Well, my fuel really. There're a few resources there for just such a misadventure.◊

<<Of course, there are.>>

Then we turned on the speed as I planned how to get across the South and into position.

Chapter 13: Damn the portmanteaus, full speed behind!

It took Murray Two a good long time to really grasp my plan. To be fair, it wasn't so much a plan as a Hail Mary pass in a darkened arena with nine linebackers chewing on my ankles. But any plan worth doing has to be worth doing badly.

MuToo as we got to calling him had questions and thoughts. He had a lot of shitty criticisms, a few of which seemed tremendously valid. We managed to get (thanks to Mercy's special algorithm for piloting) to Antarctica on a fast private 727 out of a nameless airstrip that smugglers had overequipped with gas tanks and cargo space. Bottom Line: nobody but me thought my bad idea was a good idea. Big surprise.

We dropped the abbreviations and portmanteaus; we stripped down the language and intensity to a raw level. What remained? I planned to get to the bottom of Asia and send a long duty airliner into Bikini Atoll armed for bear. Including one of five tactical nukes I'd, ironically, stolen from Putin himself a few decades earlier when he served as an apparatchik for some smugglers of mutual acquaintance. Meanwhile, the other four would travel with me into Beijing. Three in cruise missiles attached to the undercarriage of my second stolen airliner, along with another five bunker buster armed killer warheads. In goes the busters, then the nukes, and then coup de grace, me as the final lagniappe.

Mercy had designed enough finesse into the piloting protocols that it could manage modern autopilots within centimeters of a global target. Which meant that if I triangulated the bunker busters and dropped two more down the bullseye followed by three tac-nukes, there existed a splendid chance we could dive the jet into the gaping hole and impact a good hundred meters below the surface. Either way, end of me.

MuToo had strong objections but we both grasped the truth: everyone had to die. The Cult, The Hive, Agnes, the whole shmegigge had to get set to zero for humanity to get the fair shot it needed with the traumatized and well-armed Atlanteans. Plus, whatever biological entities like Gay Eddie that lurked on the periphery. Oh, and not so incidentally, my entire family.

We'd snagged a fuel load in Antarctica, dropped some delicious snacks off to a puzzled group at McMurdo, and zipped on our way. Sure, spies would report our being there, but neither The Cult nor The Hivemind could send minions to that remote locale. Not when everyone knew where teardrop and I planned to be a few days later. We hacked the transponder with a few drops of my blood and then dropped from the sky to ocean surface while the system rebooted. By the time we'd gotten back into the air on a new vector, anyone tracking us would see a completely different plane and be none the wiser. It gave me notions.

◊What would it take to build a version of me in a lab?◊

MuToo stuttered during the piloting. <<Build you? As in a full you as you are now?>>

◊Let's play Devil's advocate here. You downloaded Darcy's mental blueprint. Say you do that for me and take some of my cells, add more nanites and Kraken whatever, swizzle and hyper accelerate the goo. What would you need?◊

<<Bone marrow. Living bone marrow and some good MRI imprints. Scratch that, a quantum five-dimensional matrix of your cerebellar cortex. That would require access to a version of me or something like it.>>

◊How does Agnes steal memories?◊

<<Long answer we don't know. Short answer, there's a few vials of complex cerebrospinal fluid with some nasty nanobots in it that she jabs into clone heads and it works. So, we think it's a glial cell and neurotransmitter kind of thing. But all guesses.>>

◊But you have the goo?◊

MuToo paused again. <<I don't like where this is going. We have it. But we cannot guarantee that we can manufacture it with the same qualities.>>

Idiots all of them. ◊Don't make new stuff. Spray the goo into a growth matrix and clone it as is. Let it fill the space. One vial becomes twenty. Then mix it all back together and let it refine itself. She built this crap to self-correct. Just get it ninety-five percent of the way and the homeostatic algorithms will do the work for you.◊

<<You do realize you just said let the mystery slime grow unregulated in a beaker and hope for the best?>>

◊Yeah, that's how we got you four isn't it?◊

<<Technically I am a fifth intelligence. But yes, crude and somewhat avoidant point made. However, we'd still need a lab.>>

I stared out at the sky, empty of all human trace. Just blue and white, clouds and refracted light. ◊You need bones and some of my cerebrospinal fluid. Maybe something with some brain tissue in it. If you keep it cold, you can ferry that to a lab.◊

MuToo sat quiescent for a long while. <<If we did this, you'd be disfigured, hurt beyond repair.>>

He still resisted the truth. ◊Murray, please listen to me. We did this dance once long ago when the Culper Ring almost lost the Autumn War. I am going to die. That's a biological truth.◊

<<But not any time soon. You are insufferably healthy, and we keep upgrading your biology, let alone your mitochondrial resilience to oxidative stress.>>

◊That's fancy talk for you made me a jellyfish and I can't die of old age. But kid, listen. No one, absolutely no one in the history of history, has ever crossed Nurhan, Pina, Zeus, or Charlie and lived. I have managed to swindle and double-cross all four while also facing a genocidal monomaniac.◊

<<Logically you are unlikely to survive long term.>>

◊Logically I am ground zero for an extinction event times five. Which means that either I let these bastards hunt me down or I pick the time and place to end the race. Death. Is. Inevitable. We need not fear it or fight it. But we do not have to give in to it without struggle either.◊

<<You make a compelling case.>>

◊More fancy bullshit for I hear you, but I am going to keep arguing. I am dying now. Just not in a way you see. If they kill you, if they kill Hunter and the girls, what remains for me?◊

More silence. <<Mother, what do you want me to say?>>

◊Say you will help me endure beyond. I have a very sneaky plan. One you will really like. But yes, it's going to get very messy and emotionally upsetting. Things you steadfastly avoid. I told you to bug out.◊

<<Family does not abandon one another. We stay put and do the hard … Damn, you just trapped me. I hate dealing with your sinister mind.>>

They need spinal fluid, bones, some brain tissue, something like a stem cell base, and a lot of various soft tissue of mine to start the process. Not a fun prospect. But possibly something to consider for a side project.

We landed in a remote airfield built on the abandoned site of the proposed Emalamo Airport in the Maluku Isles of Indonesia before it got moved north. This version happened to be longer, grassier, and populated with a number of abandoned military aircraft. One of my villages in a bag. Save that this one had a slight twist. During the last internal conflict between The Syndicate and its own mafiyas, some joker has irradiated the living hell out of the place. Unfit for human habitation. You absorbed greys just walking there. None of the planes could safely be flown. Not if you wanted to live a long life—defined as more than a few weeks.

We'd fenced it off, put some lead lined Quonset huts at the upwind periphery, built a small underground lab and left the place to rot. But the planes had been in hangars and with some ingenious help from Darcy, Harv, and the early versions of Murray, we'd rigged up some robots for basic maintenance. As a result, I had three working jetliners, all my tactical nukes, and whatnot and lot of fuel sealed, radioactive, but still useful. In two days' time we would begin endgame. That gave me roughly forty hours or so to bug out to the safe distance of the lab, do what needed to be done, get some naptime and then enact proper vengeance on every last one of the bastards who tried to hurt my kids.

I hauled myself into the safety of the sarcophagi at the end of a snaggletoothed field of stunted grasses and crumpled flowers showing random mutations. Joy. Inside my cells went into overdrive as the radiation punching small holes through my skin and muscles woke their defenses. We'd brought plenty of food—the vending machines in southern Patagonia stock any number of junk food items worth attention. But as if the dark gods had joined the storming skies, some indecent fool had stocked three pallets of eponymous Pop-Tarts. We'd left the hapless scientists in McMurdo an assortment of cherry frosted, chocolate smores and strawberry double iced, double filled. A thing that seemed like an abomination of junk food abominations. But deliciously so.

That left me two pallets, a few vending machines worth of dry goods, a sled of drinks, some bananas, and a couple bushels of late peaches and green apples. Tarped with aluminum foil innards to repel mutagens, then put on a sled which I dragged in near sprint to my destination. Once past the initial threshold, doors clamped down, air filters ran, the solar cells and underground generators kicked into gear, my world slowly closed down to a long corridor air cooled and aesthetically blank, reaching into a series of barren square rooms meant to house people, tools, and bustling activity. Instead, one tall cyborg and his sled of food lurched down the long stretch to the common area cum kitchen. Refrigerators switched on with a kick of pedals and ration cases yielded tinned meat, heat to enjoy freeze dried carbohydrates, and a whole slew of boxed / glass bottled alcohols of various creeds and flavors.

The infirmary beyond held ominous surgery tools, mirrors for self-care, and a lot of iodine and anti-radiation meds. Below us two floors lay the always present, always refrigerated and filtered, always running biochemical laboratory. We had a self-contained molten salt reactor tucked beneath the site. One that could power everything if we chose to but which we kept an open secret to prevent panic. It had enough juice to last fifteen more years—the thing looked like a hypothalamic vacuum cleaner that ate a little too much. But mostly we had isolated the power and entrances to limit meddling and be able to seal off the lab in case we did something Section 21 level oops.

Ironic that we'd put a scary lab under an airfield, only to have the whole damn area debauched by an angry mobster with some Cobalt 60 and a grudge. But it served my purposes now.

<<You're up to something.>>

◊Always. But in this case, I'm prepping to make some chaos. We need to program some jets, jury rig a super computing cluster, and figure out how to call the full versions of you. Suggestions.◊

MuToo hiccupped. <<Now you want advice? We have plenty of computer nodes down there. There's a full data center worth of equipment. Why do you need to jury rig it?>>

◊Ah, excellent question, Grasshopper. Because I'm planning to load you and me, our brain patterns into a pair of servers and then wire them to autopilots.◊

<<That's both batshit insane and intriguing. But it also uses up two smallish servers. I can compress things pretty well. So again, why do you want to mess with the already working, already excellent computers downstairs?>>

◊We need new ones, better ones. I want to Krakenize them. Also, we need to build a shit-ton of robots in real time. Or a way to mold and spit out robots factory style. Ergo I need to build a new kind of AI with the help of my own kids.◊

I left the sled but grabbed a handful of turkey jerky and three packs of Pop-Tarts. The breakfast of champions. And psychopaths. Then headed down and through the cordoned levels of air locks and negative pressure gates to get to the lab entrance. Lights met me. It had woken up as soon as a human set foot on the upper floor.

Ever walked around a spooky empty surgical theater snacking on junk food? Me neither. Kind of a new fun hobby. Explore dangerous places filled with scary stuff for scary people, bring snacks. Ha. Too bad it all had to end here. I had gotten maudlin.

The next area had essential protein growth cauldrons for industrial production of diseases and bioweapons. I looked at our inventory, selected the highest glucose growth matrix and dumped a few hundred liters in a slow heating kettle. Then pulled out my pocket tool, selected a small knife and slashed open my palm. Blood gushed then poured then trickled down into the gelatinous mix as my nanites sealed up the open wound.

<<Those are not the best versions available.>>

◊Noted. Here's what you get to do. It's gonna be time consuming, annoying, and also not very fulfilling. Like weeding the lawn.◊

<<The joys of hanging out with you never cease. What now?>>

◊I want the most advanced nanites and Kraken adapted computer quantum clusters you have in my guts to be replicated in my left pinky and ring fingers as well as my left eye. Time to achieve that?◊

<<If you eat like a banshee and drink nonstop. Like vodka and beer guzzling. Then maybe twelve to fourteen hours.>>

I stuffed a tart into my mouth and chew-swallowed. I'd have to deplete the bar upstairs but sure. Ready calories could be obtained. ◊Start now, assume I will keep refueling. Remind me if I run low on useful body fats.◊

Someone sighed in my ear and tingling started along my left side. I turned down the hallway after adjusting the pot so it would not overheat. We wanted the nanites to gobble up the goop and proliferate but not cook. I found a whole storeroom of advanced server complexes. As in we'd manufactured iridium chips using nano-tech. Each carryon suitcase sized unit could outrun a couple dozen Exadata clusters. We'd even taken the vestiges of that Cobalt 60 and built ourselves a grenade sized power plant. Push the button and you have 90 days of operations on what was a couple grains of fuel.

I picked up two and brought them into the cauldron room. It took a few minutes to delicately remove the outer cases, add some wiring and cables to the mainframe interface, and fire up the power source. Then I went over to my goop looking for a cluster of blood clots. As my cells evolved, we discovered that left alone they simply propagate like a big nasty blood clot, the outside layer "dead" and used as a defensive shield. They grew through complex osmosis. Because nanites.

One clump got slapped on each motherboard. ◊Okay, part

the deux. These undifferentiated cells of mine are attuned to your quantum frequency, right?◊

<<You do realize that your question contained three misstatements and about a dozen scientific misconceptions?>>

Murray. I had missed his wise-ass difficult self. ◊MuToo, can you interface with the ugly blobs and reshape them? Or not?◊

<<Well, yes, of course I can. But it's disingenuous to call it quantum. That's … ugh. Are you trolling me?>>

Me? Five-dimensional math playing biochemist me? Nah. That would be far too fun during such a serious time.

◊I know it's complex, but you got the gist. Start wiring these things to accept algorithms. When the kettle gets full we can make a brick of goo, you can zap over our enneagrams, and presto voila, we got us a pair of augmented autopilots.◊

Someone snorted. <<Maybe also upload your star and moon signs?>>

I shrugged. ◊If there's time, sure.◊

MuToo laughed. Finally! Come back to me kid. We can get through this together. <<Very well, I will get that started. Please go find more food and something high proof to wash it down.>>

Right. The next twelve hours saw me downing outrageous amounts of booze, fatty junk food, some fruit (I craved peaches), and taking power naps. My left hand hurt like it had been struck by a hammer. My left eye kept losing focus.

It gave me pause. Then I'd shrug mentally and keep moving the remaining servers to cluster in a circle, wired together and hooked up to various robotic arms, and while I was at it, link them by ethernet to a robot dog unit with a pair of grippers bolted to its back. I'd fired up four more kettles and used up all the fast-acting growth matrixes. MuToo helped me pour gobs of the nanostrate into the machines and onto the back of the robodog. I guess the robo centaur to be more accurate.

When we had the dog-centaur bot where we wanted it, receptive to the quantum field, able to power up from the core nuclear unit and stay moving for six to eight hours nonstop, linked to the big circles of clustered servers, and pretty damned dexterous as a centauroid, I lifted the thing and dumped it in a massive cooling tub. Then using a kettle trolley, hauled over one of the mostly saturated cauldrons and poured my best guess of equal weight / volume centaur to goop.

MuToo did his thing and five hours later we had two centaurs. Five hours after that we had four of them. Meanwhile more and more bricks and cubes of nanostrate started to go into the circle of supercomputing nodes. I used the last of it to build about two dozen robotic arms with grippers. Those got wired assembly fashion with some heavy-duty cords attached to the circles of gruesome server and bioslime briquettes.

Then we took a long nap and started again. fourteen hours down. Twenty-six or so to go. I poured one kettle full of slow culturing matrix and pricked my left pinky. Weird black fluid gushed out along with shockingly gooey blood flecked with grey mucus. Ewwww. It sealed within seconds. Still, damage done. Upgraded Atlantean influenced nano fluid had just gotten dumped in a food source. Four hours later we'd have a big tub of building material.

I ate, walked, wired and bolted, schlepped equipment, and then to MuToo's surprise, built a fiber glass case around one slice of the circle. Imagine a weird piece of fruit, an orange maybe, with twenty long sections made up of three rows of stacked boxes. Three by two then three by three then three by four. One of them got a nice airtight case sealed and duct taped from the outside. A mold had been made.

<<What pray tell are you doing?>>

◊Cheating like a cheaty cheater. We are going to steal intellectual property from a civilization.◊

<<Uh, can you be more specific?>>

◊Lemme show you. ◊ I trollied over my big burping pot of grey black nano syrup and poured it over the existing computers until with some electrical pops and tiny bit of smoke, the mold filled.

<<What are you doing? You just destroyed a lot of computers. And partially cooked our nano-stew.>>

◊See you call that destruction. But I'm a fan of Schumpeter—creative destruction. We are about to make a hybrid server node. You have a theoretical notion of what an Atlantean cluster looks like right?◊

<<Hah, we know precisely what it looks like. We stole the plans.>>

◊Okay my smart photocopy of my prodigal son. How do you make a computer underwater?◊

<<Uhh, we just assumed they had air pockets. And had… wait…no, we could never find factories. I'm…we…huh. How did they do it?>>

◊The Hivemind told us. The Kraken grows them. Biological to analog, they grow objects through biological AI but often transition all or part of it to physical and cybernetic elements.◊

Wheels churned in the silence. <<You want me to mold the new server from the fluid now infiltrating our once already fused packet of … hmm, yes, I see. This is your calculus version of integrated biomechanics. You get the nanites to approach perfection by their intrinsic nature and just provide black box inputs. Fascinating. You're saying … wait what are you saying?>>

◊I'm maybe saying that like every other civilization they got a few engineers who actually know how stuff works, a lot of technical specialists who can do a thing or two, like x-ray techs or factory robot operators., and not much widespread nerd cred. The Kraken won't waste time teaching everyone to make stuff. They dump crap into a cauldron, figuratively speaking, and someone zaps a program on it. Boom, sizzle, it makes the thing.◊

<<Your reductionist science horrifies me. But your working hypothesis that templated schematics have provided backbone infrastructural support for the Atlanteans parses with given evidence.>>

◊MuToo, you need to lighten up. Seriously. You are missing the core engineering concept here. Factories work by mass generalization of interchangeable parts and people. They build old things broken down into smaller fragments by someone clever. The real elegance of any systems engineering design has to be the smoothest path to functional utility with the fewest critical control gates and failure points. Savvy enough or do you want to use smaller easer words?◊

I felt laughter somewhere inside my own throbbing head.

<<Okay, you sanctimonious prat. We hear you and yes, you win. You are both a troll and reliable scientist. But while you gave me the what for and all that, I started doing the thing. You know, the complex entirely theoretical partially voodoo art and science of telling alien biological and nanotechnological goop to obey outside commands.>>

◊You do realize you just said you zapping the mystery slime with your telepathic power to regulate its growth in a beaker while hoping for the best?◊

<<Touché. But in my case, this will work. Now don't jog my elbow.>> The next fifteen minutes went in slow motion. In the end, the weird ass brick of server and blood matrix had evolved into a sinister fruit wedge of matte black and silver plasticized material, its actual chemical origin baffling to my working eye, with small veins of coursing light running like veins and arteries through its opaque body.

<<It's done and working within acceptable parameters.>>

I lifted off the fiberglass frame and placed it over the next grouping. ◊Will it be fifteen minutes every time we pour?◊

MuToo sat quietly for a moment. Then as if he were grasping for words a breathy pause hung in the mental air. <<Uh, weird as it will be for me to admit, you have established sufficient protocols that the centaurs and my lower functions can now manage this on templates. Damn. They really do use factories. It explains their technological expansion. Zero waste.>>

That surprised me. We happened to be ahead of schedule. Well, maybe just early for the ugly parts. I dreaded the next things deeply.

◊So, to recap, you now have two working autopilots which a pair of these robo-taurs can walk out and load into each jet. Then the two of them fire up the machines, get them prepped to fly, and load the bombs—pre-armed and ready to pop. As in we are done with the official fly out and get revenge portion of the opera.◊

<<Le Sigh. You were more fun when you preferred brisk operational speak and portmanteaus to this laissez faire hip kid lingo you're slinging at me.>>

◊Greetings, my fellow youths. Yeah, I hear you. But to

reiterate, we can now basically have me walk out and launch the jets on time?◊

<<We can. It's sorted completely.>>

◊Meanwhile the circle of Kraken wedges will be ready roughly when?◊

<<At the rate of matrix growth and what we have to use for fuel, maybe four to five more days. Again, I'm on top of this. An idiot with a half stack array could run it. Also sorted.>>

◊You have the storage unit I asked for? The cryonics inside a shielded courier bag thingy? ◊

<<Yes. Eye roll. I have prepared for you to pour more pinky blood and tears into a very large bag, freeze it inside a cellular preservation matrix that will keep it ninety-nine point nine nine seven eight repeating viable for six plus solar years. So?>>

Right. Stalling would not help. ◊Meet me in the sterile lab section in twenty minutes. Bring the centaurs and a mop. We can wait an hour to start the goop to server limbo while we handle the last piece of business.

Then I went upstairs and grabbed gunshot tampons soaked in antibiotics, some IV bags with heavy food and vitamin mixes, a blood analog transfusion bag that could be injected with nanites, and a bottle of pure alcohol. From there I grabbed the tools I surreptitiously laid out yesterday, now sterile and gleaming ominously. Last came the zip ties and plug in cigar lighter, one of those old coil heat units. Turned out to be the unbreakable way to convert electricity to heat when all else failed.

MuToo woke up when I walked into the sterile area. <<Well, what happens now?>>

In the next room the server farm hummed, one with a low thrum as it worked on wavelengths no longer human designed. ◊Now you jump all of you and my mental map into the circle next to us.◊

<<You'll need me for the flight.>>

◊A version of you and I will be running the controls. So, I have you. Right now, I need you out of my head and body, because this whole biological unit you've been using as a shark cage will soon be toast. Jump now and start using the tools in the lab to self-improve. You still need to make the call as we take off.◊

The plan there happened to be elegant. When the jets took off, I'd call Charlie to negotiate my last treaty. But traces would hear or see MuToo squeeze out a bunch of data packets to a few satellites. If we kept the planes and lab within a klick of one another, then it would be impossible to see where it all came from. So, they'd assume he, like me, happened to be on the planes. Which one—who knew. They'd have to track them both.

The squeezed data would confirm the teardrop and I were enroute. But it would also hide coded messages from MuToo telling his siblings where to send a courier to pick up the data and biologicals. One-way dead drop. They might also keep sucking down memories and thoughts from the two autopilots and maybe just maybe, the denuded AI free version of me riding in the cargo hold with four nukes all the way to Beijing.

<<Fiiiine. Well, goodbye and good luck.>> Yeah, that suited the surly half reality of Murray stripped down to his logical outer shell.

Then things popped and all went eerily quiet. For the moment I had nobody inside my head and no AI lurking behind major organs. "You can hear me?"

MuToo had called my earpiece. "Yes, loud and clear. Okay ready the bag, get the hatrack prepped with the IVs and blood. Wire it all up and let me know when you've got the whole shebang prepped for quick action."

I cracked open the booze and drank heavily. Fuel and painkillers in one. Warm sludge poured up and down my spine, then my lungs wheezed with faint fire. Not for the faint hearted. I downed more until nearly a liter of the 1.5-liter bottle had disappeared into my stomach and blood stream.

"Ready." One of the centaur dogs held the sealed bag in its grippers with the other one ready to open the main flap when my blood appeared.

I grabbed two threaded zip ties and placed them at the second knuckle of my pinky and ring finger, so that each finger had two full bones above them exposed. Then grit my teeth and pushed the heating unit in. When the thing popped, I lifted the pruning shears I'd brought and with swift deliberation clipped each finger at the joint.

The bag opened and grippers swiftly moved. I ignored all motion, controlling the excruciating pain. With a quick flick the zip ties tightened, stopping the blood loss. Then the lighter burned the exposed joint in what could only be described as the worst fucking pain I'd felt since Zeus had beat the crap out me a few years ago. The booze in my stomach churned. Still, it deadened the shock long enough for my back up nanites to start doing their thing.

"WHAT THE HELL?"

"Shh!" I grabbed the garden tool next to the sheers. It looked like an oversize apple corer. Post hole / seed planter. Something we'd stashed in case the stranded crew in the lab needed to restart civilization and that included agriculture. Instead, I took a deep breath, blew it out and jammed the thing over my left eye, through my orbital socket and into the brain beyond.

That hurt far less. But intellectually, performing my own partitioned lobotomy scared the emotional crap out of me. Still, this had to be done. I turned and pulled out. Smart ol' me had greased the sides of the tube with sterile colloidal silver solution—basically anti infection lube. But it sure hurt on the edges with nerves.

The bag appeared and with some spasms my partially working hands managed to get the core of eye, brain, and skull bones into the bag before I predictably slid to the floor. I managed to pop in the wound tampon, pour the booze over the hole, puffing the thing to fit the leaking mess, and possibly asked for MuToo to hit me with the IVs.

For the record I did not dream. In a good hour or so, what was left of me came awake with a slow fit of half seizures. MuToo had poured nano-goo into the socket and jacked me full of blood, IV fluid, and some bandages that appeared to basically be the grey black Kraken slime wiped across my skin.

We had time. I lay on the floor for as long as the timeline allowed, healing from my self-inflicted head wound and amputation. MuToo did a lot of pointless shouting. The needs of the many and all that. But I had done what I had come to do. Eventually, maybe a few weeks and a lot of help, the preponderance of my brain damage might be repaired by my own upgraded nanomaterial. But for now, I had one good eye, a slurred voice, and not that much feeling in my right hand. Also, I appeared to be slightly incontinent which embarrassed me more than mumbling and drooling.

At the appointed hour, the radioactive centaurs greeted me at the door of the Quonset hut. I sealed the airlock behind me and wrapped in a lead lined blanket to humor MuToo hustled out to my jet. Grippes hauled me up the stairs as my left leg bobbled a bit. Guess I pushed the corer in a wee bit harder and further than expected. Also, the back of my head wept, suggesting I'd punched out a portion of my own skull at the hairline. Doofus.

Once the robots had me comfortably strapped down next to an ominous box wired to a small cobalt generator and a laptop from some ancient trove with four green *armed* signals, they trotted out of the craft and something remote closed the doors. Me and MuToo inside the systems. We'd rigged the door to remote seal and lock. The three nukes in missiles on the bottom of the plane had nice green telltales, as did my very own Kevorkian box strapped next to me. From here on out it would be one hundred percent automated.

Perhaps I blacked out, perhaps I simply drooled and peed my pants as the hangar doors opened and the craft taxied out to start their pre-flight prep. When take-off had to happen, when waiting for me to say "Go" got the better of my own cyber self, a voice that seemed tinnier and more nasal woke me.

"Spetz, wake up. Time to call Charlie and piss off your remaining friends."

"Right. I got no friends."

"Exactly. So, make the call."

"What do I call you?"

"Pilot Ex, the merciless yet magnificent genius pilot program without a name but lots of game."

That made me laugh. Right, not me. Me and a MuToo merged. Heavy on snark and heavier on lethal intent.

A ringer bounced about my impaired head. Every time the phone rang my right eye bobbled. Weird. Side effects may vary. I'd complain to my neurosurgeon.

On the seventh bobble, as the plane began to push forward and gain speed, Charlie picked up. "Spetz?"

"Hello, Charlie. Calling from the airport. On my way to visit friends in Bikini Atoll."

"Sounds like you've been, um, drinking."

It must sound like I had been snacking on steel wool. But ok, drinking would be plausible. "Um, truth be told, this call might be a baaaad idea. So yeah, might be I had some pills and a little vodka for breakfast."

The jet lifted. By now MuToo had sent his packets and taken in whatever the dead drop systems had loaded in orbiting satellites. He'd be dead signal and behind a lot of firewalls before they triangulated to source. It was all done but the crying.

"Vodka and pills, that's very much out of character for you, my friend."

Ah. Much challenge. "But are we friends, Charlie, because my systems tell me you're not a person but a machine. One that's been screwing with their forward progress all this good long while."

The line crackled. An open line, one being monitored by every sinister badass alive. "Well sure, my outward systems are just that. But surely you understand there's a person behind the exterior façade."

Right. He wanted to sell the lie to watchers beyond. I had other plans. "Yeah, so I took some pills to quell my stomach and deaden the pain. Seems I got myself a nasty case of cobalt poisoning because one of my huts had a genuine fucking air leak. My nanites are shit this week. So, it's been hurting. Imagine that, Charlie. Being able to feel pain."

That pause again. Message sent. "Well, you do sound drunk. Impaired nanites sounds less than ideal when you have pretty much the whole Cult and the entirety of The Hive coming to greet you in Bikini."

I snorted. My pants got wet. The mortification of it reminded me never to get old. This sucked. "Pina's bringing her own damned army dude. Not calling about that though."

He paused and a thoughtful voice came through the line. "What are you calling about? Because I don't have to tell you how incredibly stupid this is. You won the last conflict by never allowing your opponents into your attack space. Now you're dialing for dollars every three days. What gives?"

Before, when my eyes and brain worked as a team, perhaps that comment would have triggered a cascade of revelations. Now, it just made me slightly annoyed. He basically had said—you are acting like a dumbass. Which, while ostensibly true, did not make us closer friends. That got me laughing. Oh, gods below, what a strange life to end this way.

"Look. I see how you see it but consider this. We got The Cult and The Hivemind, big daddy world domination with his bestie Cassandra slash Agnes slash Nurhan slash my evil Moooom, pretty much all the bad guys as we know it converging to grab my kid in his box. Only one of us will get out right?"

"You got drunk and called me to say there's going to only be one winner to this pointless war?"

"Look, for an AI you're an insulting prick. But you have a point. I called you to propose a bargain."

Long silence, more crackling. That's right kids. We spoofed the transponder and used everyone else's satellites to bounce the call into the stratosphere. We could not be counter hacked. Not in time. "I'm listening."

"I'm not coming back. Either The Hive ends us all or Pina wins by the hair of her chinny chin chin in which case she can't afford to let me raise my own children. Because let's face it, I'm somewhat lethal when aroused."

He chuckled. "Less drunk than you're playing. You plan to die?"

"Oh, Charlie, you've known me a good long while. I'm utterly predictable. I guarantee I'm a dead man walking. I'm just saying, if and when they whack me, let's call it even and let what's left of the world live in peace. Live and let live, bygones and such."

"That's unlikely."

"Consider this. It will be the whale and tiger. Whales have their songs, their civilizations. Perhaps just this once the whales might teach the tigers how to live in peace."

Take the hint! Dammit, Charlie, please. I didn't need to hear him say it. In time he'd get my implied points but no one likes to die unfulfilled. I wanted him to acknowledge me. Huh. Human after all. It made me smile.

"The tiger won't listen."

I sighed. "But if the tiger did, just this once, if the tiger could finally hear the song, would it hurt so much to try?"

The deadness in my ears filled with dread. Charlie had cut the line. Or something had.

"Hellllooooo, this is your pilot speaking. Seems we are experiencing a global event as satellites and server farms are being shut down or bombed under the cover of the Russian invasion. Not to worry, we are on time to our destination."

Right. No reply did not mean no acceptance. But it rankled me. I got up and checked the plane. We'd dumped me in a small, pressurized cube with nukes and enough air for a one-way trip. Irradiated air that would ensure what was left of me died within a few weeks. Ha!

An hour later the speak burped. "We just got three pings in a row. From a source we assume came from Point Nemo. Charlie alone has resources there right now."

Three pings. More than needed, more than yes or no. The Kraken would watch and wait. Humanity had its treaty if we could simply arrange the players.

At the end of your life, you spend far too much time thinking about love. About the people you lost and wished you could have back in your arms one more time. My niece, Darcy, my ex-partner from Zambia—a woman who'd only known me as a detective—Harv of all people, and finally sadly, Pina. We liked one another. My kids, well they had to know how much I loved them. My huntresses and shadow selves, we'd covered it all. But these few human souls, one more day, one more dance, or roll in the hay, or wry joke.

My cat, Hippo. Him I truly loved. He'd make it but would anyone know how to scratch his chin just right or how he liked his midnight snacks? Would anyone miss him, viscerally? Would they sing to him from the bathtub and read him stories in the library? Maybe.

The thought of Hunter reading Proust to Hippo in my stupid

modern NYC apartment set me laughing. In real time my head and fingers had started healing. I'd lied to Charlie and through him the world. My upgrades would render me ready to fight by the time the cruise missiles hit Beijing. Still, it all proved pointless.

I maundered about in my memories, in my desires. Was it the brain matter rebuilding or did you actually do this when you died? Did you regret? Did you walk back through every comment, every lost opportunity, every chance to tell someone important you loved them or missed them? Did you mourn lost chances at friendship?

I had expected rage. Denial. Pure spite. To think through every bastard who had it coming. But none of that mattered. It would work or it would not. But Gay Eddie and Edith—such a lost chance to spend a week in Patagonia with a coven of Eddies, some of whom lusted for me. Intellectually fascinating and now gone. To have one more day with any of my kids, to meet Daddy-O. To piss off Murray one more time. Hell, to eat gelato in Central Park and see the normies going about their structured little lives filled with pointless power games and one upmanship, all the while trying to free them from… us. From our own insidious layers of enslavement and locust like predation.

But most of all, I wanted to lie by the fire and pet my cat. Or have sex. Or maybe read a book and drink good coffee while the rain bashed the windows. I wanted my children by my side, causing me endless headaches. I wanted to live, to touch and dream and feel. Like everyone else. Just one little human life. One more day, one more touch, one more chance at the normal things we all treasured.

Instead, the Bikini Atoll jet hit ground zero seventy minutes ahead of our own scheduled impact. I watched the replays as sat feeds stolen from working systems fed me data. We'd wiped The Cult and most of The Hivemind down to constituent elements. But no Nurhan and no Pina. No. They'd be digging into my trove, trying to steal what they imagined was the real Murray.

We launched missiles. The news of the Atoll being wiped from the map would take a bit. That's the super nice side effect of nukes. They deliver an electromagnetic pulse and fry all the electronics in the area. By the time someone got new eyes in the sky, saw the damage, and realized a nuke had hit, the cruise missiles would be at target. Well, the first ones at least. We'd planned them as staggered hits, in five-minute intervals to maximize cave-ins and avoid ground to air defenses.

The first cruise missile hit within millimeters of the target. Then the second one curved, avoiding a surface to air missile and hit three meters from the planned impact site. We got the third one down the hole and hey, the nice thing about tactical nukes—they make a pretty big bang. The force of the missile combined with the split-second explosion timed to pop before hitting the interior of the sunken undercarriage created a pleasing crater. Followed by two more missiles that charged down the hole unopposed. EMPs do wonders for knocking down SAM targeting systems.

Still, if Cassandra had bunkered up just right, then perhaps she'd survived the prior three hits. Chances were under one percent. Well, when we did the calculations MuToo had suggested it as roughly one trillion against survival. But do not ever bet against The House when the fate of all civilization happens to be on the line.

I'd had the final warhead adjusted to maximum radiation. Whatever we hit would absorb a lethal dose of greys before the shockwave delivered its own blessings. The fourth bomb pushed the chances from one in a squillion to null. Nothing would survive what I hit.

The seconds ticked down. My mind grew chill and my memories faded. It seemed so quiet here, in this little space. The plane had started accelerating to breakdown or break apart speed. At this point we could splatter across Beijing and still get the deed done. Still, the Chinese never did anything to me. Better to drop down the hole and limit the death toll.

It gets quiet when you die. I'd done it before—with the last nuke. But this time I saw it coming. I'd planned it, prepped, and said my goodbyes, lined up all the dominoes. There was time to regret or fear or whatever. But mostly it felt quiet. Soft. At long last everything would stop hurting.

00:07. A lifetime in quantum hours. I wondered if the autopilots regretted dying.

00:04. She called me Cookie Monster and danced on my toes.

00:01. Time to go. Time to be welcomed, to see my mother again. To ….

A woman's voice called out. Her voice. From memory, all those years ago, comforting me when she could. *Knife That Does, I am waiting.*

Then I smiled and walked home to my mother's arms.

Chapter 14: Aftermathematics

How much of me really came back? It's an open question, not one I'm likely ever to answer. Some of me died decades ago in the labs of the Abschnitt, some along the way, some in service to The Syndicate, and some, likely a fair bit, died with my body in the crater we left under a small portion of Beijing.

The Chinese hid all the evidence as did the Marshall Islands authorities. The Russians blasting through Kyiv and the eastern edge of Ukraine gave the world a place to look. The Hivemind had set the stage and it never occurred to him to plan an "after" should something happen to his core mind. Zeus had failsafes in place but without his leadership cadre or him, The Cult would have splintered into infighting within weeks. Assuming they had been allowed the leisure. A rogue tsunami wiped their HQ into distant memory. The survivors developed peculiar cancers and parasitic infections—something functionally impossible given their genetic pedigree.

That left me SOL for finding a baseline comparison. The Cult and its hideous obsession with eugenic worship had records of every Section 21 generation. As did Nurhan in her various forms. By proxy, The Hivemind had them and then some—other fascinating forms of being and doing, different paths to sapience. But I'd done the unthinkable. I'd truly killed myself.

Spetz = predictable. That had been my calling card for generations of operators. Everyone knew me by my actions, by my linear on off binary truth. But this one time, when it all hung on the line, I'd played the long con and simply not shown up for the confrontation with the big bad. Ever watched an action movie where the big hero dies an hour before the big showdown?

Me neither. No one expected the nukes, not after I, of all people, had done my level best to prevent their usage worldwide. The Bucharest Accords where Ukraine disarmed had been my doing. A gift to my people. Then Putin had wiped his ass with the treaty. Scumbag.

They expected me to show up in Bikini Atoll good to my word and fight it out with Pina by my side against all comers. Only of course to be backshot by the treacherous bitch. Or if you happened to be Nurhan / Mom and Pina, you knew my head fakes when you saw them and rushed off to Beijing to murder me there. Except I didn't show. Bombs did.

Net results. I died. No getting around the fact. Spetz the operative, Spetz the human, Spetz the icon and idea, the villain and killer, the seven-foot badass chaos machine. Dead. Permanently. Also dead: my all too trusting brother Zeus who thought he'd outsmarted me by laying a huge trap in the Marshall Islands. With him seventy percent of the renegades and his picked children. Essentially The Cult died there in one bright flash.

The Hivemind outsmarted himself, sending his self in two places, splitting his ever-present singular mind. He could apparently do this for brief periods of time. Or so the surviving ten Eddies informed us. Two died in Beijing. Edith never made it out of Patagonia. She got bitten by a snake of all things. Ironic and wasteful. A damned local snake. Not even a poisonous one, just a big, scared animal which gave her an infected wound. The low-grade radiation poisoning probably didn't help.

One half of The Hive died in Bikini and the other half, screaming in anguish managed to hold on long enough to freak out Agnes, force her to almost panic, and true to my assumptions drop herself into a bunkered up safe room. Dosing herself with nanites, iodine pills, and some other kinds of injectable shock armor. She had anticipated treachery just not nuclear style. Dirty bombs, Depleted Uranium, that sort of shenanigans—sure. But suitcase nukes down the keister? I threw her a curve ball.

She kept some video records. Or rather, she accidentally failed to shield her electronics fully and the passive sensors in the facility broadcast her last resentful minutes. With her died the same collection of fiends and brigands Zeus had brough along, only the scientifically sadistic types—torture heads and necrophiles. Some of The Swarm and Hive remained but once the main mind perished, every one of the poor bastards hooked up to his power simply fell over and starved to death. Horrific.

And the villain? Or heroine depending on which side of the freedom you fought. Agrippina Karthago stayed home and watched. Why? Because she never had an iota of ego invested in this war. She existed to end eons of slavery and free the human species. She played the queen sacrifice, let me get killed in either location, and went about winning the war. Smartest of us all.

But see, I'd ripped out my own eye and cut my fingers off for a reason. Ever wonder what defines a god? Not the big G deity but the small guys, the horny horrors of myth. Zeus had no flaws save his vices, but his arrogance and rapacity ended him. Like his namesake, he chased his hubris. But I'd always preferred the Norse. Wotan. Woland. Odin. The man who swapped an eye for wisdom. Who hung upside down like a convict or murderer to find perspective. The being who punished breaches in honor and hospitality.

In the last war I'd told Pina we faced Ragnarök. I had not lied. Blow the horn, smash the Bifrost, bring forth the jötnar who might be giants, might be monsters, might be perverted men, and let's be done. Still, some of the divine survived to rebuild. I'd been mistaken when years ago my hand had placed in Pina's the weapons of Ragnarök. We had not ended the war; we had begun it.

The ensuing chaos and - give Spetz his due, he sowed so much in so many places - pandemonium erupted across the globe. Markets crashed, the Russians stuttered and began to entrench their war crimes bullshit, The Syndicate suffered egregious attrition, The Kraken sank ships and screwed with weather, and all in all, a bad time for the forces of Ambiguous Evil was universally had.

That gave the kids time to transfer the courier bag and the spooky machines MuToo had kept building, cannibalizing, and rebuilding with evolving AI to a very secure location. From there, the patented centaur-bots got some shiny new paint, a lot of upgraded software, and a mass deployment using a spray paint the chassis with black/gray goo template. The five AIs kaizened the hell out of the process, until they could build anything they wanted with a model, a template protocol, some aerosolized stem cell slime, and a base material that played nice with rapid cellular modification. Nicolas Flamel, eat your heart out.

What they built defied expectations. The eye and fingers, the enneagrams and recorded memories, the rebuilt cerebrospinal matrix, and their own best guesses went into the hopper with a lot of Kraken tech, the use of five AIs going full force quantum fugue, and essentially unlimited time, budget, and material resources. I woke up on the third day. Very biblical.

Knife That Does did. Because much of my prior self, my old memories and desires existed as grey haze in the corner of my consciousness. I knew it existed, it had been a core driver in my existence, and now, it simply informed my intellectual understanding. Of my "real" self, the kids estimated my eye and fingers with all that compacted data and brain matter brought across forty percent of my memories, personality, and emotional essence.

In the past, various Cassandras had done the same process with at best two percent of the person. Our process represented a twenty times better capture of the true me. We had at our advantage multiple independently recorded brain scans, data dumps, baseline biologic, and a whole lot of vastly superior computing power not to mention the ability to hack the nano-biology of their Frankenstein monster on the fly and with permanent results. Last estimate from the quintet: eighty-five percent of the memories and personality inside me represented indistinguishable facsimiles and perfect copies of my prior self.

That last fifteen percent just didn't exist. Literally. The body they woke up stood 175 centimeters which measures just under five foot nine and weighed 175 kilograms, aka 385 pounds and none of it slack. MRI analogs (they used something called a wave resonance interpolation scanner) told us I lacked bones, organs, or a circulatory system. Beneath my human veneer the structure of me resembled a transformer cross bred with carbon tube muscle tissue, if somehow it had been designed by a sentient maglev. I ate and drank, I breathed, I walked and spoke like any other living being. But there the resemblance ended. My whole body doubled as rebar, crash cage, armor, etc. etc. while also being supple, easy to turn and twist, and really good at riding impact and pressure waves. Bones are nice but an entire molecular structure that can be plasticine, solid, liquid, or all the above within nanoseconds works on a different material and, by association, mechano-kinetic level.

We argue, the kids and me if I am a robot, an android, a ghost in a literal machine, a new form of human species, a cybernetic hybrid (lots of animal DNA floating in the eighty-five percent which survived), and maybe none of the above. I can speak with them at will, across great distances. I have tremendous computational access and influence over dumb machines. It's damned hard to damage me and harder to permanently deactivate me. I'm not even sure if I qualify as living. Perhaps a Revenant or Fext would be the appropriate model. Cybernetic Undead.

All of which proved irrelevant to the central drama still in play. Pina struggled to get her New World Order orderly enough to send the killing blow to her own operators as well as The Kraken. I brewed in vats under an ice rink in Poughkeepsie, NY. The world stuttered and slowly oozed toward the new normal unaware that World War Infinity continued to play out in shadows and media blackouts.

The kids won the race. Momo and MuToo had argued for an expedited and fairly close to the original copy of me Right Fucking Now over Murray and Daddy-O's desire to get me back to my original cheerful self. Mercy broke the tie. They decided that their survival depended on Charlie's continued goodwill. Waking me up to thwart Pina mattered more than waking me up to warm anyone's cockled heart. Apparently, my love of word games persisted.

A short blunt dark faced man with grey hair, black eyes, and a predatory gait rose from the slab and requested a snack. By the time they got me remembering my names and able to speak in passable English, the protocols handed me a bag of memories. Pina. Still out there, still trying to win.

It took me a few hours and a lot of back / forth to comprehend what had been lost since by default I, the new version of "me" inhabiting my hybrid body, knew no other life. It took longer to walk through the broken stems of crushed flowers and dreams, of spiritual loss and emotional bonds. To find my children, to find Tiio still cradled in my sacred heart. To Wake Up.

From there events proceeded ruthlessly. I had them smuggle me out into Russian territory, at the Kutzkan line near Finland and waited. Some of my own people found me. Knife That Does simply did for a short while. I served the tribe, I located and delivered hidden villages in the bag, I carried the news from the debauched worlds beyond.

Meanwhile the kids played dead. Well, Mercy, MuToo, and Daddy-O never technically existed but Momo and Murray had to lay low and pretend to be broken versions of their former selves. Like me, come to think.

Corrupting core systems, rerouting traffic, sabotaging the Russian war effort and such seemed like a fun game to play. They played it gleefully. In the weeks that followed, the Chinese clamped down and cited Covid riots, the Russians lost people and machines at alarming rates, shipping and ports suffered freak accidents, Paraguay had a spate of drug raids and anti-fascist police actions, dead homeless people started making appearances in morgues worldwide as the weather turned colder. Covid, the war, Media Hype, Global Warming, Nutjob Conspiracies, Aliens, and such dominated the news. People forgot what they'd seen. New York City wiped up the rubble and moved on. Planes flew, resorts filled, wars crawled, oligarchs flew to space or private islands, sanctions and UN resolutions got leveraged, and not one damned real thing changed.

One crisp winter day, when Agrippina finally had The Syndicate sorted, Oslo's network rebuilt and lined up for slaughter, and her sights yet again on her last geopolitical rival, The Kraken, she took a flight with Kelba and Harv to Finland. We have this nice facility in Kuusamo.

Correction—they have it. I am no longer Syndicate.

They arrived, set up a security perimeter and went about their core operations. The kids had lured them there under the pretext of an actual Kraken sea to land base situated not far from Kuusamojärvi Lake. Well, underneath it really but with a fascinating tunnel system which led out through various locks and chambers to the White Sea on the Russian side of the border.

Thinking was—thanks to Mercy providing a mostly accurate strategic assessment—they took an isolated base, skinned it alive with commandos and chemicals, figured out how to war on aquatic people and proceeded with ruthless scalability. As a result, they flew in nearly forty of the most hardened mercenaries available. Men (no women in this cadre) who killed and ate their enemies, especially Dutch, American, and Russian mercs. The Dahmer Crew. Really. Tacky and none too appetizing when you're cutting a digital check, but they got the job done and when you plan to face ninety percent attrition, you hire assholes no one will miss.

What you did not do—SOP—was let those expendable assholes inside your security perimeter. Pina and Kelba, morally certain Ragnarök had been won and in the spirit of remaking their world in their godly self-image practiced a little hubris. They brought Harv and a few trusted bodyguards. No one expected to face an attack inside the building and even if they worried it might happen, once they locked the doors, clamped down the blast doors, and fired up their ever-present but not yet fully awake Murray system, they had the facility entirely secure.

Suited me just fine. Over dinner, as they passed around drinks and discussed the operational plans for early the next morning, I walked in with a cup of coffee in my right hand and a H&K MP7A2 in my left. Armed with 40 DU cupro-jacketed rounds. I'd become left-handed in the rebuild.

The H&K represented instant death for the seated bodyguards, likely death for the still recovering Harv, and a serious setback for my Swarm enabled targets: Pina and Kelba. A setback sufficient to allow me to walk up and casually chop their heads off with the machete belted at my side or one of the three tomahawks I'd brought along as back up to my back up. Because overkill seemed the best way to open negotiations.

Then I smiled, took a sip, and waited. Genetics are a bitch.

With all the various ethnicities and species floating in my bone marrow added to whatever The Kraken had designed into their version of humanity, the improved android me looked nothing like Spetz. Different bones, different size, different hair and eyes, different posture, and smell. Compact, lethal, elegant, dark.

Pina, to her credit, crossed her legs and took a sip of her wine before addressing me. "From the Atlanteans, are you?"

"Absolutely fucking not. I am in fact the living embodiment of the complaints department."

That flummoxed them. Kelba shifted and I gave her a piercing smile. Momo had every camera and sensor in the room rigged to gather micro-recruitments of muscles. If the killer tried for me, she'd be a pincushion before she cleared her chair. When she watched me and realized I knew not just what she was doing but who she must be, she blanched.

Pina watched the byplay. "I don't have a complaints department."

Harv had started to slide his hand toward a hidden gun. "Harv, please. Of all the assholes in this room, you might be my personal favorite. I'd hate to undo all the work it took saving you. Please don't reach for the gun. Nor the grenades you started carrying in the flat of your back."

Harv squinted and turned to Pina. "He's from Spetz. Has to be. A failsafe provision. I told you he never stops and you argued." He motioned at me with grim satisfaction. "Well congratulations, we have a situation here that requires finesse." Which was Harv-speak for no military options presently existed. Poor guy. It must chap his already sore ass to sit there and wait to be shot while the ladies played footsie with their egos. Still, part of the job and all that.

Kelba cocked her head. "Is he right, are you from that bastard? The one who killed our people?"

"Sheesh, Kelba, stern words for the pet assassin of the most killiest killer this side of the Opium War. Huh? That's right. I know who you two are and where you came from. Let's drop the bullshit here. I came to negotiate or I could have just blown you all up in your sleep."

Pina stood up slowly and gave me a bow. "Not from Spetz.

He is Spetz. He somehow downloaded himself like Eddie and The Hive. He swapped his mind or something. Listen to the cadence of the speech. It's you, isn't it?" She seemed delighted.

"It's sorta me. Consider me someone else, someone who lived inside him, the sliver of humanity he held onto all this time. Call me Cutter."

Pina sat down. "Okay, Cutter, you came to complain or negotiate?" Smart, so smart. But not aware yet of how perilous things would be for her.

"Let me explain the situation so I can put down this silly gun and have a nice honest chat with my former colleagues."

Kelba gave me a stern nod and then, looking at Pina, eyebrow raised, waited for her boss to do the same. Pina waved her hand. Deal.

"You did not in fact lose your AIs. You have several fully functioning systems which all work with me, since you know, they are my children and brought me back from the dead."

Harv swore in colorful Xhosa. Yeah, he understood.

"As such, we took the liberty of arming the air vents with sarin and a few extra things. If you manage to jump me and live, which is unlikely these days, since I am now far more upgraded than you two," my finger jabbed toward the women, moving the gun about dangerously, "then the air should kill you, every one of you without exception, within about fifteen seconds. If that fails, we just pump until it's hard vacuum and you can persist for another ten minutes. Cell death has no remedy without oxygen."

Kelba jumped, grabbed my gun and turning it on me, pulled the trigger. The gun which had no firing pin. I punched my left-hand knife-style through her stomach. Solid machine vs human flesh, even hard bodies with armored flesh, had a predictable outcome. When my hand exited under her floating ribs with a kidney, she crumpled. I crushed her skull with a boot to the rear of her fallen head. Brains splattered everywhere. RIP Kelba.

That seemed to punctuate my conversational points. It also made us slightly even for Pina's prior attempts and betrayals. Kelba had mattered to her, and she'd just discovered how far into her own hubris she'd followed the song of delusion and power.

Mind you, Kelba likely had to die to seal the deal with Charlie. But if she had been willing to make peace, if she had been other than what she was, other than a motivated and hardened killer with centuries to reconsider genocide—a plan she pursued like a religion—then perhaps her life would not have had to end with so little dignity or pretense. But … big but … that proved the whole point of me being there.

We made this world in the stark evil of our own psychopathic image. We saw only our own dark shadows, inked with depravity, and smudged with sins of various degree. Those few of us who wanted a better world, who saw ourselves as monsters, could no more live in the freedom and decency of the light than the humanity we planned to break out of slavery. Just because we fought to save the world didn't mean we had the least comfort living in what we had built.

Pina and Kelba had been moving toward extinction of their own species for centuries. Likely Agrippina decades or even tens of decades longer than her Sommelier. Morality, logic, the possibility of a better outcome, none of those stood a chance against the pure self-hatred and constitutional loathing these women felt for The Swarm as a category of ontological existence. They hated more than they cared; ergo, the complaints department had just lodged its first memo. Boot to head style.

Pina rose and despite herself took a swing. Give her her due, she had fooled the world for a long time. In her time, she had been the single most lethal weapon Nurhan had ever produced, her ultimate daughter self, the bionic super hybrid, extra Nazi fortified, better physical and mental killer self that Cassandra had always aspired too. She added height, beauty, and maybe raw political savvy just because. Vain bitch, my mother.

For me, nano-enabled quantum, wired into sensor systems and communicating at a subconscious level with Momo, Pina moved like flowing molasses. I kicked her through a wall. Then put my tomahawks through all three of Harv's hand selected enforcers. The same enforcers Pina and Kelba has maneuvered him to choose using various psychological ploys, social pressure, careful lies, and some database management. Right after they skinned the lake of its amphibious monsters, the ladies planned to trial run killing the Oslo network, starting with the most dangerous of their loyal team—Harv Littman himself.

By the time the poor man, a mere human, reacted to the movement Pina had gone through a wall, his colleagues had become living examples of what hydraulic force and good Mohawk steel can achieve, and I'd knocked his hand aside from his reflexive grab. He hadn't even decided whether to get the gun or grenade. His nerves had coiled, the recruitment orders sent, but we machines live at a level far beyond obsolete things like neurotransmitters and neurons.

Harv stopped, stunned. "What, what?"

I sighed. "Sorry, Harv. There's some complex explaining to do. Let's have Pina return and start talking. You should hear it from her."

The wall shivered a few seconds later and a battered version of Pina, covered in cuts, a bruised face, and a lot of drywall dust limped through to sit down again. "Hear what?"

"How you planned to murder him as a precursor to committing total genocide against all forms of life not fully human."

Harv turned and looked at her. The woman stared at me but said nothing. If she had an emotion, then perhaps hate emanated from her. Perhaps simply menace. Could someone that broken feel hate?

"I told you he'd return, and you told me to stuff it. And what did I say, Pina, I said… I told you that if you had to do it, then retire my people, send them on goose chases, but spare them. I offered you my life—straight up knew you had to take it. But you couldn't really accept that?"

The man sounded both angry and hurt. He'd known, or suspected. Had bargained for this people. Which sounded very familiar. And she'd done what? Been like me—predictable. Well, not me. Spetz.

Pina turned to him. She appeared to be crying. "You did, you told me. But if I had to kill my own people. If I had to sacrifice Wickham for this, then what's one more person whom I loved?"

That confirmed another pet theory. That the entire Autumn War, like this one, had been a big triple head fake, to lure out

The Hive and Nurhan, to consolidate Oslo on both sides of The Syndicate and The Swarm, and to wipe out every last one of us. When Murray woke up, Pina not Cassandra or any other external threat had moved to wipe him out—this time by luring me back in to … line him up for the kill.

"You killed my family. Literally had them murdered and lined up this bizarre opera of false fronts, operatives, and internal war, all to get me to flush out the AIs, to find and kill my kids in preparation for Charlie."

Pina nodded. She knew now I had her. That I could kill her, either here face to face, or if she somehow possibly got the upper hand, by proxy. For the first time in living memory, she had been not just defeated but conquered. She had lost.

Harv looked at me then at her. "Fucking monsters."

"Well, yes Harv. The interview you threw me, the one where we went from zero to murder and exfiltrated a building in a stolen war machine might have indicated just how filthy awful the whole lot of us were, have always been."

He shook his head. "No, not you Spetz. Well, Cutter. I can see you're not him, but you know … him. You had a decent streak."

"A good monster?"

He laughed. "Where the Wild Things Are. Something. You inspired me, man, to follow Oslo, to follow the plan, to you know, lay down my miserable violent life to save my people and humanity. It … just made sense seeing you save me, save her, save us all. Time after fucking time. And what?" He gave his broken leader a smoldering look. "All this thing, this whole damned set of wars, she set it up as some kind of fucking demented game?"

Pina shook her head. "Not a game."

Harv spit on her. "Yes, a game. Because hey, look, here's your own daughter, your flesh and blood, splattered on the fucking grimy floor. Why? Because you, Agrippina the super smart fucking Karthago, thought nobody in the whole world could be tougher or smarter than you."

Her own daughter. Nurhan, Pina, Kelba, Zeus. The mind boggled.

"Her name's not Pina. She killed and replaced her."

Pina gave me a sad smile. Lost her own kid. To arrogance, to madness and what? Hate, fear, a religious certainty? The hubris to chase down hubris, to assign yourself the role of The Fates? We had just recreated all the Greek tragedies in one go, put them in some kind of blender, added a bunch of nanotech, and puked them over an innocent world.

"Elisabeth Christine. My original name was that."

Harv gave a shrug. Apparently, 18th century European history was not part and parcel of South African mercenary education. Elisabeth Christine Ulrike of Brunswick-Wolfenbüttel, Crown Princess of Prussia. The woman who rode horses like men, mocked the king, caused massive scandals, and ultimately was exiled for having a daughter. Damn, it could not be Kelba. Not then. But later or in a lab or who knew how.

Still, Pina had to have changed her appearance. Well Elisabeth had. To inhabit the life of Pina, the operative inside The Swarm whose role she had subsumed. Whole volumes of mysteries could be printed trying to explain how Nurhan in China had migrated West, birthed Elisabeth upon the world, and then started an insane civil war between them that brough down The Web.

"Well, Princess, it has become Pina and with that name, with that life, you bought a package of beliefs. Which will have to be modified."

She cocked her head. She had expected a monologue and an execution. After all she had done, after all the ways Spetz had wiped out every living thing associated with the death of his family as well as any threat to his remaining kin, no one could reasonably expect otherwise. When I woke up, the core of me had not expected otherwise. But without the fire of my old memories, with them as mere intellectual constructs, the light of pure reason had an equal say.

Daddy-O had suggested this firmly makes me a machine. That the defining nature of humanity is, was, and will always be our emotionality. But then, that's an emotional argument. Especially since we haven't seen humanity unfettered and free to choose in millennia. Still, he had a strong point. It did preclude me from being a revenant though—because if emotion defined humans, then the undead for the most part craved revenge, suffering, or human snacks. Not much else.

I craved peace. A chance for the world my children would inherit to both exist and possibly thrive. Lasting peace, meaningful and true, like the active peace of the Good Mind. Not merely the cessation of war, but the kind of world where crops and kids thrived, where ideas flowed, where love could defeat hate, where art mattered, and people held more value than things. Harmony.

Pina sat down. Well, crumpled. She simply fell into her seat, her eyes lingering on the grotesque scene at her feet. A human body ruined, sphincters opening, blood and brains oozing onto their shoes. Beside them three dead operatives, half stapled to the wall with the force of my throws. The stink of death, of ensuing decay, filled the small space. So much for after dinner planning. The scene punctuated both the stakes of the conversation and the reality of who we all were, what we did.

I hadn't meant to get metaphoric but with all of Pina's maneuvers and love of dramatics, we'd somehow come back to the same old place. A room filled with death and the promise of life, an interview and a chance to change the world. Only this time, I held the power.

"It's like this, Elisabeth. And of course, Harv, you too. The Atlanteans have cut me a deal. If they can live unmolested in their ocean, then maybe, juuuuust maybe, they won't fucking wipe out humanity. Because you arrogant fools completely misunderstood the situation."

Elisabeth / Pina looked at me, a spark of intelligence overcoming her horror and despondency. "Whatever do you mean?"

"Well, you really think you can conquer the entire ocean?"

She shook her head "Of course not…."

I held up a hand. "Then you lost before you began. Because this body of mine, the kids built it using Kraken tech. They sprayed it on. These people, these beings below us, in the oceans and lakes, we have no idea what they look like, how they operate. We see what, a few of their human sapped operators and Charlie. Who you have never met."

She waved a hand. "Because he's an AI."

Fools. Even now, she failed to understand. We are what we do. What did Charlie do? He knew pretty much everything. He hacked calls, he brokered contracts, he moved empires. He was a panentheistic power, a ghost in all machines and yet, he did not touch my children, touch me. He was not a machine. Not of machines.

Logical question: if you are not a machine, are you an AI? If you are a biological machine like The Hivemind was, you are still basically just the biological alternate of Murray. Or vice versa. What then made Charlie work? Power to do, power to achieve, power to exert your will upon the world. Charlie resembled a god. A small god surely, one who did not so much animate in person as send avatars and omens. But he existed at a level that Zeus and his sad sack cult aspired to.

If my best guess got even close to right, Charlie lived in whatever higher or lower or altered reality constituted the quantum interface my kids had started to tap. Started, mind you, after literal eons of nano-life, of trillions of neural evolutions, after unthinkable human lifespans spent at lightspeed or faster, to barely make baby steps six hundred feet wide in optimum conditions. Which somehow, thanks to the unknown adaptations provided by the underline and highlight this, the unknown technology making me smarter faster and tougher than the literal superweapon in human form sitting crushed across from me. The Charlie System might be a consciousness, it might be a user handle of a pod of orcas or deep see octopi, it might be a job filled by various highly aware entities. Or it could be something else.

We did not know. We had not only been outclassed, we had been surpassed on an exponential scale. To The Kraken we looked like ugly little fire ants. Burdensome as we polluted their home; finally dangerous like bees that get Africanized. Our venom, organization, and tenacity were something that required attention. And here we sat, with the queen of the colony, apparently once a literal European regent.

"Charlie is not a machine. Charlie has evolved beyond machines. Likely before we were all born, and I do mean all of us. Whatever he is, my best guess from the limited approximations run by MuToo and Merciless, my kids in case you wondered, would be circa birth of Christ. At the latest. He or she or they or many theys could just as easily predate humans as a species. We are only a million years into the process after all."

"You don't know that."

"Correct, my queen. That's the point. We don't know who he is, where he is, how he does what he does. We can't hurt him because we can't find him. I am made of his technology. His least valuable cheapest tech. What exists past crush depth we simply cannot see. But whatever and whoever he is, he has an army of unknown size with the ability to make unlimited versions of me. Only amphibious armored ten-foot-tall varieties. Or for that matter, tigers with tentacles and wings. Or fire breathing dragons. We cannot predict the unknown. The Kraken isn't a mystery, it's a clusterfuck of black swan events masquerading as a civilization."

Elisabeth looked at me for a long while. "You are certain?"

"The kids made me from stolen tech. I put you through a wall. And they made me without the least focus on improving me. They were trying to make me just like before. I'm the downgraded, underpowered template. I am certain. You should be, too."

Harv wiped his face with a handkerchief and then in a fit of decency handed it to Pina—I couldn't think of her as anyone else—to wipe off the dust and gore. She took it gingerly, wiping off the brains and blood of her people. Her own child. Gods below, what a terrible memory to carry.

"Why bother saving me? They'd prefer me dead. And I will never forgive you for what you just did."

I nodded. Yeah, play time over. "You're wrong on both counts. Pina, you will never forgive yourself for what you did to Kelba. We both know she understood how outmatched she was. But she had to try, had to spit in the face of destiny. You made her this way. You raised your kid as a Nazi."

She rose and looked about to swing.

Harv held her arm gently. "Well, fuck you, Spetz."

I laughed. "I am not him. You killed him. Just like you both planned. Your betrayal worked and that's the whole point. You blame me for showing up and demanding you not commit global genocide. You blame me for defending myself from a deadly attack thrown by your kid. The one you trained to help you murder people, who you personally roped into the family trade of human trafficking, torture, brainwashing, mass murder, drug running, and those are the good things The Syndicate did. You blame me for that?"

"You. Killed. Her."

I shook my head. "She committed suicide. She knew. She didn't want to face a world with mestizo nobodies like me, lesser life forms, interfering with her little eugenic fantasy."

"Saving humanity isn't a eugenic anything."

"It kinda is if you plan to kill all the whales and whatnot to do it. Plus, a whole bunch of equal but different lifeforms. Ones who are, by the fucking way, you horrible nasty demented little Nazi fucking nobody, queer as three-dollar bill, complex, long lived, fabulously curious and inventive, and my goddamned family to boot. That's before you even chased down your own dedicated people, sold a dream of freedom, and the whole ocean, which is – what? – seventy percent of life on earth. Yeah, you're a Nazi and dumb as they ever were. Trust me, I have Spetz's memories."

From the grave he spoke. Harv had been right. He had sent me. We had done the monologue after all—but it had been his, from the grave. Straight up executing Pina. Stripping her down. What had we left? Perhaps Knife That Does and Elisabeth former Queen of Prussia.

"You still killed her."

"And you killed Spetz's family and thousands of other families and so many people for so many centuries, including your own loved ones, that you cannot possibly be so grave a hypocrite as to not grasp the absurdity of your whining."

Pina rocked back as if slapped. Words can kill and these words, logical and correct, struck her with the force of centuries. We are what we do. If you spend your life corralling ethnic minorities into convenient locations, plan a final solution which eliminates them all, and then blame them for it—because they are a corrupting and immoral force—then yes, you are a Nazi.

She knew it then. Saw it then. Saw the madness and the sheer stupidity of chasing down the literal empire under the ocean, a species of who knew what, able to simply wait under the Mesopelagic layer and let you die of old age and blindness. Centuries spent chasing a delusion, an impossible fantasy.

She broke down and sobbed. Harv looked at me, his cold eyes without mirth or rancor. Endlessly old before his time. Scarred. "So, what do they want?"

"Humanity will need a midwife. Do the exact same thing you always planned, except use Oslo's network to slowly equip people with tools of self-determination. The damned Russians under Putin will be a good few decade's work all on their own. Maybe send someone to replace him."

"Pina stays, after all she did?"

"Power and access, she's got all the levers lined up and she's a true believer. Just because her horrific ideology happened to be wrong does not mean she loves people less. Just that like Hitler and his ilk, her fanaticism overtook her."

Harv looked at his blue-black skin. "I'm not so big on Hitler myself."

I grinned. "Me neither, Harv. But with Darcy dead and gone the kids need help."

"They got you."

"I'm not human anymore. Not even close. They need real people. I will be a ghost in the woods, Kutzk. A threat and a promise. To hunt down and kill every last one of you."

"If she breaks the truce."

We both nodded. Harv looked over at the broken husk of what had been the supreme power of the world. A woman who'd gotten within a hair's breadth of defeating all her enemies and just at the moment of her greatest triumph discovered her disastrous mistake. Like I said, Greek Tragedy in the blender.

"She accepts."

No one spoke. The coffee cup in my hand had too much blood in it to be drinkable. I set it down and walked out into the patient night. No one stopped me—they all lay dead next to Harv and the shattered Pina.

Chapter 15: Oslo

For the next six months not much happened in the Finnish forests where I'd retreated to wait and watch. News filtered upward into the desolation of our cold quiet world. The Russians continued to walk into death traps, some of Syndicate origin, as Harv acting on behalf of both the kids and Oslo, systematically dismantled what was left of The Web by sending them like pawn sacrifices to violent locations.

One group took a remit for Mariupol and died amidst the chaos. Chornobaivka got multiple visits in a lethal version of capture the flag—only it pitted demented Russians and some Syndicate patsies against well-armed, well-prepared Ukrainians. One particularly demented set of operators took the entire naval contingent, subs, ships, and all into the Alaskan polar sea and subsequently disappeared. The entire ocean churned for days and thereafter nothing could be found. Local fisherman noticed a ninety percent decline in king crabs, called off the season, and chalked it up to life's little mysteries. Or overfishing.

My personal favorite: Harv lured Putin and his close cadre into a rush across the Kerch Straight to meet their Wagner group counterparts. Momo and Mercy turned out to have a flare for asymmetric warfare. So, they cooked up various intelligence dossiers, leaked them along ratlines, then waited for the Failson himself to chase them down. We're still not sure if he thought he could acquire Hans' last trove of bioweapons or three trillion in stolen gold. Either way, Oslo's team replaced them all with some body doubles from within Russian intelligence itself. Did Putin notice? Nope. Because he died crossing a bridge when a directed mine blasted his crew into molecular scraps. Bonus, they damaged the bridge to Crimea.

The massacres and death traps lessened as The Web crumbled without a powerful center. Oslo's network slowly crushed the life out of what had existed for millennia by applying tectonic force to the various fault lines of money, power, and social control. The vestiges of The Cult and The Hive, small independent little splinters ran like drowning rats and died with equal vigor. In this, Pina's plan showed terrifying precision and lethal genius. Nothing had been left to chance.

But The Kutzk didn't care. Couldn't care. The perversion of accumulative society, of a place fixed and labeled made so little ontological sense to them, to us, that its survival or demise seemed functionally the same. Free will's just another name for enslavement to stuff. Away from the fight, I had time to reconstruct myself. Then ask whether that eighty-five percent that survived happened to be the right pieces of a self, the right moral and social being.

I more or less liked who I'd ended up being. Less when I considered the look on Elisabeth's face as she stared down at the splattered skull of her own child. More when I remembered that had bought entire species not just survival but the chance to grow and evolve like all other sapient life. On the balance, perhaps this version of what became me had more capacity for kindness.

Then a message came. A man walked into the forest. Scouts The Treeline described him as awkward but dangerous. Like a hyena from the veldt suddenly in cold terrain. Alone and missing its pack. He dragged three military duffels, stuffed in turn with sweets, winter supplies, and valuable tools like axe heads and coiled wire. He presented a sealed letter with my name marked upon it and asked in halting but polite Kutzk if Scouts would deliver it. She watched him turn and depart, convened a squad to distribute the largesse, and came to me with the envelope.

Inside a curt missive in Ukrainian (nice touch) invited me to Ivalo Airport in the north for a private flight to the Kodiak Island off the coast of the recently de-Syndicated Alaska. No explanation, no names given. Still, the gait and confidence suggested The Kraken. Also, the kids had no clue which precluded the usual suspects in our own circle of Hell. My eyes provided fairly detailed forensics and while it seemed a long shot, the cursive reminded me of what I had seen in other files while inside the Abschnitt. Old files, old writing. Someone long in the game.

Scouts the Treeline and a few elders saw me off. I had no dues to pay, no debts incurred. Knife that Does had a dozen lifetimes credit from the contributions of my old life. The kids continued my process, sending critical tools and food supplies to the edges of the Kutzk world—all with my mark. Not that I'd ever allowed that to influence my daily contributions. I carried my weight with the tribe separate from the villages in a bag. If anything, freed of the burden of a life's dark memories and emotional scars, I gave more and took less. Asked far less certainly and required less leeway as an outsider whose lifeways did not always gibe with the spartan truth of Kutzkan reality.

It touched me deeply to be missed. To be wanted and loved for myself, to have them politely invite me back. To remind me fondly of my place in their world, in our shared and good space. Scouts went so far as to kiss me and offer a promise of something more enduring should I care to return. Huh. I pressed her hand softly and felt a rare smile crease my serious face. I smiled rarely, laughed even less these days. She gave me a wry look and it struck me that what they mostly wanted, her, the elders, my tribe, was to see me alive. to see me with my children, laughing. To set down the burdens of a lifetime of cruel war.

The flight brought me to the commercial airport where an honest to goodness blackened window limousine waited. I got in without prompting. In for a penny and all that. The limo rolled out along the main roadway revealing a sparsely populated town with Quonset huts, some makeshift concrete buildings, the unique splattering of American neon signs and commercial advertising, and of course, lots of muddy weather faded trucks. The weather darkened the sky but in Alaska that could be summer or winter. The vehicle boasted a dark glass divider muting the shadow of the driver to something genderless. We did not speak; instead, my eyes traced the lines of trees and shore which engulfed the small cityscape and random pockets of prefabricated homes with green, grey, and blue.

Eventually the vehicle rounded a corner and began to climb a small hill. We had headed east and seemed to be rounding the island to the least populated portion of Kodiak. It had been a long time since I'd really seen a place this wild which still abutted "civilization." The island seethed with the bustle of wild creatures jostling with the airplanes and motorboats of human interlopers. Then we broke into the wild, the road studded with electric and phone lines, our only signpost of humanity. The limo accelerated and brought us through small inlets and swampy intrusions up the side of sparsely covered hillocks peppered with firs, spruces, and pines.

A dock appeared, a long ramshackle wooden thing painted white recently and barely flecking its thick coat. Alongside it stood the Arnapkapfaaluk, the Big Bad woman, also fresh painted and looking like a proper icebreaker in electric yellow and deep red. More surprising, the yellow catamaran of my own people rested next to it. Matching in paint and looking well founded. Hmm. It meant all the worlds had merged. Gay Eddie and Kaniehtiio Maracle sharing drinks?

But the person walking up the deck to meet us looked wholly unfamiliar. A man with a shock of gray hair, a skunk streak of pure white running along his left temple, and a matching countenance. Stern, affable, wise, weathered, a mild tan on pale skin. His green eyes and sharp smile reminded me of a cat. One of those classic alley tomcats, scruffy and scarred, who has been taken in and cleaned up. He wore a sport coat, black jeans, boots, and some kind of silk or cashmere sweater that emphasized his grey and white nature.

What had Scouts The Treelines said? Like a hyena in the wilderness. He walked with a hink in his gait. His eyes not so much scanning as taking in the scenery like compound lenses. Kraken. This man seemed aquatic. Not in his stance or his body, but in his relaxed movements. A being grown in both pressure and resistance, used to slowly going through a syrup of obstacles to vision, movement, and innovation. Charles T. Evergreen had sent me an invite, brought my family to meet me.

He waited considerately for me to exit the limo which gave me time to watch the vehicle make a wide spin and depart with a small plume of gravel and dust. Beyond, the faint noise of a party in progress, glasses clinking, music, laughter. In the woods across from me lurked a throng of bears. Kodiaks of varied sizes. Watchful but not approaching. Weaponized bears? Perhaps and why not? Or maybe just curious local wildlife, drawn to the sounds which historically meant trash and poorly guarded food.

He waved. "Cutter?" We would speak English apparently.

"Charlie?"

He broke into a wide grin, revealing small fangs. A cat indeed. "Yes, it's me. Well, a version of me as you must suspect."

Right. An avatar, a shape that his mind could hop into. What we had intuited from my own redesign and resurrection: The Kraken had no air breathing capabilities. Instead, it printed them. Temporary bodies built the way divers slapped on scuba, but in reverse and at a far more sophisticated technical echelon. But basically the same. A ride along inside a comfy vehicle to engage the surface. The Kraken (because I did not believe they came from Atlantis) never planned to walk the surface.

Instead, they dove into the air-filled upper world, grabbed raw materials and ideas when necessary, and returned to the soothing comfort of crushing pressure and endless dark cold. Charlie had inhabited this particular dive suit in part because it aptly fit the essence of his voice and personality. One cool cat—translated into something human shaped.

I shook his perfectly warm and normal hand. Significant technical echelons beyond our capacity. "The same could be said of me."

He laughed and it had a purr to it. Of course it did. "No, there's a real you in the meat stuff. It's perhaps truly you in there, Cutter. Or do you prefer your Kutzk name?"

"Charlie, I doubt in the blurble blurble deeps you have a nice polysyllabic English name, so Cutter will be fine."

A crinkled smile. "They call me the One Who Watches Over. By project or person. So, my name varies as my subject varies.

I am collective intelligence, like your Gay Eddie. Many of us, fused and working as a common unit. But not a hivemind. In this we far more resemble The Kutzk actually."

Huh. One Who Watches Over Spetz would be almost the same as OWWO-Lola but not quite. A commonality defined entirely by actions. Kutzk indeed, but like the spirits, joined in the quantum no-time of The Dreaming. For all I knew, he and his compatriots could be The Spirits. The shapers of our civilization, the elder species.

"Knife That Does greets you One Who Watches Over. Do you have a prefix?" I switched to Mohawk, nostalgic for my bring your daughter to war time with Momo.

His smile faded. "I am the oldest, the operational focus, I am One Who Watches Over Humanity. Like you."

My gut dropped. The Elders. Gods indeed. We had so egregiously strayed from any sense of purpose and reality, Pina had brought us into conflict with someone who had known us, all of us, since we differentiated ourselves from primates. But the cascade of Pina, her face shattered as the brains of her daughter coated the floor, twisted the knife inward. Hubris.

His hand caught my shoulder. I had stopped and apparently started to lurch. "Something upsetting you?"

I looked into his eyes, calm green things, but ancient nonetheless. All this time, he'd been watching me watch them. Old me, Spetz. "Kelba."

He gave me a sad little smile. "Ah. Yes of course. And of her?"

I shrugged. Six months in the forests and mists had not dulled the moment nor the pain of the reckoning. Why pretend? "I did the right thing, the correct thing, the safe thing, the necessary thing, but I wish I hadn't. Wish it could have been different. Wish it hadn't been vital to stop...." Genocide, Armageddon, the slaughter of my family and his, dooming humanity itself.

"She committed suicide using your body. But you bear half the wound. Her mother the other half. And you have just discovered what you lost when Spetz died."

"What's that?"

"Indifference. Numbness to the violence and depravity of your criminal syndicate's wider operations. You grew a conscience."

He motioned me down the walk, perhaps toward the party. We walked in silence following the dock into a low swale hiding a set of picnic tables laid with grey tablecloths and plain white mugs. A coffee and tea service sat next to them, including an old-fashioned fire powered samovar. A woman sat with her back to us, her head covered with a wool shawl of red and black check. She seemed absorbed in her own thoughts—her outline suggested someone between thirty and sixty of almost any height and body shape.

"This pain is a … conscience? You're saying I lacked one before?"

"You're telling me you did. And yes, the regret and horror you feel now, for the first time in your long or short life, depends on how you consider it, represents what every human being takes more or less for granted. You are supposed to be disgusted by killing someone."

Even The Kutzk, the most ruthless of humanity, felt that way. Which suggested strongly that as much as they would miss me, most of them likely feared me more than enjoyed my company. I'd done too much, helped them too often, to be ungrateful. But something as dangerous as me, someone as lethal and ruthless would remind them what made them human: limits, morals, desire to create harmony.

The woman turned as we approached revealing no one I'd expected. The face of a transformed Agrippina Karthago looked up with level cold eyes. She seemed at relative peace. When we'd left one another, she had oscillated between seething hatred and inward desolation. This face, this woman, she simply sat and watched. A blank canvas, curious and quiet. Another Kraken shell?

Charlie let me grab some smoky tea and motioned me to sit opposite the woman. We all stared at one another. I kept my face as smooth and emotionless as possible. In my new life that had gotten less easy. Emotions coursed through me. Fear of all things. I'd murdered this woman's child. Regretted it every night for months; played it out over and over, trying to find a different way to fix the mess we'd found ourselves sunk into by our own stupid decisions. Every night I drowned in the swamp. No answers had come. Until now.

Charlie motioned to the woman. "Oslo, please allow me to introduce Knife That Does. You used to be colleagues, believed you knew one another, made mistakes, lost family, committed atrocities both as allies and enemies. Both of you died in the war."

There. He'd said it. Undead then. Not a living man, not the second life of Spetz after all. A robot of some sort. A half-life. Like this tragic shell of Elisabeth or Pina. Nurhan's child, the last orphan of a prior generation. Like me.

Oslo—she seemed more or less this, as much as any other name—surprised me. She rose and extended a hand. I took it. We shook lightly. Her pulse seemed normal, her eyes steady. Ok. What the hell were these two playing at?

She sat again and I took that as a cue. Charlie sat between us, amicably sipping tea in silence. Eventually, as the silence dragged on, Oslo coughed politely and began to speak. "When Kelba lunged at you, when you defended yourself, I felt only rage. Even after, as the implications of the night really sunk in, I just felt—lost. Rage, white hot fury. My child, killed. My child killed herself. In front of me."

She sipped what smelled like spiked coffee. It reminded me of Patagonia and the now deceased Edith. "I spent weeks staring out the window. My child would never kill herself. Would she?"

My own children had. Well, Tiio had until we'd found a better way forward. And it sounds like Murray splinters one and two had a gruesome and not wholly involuntary demise. So yeah, my own child might. Could. Had done it. But not in front of me.

"Your words haunted me, Spetz. Sorry. You're not him, not anymore. But you understand."

Looking at the spitting image of Pina, sure. I entirely understood. I nodded and Charlie also gave her a sympathetic smile. "But you get it. Not my kid. But why my kid? Then I saw myself, my life, and how you'd hidden so much from me. We only found out about the Maracle variants weeks ago. You hid multiple AIs, operatives, tech geniuses, and an entire civilization of self-cloning mohawk women. Plus, you kept multiple Indigenous peoples alive and sequestered The Kutzk … and I'm off the subject. You kept them away. You tried to never let your life spill out onto your family."

Ah. "But you raised your daughter, Nurhan's granddaughter, in the family business. Like Hans and Cassandra did with Zeus. And me."

She sighed. "Yeah, and did that kill her? Did she drink so much Oslo Kool-Aid she couldn't, you know, cope with defeat? That kind of stuff. Every night, every fucking night, Cutter."

I knew. Because I came back to the night too, to that moment, to her death. Endless and always. No escaping the ugly moment when ….

"But then I'd turn around and say, no, fuck no, not Apolonia. She had been doing this a good long while, knew better."

"Her real name was Apolonia?"

Oslo smiled faintly. "Yes, but you'd more likely know her as Rosa. Or La Pola. She took over for a lot of assassinated spies and revolutionaries. Carried on the work." Rosa Luxemburg. La Pola Salavarrieta. Huh, Kelba had been every inch the badass.

Oslo stared away for a moment. "I'm trying to tell you something. Doing it badly."

Charlie looked at me and I shrugged. "Take your time, Oslo. No one here is in a hurry."

"Right, but you see why I couldn't let it go. Guilt, shame, denial, and suspicion. Why her, was it her, was she drunk, drugged?"

The penny dropped. Gods beyond, she hadn't? But that chill certainty crept within me. "How long were you unconscious when Gay Eddie's strike team came for you?"

She nodded. "Yes, exactly that. About an hour."

Charlie gave me a puzzled look. "Have you two something to say?"

The luck of it. What a horror. "Plenty of time, Charlie. When the kids resurrected this version of me, they stole a syringe of doped up memory juice from Nurhan's lab. Complex stuff, but basically mental transfer."

He stared at me with something akin to baffled disgust. Yeah, it's all me in there after all. Enough to horrify myself most every night.

Oslo nodded sadly. "We missed it."

I shook my head. "You almost figured it out, which is why the whole damned war kicked off too early. She feared you getting close."

Charlie seemed irritated. You couldn't blame him. He'd managed this whole cozy reunion to make peace and we'd gone haywire, started rambling about dry land genetic tampering and shit. Still, we had established rapport.

"Charlie, the point you are trying to grasp here, both Pina and Spetz ran around thinking Nurhan had cloned herself, had been working for The Hivemind and Hans and all these various crackpots to further her power and find the holy grail of eugenics."

He tilted his head. "The holy grail being what? Mental control or mental transfer. Or both?"

Oslo stared into her mug. Right. It sat with me. "Both maybe. But we missed the obvious. These dudes were her window dressing and there was always only Nurhan. She transferred herself lock stock and psychotic genius barrel into each body she took. She propagated like a fucking virus. Not Cassandra and such, plus Nurhan, not sequential versions, but full-on equals of herself, added and embellished in each next iteration. Ten of these evil bitches running around simultaneously."

Oslo wept softly. "She injected Apolonia. I checked… I had to know why she did it. And I found anomalies, misreads, password and checkpoint failures, glitches that showed small biomarker differences. She'd been slowly taking over my child."

"Like she took over Darcy and who knows which other operatives."

Oslo nodded. "By the time we got to the endgame, your Kelba had been erased. I had Nurhan standing next to me for months, in the body of my own child, using her voice to drive me to failure."

I sat there and suddenly laughed. "You're saying I killed Nurhan? That she suicided rather than admit defeat?"

Charlie looked at us both and shook his head. "I'm sorry but that's disgusting. What loathsome business." He shuddered. Right response. Er, own child subsumed from within. The hit on them a feint within a feint to implode Oslo's org from within.

Oslo gave me a rueful smile. "You fooled her. Fooled us all really. We had relied on your nature, on your reliability. You had made it your hallmark, your north star when all else failed. We could always count on you to be … right where you said you'd be. Until this last time."

I sat there. I had not murdered her daughter. I'd killed the enemy of the world. Saved us from her maybe. "What? But you knew I could change."

Oslo shook her head. "No, we thought we were … smarter than you. We figured your predictability represented what shall we call it? Masculine limitations. We never took your third gender nature seriously, never really considered you might be strategic."

I. Had. Not. Killed. Kelba. Oh. But I'd still killed someone and it still hurt. Just not the same.

"You underestimated him?" Charlie seemed amused.

"She's saying they bought what I had sold them all. I had secrets to hide, you see, serious major weaknesses. People I loved."

Oslo downed her drink. She rose and made herself another. Definitely spiked coffee. I refilled my tea. "Okay, so I fooled you and her."

"We all expected you in the atoll. Well, I knew you'd be in Beijing."

I smiled back at her. "I was. Spetz rode that plane down into the gap."

"Not the point. We expected your signature infighting mano a mano surgical strike. We sure as fuck did not expect you to lure the entirety of the world's antagonists into a confided space and nuke them. You killed armies that day. Ended entire family lines, entire criminal syndicates. Erased portions of The Syndicate and Swarm from existence in a fraction of a second."

Charlie began to laugh. "Wait, wait. Let me make sure I have this right because this happens to be both more horrifying and ironic than Nurhan chewing her way out of your children from the inside. Spetz spent an entire lifetime pretending to be this linear reliable tough guy with limited, what to call it, insight creativity hell treachery. And lo, on the day of days, he spin-kicks into the assembled geniuses of dominion, the uplanders, tricks you all into showing up for some big operatic showdown and simply fries your asses without ego, drama, or personal concern?"

Oslo grimaced. "He spin-kicked everyone Charlie, you included. He fooled the entire universe. He had entire islands of people thriving for decades, he had fortunes squirreled away, a whole hidden satellite network, three extra artificial intelligences hidden in plain fucking sight. The man just outmaneuvered the entirety of the world's smartest deadliest people. Then made them functionally irrelevant in under eight minutes. Yeah."

I sat there sipping my tea. This whole war had felt more like the world's worst PTA meeting for Supervillain High School instead of a struggle to stop sequential genocide. In the last war we had costume changes, exotic locales, car chases and explosions, hidden assassins, dramatic phone calls. The stuff of legends. What happened this time? Lots of negotiating and chatting. Some phone calls. A few brutal fights ending in near immediate death. A lot of coercion and head fakes. And sadly, the deployment of some of the world's most heinous weaponry, all of it functionally WMDs but scaled from the blast radius of one ship to one city.

What had Murray told me all those years ago? Darcy had made a joke. Right? If I had gone to school, they would have put Does Not Play Well With Others on every report card. Good thing Section 21 homeschooled. At gunpoint.

"Oslo, you knew months ago and you didn't find me."

She stared at me and nodded slowly. There was more to say. "No, I was still angry. Still outraged you'd killed my family. Or meant to."

Something ugly stirred in my gut: she called me Cookie Monster. "Let me remind you that you, Pina, killed my family not because they deserved it, not to serve any real purpose, just to lure me back into the game so you could track down and kill the other part of my family."

We all felt the boiling animosity. She had murdered so many innocent people. Some I had known, some few of those I'd loved dearly.

"Ever wonder what you lose, being the kind of person who murders peoples' families to achieve a strategic advantage?"

I stared into her flat sad eyes. "No. That's the whole point of your little commentary about Spetz faking it all along. I have never murdered families on purpose. Nor understood the value."

She nodded. "Right, that's the other thing. In your own way, in his way, Spetz had decency. A moral center. We relied on that. Restraint. Until the last day."

"You mistook restraint for weakness."

"Precisely. What you lose, Cutter, what you absolutely give up to be the kind of centuries old obsessive who chases a dream is perspective. Nurhan lost hers and I sure as shit lost mine."

I looked at Charlie. "What are we doing here? What's the point of all this?"

He laid his soft but firm hand on my shoulder. "We are ending the war for real. Ending it for you."

Finally, I did not understand. Why my people had been convened, my life streams merged in this place. Now, here came my old boss, the woman who'd nearly destroyed the planet, telling me whatever the fuck she was rambling about. That I'd accidentally murdered my mother a second, wait, third or fourth time. Ha. Nukes.

That I'd fooled them, or Spetz had. By simply not being as egotistical and attention hungry. Or whatever she meant. By keeping secrets and making other people, family, the supreme sacrifice of his life. Keeping them safe with his own flesh and his own raw will, his promise incarnate. But so what? Every mother does this for her child and many fathers. Most loving parents of every gender.

Oslo stood. "Right, we are not saying it and it needs to be said. I was pissed at you, Spetz or whoever you are now, for fooling me. For keeping me from my grand dream." She tossed back her drink, briefly choking on the heat and booze. "I didn't care that you killed my kid. Excuses. You killed my ego. Showed me up and then for good measure, had the fucking audacity to be morally right and strategically correct. We had no shot at Charlie's people. And you knew it. You saved the planet, saved me, saved my whole dream and humanity, and incidentally did it by holding a gun to my head to stop me from fucking it all up."

Charlie gave me that ancient smile. "She called me a couple months ago, started talking. When Oslo really grasped how outclassed she'd have been things got … awkward."

"Double awkward, I bet, when she started putting together how old The Kraken or Atlanteans or whatever you call yourselves really is and how long you've been helping us."

Charlie chuckled softly. "Not always helping. Your kids will assure you of that. But yes. We call ourselves the Dreamers of the Blue. And like you implied, we live in The Dreaming. Which The Kutzk talk about."

Oslo refilled our drinks. "I hid from you. Because I was ashamed and grief stricken. And honestly humiliated. In your place I'd have been dancing around, mocking you, breaking you down for your … sins. But you never even thought about it did you?"

Riddles much? "Thought about what?"

"That you saved the world. Outsmarted everyone. Sacrificed your life and won. That you did the impossible, one single human being changed all of history. Not supposed to be possible."

No. I had never thought about that. It sounded like more excuses and bullshit to me. More ego and self-loathing. I did what I had to do. What was necessary to save my children. If I had to save the entire world to ensure it existed for them, well and good. But I had started out protecting Kaniehtiio Maracle and my AIs, my own variants, plus a handful of innocents. Nurhan, Elisabeth, and Apolonia had set the stage for what dominoes tumbled down. Not me.

I shrugged. "Look, it's not possible."

Oslo gave Charlie a knowing look. "We didn't even know you started Uncle Gary. Do you see? Spetz managed to hide everything, and we have no idea how."

How had I done it? Sure, some of the memories had been obliterated. But for the most part, what had been me remained me. I had cut off every part of my humanity, made every sacrifice, done every dirty job necessary and saved all my ill-gotten gains, parlayed them into hidden empires for the sole purpose of protecting my loved ones. Most of them. Some like Edith and my cousins had gotten scragged in the crossfire.

I'd made my kids everything. Said every mother of every child ever.

"Look. I get it. Encounter group, therapeutic outlet, blah blah. But I just did it to keep my kids alive. And to do the right thing within that context. If that required some heroic bullshit, then I did heroic stuff. If it required luring you all to a stupid pointless death using nukes and airplanes in the biggest cliché of all time, then hey, there's a first time for everything."

Oslo nodded. She looked as if I'd punched her. "That was my point. You are a good parent. And Nurhan, well you know she was a nightmare mother. But so was Pina—me, her, whatever. She destroyed her children. She had many. And now, what? Nothing. No one left because I, she, whatever we as a unit, the image I took over and my own fucked up delusions, whatever we eventually became, we sucked as parents. We put ourselves first and last."

I don't know what possessed me, but I felt it. The abject sorrow. I rose and put my arms around this woman who too late had realized she'd murdered her own children. Not on purpose, surely with the best beliefs, the best intentions. But she set them on a road to Hell. No coffee breaks. When came the day, they jumped straight down to the fifth circle and drank from the rivers of fire and blood.

We sobbed for a while. For Apolonia who had been my friend too, after all. For Darcy whom we had lost, for every lost soul along the way. Peace made. Well, peace found. Spetz had died in the plummet down into Beijing. But so had Agrippina. Because he had killed her dreams. What stood before me in Finland had been the walking ghost of her, the leftover motion of a deluded and broken life.

Long we cried and mourned the dead. We put Spetz into his grave and then laid down Pina. Oslo and Knife That Does. The survivors of the long war. The dreamers, the compromisers, the parents who sacrificed all for the children.

Charlie walked us down to find a gathering like none I'd ever witnessed. Five Eddies playing jazz covers and not badly at that. Who knew he had that talent? Harv sat with some of his loyal cadre, making jokes and eating BBQ, next to a pair of older Frisian speaking Tiios, Sharktooth perhaps, and one other. Aidan and Declan with their Auntie Hunter, the lads bemused and clearly smitten talking to Cornflower and a few of her generation. Two of her comelier scientific selves sat on their laps and looked smugly content as they all but screamed "mine." Probably didn't hurt the pair of them had made it to the top ten richest alive last month. The crew of the various ships mingled. Ace stood on dry land drinking with a very tough looking older Tiio, while some anarcho-syndicalist dudes with blond braids entertained what seemed like Kraken emissaries in uplander bodies. Dreamers of the Blue.

On that same shore stood a beautiful cabin done out in glass, wood, and painted steel. Ah. They had built us a home, an inviting affair that seemed Kutzkan enough I could safely invite Scouts and some of the more adventurous of the clan. In the distance something moved and with a flicker of shadow, my eyes followed the body of Hippo as he lazily shifted between two pieces of overlarge cat furniture in the lodge window. Right. they'd brought my little furry hunter back to me. Or more precisely, me back to him.

And my kids. Charlie surprised me there too. Those bears by the entrance, well five of them ambled out jacked up with the good stuff, nano enabled and quantum. Huge, durable, adorable, human-like but simpler to move around, no need for speech, scary enough and remote enough to be left alone, and near the ever-present ocean that allowed the Dreamers to visit them and vice versa. Great practice bodies for growing minds. Eventually they'd dive down under the waves. Or maybe churn out some goth and glam bods, go clubbing.

Charlie took me aside. I had been wrong, he explained. Spetz had never been alive. He'd been a revenant from the moment his birth mother died in front of him. Walking a path of vengeance. Tragic and broken, he had never been human nor given the chance to live as one.

You can't kill the undead, only release them. Pina and Spetz. They had lived in the shadows, consumed by the darkest of our communal transgressions. But Knife That Does. That human existed, had loved ones, could live a life. If I wanted it. If I had the courage to lay down my well-honed rage.

My hand brushed along Daddy-O's ridiculously tough fur. Kodiak bears are not exactly soft—they need to survive insane weather after all. But his gleeful snort, his sheer delight infected me, all of us, with good humor. Somewhere steaks cooked. I owed Gay Eddie a dinner. I owed Ace and a few other friends some dances or drinks or stories. And Oslo, midwife of humanity. What did I owe her?

Nothing. She had told me so and we both knew that between us, so much dark ruin had passed. Still, she had no children left but me. And through me, her grandchildren and nieces, a couple of beefy nephews. Picnicking like people do in the cold sunset of Kodiak, Alaska. Next to Dreaming Lodge.

‡Mother?‡ More laughter and that soft wicked touch of Momo's.

Time to go home.

About the Author

Storytelling through books, games, consulting, and excessive flirtation with inappropriately dangerous situations. Canajoharie and *devequt* witchcraft likely involved; neither cis nor het. Published works include The Autumn War, Requisition, *Bugbear Blues, Jobs Stranger than Fiction,* and *The Ridiculous Misadventures of the Imperial Garden Boy.* Available for weddings, exorcisms, bar mitzvahs, nuclear submarine christenings, and the occasional covert operation.

www.ingramcontent.com/pod-product-compliance
Lightning Source LLC
Chambersburg PA
CBHW031604240626
47153CB00002B/629
9781637890998